THE LUNA'S PACK

THE LUNA'S PACK

Book #1 of The Luna's Pack Trilogy

L M LISSETTE

Dreams In Ink

For those who desire an adventurous fantasy worthy of dreams and a beautiful romance stronger than a bully.

Contents

I

The sun's rays slowly filter into the café as it climbs to start the day. My bitter coffee lost its warmth a while ago, yet I'm still cradling it like we're friends. Some framed clippings of old newspapers hang on the wall behind the counter. On one of them, an old man waves as he exits a car. The heading above his picture says, "The President Has Died." That was 36 years ago. Twelve years before I was born. Where I live was called the United States, and we had a President. *A whole lot of good that did us.*

They called it the War of Worlds, only it was just our world. Militias rose and grew in numbers so fast that they overthrew nearly all of the governments. Countries began destroying all the war machines they could find when the militias started bombing one another. In an attempt for peace, the militias met in neutral territory and agreed to ban electricity. They said they needed to remove power from every entity, so they literally removed power. *I wonder if they were as stupid as they sounded.* When I was a little girl, I used to ask about how things were then, but now I don't care.

I'm exhausted. It was a long night, but the horses made it to the buyer, and I'm still alive. I wish I could focus on that, but I can't stop obsessing about the unknown.

"Need some more?" A familiar voice pulls me out of oblivion with a jolt. "Coffee, Darya." Rosalee is standing right in front of me, across the counter. She smiles, tapping on her tin coffee pot. "You're about a million miles away, girl. What's eating at you?"

Sighing, I push my cup toward her and rub my eyes. "I haven't been sleeping well lately. Maybe I need to lay down for a while."

She tops off my cup and sees my grandmother's ratty notebook before I can slip it under the counter. "I don't know why your father gave that to you," she says, frowning. "Your mother would have had a fit if she were still alive."

My father found the notebook after my grandmother died. It details quite a bit of our family history. The strangest fact was that the gender of the children flopped with every generation. The men had little girls, and the women had little boys. If there were multiple children, only one could have a family. I'm sure that's why Rosalee couldn't have children, but she is the only family I have left.

"She was your sister, Rosalee. Are you sure you don't know anything about this?" Truthfully, I've always felt like she's hiding things from me. I have nagged her about our family for years. According to my grandmother's notebook, all women who marry into my bloodline die giving birth. Rosalee says it's just a coincidence, but it would explain why we both grew up without a mother.

She shoves my cup back at me rather abruptly, spilling some onto the counter. "She was my half-sister, Darya. She got all her crazy from her mother," she snaps. "I have told you so many times that it's nothing but nonsense."

"But there's another language in here, Rosalee," I spit out as if it's a factual statement toward its validity. We have this argument frequently. I'm not even sure why I bother at this point. Rosalee continues to look down at the counter as she wipes up the spilled coffee, shaking her head and frowning. Sighing, I change the subject. "Rosalee, can you tell me about my mother?"

My question makes her smile broadly as she leans on the counter. "Your mother was kind and gentle," she says. She hooks my hair behind my ear. "She had beautiful long brown hair like you but always wore it in a braid." She tugs the end of my hair with a smirk. I twist it out of her hand and flip it back behind my shoulder.

"Did she know what would happen?" I ask. I rephrase the question when she frowns, raising her eyebrow. "Did she know that she would die?"

"Darya, we're not doing this. Your mother was beautiful and sweet, and she was so very excited about you." She slaps her rag on the counter. "She would've been an amazing mother." She nods, nearly snorting at me, and I suddenly feel horrible for making her angry again.

I frown. "I'm sorry."

"Good." She nods again, straightening out her gray-haired bun and dabbing the sweat on her wrinkled brow. "Now I have something I think you'll want to see."

She curls her finger, beckoning me to follow her. She walks around the counter, directing me down the dark hallway to the back door. The only thing behind the café is her house.

"Rosalee, I've seen your house," I grumble, unimpressed.

"Hush, child," she scolds. "A stranger rode into town today."

"Oh, goodie," I say sarcastically.

I have never been interested in her gossip and am not in the mood now. I'm too tired to hide my irritation at this point. I sigh and roll my eyes just in time for her to turn around and see me do it.

She scoffs. "This is not about the stranger, Darya. It's what he rode in on." She flashes a crooked smile, opening the back door.

My eyes land on the most beautiful horse I've ever seen when I step onto the porch. Tied to Stanley's hitching post is a large, black Friesian mare. Rosalee's husband is pounding nails into her massive hooves to secure her shoes. Her head is down, her chin resting on the post, and she is nearly asleep. She's clearly no stranger to hard work.

Rosalee raises her eyebrow and puts her hand on my shoulder. "I know what you're thinking, but it wasn't an officer."

"A civilian rode in on her?" I lean down on the railing, staring at the mare. I've never stolen from a civilian, but she'd fetch a high price in the city.

"A rather nice-looking young man."

"Polite, too," Stanley chimes in with a wink as he stretches his back.

"But does he have a rear end as nice as the one on her?" I ask, grinning.

Stanley shakes his head and returns to work. He knows I only say things like that to push Rosalee's buttons.

She slaps my shoulder. "Why would I be looking there?" She clicks her tongue in disgust. "He had a nice face and clean hair. Although, like you, he could use a haircut."

"Sounds like a match made in heaven." I wrinkle my nose, winking at her. Rosalee tries to be old-fashioned, but it's not my style. She wants me to find a husband and have kids, but I'm a wanderer. I have yet to feel like I belong anywhere.

Rosalee frowns, showing all her years in the wrinkles around her eyes. "I wish you would stop running off and settle down. You'll get caught one of these days, and I don't want to think about what they'll do to you."

Reaching out for her shoulder, I flash her my cocky grin. "They haven't caught me yet."

There's a loud crash inside the café. I pull the door open and peek inside. Not seeing anything, I open it wide for Rosalee and follow her inside. I attempt to close the door quietly behind me, but Rosalee pulls me by my shirt, so the door slams shut. She shoves me into a closet beside us and gently closes the door.

My head knocks into a box of old linens as I land on all fours. Pushing myself up off the floor, I look around. I haven't been in this closet since I was a kid. When I worked for Rosalee as a little girl, I hid here whenever the soldiers came into town. Rosalee said little girls shouldn't listen to their inappropriate language.

I creep over to the door, cracking it open to try to hear what's going on. With my ear against the crack, I can make out some of what Rosalee is saying.

"I'm not sure why you'd think I'd know where she is," Rosalee says.

"I don't have time for you, old woman," a gruff voice I know all too well growls. "Where's Darya?"

Well, shit.

"Commander, I can assure you —" Something stops her from finishing that sentence. There's a shuffling on the floor in the café, and I swing the closet door open. A resounding slap travels down the hallway. I start walking, but my anger takes over as I near the café. I jog past some militia soldiers, shoving one against the wall.

When my eyes land on the Commander, his back is facing me. "I'm right here, asshole," I growl. He turns toward me as I hit a dead run. There's a chair close enough that I jump on it and launch myself at him. With my weight behind my fist, it slams into the side of the Commander's face, knocking him over a table. It breaks under his weight, causing an oddly satisfying thud when his body hits the floor.

By some miracle, I land on my feet and use the momentum to launch myself at him again. He puts his arms up to block me, but someone grabs me by my hair before I can get near him. The soldier holding my hair stretches his arm out so I can't hit him, but I smile and swing a boot at his kneecap. He yanks down on my hair and bends me backward, rendering me nearly helpless.

"Darya," the Commander snarls through his teeth. "I am so damn tired of you making me bleed." He climbs out of the table debris and brushes off his uniform. His olive skin does little to hide the bruising that is developing beside his eye. One of his men hands him a rag to mop up the blood. "You're gonna regret it this time."

Looking over his bleeding eye, I can't help the smile that spreads across my face. "No," I say, giggling. "I don't think I will."

A look of pure, unadulterated hate flashes across his face. "Get her out of here."

The soldier that has my hair slings me around toward the door. The other men scramble to get out of the way as he shoves me through the doorway. He throws me down in the street onto my hands and knees.

I move quickly to get back on my feet, but the Commander is already in front of me when I turn back toward the café. He catches me firmly by the throat and looks down at me. Truthfully, I'm pretty short. It's never really bothered me until now. I can tell the Commander feels a sense of power, being able to tower over me as he does.

He smells like he hasn't touched soap in quite a while, and he's been hitting the moonshine this morning. He leans down and puts his cheek against mine to whisper into my ear. "Where are my horses, woman?"

"I'm going to need you to be more specific. Which horses?" I instantly regret saying that as his hand closes on my throat. His eyes travel over my body and stay too long on my chest. "They aren't in my shirt," I add, lifting my eyebrow.

He relaxes his hand and laughs. "I'm nothing if not thorough."

The Commander steps closer when something behind me catches his eye. He pushes against my throat, causing me to step back. I suddenly turn into old news as the Commander groans with a sly grin. He slings me out of his way, snapping his fingers and pointing at me without looking in my direction. His men approach me but stay at a distance, eyeing me apprehensively.

The Commander marches through the crowd, stopping at a man I've never seen before. His features are handsome, with smooth cheekbones, and the scruff's shadow on his face compliments him well. His hair is as black as night, falling over his ears and touching his eyes. As he moves to fold his arms across his chest, every muscle flexes beautifully. I let my eyes wander over his body, and my lower lip pulls between my teeth.

"Dax," the Commander slips the name through his teeth, dripping with disdain.

"Anthony," the stranger says calmly. "How are the kids?" His tone is light, as though he's talking to a friend. They both stand a few inches taller than most of the crowd, making them easy to see.

"I wouldn't know," the Commander complains. "Been chasing this damn horse thief up and down the mountains for nearly a year straight now." He jams a thumb back in my direction. "Hasn't left much time for family life."

The stranger's eyes shift behind the Commander and lock onto me. His gaze travels up my body in a way that has my breath rushing from my lungs. When he reaches my eyes, something on the back of my neck begins burning. I attempt to swat at the bug, but my arm stops before reaching my skin and falls lifelessly to my side. I can't take my eyes off the dark-haired man.

"Looks like you probably should've just stayed home, Anthony." The stranger laughs, pointing to the Commander's eye. He quickly turns his gaze back to me. My confusion must be showing on my face. If the stranger notices, he doesn't seem to care.

The Commander scoffs. "She's feisty."

I look around for an escape route and notice my feet are moving. My breathing becomes short and shallow as I hyperventilate. I flick my eyes in the direction my feet are taking me and see the stranger still staring at me. *I'm trying to get away from them. Why am I moving in their direction? And what is with this Dax guy? I'm losing my damn mind.*

Dax shakes his head, and my feet stop. He reaches up for his neck and stops just before touching it. Dax balls his fist and jams his hand back down by his side. He winks in my direction as if that should have some powerful, calming effect on me.

"Don't suppose you could just forget about seeing me today?" Dax grins, but it is unclear who he's flashing that at since he's still looking at me. Every time he speaks, there is an unmistakable flutter in my stomach. His blue eyes seem to dance in the sun. My neck sears a little more, and I suck air through my teeth from the pain.

"Now you know that bounty is too high to watch you walk away, Dax." The Commander snaps his fingers, and more soldiers emerge from the crowd with rope. They cautiously approach Dax as if anticipating trouble from him.

Dax looks at the men with an annoyed sigh before shifting his gaze back toward me. He puts his hands out, wrists together. "I guess you have to try at least, right?" He winks at me again. Or maybe he was winking at the Commander. Right now, I don't give a damn.

The burning on my neck intensifies to the point that my vision blurs. I hold my hands out but lose my balance as the ground spins. I stumble slightly to the side without anything to grab onto to steady myself. I can't focus my eyes on anything because of the spinning. My knees buckle under me as I hear a shrill whistle, and my vision blacks out completely. I should have hit the ground, but something grabbed me before I passed out.

2

In the darkness, voices begin to materialize over the sound of blood rushing in my ears. There are multiple voices, but none I'd consider familiar. The only one I recognize belongs to Dax. The others belong to women who seem to be arguing. I leave my eyes closed, pretending I'm still unconscious. *I need to know what I'm dealing with.*

"Why did you bring her here," one woman asks.

"You shouldn't question him," the second woman whispers.

Something scrapes across a wooden floor.

"Nobody's talking to you," the first woman scoffs. "Why are you even here?"

There's a sigh, and my neck flares again.

"She's awake," Dax says.

Dax is sitting in a chair beside me when I open my eyes. He's leaning with his forehead in his hands and a large ice pack over his neck. My eyes drift around the room, seeing stone walls without windows. The single light source is a lantern sitting on a table beside the bed I'm lying on.

The women stand behind Dax. They both look puzzled as they stare at me.

"How is this even possible?" the first woman sneers. "You should've been out for hours." She flips her long black hair behind her shoulder and folds her arms across her chest.

"Get out," Dax grumbles from under his hands.

"But Dax, no," she tries to argue.

He sits back, dumping the ice pack on the floor. When he lifts his eyes, they no longer dance as they did when I first saw them. "Now," he growls.

The woman grabs a few items from the small table beside the bed and leaves the room, closing the door behind her. Dax studies me quizzically. As he stares at me, my neck burns more intensely. I try to reach for it, but my hand stops and falls to the bed.

I scowl. "What the hell is going on?"

"Don't touch it," Dax says. "It makes it worse."

"That's not an answer."

The second woman grabs an ice pack from a cooler, handing it to Dax. "Here, put this on her." She flips her hands at Dax, urging him along.

Something holds me down on the bed, so I can only writhe in pain as Dax moves toward me. The closer he moves, the more intense the pain becomes. *I bet this is how animals feel when we brand them.*

"What the hell?!" I thrash around as much as I can against whatever is holding me. The only thing I accomplish is losing my breath and wearing myself out.

Dax puts his hands up, showing me the ice pack. "Easy, Darya. I'm only trying to put this on you." He moves at an excruciatingly slow pace toward me. Every step is a new level of pain. By the time he retreats, I'm close to passing out again.

I narrow my eyes when the room stops spinning. "I'm done," I snap. "Why can't I move?"

Dax sits and leans against the back of the chair with a sigh. "I'll let you go, but don't touch your neck." He stares at me with complete indifference as I furrow my brow. "I mean it, Darya."

"You're doing this to me?" I spout angrily.

Dax ignores my question and holds his hand up. Somehow, the remaining woman knows to give him my grandmother's notebook. He holds it out for me to see. The book is close enough that I could snatch it from him if my arms weren't useless.

"Where did you get this?" Dax barely acknowledges the book he's holding.

I look at the notebook, quickly running through my options. *I could tell him the truth, but would that make me a target? Is it a bad thing that this is part of my family history? He might know something that could help me understand my family and what is happening to us.*

I raise my eyebrow, deciding to go with what I know. "I found it on the street."

Dax looks surprised for a moment but then narrows his eyes. "And you were just carrying it around? For what? A bit of light reading?" Although he's looking at me as if he wants to put me through the wall, his tone has a hint of humor. Nevertheless, he's still expecting an answer.

I chew on the inside of my cheek and try to come up with something that would make sense. Unfortunately, my head is in a fog. It feels like someone else's thoughts are arguing with mine. Part of me just wants to give up the ruse, and the rest has an excellent lie for him.

"It looked interesting," the criminal in me says, grinning. I look down, acknowledging my shame, as he chuckles. I'm usually a much better liar. Dealing with the militia for years has taught me to believe my lies to pass them as the truth. I'm not sure where that skill went.

"Why don't we agree not to lie to each other?" Dax sighs and leans forward in his chair.

"I try not to make promises I don't intend to keep." I snap back at him.

Dax stands up and steps toward me, sending searing pain across my neck. It gets worse with every step until it's too much.

"Alright, fine," I growl. "It's my grandmother's. She wrote it."

He steps back and falls onto his chair. My eyes stay on him as the pain fades slightly. I can almost see wheels turning in his head.

"Have you read it?" Dax asks.

I have no plan for what to say, but words spill out when I open my mouth. "I've been reading it for years. Most of it doesn't make any sense." My eyes widen in surprise. *Did I just say that?*

Dax ignores my minor panic attack and opens the notebook to flip through the pages.

"Are you gonna let me go?" I bark, glaring at him. "I'm getting stiff here."

Dax flashes a cocky grin, and suddenly, I'm free. I swing my legs off the bed and glance behind him. Granted, moving closer to Dax has heightened the burning on my neck, but that is the direction of the door and my only exit. I hiss through my teeth at the pain and reach up.

Suddenly, there's an ear-piercing scream. I feel torn between grabbing my neck and covering my ears, but then I realize I'm the one yelling. This moment is the closest I may ever come to an out-of-body experience. I feel like I'm listening to myself scream from somewhere else. I slide off the bed and land on the floor.

Dax falls onto the floor with me and grabs my arm. As I stare into his eyes, the woman throws an ice pack, bouncing it off my forehead.

"Dax," she squeaks. "The ice." She points to the ice pack lying on the floor between my legs.

Dax and I just stare at each other. The pain is gone. A wave of relief crashed over me when he touched me. My breath catches as his piercing blue eyes captivate me. I see my hand reaching up for his face from the corner of my eye. It stops an inch from its target.

"I don't think she needs it," Dax whispers. Breaking eye contact, he looks at my hand before it drops lifelessly onto my lap. I openly appreciate his hair cascading down his face while he looks at me. The different lengths touch the corners of his eyes and his cheeks. *Something inside me is desperate to touch his face.*

"What's happening to me?" I whisper.

Then, my relief is gone as Dax stands up and takes his hand off me. I double over in pain but know better than to reach for the burning skin this time.

"Stay with her, Cass," Dax tells the woman, stepping toward the door. "I'll send Marianna back with something to help." He pats her shoulder and reaches for the doorknob.

When Dax opens the door, he looks back at me. This time he's not as guarded, and I see his confusion. I don't feel alone in this for the first time since I passed out. He exits the room, and I can tell he's moving further away because my neck is burning less and less. I pick up the ice pack, placing it over the searing skin.

"So, Cass, is it?" I look up at the woman with a small smile.

"I'm sorry about Dax. He can be a little rough around the edges." She offers her hand to help me off the floor. "How about we get you some fresh air before everyone returns?"

She keeps hold of my hand, pulling me out of the bedroom. I follow her down a short hallway and into a kitchen. Candles light the counter area, and a few are burning on a table surrounded by mismatched chairs. To our left are several dirty windows.

"Oh," I say, looking at the windows. "I thought we were underground."

Cass smiles. "I can see why you'd think that." She opens the door to the back porch. "Dax normally sleeps during the day, and he likes it dark, so it makes sense not to have windows in his room."

I woke up in a strange man's bed. I roll my eyes, sighing. *Great.* "How long was I out?" I ask, stepping off the porch.

"About twelve hours. Dax said you passed out." She frowns and guides me to a small trail in the woods. "He had Nate bring you back here while he led the militia away. You're safe here, Darya."

Safe is not the word I would use to describe how I feel. "Cass, do you know what's wrong with my neck?"

"I'm sorry, I don't," Cass says. "Whatever is wrong seems to be affecting Dax too, though." She seems genuinely bothered by Dax's discomfort.

"Do you know how Dax is controlling me?"

"I would guess it has something to do with the curse," Cass says, sighing.

Of course there's a curse. I stop, pulling her arm to turn her to me. "What curse?" I ask.

She shakes her head. "I'm not supposed to talk about it." She raises her eyes to the woods and grabs my arm. "We need to go. Nate's back." She pulls me back toward the house.

"Don't leave on my account," a deep voice says behind us.

A tall, dark-haired man emerges from the woods. *This must be Nate.* He pulls on a shirt and puts his hand out to shake mine. I uncomfortably stare, unable to decide whether to shake it.

"Way to make that shit awkward, new girl," Nate says, laughing. "Nice to see you awake, at least, Darya." He motions his hand like he's shaking mine and pulls it back. "Cass is right, though. We need to get you back to the house."

Nate holds his arms out to us. Cass smiles, hooking her arm with his. They both turn to look at me, waiting for me to join their antics. I try a small smile, but I'm pretty sure it displays on my face as a grimace because Cass frowns. Clearly, this is something normal for these people. I clumsily jab my arm in Nate's and turn to face the house with them.

"Alright, ladies," he starts, standing tall. "Let's get you home safe and sound." Nate leads us to the house, practically skipping the whole way. I can't be certain, but I'm pretty sure it's unhealthy to be that happy. He jogs up the steps and across the porch, dragging us along. Cass laughs, seemingly enjoying herself. He stops at the door and bows with a grand flourish, waiting for us to enter.

Nate closes the door behind us. "So, Darya, you pissed off Mari tonight. What did you do?" Keeping his eyes on me, he walks to the table and pulls a chair out.

"Me? Who the hell is Mari?" I don't even have to play stupid at this point.

Cass approaches the table with a teacup. She ushers me toward the chair but then smiles at Nate. "She woke up," she answers him.

Nate's eyebrows furrow. "And that's... a bad thing?"

Cass flips her hand while walking back to the kitchen counter. "You know your wife. She likes to believe she's the only badass alive."

Nate taps his fingers on the back of the chair next to me. "Yeah, that I'll agree with."

Things start to come together in my head. When I woke up, the angry woman in the room was named Marianna because Dax had said he would send her back. She was upset that I had woken up and... *wait,* "You're married to her?"

Nate laughs at my surprise. "I know," he says, nodding. "We're complete opposites, but it works. Life is about balance, Darya. You can't have good without evil, so it would make sense that you can't have happy without pissed off."

He wanders to the stove for a cup of coffee. When he comes back, I take the opportunity to try prying more information out of him. "Where are we?"

He sips his coffee and exhales loudly as if the hot liquid will allow him to breathe fire. "A few miles off Moonlight Lake." He sets the cup down, pushing it away. "Don't worry, Darya. You're safe here."

It's funny that he chose Cass's exact words because I feel more like a captive than I did when she said them. Since these people are just the guards and my jailor is off doing God knows what, there's only one more question. "Where's Dax?" I blurt out. It was clearly my voice, but I'm not sure I was the one who asked it.

Nate sighs, sitting in the chair next to me. "You know curiosity killed the cat, right?"

I roll my eyes and look at Cass.

"Oh no," she says, shaking her head. "I'm not privy to the dealings of Dax. I don't know where he is."

Nate claps his hands loudly and laughs. "There," he says, standing up. "Now that that's settled." He walks to the back door and swings it open. "It's impolite to lurk, Mari."

A moment later, a very irritated Marianna walks through the door glaring at Nate and me. "I wasn't lurking."

Nate leans against the edge of the door, smiling at her. "Whatever you say, my dear."

Marianna holds out a flask. "This should knock her out until Dax gets back." She slaps it into Nate's palm and glares at me once more before stomping out the door.

Nate slings the door shut behind her. "And that, ladies, was the love of my life," he announces. "No need for applause."

He bows to Cass and then me. I can't help laughing. *Maybe they're not all that bad.*

Nate comes to the table and sits down with me. I grab the flask, twisting the cap off. "That smells awful!"

"Yeah," Nate says, laughing. "The best ones always do."

"It'll help you sleep, Darya," Cass says. "You're gonna need your rest." She sets some plates down in front of Nate and me. They overflow with the best-smelling food ever to grace my nose. My stomach growls in response. "Eat, you two. It'll be dawn soon."

I stop the fork halfway to my mouth. "What happens at dawn?" I look from one to the other as best as possible while shoveling food into my mouth at an embarrassing speed.

Nate frowns. "It's just been a long night, Darya," he says. "We all could use some sleep."

He's not wrong. They both look exhausted, and the burning on my neck has taken a lot out of me. I should also lie down after eating all this food so I don't pop.

It's not until I'm scraping my fork against the bottom of the plate that I realize Cass hasn't eaten anything. I watch her clean the kitchen counters for a moment. "You're not hungry, Cass?"

Cass waits for Nate to nod to her before answering. "It's not my place, Darya."

Her words twist and turn in my head until I finally conclude that they would never make sense. "What does that mean?" I ask, thoroughly confused.

Cass opens her mouth but stops when Nate lifts his hand slightly off the table. She closes her mouth, looking at the floor.

Nate takes a deep breath, placing his fork on his plate. "Darya, our world is a little different from what you're used to." He nods to Cass, who takes his plate from the table. "We maintain order by knowing our place."

"So Cass isn't allowed to eat with us?"

"Darya," Nate starts with a deep sigh. "Right now, you are a guest here. Don't rock the boat if you don't know what's in the water."

I feel like Nate is warning me versus issuing a threat. "You're ok?" I ask, looking at Cass.

"Yes, I'm fine, Darya," she assures me. She takes my plate and brings it to the washtub.

Nate casually spins the bottle of concoction his wife had brought until Cass finishes the dishes. She grabs it just as Nate nearly twirls it off of the table.

Pouring the disgusting liquid into a glass, Cass ushers me from my chair. "I think it's time we get you to bed, Darya." She places her arm around my shoulders, escorting me back to Dax's room. Cass closes the door and urges me toward the bed. "Don't worry about me. I'm well cared for here. They have always been good to me."

She hands me the glass of nasty-smelling liquid. "Nothing to make it taste better?" I ask, wrinkling my nose.

"Maybe it'll be easier if you drink it fast." Cass sits in the chair and swings her arm toward the bed, encouraging me again to sit there. "You need your rest, so drink up."

My face cringes as I bring the glass to my mouth. I open up and chug the vile liquid as fast as possible. I can't hold back the gag as I pull the empty glass away from my mouth. "That shit is horrible."

Cass smiles, pulling a thick blanket from a drawer. "Lay down, Darya. It won't take long to kick in." I lie on the bed, facing her with my head on the pillows. She throws the blanket over me to help combat the cold of the stone room.

"Will you stay with me?" I feel like a child, but I have no idea what I'm dealing with regarding these people. I can't help feeling like she is the only person on my level who might be able to help me.

Cass grins, sitting in the chair. "My orders are to stay with you and make sure you don't touch your neck. How is it, by the way?"

I touch the nearly useless ice pack. "It's still there, with enthusiasm. I think I might be getting used to it, though."

She reaches out to pat my shoulder. "Sleep, Darya."

3

I'm not sure when my eyes closed, but I don't remember anything after Cass told me to go to sleep. It takes a moment to remember where I am when I wake. The bed is comfortable and warm, making me want to stay, but the empty chair in front of me means a clear shot at the door. Smiling, I grab the side of the bed and pull.

"Go back to sleep, Darya," Dax grumbles, closing his arms around me.

Clawing at the bed, I pull with all my might, but it's pointless. My hand lets go of the mattress's edge. I'm not just fighting Dax. I'm fighting whatever is inside me that wants to be here with him. He's going to win this battle.

Dax sighs, pulling me back against him. "Darya, stop."

I shake my head, trying to clear it. "Dax, what the hell?" The heat radiating off him soothes my body, but my brain still wants to leave.

"Darya, I haven't slept in three days," Dax grumbles into the back of my head. "Just be still and let me sleep." He buries his face in my hair and hums a relaxed sigh.

"No, don't you dare hum!" I yell, literally scolding the man for feeling relaxed. "Why do I have to take part in this? Sleep by yourself or with someone who actually knows you. Perhaps there's someone out there that even likes you!" I flop around until he loosens his grip, allowing me to turn over. He opens his eyes and stares at me. *His eyes truly are gorgeous.* I shake my head to clear it and glare at him.

"The burning, woman. The only time my neck doesn't burn is when we're touching."

Ok. I didn't think about that. My nose always wrinkles when I'm lost in thought. It's embarrassing and annoying, and now Dax reaches out to bop me on the nose like a damn child.

"You look like a bunny," he mumbles sleepily. With a yawn, Dax rolls onto his back and curls his arm under my neck. "Come here."

My brow furrows as I look at him in disgust. "What? No," I say defiantly as my body rolls over to him and curls up against him with my head on his shoulder. *What the hell just happened?*

Dax sighs with a smile as my face nuzzles into his chest. "It doesn't matter. I can make you do whatever I want." He runs his fingers through my hair.

"How can you control me?" I tell my body to move away from him, but nothing happens. I stay curled up against him like a lost kitten.

Dax turns his head and rests his lips against my forehead. He's talking, but I can't hear him. His short stubble tickles my skin, and his warm breath sends shivers down my body. When Dax moves away from my forehead, I realize I still want to know his answer.

"I think I dozed off," I lie. "What did you say?"

Dax clicks his tongue in irritation. "Darya," he starts, somewhat annoyed with me by now. "I'm tired and didn't want to answer you the first damn time. I don't know how I'm controlling you, but I like it. Now go to sleep." He wraps his arms around me, holding me against his chest. I want to fight, but there is something I can only describe as a tidal wave of exhaustion that crashes over me, and my eyes close on their own.

* * *

The lantern is running low on oil when I wake. Dax is twitching and mumbling. It's impossible to understand him, but he seems pretty upset. That uncontrollable urge to touch his face rears its ugly head, and my hand wanders to his cheek. Life these days is hard enough without having to suffer through bad dreams, no matter how much the person having them annoys me.

Dax's scent reminds me of the forest after heavy rain. I try to snuggle a bit closer without waking him. He leans his cheek against my hand, making me jump against him.

"Darya, if you get any closer, we'll wear the same skin." Dax rolls and closes his arms around me. He puts his chin on my head and sighs.

"I didn't know you were awake," I stammer. "You had a bad dream."

Dax works his jaw a few times against the top of my head, and I feel him look down. "Whatever it was, it ended when you started moving. It doesn't take much to wake me up." He pushes my lower back to roll the rest of my body closer to his. "This is comfortable."

I tangle my legs with his, unable to disagree. This feels comfortable to the point I might call it natural. That's when it hits me. "You're making me feel this way, aren't you?"

Dax sighs, looking down at me. "Feel what way, Darya?"

"All comfortable and shit!" I narrow my eyes.

Dax stretches his arms out to his sides. "Darya, did you ever feel comfortable when I was making you do anything?"

Well, damn. He's right. It actually made me pretty angry.

"It just feels right, Darya, and I'm not interested in questioning it right now." Dax runs his fingers lightly over my back with his eyes closed. "Besides, I haven't been controlling you since I made you go to sleep earlier."

"Wait. You did that?" I prop myself to look down at him.

Dax sighs, opening his eyes to look at me. "You seem like you want to be mad at me about something." He pushes some hair behind my ear. "I don't think that's our thing. I'm not interested in fighting."

He closes his eyes, laying his head to the side. I don't even know what to say to that. None of this makes sense. I'm more comfortable in this stranger's arms than I've felt with someone I know. I don't feel like I'm making these decisions, but something inside me clearly wants this man.

After a few minutes, there's a knock on the door. When it opens without waiting for permission, I duck into the blankets as quickly as possible.

"Sorry to interrupt, Dax," Cass whispers. "It's almost time."

"Thanks, Cass. Is there any food?" Dax rolls toward me as I try to crawl into his chest and disappear.

"Not yet," she responds. "I'll throw something together. Do you want breakfast, lunch, or dinner?"

Dax leans back and looks down at me. "What do you feel like, Darya?"

I feel like I'm ridiculous. I'm in bed with a stranger, and some woman just asked what I want to eat.

"Breakfast?" I mumble.

"You heard the lady," Dax says, chuckling as he rests his chin on my head. "Oh, can you grab that, Cass?"

When Dax rolls onto his back, he has my grandmother's notebook. He begins shifting us around the bed so he's lying on my shoulder and can hold the notebook with both hands. Dax opens it to some pages in the middle, and I close my eyes, yawning. My arm is across his chest, and when I open my eyes, I see my fingers drawing circles on his skin.

What am I doing? Once I stop my hand, I realize my bottom lip is in my teeth. *Shit.*

"So I looked through some of this last night," Dax says. He looks at me with his eyebrow raised curiously. I can't even imagine what I must look like, but judging by his face, I probably don't want to know. "Are you alright?"

"This is weird, right? I can't be alone in these strange feelings." I try to laugh it off, but I lick my lips instead, and his eyes lock on them.

"Yeah, sure, weird," Dax stammers before quickly shaking his head and turning away. "So, anyway, does your grandmother speak Drueidan?" He holds up the book and shows me some parts I've seen but can't read.

Sighing, I relax back into him. "I don't know. We didn't find the notebook until after she died."

I feel Dax turn to look up at me. "I'm sorry."

For some reason, I didn't expect that from him. He doesn't seem like the kind of person that cares about death or family. I curl my arm toward his head and run my fingers through his hair. It's softer than I thought it would be. It seems he's determined to surprise me in every aspect.

"I haven't seen the dialect since I was a kid," Dax whispers. "I'm not great, but this here says 'the Lunar Pack.'" I hear him flip the pages. "This says 'true heir,' and this one says 'curse.'" He flips some more pages. "This is 'arrive' or maybe 'birth.'" He groans quietly, turning his head to the side so I have more of his hair to twist in my fingers.

Another knock on the door makes us both jump. Cass comes in with a tray of eggs, sausage, and biscuits. In her other hand, she holds two steaming coffee cups. Dax lifts off me to take the cups from her. We shift around so she can put the tray on the bed, and I smile as Dax hands me one of the coffee cups.

"We're gonna need a change of clothes for Darya, Cass," Dax says, staring at me. "Tell Nate to bring me the white mare. We'll be leaving soon." He winks at me and then looks at Cass. "That's all."

Cass bows and leaves the room, closing the door behind her.

My eyes stay locked on the door. *That woman just bowed. I'm pretty sure I saw that.* I turn to Dax. "So, she just bowed, right?" I ask with my eyebrows knit together.

Dax shrugs.

"No, this is not a shrug kind of question," I spit out. "Why does it seem like you have a servant, Dax?"

He pops a sausage link in his mouth and smiles. "It's not like that, Darya. She works for me, and in return, she has my protection."

"Dax, she bowed," I say slowly, frowning.

"Oh, baby girl, your world is about to get much bigger." He runs his hand up my arm and squeezes my neck.

I narrow my eyes, studying Dax as he props the notebook against a pile of blankets. Some of his hair falls into the corner of his eye as he leans forward, but he doesn't seem to notice. I can't help licking my lips as he takes a bite of a biscuit. He looks up to catch me staring.

"Here, you look hungry," he says, holding a sausage link out. *Yeah, hungry. I'm sure that's how I look.* I turn the entire situation awkward by just staring at him. "It's food, Darya. Some people eat it." He shrugs at my display and jams it in his mouth. "So, listen, I have some stuff to take care of before we leave. This is gonna hurt like hell until I'm further away. When I get back, we'll visit a friend who should be able to translate this."

Recalling the pain, I cringe. "You think your friend will know how to stop the burning?"

"I don't know. Cass will bring you some warmer clothes," Dax says. "We're going into the northern mountains. I know it's summer, but it does get cool up there at night." He piles some eggs onto a biscuit and takes a bite. He seems so relaxed, as if hanging out with me in bed is normal. "I hope we'll find some answers."

My lip is sore from how much I've been chewing on it. *Maybe Dax's friend will know why my body seems to crave a man that my head doesn't want.* "I'm ready when you are." I smile, steeling myself.

He shifts around on the bed, stepping off to stand as close to the door as possible while still touching me. He nods and then darts toward the door.

Before Dax reaches the handle, I'm screaming in pain. I clench my fists to keep them off my neck because that was horrible last time. I look up, breathing through my teeth, and watch him leave. Cass crashes through the door he'd left open and slaps an ice pack onto my neck. I think Dax only told her it helped to make her feel good. It certainly is not helping me, but the pain subsides as he moves further away.

Cass pats my shoulder. "I hope you can find a way to end that. It seems terrible."

"Yeah," I grumble. "Terrible. That sounds almost accurate."

She holds up the clothes she'd carried in. "We need to find you something to wear." She sets them out on the bed. They have a commonality, and Aunt Rosalee would be proud of Cass's skin-covering selections.

"Oh, um," I say awkwardly. I dig around, finding a tank top and some shorts. I see an oversized zip-up sweater at the bottom of the pile.

Cass holds up a pink sweatsuit. "I would've gone with something like this. It gets cold up there."

I grimace at her. "I don't think it gets that cold, Cass."

She busies herself, collecting breakfast dishes as I sit down, reaching for my shoes. I shift the ice around, trying to make it effective, but the burning is getting stronger. I stand up, stomping down into my boots, just as a door slams somewhere in the house.

"Darya," Dax yells. "Get out here!" His voice sounds strained, as if he's gritting his teeth. I can completely understand because I'm sure the ice pack is boiling in the heat from my neck.

I fling the door open, falling into the hallway. I stumble as my vision blurs, but I reach my hand out to something that looks like Dax. He grabs my hand and attaches it to his waistband as I catch my breath.

I close my eyes and lean on Dax like we're friends. "Jesus, that's better than sex." My jaw slacks, and my entire body participates in my cringe. *What in the name of all things holy did I just say?* I peek around Dax's back to see them staring at me. *Yep, I said that out loud.*

I can feel the grin that creeps across Dax's face in my soul. "I hope that's not true," he says, winking.

As if my dignity needs another hit, Dax drags me across the kitchen by his pants. He grabs a set of saddlebags and stops at a bow leaning against the doorway. "We'll be gone for a few days, Cass. You'll need to keep an eye on Nate. You know how he gets." He loops the bow over his shoulder and pulls me out the front door.

After the dense forest outside the back door, I didn't expect the beautiful, lush field outside the front door. It's so bright that I nearly miss the big white mare near the porch. Besides stomping at flies, she waits patiently, just like the Friesian did.

"Now you're speaking my language," I say, allowing a smile to spread as I look over the mare.

Dax slows to let me walk beside him. "I thought you might like her."

"That Friesian in town wasn't yours?" I ask, frowning. I can't help feeling disappointed.

Smirking, Dax looks at me from the corner of his eye. "Oh no," he says smugly. "She's mine. With your reputation, you're not getting anywhere near her."

I set my jaw defensively. "I only steal from the militia."

"Mm-hmm." Dax pulls my hand from his waistband, throwing me in the saddle. He slings up behind me and slips his hand into my sweater. The sensation of his hand sliding across my skin has air rushing from my lungs with urgency. I'm still recovering from the blended feeling of fire and ice he left on my skin when he hisses at the horse, sending her galloping toward the mountains.

Even carrying two, any horse I'd ever ridden could not have matched her speed. We're all out of breath when he pulls the mare up, steering her into the woods. Dax lets his thumb run down my hip, lighting up my nerves. I let out a groan without realizing it until Dax reacts.

"Feels good, right?" He flicks his thumb again for effect.

I swallow hard and shift uncomfortably, trying to find a way to create some distance between us. Dax doesn't seem to notice as he digs around in the saddlebags. He pulls out my grandmother's notebook and hands it to me.

"Little bit of light reading while she cools down," Dax says lightly. I can hear the smile on his face and don't need to turn around to see it. He's enjoying the fact that he's making me unbelievably uncomfortable.

Although I'm probably blushing like a teenager, I square my shoulders and take the book in my most professional manner. Picking a random page, I hold it up. "Where should we start? Is there any more Drueidan that you recognize?"

Dax leans forward to see what I'm looking at, putting his cheek against the side of my head. As he speaks, his lips brush against my ear. My nerves fire down my body, and I can't hear him anymore. I'm sure he's still talking because his lips are moving, or maybe he's just breathing. *Oh, fuck it.*

I slap the notebook shut and jam it under my leg. Surprised, Dax starts to lean back as I twist my upper body around and grab his face. My fingertips hook onto his jaw, pulling him to me. Dax curls around me and crashes into my lips, leaning me back over his leg.

As Dax slides his tongue over mine, I become aware of a strange sensation on my neck. It feels like something's running down it. I push Dax away and pull my hair off my neck as I sit up.

"Dax, is my neck bleeding?" I shove my neck in his face.

He pushes the rest of my hair out of the way. "No," he says, sounding confused and out of breath. "It's just a birthmark, Darya."

I drop my hair and look at Dax. "I don't have a birthmark." Biting the inside of my cheek, I pull the notebook back out. "We need to figure this out."

Dax leans against the side of my head again, but this time I'm careful to ensure his lips won't slide against me. "That's not really where I was going, but fine, we'll do it your way," he whispers.

We flip through the book as we ride along. I land on a page with a few confusing phrases. Dax says he can't translate more of the Drueidan text, but there's plenty in English.

"What does it mean that the 'forgotten heir will remain?'" I turn to look back at him.

Dax sighs. "I think that refers to the illegitimate child of a pack leader."

"A pack leader? Is that like a tribe or something?" I ask, turning away from him.

"Something like that."

When I feel Dax sigh, I look up at him. My gut starts to flutter and heat up again when he looks down. *No, I'm figuring this out, not making it worse.* I shake my head, turning back to the notebook. "How about 'Forsaken members shall forfeit their right?'"

"I don't know," Dax barks. He hisses, sending the mare galloping up the trail again.

Although Dax eventually lets the horse slow, he keeps her pace moving too fast for me to look at the notebook again. I don't particularly like the angry silence between us, but I'm unsure how to fix it. Rosalee yells at me when I disappear for more than a few days, and the militia officers yell at me when they get close enough to be heard. I usually just laugh at them. That doesn't feel appropriate right now.

Dax slows the horse to a walk once the sun has set, so it's too dark to read, not that I'd chance it. It's evident that Dax is not in an excellent mood, and this book seems to be making it worse.

"We still have a few more hours to go if you want to get some sleep." His voice is much softer than I expected, based on how stiff he feels against my back.

I frown, feeling brave enough to confront him. "I feel like you're not telling me something. Maybe a lot of things. I don't like it."

Dax stretches his back and rests his chin on my head. I relax into him and soak in his unnatural body heat.

"You're not going to tell me, are you?"

Sighing, Dax relaxes his body. As he does, it feels like our bodies just melt together. "Not right now, Darya."

We travel for the next few hours in silence. The horse moves with a slow cadence, and I lean back against Dax's chest. With the gentle rocking of the horse and the heat coming off of Dax's body, you'd think I'd be able to sleep, but any time I doze off, Dax moves. He rubs his cheek along the side of my head, slides his hand on my skin, or runs his finger along my hip, and my body ignites like he's poured oil onto a fire.

My exhaustion is nearly at the level of tears when he tips his head to whisper in my ear. "We're here."

4

A gorgeous two-story cabin stands before us. The moon shines down on its wrap-around porch filled with swinging benches and half barrels containing colorful flowers. Dax directs the horse to the side of the building where a few hitching posts stand.

"This is beautiful." There's no disguising my awe and surprise.

Dax snorts as he slides off the horse. He lifts the bow from his shoulder, letting go of my hand. My neck fires up instantly, and I dive off the horse, landing on Dax to find relief. He crashes onto the ground, brushing my hair off my face.

"Are you ok?" He searches my eyes as if they'd contain the answer. "I forgot. Shit, it's getting worse."

"Yeah, that's getting old." Standing up, I pull him with me. Dax scans my body for injuries before running his hand over my cheek. Blood rushes to my face, and my heart pounds as he steps closer. He's a few inches away from me, and I'm fighting my body because it just wants to crash into him like a mare in heat.

I take a deep breath, about to lose this battle, when the door beside us opens. A middle-aged woman with her hair pulled back in hundreds of braids steps out. The woman raises a lantern. "To what do I owe this honor, Alpha?"

Holding her lantern, the woman stands calmly at the top of the steps as a rumble erupts from Dax's direction that sounds like a dog growling. *Is he growling? Where the hell is that coming from?*

Dax has turned his head to glare at the woman. "Jules," he says through his teeth. He slides his hand around my neck, stopping me from moving away.

"I didn't mean to disturb you, Alpha," the woman apologizes.

I finally turn to look at her as a much louder growl fills the air. The woman bows, backing into the house. I watch the door close and then turn back to Dax with my eyes so wide my forehead hurts.

He runs his thumb along my jaw and waits for me to close my mouth. "It's ok, Darya," Dax starts. "You don't have to be afraid." He sits on the steps and pulls me down with him. Dax scoops my legs in his arm, places them over his lap, and slides his hand into my sweater along my back to keep contact.

"You growled, right? I didn't imagine that." I'm sure I could focus on other, more critical facts, but I'm stuck on the noise of unknown origin.

Dax shifts his eyes upward, sighing. "Darya, what have you heard about werewolves?"

Suddenly an entire childhood of horror stories comes flooding in. Nothing but blood and death has ever been part of a story that included a werewolf. I swallow hard and study his face, looking for any sign of those stories. If any of it is true, I'm as good as dead.

"Only the fairy stories told to children to keep them indoors at night." I bite my lower lip and cringe, hoping none are true.

Dax smiles and slides his thumb under my lip until I release it.

"They're not true." He gives me a moment to process his short statement before taking a more serious approach. "Do you trust me?"

I pull my head back, considering his question. I don't even know this man. I have no reason to trust him.

"Yes." *Who the hell just said that? Did I just say I trusted him?* I shake my head and focus. "What are you hiding from me? If those stories aren't true, what is?" I nod, satisfied with my recovery.

Dax frowns, clearly not interested in helping me understand my current situation. I brush the back of my hand across his cheek. He closes his eyes as he leans onto my fingers.

"I can't concentrate when you do that," Dax says, looking at me through half-opened eyes.

With my eyebrow raised, I pull my hand away at a cruelly slow pace. Watching Dax's eyes roll and hearing him groan after he wouldn't let me sleep on the ride gives me great satisfaction.

"You are the devil, woman."

"Dax, tell me the truth."

He straightens up and holds my hands in my lap. "I'm not even sure where to start."

I turn my body toward him, curling my leg underneath me. "How about at the beginning?"

Dax raises his eyebrows and takes a deep breath. "Ok, well," he starts, letting his breath out slowly. "My father was a werewolf, the Alpha of his pack." He shifts a bit and laces his fingers with mine. "Werewolves have mates. It's a pairing that naturally happens. His mate died before they could bond. My grandfather saw this as a pack-expanding opportunity. He forced my father to marry the daughter of an Alpha from a smaller pack."

"Like the stories of the kings and queens in Europe?" I wrinkle my nose, not liking this story very much.

"Yes, actually," Dax says, squinting an eye. "It was a lot like that. My father hated the whole idea of it. He gave her a son and then left her."

He pauses, looking down at me as I frown. *How horrible to be forced to marry someone you don't love. His wife must have been lonely.*

"That's so sad," I whisper slowly.

Dax tips the corner of his mouth in a pained grimace and slides his hand around my hip. He pulls me closer as he continues. "He met my mother after that and fell in love. I came along sometime later." He smiles and rubs my arm with a faraway look. "They were so in love. I remember watching them and thinking, 'I want to have that someday.'" Dax tightens his arm around me.

When this started, he told me that werewolves weren't so bad, and now I feel like I'm intruding on a personal moment. Under normal circumstances, I would probably try to tiptoe my way out of the room and never speak to the person again to avoid this particular situation.

However, I'm a little stuck with this man for the foreseeable future, so I wait awkwardly until he continues.

"When my father took over as Alpha, he denied my half-brother and named me his heir. So, my half-brother killed my father to take his place as Alpha, as was the custom in his mother's old pack." Dax looks down at our hands. "My mother died shortly after that."

I'm unsure when my jaw flopped open, but I had to close it when he finished. "Oh, Dax," I manage to squeak out. "That's horrible. I'm so sorry. I asked you for the truth, but this is not where I thought this story was going."

His lips curl into a small smile, and he wipes a tear off my cheek. "After that, half the pack stayed with me at Moonlight Lake, and the rest went with him to the other side of the mountain."

"So, you're a werewolf?" I start piecing the story together in my mind so that it begins to make sense. "Are you an Alpha, like your father?"

Dax narrows his eyes. "I'm not a werewolf, nor am I human. I'm something in between. I am, however, their Alpha."

My curiosity starts getting the best of me. "So, Nate and Marianna, and Cass?"

"Nate and Marianna are a mated pair in my pack," Dax answers, leaning away from me slightly. "Cass is human."

"You said you protect her," I say, trying to lead him to give me more information. "What do you protect her from?"

Dax smiles. "She had an abusive husband. One horrible night, she killed him. We protect her from the militia." He slides his hand over my cheek. "Do you still trust me?"

I'm pretty sure I didn't trust him in the beginning when some crazy person inside of my mouth said yes. How am I supposed to answer now? I look up into his eyes and instantly become captivated by them. They are alive with every emotion imaginable, dancing from side to side, bouncing between my eyes as if one will say something the other hides.

"I don't know why, but I do trust you." As I acknowledge my confusion, a clear shove in his direction seems to come from inside me. My chest feels tight, like I can't catch my breath. Whatever is yearning for this man is going to win this fight. "Dax, is this real?"

He threads his fingers into my hair as he licks his lips. "God, I hope so." Dax slides me onto his lap and holds me against his body. I claw at him as his tongue plunges hungrily into my mouth. My hand snakes up his sleeve and eases across his back. I can feel his muscles contracting under my touch. Every nerve in my body wants to experience him.

"Dax?" I push my forehead against his to pull my mouth away. My chest is working hard, trying to heave air through my lungs.

Dax pulls the tank top strap down as he slides his teeth along my neck. He bites my shoulder, causing a need to settle deep within my core. My head rolls back as a moan escapes my throat.

With a deep breath, Dax tenses. He drops his forehead onto my shoulder and lets his hand slide from my neck. "We're not alone," he mumbles, sighing.

I would probably be frozen if it wasn't for my lungs working so hard to pull air. Somehow, I manage to push through my muddled-up thoughts. "What?" I can't see any movement in the cabin windows. The door hasn't opened. "I don't see anyone."

When I look at Dax, he nods toward the woods. "Nate's here."

I narrow my eyes, squinting against the dark to scan the tree line. I start to shake my head, but then I see it. A large, brown wolf slowly steps out of the trees. My eyes widen as my jaw drops. His back is at least the height of my hips, but he hangs his head low to the ground as if he's in trouble. A smile spreads across my face, and before I know it, I'm reaching my hand toward him.

"Nate?"

A growl resonates from somewhere deep within Dax.

I turn my smile toward him. "Oh, come on, Dax. Look at him! He's adorable." Nate lifts his head and happily pants a few times. "Is it crazy that I want to pet him?"

Dax glares at Nate, which makes him drop his head back down. He turns back to me and raises an eyebrow. "So listen," Dax starts, almost confused. "I'm glad you're taking this so well, but do not pet the wolf, Darya."

"You're sure?" I laugh in my excitement. "Just once, Dax. Let me get it out of my system."

Dax rolls his eyes. "We can make this uncomfortable, and I can make you leave him alone, or you can just keep your hands off the damn wolf."

His change in tone stops me. *Ok. Don't pet the wolf. Check.*

He turns to Nate, glaring at him again. "I told you to handle it." Nate continues moving up the steps, looping behind me. Dax said he would make it uncomfortable if I pet Nate, but I'm not sure it would be worse than watching them stare at each other.

"So," I say, drawing out the word. "What's going on?"

"Pack business," Dax barks, looking behind me at Nate. The wolf rests his cold nose on the back of my bare shoulder, which makes me jump. "Go. I'll take care of it later." Nate jumps back and runs down the stairs. "And stay home!"

Dax stares at the woods momentarily before turning to me. His eyes are considerably softer than when he looked at Nate. He takes a deep breath, pulling my sweater and tank top back over my shoulder. I can still feel the cold spot that Nate's nose had left.

"You can hear him?" I ask, reaching for his chest. "When he's a wolf, you hear him?"

"I can hear all of them," Dax grumbles. "It's not a blessing."

I try to frown to match his mood but can't stop my smile as I wrinkle my nose. "I still think he was pretty cute."

Dax stands up, putting me on my feet. "Whatever." He rolls his eyes at my childish grin and grabs my hand. "Let's go before we have any more unwanted visitors."

He pulls me through the door at the top of the stairs. The room we enter is enormous. A few colorful couches face each other in front of a grand fireplace, and there's a large dining table with twelve chairs to our right. To the left is a wall of glass offering a raised view over the forest as it cascades down the mountain.

"This is amazing," I whisper.

Dax winks at me as Jules enters the room from beyond the dining table. She gestures toward the couches, settling across from where Dax is dragging me. Dax sinks onto the sofa with his back to a staircase and pulls me down. As I have no grace around him, I trip over his boot and crash into him.

"Seriously, Dax?" I grumble. "A little warning next time."

He chuckles and moves me around to sit beside him, leaning against his chest. Dax runs his hand slowly across my midriff underneath my shirt. I feel an unfamiliar nervous heat rush down my body.

"How may I assist you tonight?" Jules stumbles over her words. I can tell she is desperate to refer to Dax as his title but is now afraid to do so.

Dax pulls the notebook out of his back pocket and leans over to hand it to her. "I'm hoping you can help us out by translating this."

Jules raises an eyebrow and opens the notebook. She turns page after page, her eyes getting wider with each turn. I'm watching her act shocked when my eyes close as Dax leans against the side of my head. I try to force them open, but they are stuck. I want to say something to Dax about this, but I'm pretty damn sure I'm going crazy. *How can someone not be able to open their own eyes?* He rubs his cheek lightly against my hair, and my head leans back to put my cheek to his. *What the hell is happening?!*

Jules speaks up suddenly, snapping me out of whatever has me cuddling with Dax. "This is talking about the Lunar Pack curse," she says excitedly. "Where did you get this?"

"Found it," Dax grumbles.

She frowns, knowing that's a lie, but Dax doesn't seem like someone you should question. "I think this is the prophecy about your brother."

Dax scoffs. "He's no brother of mine."

Jules slaps the notebook shut and fixes her gaze on him. "I'm going to stop if you're just going to get angry at me for what is in this book." I feel him tense behind me. "I will tell you what I find, but you cannot get angry at me for someone else's writing."

I look up just in time to see Dax roll his eyes. "Continue."

Jules nods and opens the notebook again.

"The prophecy states that the blood of the blended pack will end the line of the rightful heir." She keeps her head down, reading to herself.

"What does that mean?" I ask.

"Markus thought that it meant Miles would end his line, so he named Dax his heir." Jules looks up with a thoughtful expression.

"But that wasn't right?" I press. *Why do I feel like I'm the only one interested in what's going on?*

Jules shakes her head. "I have no idea. Prophecies are no more than a pain-in-the-ass prediction. I think it foretold that Miles would kill Markus, but none of that matters now." She looks back at the notebook. "Mira, Miles' mother, was furious at Markus. She sought a witch to create a curse. This part says she rode south for ten days to find a witch who would defy him."

She runs her fingers over the pages. I recognize the section she is in as a part written in Drueidan. I slide my hand along the arm Dax has slipped into my sweater and look up at him. He sighs, giving me a weak smile as he kisses my temple. *It is truly unnerving how normal that feels to me.*

"According to this, Dax, the curse was meant only for you, not your whole pack." Jules continues to slide her fingers over the text. "Activated by Mira's blood, you were to pay for your mother's sins for all eternity."

My nose wrinkles in my confusion. "His mother's sins?" I swat at Dax as his finger pokes my nose. I'm turning to glare at him when Jules answers my question, distracting me.

"Mira, and many others, saw Dax as an abomination, the half-breed son of their Alpha." Jules doesn't even look up from her reading. "The curse was to be activated upon Olivia's death. The longer she lived, the more sins she'd commit. After Markus's death, Olivia learned of the curse. In her search for a way to stop it, she found Estrella, a hedge witch. Estrella told her that if she sacrificed herself on the day of your birth, that salvation would come." She pauses, moving the book closer to her face. "Or maybe that's meant to be 'enter?'"

She puts the book on her lap and runs her fingers across the top of the page again. I sneak a peek back at Dax. His eyes cast down to the floor, and there's the tiniest hint of a frown. I can feel his fingers digging into my hip, so I slide my hand down his arm and push on his hand. Dax takes a deep breath and lifts his eyes, opening his fingers to thread them with mine.

"Born," Jules just about shouts with a satisfied smile. "It's born. So it would be, 'Your end will be his beginning, prompting his salvation to be born.'" Her smile fades, and she looks up at Dax, confused. "Dax, this doesn't make any sense. Olivia died over 150 years ago. Wouldn't that mean your 'salvation' would have come and gone?"

Even with my skin burning and freezing together at once under Dax's touch and my brain all muddled up as I crave him, I still add this information up in my brain. I straighten my back, lifting my body away from Dax. My brain wants to look for an escape route.

His mother died 150 years ago. That means he's over 150 years old. He's, what? Just about my age? 25, maybe? He can't die. The man can't die. I need to get out of here. We have now exceeded my comfortable level of crazy. I just need to move. Come on, body. MOVE! But my body isn't interested in leaving Dax. So I remain seated on the couch like I'm the one who made this decision.

When Dax casually slides his hand up to my ribs, my body falls back onto him against my will. "Easy, Darya," he whispers. "I'm immortal. That doesn't make me dangerous."

Jules snorts. "Yeah, that's not the reason." Her eyes widen as she looks back up at Dax. "I'm sorry, Alpha. I didn't mean that." Even with her dark skin, I can see her cheeks fire up as she looks back at the notebook.

Dax lifts his head off the back of the couch and leans over to put his forehead against my temple. His lip brushes against my ear, and my chest heaves to release a deep sigh. My body starts to sweat as if set on fire when I hear him lick his lips. Right now, my mind rests between wanting to rip his clothes off and fearing what is happening to me.

"Dax, I'd like to take this to Celeste," Jules interjects, shoving my senses back into my brain. I silently praise Jules for stopping whatever embarrassing thing my body was about to do.

Dax sighs and turns away from my ear. "No."

Jules stands up. "But Dax, she could translate the rest of this and decipher the spell."

Dax growls. "I said no," he yells. "That book does not leave this cabin." He jumps off the couch to snatch the book from her hands and dumps me on the floor.

The burning starts instantly. I fall in a heap at Dax's feet. My screams echo as he crashes down on me. Dax holds my face in his hands, putting his forehead against mine as we both work hard to catch our breath. He pulls me into his lap, stroking my face.

I shake my head, clearing my thoughts as I pull his hands off my cheeks. "We need help to figure this out."

Jules moves around the coffee table and sits on the couch near us. "What was that?"

Dax's eyes scan my face. "You can bring her here, Jules," he says without looking at her. "Leave the book." I hear him talking to Jules with my ears, but as he looks me over and focuses back on my eyes, I feel like he's asking me if I'm ok.

"I'm alright, Dax." I hear my voice, but I'm not sure I said it. My eyes widen, and I raise my hand to my lips.

Jules hands Dax the notebook and quickly leaves the room. I'm still staring into Dax's eyes when a heavy door opens and closes, signaling her departure. Dax grabs my wrists and hauls me to my feet. He does another scan but takes in my whole body this time.

"Come on, Darya," he whispers. "I think it's time I let you get some sleep."

He leads me up the stairs and down a very short hallway to a bedroom. I step into the room, and he closes the door behind me. As he walks across the floor with me in tow, he kicks his boots off and lays my hand above his hip to pull his shirt off. He grabs my arm again and dives onto the bed, pulling me with him.

"Dax," I whine. "Let me take my boots off."

Chuckling, Dax slips his fingers into my waistband to free my hands. I kick off my boots, letting them fall to the floor with a thud, and remove the oversized sweater. Dax rises to his knees behind me. His fingers slide inside the tank top I had borrowed, and he slowly pulls it up, waiting for me to lift my arms. I decide there is no way I am letting Dax take my shirt off a moment before my arms raise on their own and let him.

Dax lifts the shirt off me and presses his bare chest to my back. I spin around and put my hand on his chest without breaking contact. When I look up, Dax's eyes are on mine, not my body as I expected. They are soft and curious. Everything inside me starts to melt in the heat they are creating. I hear him take a deep breath as he gently runs his hand across my cheek to the side of my neck.

Dax pushes against my hand until I move it, allowing him closer. He doesn't stop until his chest is against mine. Looking up at him, I can't help noticing that my lungs are heaving, trying to move enough air in my foggy state. Dax pauses with his hands on my neck and breathes out slowly.

"I have never wanted anything as much as I want you, Darya," Dax whispers, not taking his eyes off mine. "I don't know if I can fight this anymore. I'm not even sure I want to."

I move closer so his breath tickles my lips. "Then don't."

Dax crashes onto my mouth, making me gasp. Our tongues meet, and my body heats up as if set on fire. I slide my hands over his arms and around his back. His growl has me smiling into his kisses, but I know what he means. Dax's touch is like a celebration on my skin.

There's a moment of clarity when Dax's hands rest on my waistband, which has me questioning what's happening to me, but then his mouth lands on my neck. Suddenly, I'm not in control anymore. I attack him with animalistic needs, stripping him of his clothes. We pull at each other and enjoy our bodies as if this were normal.

I want to be upset about my lack of control, but Dax feels amazing in my arms. I'm not interested in ending these sensations. He pulls at my hips until I collapse onto his chest, slowly catching my breath as he runs his fingertips along my sides. Dax is still growling, but it's become more of a hum.

He inhales deeply and cuts the hum off. "I needed that." He kisses the top of my head.

I lay my hands on Dax's chest, resting my chin on them. "I just want you to remember the day you, mister big bad Alpha, needed me." My tongue slides between my teeth as I smile triumphantly at him.

Dax raises his eyebrows. "I think you might need a lesson in the pack hierarchy."

"I am not in your pack." I grin through my response. "You are no Alpha of mine."

He smiles. "Shut up and get over here."

I giggle as Dax rolls over, wrapping his arms around me and holding me against his chest. He rests his chin on my head. As the familiar wave of exhaustion crashes over me, I reach my legs out to tangle them with his. This time, I'm ready and welcome the relief that comes with it.

5

❧

My sleep is restless at best. The dreams come in waves. Men are fighting; babies are crying; women in white dresses and wolves are running across every scene. My mind settles on Nate as he strolls up the porch steps toward me. Dax isn't there, so no one tells me not to pet him. He looks gentle and calm. I can even hear him humming as Dax does, which makes me think he wants me to touch him. I reach out and push my fingers through his long coat. That's when his hum changes to a snarl. I pull back, but his teeth clamp down on my arm.

I jump awake, and Dax's arms tighten their grip on me. He ducks his head in the blankets, whispering into my ear. "Easy, my beautiful, it was just a dream."

That's not good enough. I need air and light, so I pull the blanket off our heads and try to roll away. Dax stiffens his body against mine. He pulls the blanket back to my shoulder, holding it in place. I duck into his chest as he growls.

"Celeste." He lets the name creep slowly from his mouth.

I jump when my grandmother's notebook slaps shut behind me. "Get over yourself, Dax," a woman says, sounding annoyed. "You don't scare me. Get up. We need to talk about that Blood Mark."

Dax remains tense, firmly holding me against him until the door closes. He sighs, relaxing back into the bed. Dax rubs his hand over my skin, sliding it over my hip and grabbing my thigh. He pulls my leg and hooks it over his hip, shifting my body.

Gently brushing his lips against mine, Dax rekindles the sensations

40

of last night. His cheek glides across mine as he pulls my hair off my neck. Exhaling, he opens his mouth to put it on my skin. My body comes alive with anticipation, but Dax's mouth never lands on me.

I wait a moment, holding my breath until finally, I roll away from him and see that he's staring at my neck. At this point, I'm desperate to have his mouth on me and don't care what's caught his attention. "Dax? What are you doing?"

His eyes flick toward mine. "Come with me," he mumbles.

Before I can protest, I'm pulled from bed and across the hallway. Dax inspects himself in the bathroom mirror before moving me in front of it. It takes a moment, but my eyes fall on his neck first.

I turn to Dax and shove his head to the side. "That wasn't there last night."

Rolling his eyes, Dax turns me back to the mirror. "It matches yours." He moves my hair and tips my head.

Looking at the image spread across my neck's left side, I feel sick. I touch it and pull at my skin, leaning toward the mirror to see it better. My eyes flick from my neck to Dax's in the mirror. Mine is on the left; his is on the right. I turn back to Dax and push his head forward to look at the back of his neck, finding a large circle.

I release his head and stare into the mirror. "Dax," I say on the verge of blinding panic. "Why is there a wolf on my neck?" I clutch my chest as my breathing speeds up.

Grabbing my shoulders, he spins me to face him. "Darya, you need to breathe," Dax says soothingly. "Easy now. You're not alone in this. I have it too." He lifts my chin until my eyes meet his. Wrapping his hand around my head, Dax pulls me to hold my ear against his chest. I can hear him hum from his gut, and the steadiness of his heart begins to calm me.

When I finally look up, Dax lifts me onto the bathroom counter. He slides his hands down my jaw and spreads his fingers along my neck. His thumb pushes my chin up, shifting my eyes to his face.

The problem is that Dax licked his lips while shifting my gaze. Now my eyes are fixed right where my lips want to be. Panicked or not, I can't control this need, and I'm ready to give up trying.

Dax's eyes close as he exhales and puts his forehead to mine. He takes a few deep breaths while I raise my hand and brush my fingers over his lips. On the third deep breath, Dax gives up. He pulls my head to the side and puts his mouth on my neck. His teeth slide down my skin as he inhales a deep breath of my scent. That might have bothered me a few days ago, but it has my entire body excited today.

I wrap my legs around him, inviting him closer to take more. Dax's hands drop to my thighs, squeezing them as he rests his forehead on my shoulder. I lick his neck and rest my mouth beside his ear. His back contracts with each breath as he begins growling.

"Sometimes it's ok to have what you want," I whisper, letting my lips gently slide over his ear.

Pulling away from me, Dax grabs my face again. "I'm a hundred and seventy-six years old, and you, Darya, will be my undoing." He pulls me to his lips, claiming mine as his own. In my head, I have no desire to have sex with this man that I barely know, but the rest of my body disagrees. I claw at Dax and try to bring him closer to me.

"I'm not waiting all day, Dax!" Celeste's voice yells. "Get your ass down here!"

Dax leans back and puts a fist to his forehead. When he straightens to look at me, he appears annoyed. "If we don't go down there, she's just gonna come up here." He leans forward to scoop me off the counter, and I rub my lower lip against his cheek as I breathe out, stopping him.

"Dax!" A very pissed-off voice screams from downstairs.

Dax works his jaw against my cheek, letting me feel his lip and stubble. "If we don't leave this room and put clothes on right now, I will not stop, and we will have an audience by the time I've had my fill of you." He pulls back and puts his forehead to mine. "And you deserve better than that, so stop making this so damn hard."

With his plea, my head takes control of my body, and I follow him back to the bedroom. To keep physical contact, we help each other dress. Clothing me proves extremely difficult for Dax. He seems more practiced in taking clothes off of women, so when I notice he's struggling, I can't help making it more challenging by distracting him. I run my fingers over his body and brush my lips against any skin I can casually touch. After his hands take my top off for the second time, Dax sighs and pushes me away.

"This," he waves his free hand to indicate my entire body, "is not helping."

"Fine, I'll do your job for you." I laugh and finish dressing. "Let's find out why I have a wolf crawling across my skin." I wink at him, feeling more confident than I have in the past few days.

Dax rolls his eyes, leading me downstairs. Jules greets us at the bottom of the steps holding two cups of coffee. She hands one to each of us and sweeps her arm toward the large table. Dax leans to kiss her cheek and pulls me across the room.

He holds a chair out for me as Celeste walks in from outside. She strides straight to a chair opposite us, slamming the notebook on the table. "Are you stupid?" She's staring at Dax. I'd have assumed I was the stupid one. I'm hanging around with a damn werewolf, but I'll go with being the smart one. I lean forward as Dax grabs my leg, pulling it across his lap. *This should be interesting.*

Dax leans back in his chair and sips his coffee while running his thumb over my knee. "Watch your tone, Celeste," he says casually. "You're a guest right now. That can change."

Celeste waves the notebook around. "This is a map, Dax," she sneers. "According to this, the greater the connection, the stronger that mark grows. The book doesn't say whether it's good or bad, and you're sleeping with her? Where's your head at?"

Dax grins. "Well, that shit's obvious, isn't it?" He sits up, squeezing my leg. "I didn't allow Jules to bring you here so that you could judge me. Can you translate that or not?"

Celeste settles into her chair and opens the notebook. She has long white hair that she collects neatly into one braid. Her already-tanned skin seems darker near its contrasting color. Celeste acts as though nothing could faze her, and those dark eyes command attention when she looks up.

"Mira meant this curse to play the long game. Olivia cut that short and warped it." She pauses and looks down at the book again.

"So she caused it to change to something else?" I ask, unable to wait for her.

Celeste looks up with narrow eyes. Her face clearly states that she wants to know why I dared to speak in her presence. "Yes," she snaps. "At least fate sent you a smart one, Dax."

I want to have something sharp to say back to her, but Dax is running his damn fingers up the entire length of my leg, and I can't hear my thoughts over my body's needs. Dax frowns at me. I snap my teeth at him and then glare in his direction over my coffee cup.

Celeste starts talking again, bringing us back to the moment.

"The original curse was on you alone, Dax. You were to 'walk the earth alone forever, paying for the sins of the mother.' According to Estrella, by Olivia sacrificing herself on the day of your birth, she created a way to break the curse." She runs her fingers over some more text before looking back at us. "On the 25th day of March 1910, Halley's comet was close enough to Earth to be seen with the naked eye. The power of that celestial event altered the curse."

For the first time since I laid eyes on Dax, I feel like I have all my faculties. *This woman must know how to stop what's happening to us.* "Altered it to what?"

Celeste glares, clearly hating everything about me. "I'm getting to that. Keep your pet quiet, Dax."

Dax has been focusing on my leg, watching his fingers drift lightly over my skin, marveling at how it reacts to his touch. The air thickens when his hand stops and lays flat against my skin. His growl is so deep that it travels through his arm, shaking the table. "Watch yourself, witch."

Celeste rolls her eyes. "Whatever," she snaps. "Instead of affecting only you, this text says, 'Those who follow the fallen shall lose themselves to the waters.'" Her eyes squint. "This would explain why your pack must stay near the lake, or they'll shift."

My eyes widen in realization. "That's why Nate —?"

"Yes," Dax whispers with a sigh.

Celeste turns her attention to the notebook, and Dax slumps a little in his chair. I trace my finger over the circle's edge on the back of his neck. His skin reacts with the same raised bumps as mine. Dax grips my thigh, shaking his head slightly. This seems to be his way of requesting that I stop.

"Halley's comet comes by approximately every 75 years. I don't know why it didn't happen last time, but it's 151 years this year. Some of this is smudged, but this says, 'Find salvation in pairing through the mark of the eldest pack.'" She looks up at Dax. "So it's saying that the mark creates a relief, maybe? Then it's followed by 'cured only by sacrificing salvation on the day of its birth.'" She turns to me. "You, girl, when were you born?" Her eyes land on me with the full intention of hearing my voice for the first time since we met.

Dax begins to growl again as he straightens himself in his chair.

"July 29th," I mumble.

Celeste lifts an eyebrow as the final puzzle piece falls into place. "Well, there you go," she says plainly. "You just need to kill her on her birthday."

Dax jumps up, leaning across the table. His hand rests on mine, a little heavier than I'd like, but I'm sure this is not the moment to complain. Somehow his growl begins to shake the walls, and a framed picture falls, shattering its glass. Celeste slides her chair back, standing up slowly.

"Get out!" Dax's voice rumbles with the addition of his growl.

Celeste jumps in surprise, darting for the door, and I can't blame her. After that, I'm considering leaving my hand behind and bolting myself. I pat my cheek a few times, trying to wake up. *Come on, girl, wake up. You can do it. You can't play with the pretty wolves anymore, Darya. It's time to return to the usual scary shit you can explain.*

"Darya?" Dax is watching me slap my face. "Are you ok?"

No, I'm not "ok"! You growl! There's a curse that I have to die to lift. Why me? How in the hell am I supposed to be ok?

I look up from my blinding panic and find his beautiful eyes. My mouth opens, and someone else's words fall out in my voice. "I'm ok, Dax." *The hell I am!*

He brushes my cheek with the back of his fingers. "I won't let anything happen to you," he promises, smiling. "If there isn't another way, we'll just stay cursed."

My brow wrinkles, and I bite the inside of my cheek. "You're sure this isn't a dream?" My eyes shift from Dax to Jules.

Dax only gives me a confused look, and Jules comes to his rescue. "I'm afraid you are in this just as much as the rest of us, my dear," she says, politely smiling. Jules opens a drawer and pulls out a roll of paper. As she spreads it over the table, she reveals a map of the valley. "According to the notebook, Olivia's hedge witch was from just here." She puts her finger on the map.

Where she indicates makes Dax groan. "That's across the hollow."

I lean over the map, squinting at its small print. I know this area well. The militia usually tries to set traps for me by keeping horses around the basin.

"There's a militia base over here." Jules points to the west end, which houses an expansive base. "You should be able to go around. It'll take longer, but you might find a descendant of Estrella's who can help."

"I can get us through there," I announce.

Dax looks up and studies my face. "You have a route through there?"

"A few, actually," I say, smirking. "I am more than just a pretty face, you know."

Dax shakes his head. "I've heard your reputation, but you don't have to do this, Darya."

"Oh no," I say confidently. "You somehow roped me into this. I won't sit around and hope you find a way out. We're going."

Dax chuckles as he rolls the map. "Thanks for everything, Jules." He looks around the room. "The cabin looks great. Thank you for taking care of it."

Jules nods to me before placing her hand over Dax's arm. "Be careful, Alpha."

"Always," he answers.

Dax slides his arm around my waist and guides me outside before I realize we're leaving. He marches us straight down the stairs to where the mare is still tied, chewing on her hay. Dax lifts my hand to his shoulder as he takes her bridle off the saddle horn.

"So, am I allowed to know the plan?" I ask, confused.

Dax lifts his eyebrow, but then his face softens. "For more than a century, I've traveled with nothing but a team of wolves that can hear my thoughts." He smiles, pushing some of my hair behind my ear. "You, my beautiful, will take some getting used to." When I raise my eyebrows, he continues. "We've gotta run back down to the lake. I have something I need to handle. Then we'll put your skills to the test, horse thief."

Stepping into the stirrup, Dax swings into the saddle before pulling me behind him. It's cute that his shirt is neatly tucked into his waistband, but that won't make it easy for us to keep skin contact, so I pull it out and run my fingertips across his skin. I flash my proudest smile as Dax sucks air through his teeth at the sensation.

He claps his hand over my thigh, catching some of the horse's flank. The mare tries to jump forward, but Dax holds her back.

"You better hold on, Satan's spawn," he growls before hissing to the horse as he drops her reins. She darts into the woods at a blinding speed.

* * *

After hours at the grueling pace, the mare stumbles through the dark field in front of the house. Dax throws his leg over her neck, dropping to the ground. I make a valiant effort to dismount but fall on top of him.

"Easy tiger," Dax says, chuckling as he catches me. He keeps his arm around me and helps me walk up the few stairs required to reach his house.

I smile when we open the door to an empty kitchen, thinking we're about to have a quiet evening so I can relax my aching muscles and sleep. That is until the back door crashes open, and Cass plows through with bags of food. I know it's rude, but I huff loudly and roll my eyes.

Dax turns me around and grabs my chin, making me look at his concerned expression. His eyes shift from one eye to the other. "You ok?"

"I'm just tired, Dax." I smile sweetly, placing my hand on his chest. I didn't need a lie to cover up what I'm pretty sure I didn't tell my body to do. I'm sarcastic by nature, I will laugh at a funeral long before I'll cry, but I'm not blatantly rude. I'm also not crazy, but the more I can't explain what I say and do, the more I doubt my sanity.

"Well, let's get some food in you, and then we'll sleep."

Cass busies herself about the kitchen, plating the food she brought. Dax sits down at the head of the table and pulls me into his lap. At this point, I don't care. One seat is as good as another. At least Dax wants to rub my back. I've never sat on a chair interested in doing anything but holding my butt.

Cass slides plates in front of us. I smile in thanks while Dax lifts his finger, signaling her to stay put. I jam a fork full of pasta into my mouth and raise an eyebrow. He seemed lighter or maybe younger when we were away from the pack. Now that we are back at his house, I can see the weight of the crown Dax wears. He pushes the food around on his plate like he's trying to find his words buried in the sauce.

Smiling, I stab some meat with my fork and hold it up for Dax. He shakes his hair out of his eyes and opens his mouth. Dax smiles and chews the meat before kissing my cheek.

"When I said keep an eye on Nate," Dax says slowly, turning away from me to look at Cass. "I feel like that should have included keeping him home."

It's clear from the worry on Cass's face that she regrets Nate's actions. I have fun with Dax, but knowing what he is, I would never defy him.

I put my arm around Dax's neck, hoping to smooth things over for Cass. He doesn't take his eyes off her. They aren't even blinking. *Do immortal men have to blink? That's probably not important right now.* I slide my fingers up the back of his neck. Dax sighs, slipping his hand up the back of my shirt, never averting his eyes.

"There were issues," Cass finally says. "We felt that you should know right away."

"What the fuck am I going to do about it on the side of the mountain, Cass?"

Cass nervously flicks her eyes between us before continuing. "We have him tied up in the barn now," she mumbles.

"At least he fixed his screw-up," Dax grumbles. He releases Cass from his stare and puts his forehead on my temple. Dax raises his hand slightly, indicating Cass can leave. She hurries away while Dax opens his mouth and runs his lower lip along my jaw. His hot breath sends shivers across my skin.

I close my eyes, letting Dax distract me for a while. I've only felt satin a few times in my life, but I remember it feeling a little rougher than his touch at this moment. His hand moves across my back while his lips apply no more pressure than his breath on my neck. Air rushes from my lungs, and my eyes roll painfully under their lids.

Dax slides his arm under my legs and lifts me off his lap. He curls me against his chest. "I thought you might like a bath," Dax whispers, carrying me into the bathroom, where a freestanding tub filled with steaming water greets us.

"I suppose you'll be joining me?" I raise my eyebrow as he lowers my feet to the floor.

The past few days have been strange. I don't know what is bringing us together, and my body seems to have a mind of its own when it comes to this man, but he's done nothing but adore me. It's almost a relief when Dax begins removing my clothes and says, "There's nowhere else I'd rather be."

We quickly undress each other and slip into the hot water. I lean against Dax's chest, putting my feet on the tub's edge. He gently runs a rag over my skin as I close my eyes and relax into him. I've always just washed my own body. Clearly, I've been missing out. Dax carefully finishes cleaning my entire body and rewashes my arms before I finally speak up.

"Do you think we can find a way around this as your mother did?" I ask.

Dax sighs, running his hand down my arm. "I'm no stranger to curses being cursed myself, but I've never tried to lift a broken curse." He slides me to the side to look into my eyes. "We have two months to figure this out, and I'm not giving up until we're out of time." He gently kisses my lips. "As I said, if we can't find anything, we'll just stay cursed."

Frowning at him, I shake my head. "Dax, I'm not interested in dying, but I can't just leave your pack cursed, either."

Dax stands up, pulling me to my feet. He turns me around and holds my face. "Then I guess we better get to work, huh?" He smiles and leans down for my thighs. With one swift move, he lifts me to his hips. I wrap my arms and legs around him, trying not to fall.

"What are you up to?" A smirk plays across my face.

"So there is one thing I can do that doesn't hurt anyone," he says, smiling. His eyes dance in the candlelight as he slides his arms around my back to pull me snugly against him.

After a moment, I lift my head off his shoulder and look around. Nothing is happening, and I wonder if I've missed the big event. That's when I notice that I'm getting warmer. *Is he heating up?* I pull away from Dax to look at his face. His eyes are closed in concentration.

"Be still," he whispers. "I can't remember the last time I did this with a human."

Steam rises off both of us as we dry in his heat.

"There you go," he declares with a broad smile.

I dramatically throw my arms back around him and kiss his neck. "My hero," I exclaim.

Dax blows out his lips and carries me to the bathroom door. "I'm just doing my part, ma'am." He playfully bites my shoulder as he opens the door. Dax brings me across the hall to his room, and I barely slide my leg out of the way as he rolls onto the bed with me. "Behave yourself tonight, woman," he mumbles into my forehead before kissing it. "My ass is tired."

He wraps his arms tightly around me, holding me against his chest, and his chin rests on my head. There's an overwhelming sense of comfort and security when I lie in Dax's arms. I'm pretty sure no one would dare to harm me when I'm with him, but there is something else there. Something doesn't feel right. *I don't think this is where I'm supposed to be.*

6

It feels like I've only slept a few minutes when a knock wakes me, followed closely by someone entering the room. I pull the blanket over my head. *That seriously needs to stop.*

"It's first light, Dax," Cass whispers.

Groaning, I claw at Dax's chest. "Wouldn't noon have been a better time to wake up?"

"Thank you, Cass," Dax says slowly, leaning back to look at me. "Can you tell Nate I'll be down there in a bit? Leave some food in the kitchen."

Cass's footsteps travel toward the doorway. "Sure, Dax," she says quietly. "Darya, I washed your clothes and left them on the chair for you."

"Thank you," I mumble.

When the door closes, Dax pulls the blanket off my head. "Not a fan of mornings?"

"I'm not a fan of being woken up." I snuggle my face between the bed and his chest to block out the light from the lantern Cass had left behind. "I also don't like random people coming in the room while I'm sleeping, which seems common for you."

Dax slides down the bed to bring me face-to-face with him and smiles. "That does seem to happen to me a lot, doesn't it?"

I can't help smiling back at Dax. He's so different when we're alone. I must have wrinkled my nose because he bumps it with his finger. I swat him and rub my nose.

"Come on, woman. Curses to break, people to hit. It's gonna be a great day." Dax rolls over the top of me and drags me out of bed.

I'm too tired to distract him while he tries to dress me, but I still get my giggles from not helping him. My top is a fitted leather vest that Rosalee made for me. It has eight brass buttons up the front, and Dax saves them for last. By the time he gets to them, he's annoyed with me.

He pushes me down on the bed, runs his tongue from my belly button to my throat, and bites my neck. My back arches, and I take a deep breath to hold as my body switches from tired to wide awake.

Dax turns to sit between my knees. He wraps my leg around his ribs so that he can pull on his boots. "Do your own damn buttons, woman."

I giggle and whimper, but he just laughs at me. I let him tow me to the kitchen once I've finished dressing. We quickly make sandwiches with the eggs and toast we found in the kitchen before leaving out the back door.

"Where are we going?" I ask once I finish my food.

"We need to stop by the barn to see an old friend this morning," Dax says, smiling.

"How far is it?" I ask. "I didn't see it when I was walking with Cass."

Dax frowns. "Cass had you out here?"

He wasn't supposed to know about that? Why do these people test this man? By now, I've completely embraced my inability to lie to Dax, so I just say the first thing that comes to mind. "It's a nice day today."

"I agree," he says sarcastically. "It'll be a blessing for them when I string them up by their wrists for disobeying me."

My jaw drops. "You wouldn't do that to Cass, would you?"

Dax sighs. "No," he grumbles, glancing at me. "She wouldn't survive. I'd just tie her to a tree trunk. My word is the law here, Darya."

Sliding my hand into his waistband, I step away and let his hand fall off my hip. Dax stops and turns toward me. He cups my cheeks and turns my face to look into his eyes.

"I will talk to her this time," he promises.

"Thank you." I don't know these people, so I'm unsure why I'm concerned about their well-being, but I feel on the verge of tears thinking about them being punished for anything.

Dax scans my eyes as I open them, no doubt trying to ensure that I'm taking him seriously. He slides his thumbs over my cheekbones. "I know you see them as people, but try not to forget that they are wolves. I have to keep them in check."

"I understand," I whisper with a small smile. "I'm sorry."

He takes my hand from his waistband, threading his fingers with mine. "We're almost there." He kisses my fingers and leads me down a short trail to the left.

We emerge from the woods, entering a field of dry straw. In the center stands a dilapidated building that was probably a house at one point. Dax is leading me to this building that looks nothing like a barn. Boards are falling off, the windows have no glass, and parts of the roof have collapsed.

"Is this what you were calling 'the barn?'" I look up at Dax, confused.

He snorts. "It's where we keep all the stubborn mules."

I raise my eyebrow. *I can't even tell if he's being serious right now.*

Dax pats my hand and leads me up to what I assume is the front door. "Come on, my beautiful," he says, smiling. "Time for us to say hello to an old friend." He turns the handle, making the door's hinges creak loudly as we enter. Inside, the building looks how I pictured it. The floor has years of dirt and dust covering it, broken furniture is lying about, and the walls have holes and broken boards everywhere.

The large room we entered is off a hallway that leads straight down the length of the building. As Dax pulls me through the house and down the hallway, I notice a sound coming from further inside. It sounds like a banging but then becomes more of a grunt. He reaches a door at the very back of the building. It has a large slide lock that Dax grabs and pulls back. He looks around at me and winks as he pushes the door open.

This room is very different from the rest of the house. It's almost out of place. The door is much thicker than it looked like it was from the outside. The room has wide reinforced wooden beams and bars over the windows. There's a metal frame of a bed in the corner and a small table against the wall.

My eyes land squarely on Nate. He's standing near the middle of the room in shorts and boots. The sweat on his skin glistens against the light from the windows. He turns toward us, looking shocked to see me. Something in me wants to check him for injuries when I'm distracted by a laugh I know all too well.

"If it isn't my favorite horse-thieving bitch!" My eyes jump to the man tied to a post in the middle of the room. The Commander glares at me through swollen eyes.

"Don't talk to her, Anthony," Dax says casually.

I've never felt any love for the Commander, so when Dax pulls me over to them, I take the opportunity to poke at him. I flash the Commander my sweetest smile as he ignores them to look down at me. "You got a little something," I say, pointing to a spot on my cheek to show him where he has blood on his, "right there."

The Commander narrows his eyes. "You're so damn stupid. You have no idea who the hell you're dealing with," he sneers.

Nate shoves me back and slams his fist against the Commander's jaw. "We use manners around here, Anthony," he barks. "Show some respect."

The Commander spits blood on the floor by my feet, and Dax hauls me across the room to speak with Nate.

"So, hey, Darya," Nate stammers. "Great seeing you again... in the barn... where I'm beating on some guy that apparently knows you." He grows more confused as the words come out of his mouth. *I can't blame him. I'd be wondering why I was here too.*

I smile, shaking my head. "Hi, Nate," I say. For some reason, I have to fight my hand because it is desperate to cup his cheek. *Knock it off hand. That can't be appropriate. And now I'm talking to my hand. At least I'm winning this battle. That's new.*

"Did you get anything out of him?" Dax sits on the small table and pulls me sideways between his legs, letting me face Nate.

Nate's eyes dart between us as he answers. "He was just looking for

Cass," he says, continuing his confused tone. "He says he didn't know we were here."

I lean my hip against Dax's groin accidentally. "Darya..." Dax starts, sighing.

I move away and put my hand up to stop Dax. "Wait," I say, like I'm part of this conversation. "Why was he looking for Cass?"

"That bitch killed my brother," the Commander answers me from across the room.

Dax drops his head and sighs, moving me out of his way so that he can hop off the table. He jams my hand into his waistband and storms across the room to lift the Commander by his throat. "I told you not to talk to her, didn't I?" Dax calmly stares at the Commander as he turns beet red from the lack of oxygen.

The Commander leans forward against his bindings when Dax finally releases him, gasping for air. "What the fuck, Dax?" he coughs out. His legs shake as if it's been days since he was allowed to sit. *They may not be friends, but he obviously knows these people. Why would he even be tempted to piss them off?*

Dax puts his hand out to move me with him as he takes a few steps backward. "Did you come alone?" He looks to the Commander, who glares back at him while noisily heaving air. Dax sighs. "Anthony, shall I go get your kids? We can all sit around and have a nice chat."

"It's just me," he spits out.

Dax raises his eyebrows. "And did you tell anyone where you were going?"

"No," the Commander sneers through his teeth.

Dax runs his tongue over his teeth, clearly trying to stop the grin threatening to creep across his face. "Anthony, why are you so angry? You're the one who trespassed on our land."

I've never seen the Commander look dumbfounded before. "I don't know, Dax, maybe because your guy chained me up and has been beating the shit out of me."

Dax tilts his head, nodding. "Alright, you've got a good point. I'd be pretty pissed too." He steps forward to pat the Commander's chest. "Thanks for the chat, though. I'll pass my condolences to your kids."

Lifting his arm over my head, Dax presses his hand against my lower back and guides me toward the door. He doesn't look at me but applies steady pressure on my back to move me forward. Nate keeps his eyes on me as he opens the door for us. Dax stops beside him. He puts his hand on Nate's shoulder and looks back at the Commander. "Kill him."

With that, he pushes me out the door and hooks my hand in his waistband. I hear the lock slide back into place, and then a punch connects with a grunting noise. Dax marches straight through the house, pulling me along behind him. If I trip, he'll probably just drag my body and might not even notice. Dax opens the front door, walking through the clearing and into the woods.

As soon as we're surrounded by trees again, he stops and turns to me. "Are you ok?" Dax asks, sliding his hand over my cheek.

I stare up at him. My mouth opens and closes several times without producing words. *He threatened kids and ordered Nate to kill a man like he was ordering a coffee. I've tangled with the Commander for ten years but never considered killing him. It was so easy for Dax.* I sigh and look into Dax's eyes as he leans down. *Look at him. He seems to care about me. Why would I be afraid of him?*

"I don't know, Dax," is all I say.

Dax breathes deeply and pulls me to his chest. His arms wrap around me, holding me tightly. "I'm sorry, Darya," he whispers. "I didn't have any other choice. I had to bring you with me. The last thing I expected was for that fool to find us."

He's right. The Commander found his people. He's not just going to walk away and leave them in peace. He'll bring his unit back and attack them. Dax was making the only decision that protected his people.

I pull away from his chest and smile up at him. "I'm ok," I say calmly. "You make these decisions so fast, and it's gonna take me a moment to process them."

Dax runs his hand across my cheek and bumps my nose. "Well, my beautiful, from now on, I will go as slow as you need me to." He traces my jaw and spreads his fingers along my neck. Licking his lips, Dax pushes my chin up with his thumbs.

"Why do you call me that?" I ask, interrupting his advance.

Dax stops with his lips barely touching mine. "Because you're mine, and you're beautiful." He kisses me, sending the familiar pulse of heat he generates throughout my body.

With an intense moment of clarity, I push firmly on his chest, and his lips move away from mine. "You're lying," I state accusingly. "Tell me the truth."

Dax tries to reclaim my lips, but I hold him off and give him a stern look until he gives in. "It's something my mother used to call my father," he admits, sighing. He slides his arm around my lower back and guides me down the trail. "Every night, my mother would sit on the back porch, waiting for my father to return. He almost always came home as a wolf. He'd run into her arms, and she'd ask, 'What have you been up to today, my beautiful?'"

I smile as I watch the scene play out in my mind so vividly that I can just about reach out and touch Olivia's shoulder. "I'm honored to share the name with him."

Dax looks off into the distance with a thoughtful expression. "He used to ask her how she could ever love a wolf."

How could anyone resist a wolf? "What did she say?"

"She said she needed him like he was a cool drink in the desert sun." Dax turns to face me. He slips his hand over my neck, and my core fires up instantly, causing me to shudder as I inhale sharply. Dax backs me into a large tree and presses his body against mine. I stare into his eyes as even their blue color has darkened. He rubs his lips lightly over mine. "Darya," he whispers. "I'm thirsty."

I grab Dax's neck and pull him to me as he tugs on my belt buckle. I tip my head to the side and slip my tongue past his lips. My hands tear at his pants, but I'm sure I didn't tell them to do it. I barely feel my body's movements. My nerves sizzle under Dax's hands as they relish his touch, and my chest heaves with each breath. The moans are in my voice, but I'm listening to myself from somewhere else.

Dax claims me until he falls against my body, holding me to the tree with his chest. His touch is soft as he gently caresses my thighs. I'm exhausted when I regain control over my faculties and lift my head from Dax's shoulder. I test my limbs as we catch our breath, ensuring they move as I tell them to. *That had to be my imagination.*

"We need to head back to my house," Dax whispers, gently kissing my lips and putting me on my feet. He leans down to bite my neck while he pulls up his pants. "We have people waiting for us at the house."

I reach for my shorts. "Sure," I say cheerily, hiding my confusion about what just happened between us.

Dax takes my shorts from me and pats my butt with a grin before pulling them up. "You'll like these guys. They're all wolves. I know how much you like my wolves." Dax smiles as he hooks my arm in his. We walk back to his house, silently enjoying each other's company like ordinary people.

When we reach the house, Dax opens the back door, and we step into the kitchen together. Cass is at the wood stove cooking up a feast, and three new faces are sitting at the dinner table. All three stand up and bow their heads at Dax. He sweeps his arm slightly, and they sit back down, returning their attention to their food.

Dax pulls out the chair at the head of the table. "These lovely ladies are Storm and Mason," Dax says quietly. The women look up and nod. They look like sisters, sporting dark brown hair with red highlights and dark brown eyes. I don't know which is which, but they are both beautiful. "They're in charge of our hunting teams."

Dax sits down and kicks a chair into the younger man sitting with them as he pulls me into his lap. "That pain in the ass is Tarq."

The young man rises from his chair and narrows his eyes at Dax before smiling at me. He's only three or four steps away, but it takes him an eternity to close that gap. His sandy blonde hair falls neatly toward the back of his head, except for a few locks on each side. Those curl around to touch his cheeks just below his eyes.

I take a deep breath and hold it until he is in front of me with his hand out, waiting for mine. I don't know why, but I desperately need to touch him. I reach out to accept his hand and get caught in his eyes. Their light brown color captivates me in a way I can't describe. I want to stare at them until the moment of my death. When he finally touches my hand, an internal burning spreads over me, starting from my fingers and moving down my arm. It's soothing, like a hot bath on a cold day.

He brings my hand to his lips as he stares into my eyes. The moment his lips touch my skin, the Blood Mark sears with such intensity that I snatch my hand from Tarq and slap it over my neck. Dax sucks air through his teeth as he grabs his neck and growls, glaring at Tarq. The young man's smile fades as he drops his hand and bows his head.

"I'm sorry, Alpha," he whispers, defeated. He returns to his chair and sits down, staring at his plate.

Dax kicks a chair away from the table and nods for me to sit there. He lifts me off his lap, and I sit in the chair opposite Tarq. Dax talks to the women, but I can't hear him. I can't take my eyes off Tarq. My chest hurts, and I'm on the verge of tears. When Cass brings a plate of food and sets it before me, Tarq glances at me for a second. The air catches in my chest. *Why am I over here when I want to be over there? I can't breathe. I need to touch him again.*

Dax growls at Tarq, louder this time. Tarq stands up and leans on the table, glaring at Dax. His growl starts low but quickly matches Dax's intensity.

One of the women clears her throat. "You can leave, Tarq," she says, lifting her glass of water to her lips.

Tarq stops growling and looks down at the table for a moment. He throws his glass against the wall before spinning toward the open door and leaving the house.

I stare at the door as Dax reaches under the table for my leg so he can let go of my hand. Something in me knows Tarq is still close. *Please come back. What was that?* I can't move my eyes. If I do, I'll miss him walking through the door.

I slowly become aware of Dax's fingers running over my leg. At first, it's annoying, but then it takes on its beautiful feeling of fire and ice, commanding my attention. I take a deep breath and relax into the conversation happening around me. *I'm obviously losing my mind. Why would his touch create heat?*

"You're sure you can control him, Storm?" Dax asks before he pops a piece of ham in his mouth. He catches me looking at him and motions toward my plate of untouched food. It does look delicious, and my stomach growls, asking for some of it. *Welcome to your reality, Darya.*

"Alpha, he's the best tracker we've got," the woman in the red shirt, who is probably Storm, says. "He's quite taken with her." She jabs her fork toward me. "He'd probably listen to her more than you. She could make it easier to control him."

My fork stops in my food. "Me?"

Storm snorts. "Tarq's got a thing for pretty faces."

So I'm just one of many? That solves that. I shove a fork full of potatoes in my mouth while I pout. Cass brings a cup of hot tea to the table, setting it before me. She smiles politely and then bows. It takes a moment to register that she bowed to me, not Dax.

I snap my head up and look at Dax. He's arguing with Storm about Tarq. "Dax?"

He raises his hand in the same manner Nate had used to silence Cass. *Oh, hell no. I know for a damn fact that fool did not just tell me to shut up!* I narrow my eyes at him and open my mouth, but when he turns to look at me, I instantly close it. His look alone could kill a faint heart.

"Later, Darya," he grumbles, returning his attention to the other women.

They talk about how no one wants to go through the hollow while I angrily jam food into my mouth, making a show of it. Dax finally lifts his hand, dismissing the women, and turns his attention to me. He grins at my display and pushes his plate away, leaving his eyes on me. Cass approaches the table to retrieve it, and Dax kicks a chair across from me.

"Sit," he barks, turning away from me to watch her drop slowly onto the chair. Cass nervously flicks her eyes between Dax and me, waiting for him to speak. "Darya tells me that you disobeyed my orders."

Cass instantly begins to stammer, trying to find a way to explain her actions. My jaw drops, and I try to pull my leg away from Dax, but he holds it firmly on his lap.

He flexes his jaw and licks his teeth. "What were your orders?"

Cass swallows hard. "To keep Darya inside and make sure she didn't touch her neck," she says quietly.

Dax taps his fingers on the table. "And what did you do?"

Cass looks down at her hands. "I took her outside." Her voice is barely a whisper. I have to hold my breath to hear her. Dax was hardly paying attention. He already knew the answer anyway. I try to pull my leg away again, but Dax digs his fingers into my skin.

Dax frowns and takes a deep breath as he turns back to me. "You have Darya to thank for this conversation," he says calmly. "She asked me not to punish you." Cass looks up at me with a pained smile. "Don't let it happen again."

"Thank you, Darya," she whispers. "Thank you, Dax."

Dax raises his hand again, dismissing Cass. She jumps up and runs out of the house. He leaves his blue eyes trained on me.

"Let's take a walk." Dax grabs my hand to pull me to my feet and leads me to the field. Sliding his arm around me, Dax pulls me to him as we walk through the tall grass. A few horses are grazing, but nothing else disturbs the view for miles.

I want to know why Cass bowed to me, but I can't stop thinking about Tarq. "Why are we taking your pack with us into the hollow?" I know better than to ask about Tarq directly after how they interacted in the house, but I still want to see if I can get any information about him.

Dax leans down to kiss the top of my head. "There's no safer way to travel than with a pack of wolves," he says, chuckling. "Besides, we're not taking the whole pack. Only a few wolves are going."

"It's gonna be hard to sneak them in and out of some areas." I have no idea why I even said that. I'm not trying to talk him out of bringing them.

"I've got it covered, Darya." His tone tells me to change the subject.

"Cass bowed to me, Dax," I say, frowning.

Dax stops and pushes me around to his chest. He wraps both arms around me, resting his chin on my head. "When you're with me, you'll have a certain level of respect from the pack."

"Do I have a choice?"

Dax sighs. "No."

He holds me for a bit longer before we start walking again. The field seems to be a calming place for him, and I don't mind having quiet time to think and clear my head. This day will probably be the most confusing day of my life. Yet somehow, I must pull my shit together and safely guide one very confident Alpha and his three wolves across the hollow tomorrow. I yawn, thinking about how exhausting this is going to be.

Dax notices my yawn and looks down at me. "Why don't we get to bed early?" He slides his hand over my hair. "I know I could use a solid night before we hit the trail again."

I smile up at him, grateful for his suggestion. "That sounds like an excellent plan."

7

〰

It doesn't surprise me when I wake up to someone barging into the bedroom. Dax grabs the blanket, pulling it up over me quickly. It was hot at night, and Dax's overheating body didn't help, so we slept naked and uncovered.

"Stop," he growls.

"Dax?" Cass sounds nervous.

Dax smooths the blanket over me as I smash my face against his chest. "Darya has asked that you wait outside the door until she gives you permission to enter."

What the hell? I start laughing as silently as I can, but there is no way either of them misses my body shaking.

"I'm sorry," Cass whispers, closing the door.

I pull the blanket off my head and find Dax in the dim light. "Dax, that is not how I meant what I said."

Dax lays back, pulling my head to his chest. "I don't understand," he says frankly. "You wanted people to wait until they had permission to enter. Now they will. I see no problem."

Of course he doesn't.

Another knock at the door causes Dax to look at me. His teeth shine in the meager light as he smiles, waiting for me to tell whoever is at the door they can come in.

"Seriously?"

Dax groans, rolling back into me. He rests his chin on my head and

64

slides his hand over my thigh. I put my leg over his hip as the knock sounds again.

I'm glad he's having fun. "Come in," I grumble.

I attempt to turn around as light floods into the room, followed by at least a few pairs of boots. Dax shifts his grip on me, stopping me from rolling away. He adjusts the blanket slightly, and his hum turns into a growl.

"Let's just have a fucking meeting," he snarls. "Clothing optional! You all wanna get naked too?"

Someone snickers, and then Nate speaks up. "So you want us to wait outside?"

As Dax raises the volume of his growl, I begin laughing into his chest again. I cannot maintain any seriousness between his frustrated growl and Nate's snarky question. The boots move out of the room, and the door closes. Dax rolls over, pulling me on top of him. Someone has left a lantern on the table, so I can see his smile now.

"I don't think your new rule had the desired effect."

"Ya think?" I say, laughing.

Dax stretches, pushing against the headboard. "Come on, Darya. They aren't known for their patience." He rolls us over and pauses to look over my body. I run my hands up his arms, trailing my fingertips over his shoulders and back down his chest. "A little longer wouldn't hurt."

Dax lowers his mouth to my chest as someone knocks on the door again.

"Go away," he says, making me giggle.

"Dax, it's time," Nate says through the door. "You need to go."

Sighing loudly, Dax kisses my neck and sits up. "Alright," he grumbles. "We'll be right out." He grabs our clothes and quickly dresses me before I can distract him.

When we reach the kitchen, Nate stands at the front doorway, leaning against its frame. He offers me a steaming cup of coffee as we approach him. I accept it and take a few sips while he talks to Dax.

I tune them out and try to move around Nate as I glimpse the black Friesian through the doorway.

Dax notices and takes the coffee cup from me. He hands it to Nate, causing him to move just enough that I see what they are hiding.

"What the fuck is he doing here?" I sputter as my eyes fall on the Commander.

Dax shoves Nate through the door and slams it behind him, closing us in the kitchen. "Knock it off," he snaps. "We need him." His eyes narrow into a glare, which I have no problem returning.

"What the hell do we need him for?"

Dax grabs some saddlebags off the table and throws them over his shoulder. "Wolves attract attention, Darya." He grabs my chin, making me look into his eyes.

I pull his hand off my face. "I told you I could do this." I roll my eyes and scoff at him as he pushes against me. "I'm supposed to trust you, but you don't trust me."

"Darya, please." Dax softens his tone and rubs his thumb over my arm. When I look at him, his eyes are calm and gentle again. He puts his other hand around my neck and gently pulls me until I lean against his chest. "I have over 150 years on you and know my wolves. We're gonna need him."

I pull back from him, looking into his eyes. "We do this my way?"

"Yes, Darya," he says, smiling as he tucks my hair behind my ear. "Your way."

I step back from him and open the door. "How do you know you can trust him?"

Dax winks, leading me through the door. "Because I have his kids."

Wait. What?

I stumble after him with my mind completely jumbled up. The Commander is sitting on the Friesian, quietly glaring at me.

"Isn't that right, Anthony?" Dax smirks, tying his saddlebags to the white mare's gear. "We're on the same team now, aren't we?" Dax helps me mount the mare and jumps up behind me.

The Commander shifts his glare to Dax. "One of these days, I'll figure out how to kill you, wolf."

"Well, until then..." Dax laughs and hisses to the horses, sending them galloping through the fields.

He aims them north until they enter the woods, and then the trail he puts them on curls to the west, toward the hollow. After a few miles, a large sandy wolf falls in with the horses. Normal horses would shy away from a wolf, especially one this size, but these horses seem to follow it.

"Easy girls," Dax says to the horses. The white mare slows, but the Commander kicks the Friesian, pushing her up the trail. The wolf looks up at us, but Dax just chuckles. "Damn, that man is thick."

He gives a shrill whistle, and the black horse drops her head as she slides to a halt. The Commander sails straight over her shoulders and lands with a thud on the trail. He hides behind the horse to wipe the dirt off his clothes. Dax allows the white mare to continue her calm walk beside the wolf.

"Convenient," the Commander says sarcastically.

"Isn't it?" Dax chuckles while the Commander climbs back into the saddle. Then he turns to him with a more serious demeanor. "As priceless as that was, knock it off. I need you to heal so you don't look like we beat the shit out of you."

The Commander scoffs. "Well, then maybe you shouldn't have beat the shit out of me in the first damn place."

They glare at each other and comfortably exchange banter as I look down at the wolf. It's laying off the trail between some trees. The sandy fur looks familiar, but I gasp when he looks up at me.

"Tarq?"

The wolf sits up and pricks its ears.

Dax sighs, and I feel his chin swipe across the top of my head as he turns to look at the wolf. His thumb rubs my hip. "Don't encourage him."

"Their fur matches their hair," I say slowly, watching Tarq as Dax urges the white mare forward.

The trail is wide enough for the Commander to ride beside us while Tarq jogs ahead. Tarq had fascinated me, but now I can't stop staring at how beautiful he is as a wolf. He's larger than Nate was. Tarq doesn't seem taller but has a much thicker build even though, as men, their bodies are similar. He puts his nose in the air, and Dax growls.

"Is something wrong?" I pry my eyes off Tarq, looking up at Dax.

He glances down and then does a double-take, confused. "What?" He narrows his eyes and shakes his head slightly. "No, Darya," he says, forcing a smile for me. "I can hear them. That one," he nods toward Tarq, "works extra hard at pissing me off." I turn to see Tarq bound a few strides, springing like a deer, before darting off the trail and disappearing.

The trail doesn't stay along the river long, but tonight's campsite requires us to keep beside it for the rest of the ride. When we reach the part that brushes the bank, we find Tarq lounging on a boulder, waiting for us. I adjust the horse to have her stay by the water, and Dax sighs loudly.

"I need to know where we're going so I can send the girls in the right direction to scout, Darya." Dax pulls back on the horse's reins to stop her.

"Dax..." I start uncomfortably, looking at the Commander.

Dax sighs and turns to Tarq. I follow his eyes, watching the wolf jump down and jog to the Friesian. He reaches up for her rein, snatching it out of the Commander's hand, and leads her further up the river.

I watch them disappear around a sharp bend before turning back to Dax. "I'm not the only one that uses these hiding spots. We would all be in danger if he stopped being your prisoner."

Dax brushes his hand over my cheek. "If he stops being my prisoner, it's because he's dead."

I take a deep breath. "A waterfall up the river will protect us for the night."

"You couldn't have just said we needed to follow the river?" Dax flexes his jaw, annoyed, and hisses at the horse.

It doesn't take us long to catch up to the others. Tarq is lying on his back beside the Friesian, still holding her rein in his mouth.

"Get up, you fool," Dax growls.

The Commander smirks at Dax's annoyance. "Trouble in paradise?" he asks, raising his eyebrow. I hear him snickering as he reaches for his horse's rein while Tarq bounces back to his feet.

"Nobody rang your bell, Anthony," Dax sneers.

The Commander points to his face. "That's a lie."

As his finger circles his face, I take a closer look. I've been so busy hating that he's here that I didn't even notice he has several bruises on his face. The longer I look at his wounds, the funnier his statement becomes. "Ok," I say, laughing. "That was funny."

Dax grumbles and pushes the group forward. We travel in silence for the rest of the day. Tarq stays beside the white mare for the most part. Every once in a while, I hear Dax growl. *Tarq must be the one wolf that Dax can't control.*

Just before sunset, we drop off the trail beside a pool that collects water from the waterfall. I tap Dax's leg, pointing to the ground. He slides off the horse and holds my hips as I dismount.

I nervously glance at the Commander before turning back to Dax. "Are you sure about him?"

His eyes are soft as he looks down at me. "I'll kill him myself."

I feel something brush against my hand and snatch it up. My jaw drops a bit when I see Tarq beside me. I reach out to him, running my hand over his muzzle and down to his jaw.

"You too, huh?" I ask, smiling.

He opens his eyes and nods his head slightly.

I know I've turned this moment about as awkward as possible, but this is my first time touching one of them, and Tarq is the most beautiful thing I have ever seen. As I'd suspected, his back is as tall as my hip. Although his fur looks like it would be rough, it is as smooth as the fine silk I steal from the militia. As I slide my hand under his jaw and over his throat, I feel a vibration, and somehow, I just know that he's humming as Dax does.

Then suddenly, my hand is moving away from him. We both watch it drop to my side. *What? No. I want to touch him.* I snap my head toward Dax, assuming he's making me move, but he's arguing with the Commander. I turn to Tarq as he steps toward me, his gentle eyes fixed on mine.

"Darya, let's go," Dax barks. "Didn't I tell you not to pet the wolves?"

As he pulls me away, I reach my hand toward Tarq, but he's already backed away. I frown as I lead them along a hidden trail beside the pool. Once we step around a large boulder, the opening behind the waterfall appears. I show them in, and we swing to the left into the cave.

It's mainly a sandy dirt floor, but at the mouth, on the right, some tall rocks hide a fire pit several of us dug out a few years ago. The stones cover most of the light the fire makes at night. There's chopped wood stored near the fire pit that Dax and the Commander use to make a fire.

As they finish, the Commander scoffs. "This is how you got away from me last fall, isn't it?"

I can't help laughing. "Yeah," I say, smiling broadly. "Ain't it great?"

The Commander shakes his head. "Sneaky bitch," he grumbles loud enough for everyone to hear over the water.

Tarq steps between me and the fire. He begins to growl with his eyes fixed on the Commander. Tarq sidesteps toward me, bumping his leg into my knees. *Is he defending me?* I've seen dogs growl and snarl, but Tarq is on a different level. *Even if his size doesn't bother you, his teeth should.* His canines are easily the length of my pinkie fingers. *And all I want to do is hug him.*

"Anthony, shut up," Dax barks. "Tarq, knock it off." Tarq continues to escalate, pulling his lips back to snarl at the Commander. Dax rolls his eyes. "Darya, would you please?" His eyes fix on Tarq.

Tarq backs up, closing his mouth. I run my hand along his jaw, from his chin to his throat. When he sits down, the height of the rock I'm sitting on puts me at his eye level. Tarq's eyes are nothing short of gorgeous. As he stares at me, I can see the black specks in the tan color. I find myself easily getting lost in them.

I'm absentmindedly running my fingers through the fur on his throat when I shift in my seat, nearly pulling my hand off Dax. He snatches my hand quickly before I break contact with him and turns abruptly to glare at Tarq. "If you don't go, you're going home."

Tarq narrows his eyes at Dax but then looks back at me as calmly as before.

I run my fingertips between his eyes and rub his ear. "You should listen to Dax before you get us both in trouble."

Standing up, Tarq slowly slides the tip of his nose along the left side of my jaw. Dax growls so profoundly that he vibrates the air around us. Tarq jogs to the mouth of the cave and looks back one more time before leaving.

"He was asking for your permission," Dax grumbles, sliding down into the dirt. I raise my eyebrow in confusion. He points to his ear. "I can hear him, Darya."

"So why does he try to do things behind your back?"

"'Cause he's a dumbass."

I slide off the rock to sit beside him. "How does it work? Can he hear all your thoughts too?"

Dax pokes at the fire and takes a log the Commander holds out. "In the beginning, they could." He throws the wood into the pit. "I had to learn how to control it."

I turn to him slightly, curling my legs onto his lap. "But you can hear their thoughts when they're wolves?"

Dax puts his arm over my shoulders, falling back into our easy companionship. "I hear when they're talking, not their thoughts," he tells me, brushing his lips over my forehead. "It's easy when they are close. When they're further away, I have to focus on the specific wolf." He turns to face the Commander with a smirk. "I hear Anthony's kids are just sitting down to dinner. Want me to tell them hello for you?"

The Commander gives Dax a look that is all too familiar to me. He smiles, but his eyes narrow. It's a look that he uses when he's planning your murder. I've seen it every time I've found myself cornered by him. *At least this time, he's aiming it at someone else.*

"I might not be able to kill you, wolf," the Commander sneers. He flicks his eyes up at me. "But I can kill your little lap dog there if you touch a hair on my kids' heads."

I've been listening to the Commander's hate for ten years. Most of the time, it just makes me laugh. Something about being called Dax's dog sets me off, though. Forgetting that Dax still has his arm around me, I attempt to launch myself at the Commander. Dax scoops his other arm around my waist and hangs on to me so I end up on all fours across his lap. I claw at the dirt, but it's no use. Dax is not going to let me go.

"Easy there, killer," he says, smiling. He pulls me back and grabs my face, pulling it to him. "Darya, I need you to dial down the crazy."

I roll my eyes as he chuckles at me. I don't know what made me so angry about the Commander's words, but I sigh and sit down, knowing Dax won't let me past him.

"Now that we've settled that, Tarq is returning with dinner," Dax grumbles. "Apparently, he thinks it should be a surprise."

I can't stop the giggle that sneaks out. "Why did you bring him if you two don't work well together?"

Dax keeps his eyes focused on the fire. "Tarq's the best hunter."

That's not it. "And?"

Dax rolls his eyes as he shifts them in my direction. He licks his teeth as if he's about to say something that will leave a bad taste in his mouth. "He's the only one I'd trust to put his life on the line for you."

Excuse me? My jaw drops in shock, and I lift my hand to question him when he turns back to the fire.

"Speak of the devil," Dax grumbles.

Tarq enters with three pheasants hanging from his mouth. He's jogging proudly with his head high, coming straight to me. He drops the pheasants in my lap and sits down.

Dax laughs heartily, shaking his head.

Tarq's eyes shift to me, and I smile reassuringly. "It's ok, honey," I say, reaching out to tug the fur on his throat. "I bet Dax would love to strip these birds for us."

Dax scoffs, but Tarq moves them to his Alpha's lap before returning to my side. He lays down with his nose touching my calf and stares at the Commander. Although three to four times the size, Tarq is like a big Labrador retriever. It would be tough to dislike him. It probably pisses Dax off, but I can't take my eyes off the large wolf as he relaxes near me.

Dax prepares and cooks the birds. He rolls his eyes at me every time I throw some meat at Tarq, but the wolf nudges my leg for another piece as soon as his Alpha looks away. *You are one large troublemaker.* Of course, I still give him more. *Why can't I say no to you?*

Once we've eaten, two wolves enter the cave. I assume they are Storm and Mason. They stay near the mouth of the cave, and there's something off about how they act. They stand with their legs squared, and their lips quiver in a snarl.

They've aimed their aggression at Tarq. He lifts his head to look in their direction but simply turns away to lay his head back near me. His eyes look from me to Dax. When I follow his eyes, I see the Commander smiling on the other side of Dax. *Why the hell is he smiling?* Then Dax growls loudly, and the women instantly stop. They move to different posts at the mouth of the cave, turning their backs to us. *What the hell just happened?*

Dax pulls me to him, away from Tarq, and leans back against the rock pillars. "Let's get some sleep, my beautiful," he says. "The sisters will stand guard tonight."

I curl up against him with my head on his chest. Tarq moves to lie down against my back. I hear Dax's growl through his chest. "Leave him alone," I tell him. "It's been a long day."

With the two of them heating up against me, I don't stand a chance and fall asleep within minutes.

* * *

When I wake in the morning, the first few rays of sunlight hit the waterfall. Tarq is kicking behind me, so I scratch his neck until he stops.

"Didn't I tell you not to pet the wolves?" Dax asks, his lips resting against my forehead. It takes me a moment to register his question because my mind suddenly races. *Why is that not affecting me like it was? I nearly wanted to eat him just a few days ago when he ran his lips against my skin as he talked. Now, I just hear his words and feel him move like it's nothing.*

I shake my head to clear it. "He had a bad dream," I say, defending my actions. "I was nice to you when you had a bad dream."

When I look up at Dax from his chest, his eyes are barely open enough to produce the glare he's giving me. "That kid did **not** have a bad dream. Quit petting the wolves." He pulls me upright and stretches his back. The sisters stand up from their posts and nod to Dax before they dart out of the cave. *I will never get used to all this thinking instead of talking.*

Tarq rolls over and pushes my leg with his paw.

I shake my head at him. "You're a bad influence."

"Where are we going today?" Dax's voice pulls my attention away from Tarq. "I need to send the sisters ahead of us."

I bite my lower lip as I look back down at Tarq. He lies with his muzzle resting on my thigh and his legs tucked neatly into his chest. He blows out his lips in a sigh and rubs his nose against my skin. *How am I going to get this enormous wolf safely through the hollow? I'm not sure I could handle something happening to him.*

"She's going into Silverton," the Commander says, answering for me.

Dax raises his eyebrows. "Is he right?" He tries to hide his doubt by acting surprised. "Right into town?"

I stand up and pull Dax with me. "If you're on the run, you avoid towns," I tell him, wiping the dirt off my clothes. "So, we go straight through it. It's the safest way."

Dax furrows his brow and looks down at Tarq, who has moved to stand at my hip. "Darya, I don't —" he starts.

"I told you I could get you through the hollow," I bark, my eyes narrowing. "If you need a second opinion, ask him." I angrily jab my finger at the Commander.

With a grimace, the Commander rolls his eyes. "She gets through the hollow with a dozen stolen horses at a time. If anyone can get your wolf through, it's her."

I arch my eyebrow at Dax and pat his chest. "There you have it," I say triumphantly. "Get your shit. Let's go."

We do our best to return the cave to how we found it, cleaning up the bird carcasses and the horses' droppings. Even the Commander helped by cleaning the fire pit, removing the extra ash, and restacking some fallen wood.

Once we're outside, Tarq leans against my hip just as I'm about to mount the mare. "What?" I ask him, twisting my head to the side. He gently takes my hand in his mouth and tugs it. *How is this not scaring me? I just let a wolf put my hand in his mouth.*

"He doesn't think we can make it through town," Dax tells me.

Tarq backs up, letting me go. I place Dax's hand on my shoulder and kneel before Tarq. "We can do this," I say, reaching out. He steps forward, putting his chin in my hand. I pull him to me and press my forehead to the top of his head. "I promise I will get you through there safely."

I run my hand down Tarq's jaw, feeling his hum vibrate from his throat. With a sigh, I lean back and look into his eyes. "Ok," I say, smiling. "Are you ready now?"

Tarq nods his head, eyeing Dax.

I wish these two would stop fighting.

Dax grabs me and throws me up in the saddle before stepping up in the stirrup himself. He nods to the Commander, who leads us back to the trail that will take us to Silverton.

"He's just scared, Dax." I look at Tarq, who's calmly jogging out front.

"Tarq's a wolf, Darya. Stop forgetting that," Dax responds angrily.

I twist my shoulders around to Dax so I can cup his cheek. I know he misses what we had before. Whatever was pushing me toward him has backed off. I can still feel it, but it's nowhere near as intense. *I assumed he was as confused as I was, but his eyes now say he is hurt by what is happening.* I want to apologize, but what would be my reason? *I didn't ask for any of this.*

"Dax?" I run my thumb over his cheekbone until he looks at me. "We're ok, right?"

His face softens almost to a sad expression. He leans down, kissing me gently. "We're ok, Darya."

"Good," I say, smiling. "I need you to time hitting town right at dusk, so we might have to push it a little to make it on time."

Dax wraps his arm around my waist, his hand finding its home on my hip. He hisses to the horses, sending them both cantering down the trail.

8

Dax pushes everyone throughout the day with only a few breaks. At one point, we stop by a creek to water the horses and refill our canteens. It's a hot day, so I pull my boots off and sit with my feet in the water. Dax lies behind me, allowing me to use his body as a pillow. His slight grin indicates he's settled back into whatever we've become.

I watch Tarq run through the water, chasing after some geese eating by the creek. As he splashes around, he kicks water at us. I hold my lips between my teeth to disguise my smile, knowing this must drive Dax crazy. *I'm pretty sure Tarq knows he's doing it, too.*

When Tarq lays down across the creek and fixes his gaze on me, I turn to Dax. "I don't understand how you can see him as anything but a kid. He's so damn goofy." I smile, looking back at Tarq as he flops to his side and rubs his face on the grass.

"I've seen him at his worst. It's not something you forget," Dax says quietly.

After that, Dax isn't in the mood to talk. He pushes the group, perfectly timing us to hit the edge of the town as the sun sets. *I couldn't have timed this any better.* We drop from the horses, and I lead them up beside a small building with a steeple.

"We need to stick to this back alley. Most of these families know me and won't bother us," I tell them, slipping around the back of the steepled building.

I hold my hand out, and Tarq slides his head under it. I wrap my hand around his muzzle and curl my fingers under his jaw. It feels like he belongs here. *How did we know to do this?*

I shake my head and concentrate on getting them through town. We skirt along the back of the six buildings bordering the alley. There is a large courtyard after the last house that the community turned into a garden. No one is tending to it at night, so we easily slip through unseen.

Just beyond the garden's fence stands a large livery stable. I bring the group to its sliding door that leads to the stalls and wagon storage. A single lantern hangs beside the door and barely gives off any light, allowing us to stay in the shadows. I bang on the door in a way that will let the owner know I'm a friend—two quick bangs, then a pause followed by a light knock.

"I should've known," the Commander sneers.

"You really should have," I say, smirking. "Where better to hide a herd of horses than a livery?"

Tarq nervously glances at me in the faint lantern light. I rub my thumb behind his whiskers and smile at him. Tarq closes his eyes, leaning on my hand. This time it's quiet, so I hear his hum, which explains why Dax puts his arm around me and pulls me away from him.

As the door slides open, a familiar face appears. "Well, I'll be damned!" Micah, the livery owner, steps through the sliding door. His dark skin keeps most of his features hidden in the low light, but he's always had the whitest teeth I've ever seen, and they flash when he sees me. He steps forward, grabbing me in a bear hug and causing Tarq to growl. "Woah, seems you're traveling with some guards?"

I smile as Dax pulls at the back of my waistband. "Don't worry about them," I assure Micah. "They'll start to behave shortly or spend the night in the woods." I turn to glare at Dax and Tarq until they stop. "This angry-looking one is Dax. The jackass over there is Anthony." I reach for Tarq. "And this guy here is Tarq. We need to lay low for the night."

Although towering over me, Micah is the same height as the men. He studies each one and then focuses his eyes on Tarq. "Darya, you know

I'll do anything for you," he starts slowly, his eyes never leaving Tarq. "But that is a huge wolf. And since when do you travel with militia?"

"Anthony's reformed, sort of," I say before tugging on Tarq's head. "And this guy is just a huge dog. He knows lots of tricks."

Dax steps up so that his body is against my back. His muscles are tense as Tarq circles beside me and sits with his head in my hand. I push back on Dax and shake my head slightly, letting him know I'm not impressed with his show of strength.

"Micah, can we please come in before someone sees us?" I fake a smile as I notice anger radiating from Dax. *Why the hell is he so damn mad?* That's when I feel Tarq's nose slide down my leg. *Well, that explains that.*

Micah steps back, sliding the door open. He helps the Commander settle the horses in empty stalls while Dax and I grab the gear from them and stack it in the aisle.

"Thank you, Micah," I say, squeezing his arm as he stops to appreciate the Friesian.

Micah turns to face me, but his eyes drift down to Tarq, who hasn't left my side. "I'm always here for you." I know he's talking to me, but he's nearly as focused on Tarq as I was when I first met him.

I sigh as I look over at the Commander. "I have one more big ask," I say, cringing. "I need to chain him up." I point to the Commander, who's standing behind him.

Micah raises his eyebrows. "What have you gotten yourself into?"

I shake my head. "I don't trust him, and my wolf needs sleep," I tell Micah. I brush my hand over Tarq's face and tug his ear.

Micah curiously looks over Tarq and me. "I think I've got some dog chains in the tack room," he offers.

The Commander scoffs. "You have got to be kidding me." I'm familiar with the glare he gives me.

"No, I'm not kidding," I growl back. "Act right, and I will treat you like a real person." I return his glare for a moment before smiling at Micah. "Can you grab them for us, please?"

As he leaves to retrieve them, I feel Dax's eyes burning into my skin.

When I look at him, his eyes are dark with desire. He's leaning against the stall door beside me and pulls me to rest against his hip.

"Did you want to add something?" I arch my eyebrow, smiling crookedly.

Dax rolls his eyes and matches my smile. "I'm just enjoying the view," he says.

I elbow Dax and kneel to Tarq. The wolf curls around to sit directly in front of me. "Hey, Tarq," I say gently. "I need you to stay down here with the Commander."

Tarq stands up, looking at Dax. When Dax doesn't react, he growls.

"He doesn't want to leave you," Dax grumbles.

I reach for Tarq's jaw. "I need someone to watch him," I plead. "We'll be up those stairs right there." I point to the stairs beside the feed room. They lead to a bedroom that Micah lets me use.

Tarq doesn't look any more agreeable. If anything, he seems like he's panicking. I frown and look to Dax for help.

Dax chuckles. "You kept questioning me. Now you understand why I have so much trouble with him." He leans his head against the wall, closing his eyes. "I'm not your damn translator."

I turn back to Tarq. Grabbing his chin, I pull him to me so that he's looking into my eyes. "I can't protect you from him if you don't listen to me either."

Tarq licks his lips, sliding his tongue over my wrist.

"So, will you stay here and make sure he doesn't get loose?"

Tarq lifts his chin off my hand and nods his head.

Dax scoffs, glaring at Tarq.

With excellent timing, Micah appears with the dog chains. He leads us to an empty stall nearby and helps me chain the Commander to the back wall.

"Now behave yourself down here, Anthony," Dax warns. "You know what will happen."

"You don't even have anyone there, do you?" the Commander sneers.

"Luke is reading to Gabby right now. They are both lying on Gabby's bed," Dax says, grinning. "They are reading by flashlight." He opens his mouth, pretending to be shocked.

I giggle and play along. "A flashlight, Commander?" I shake my head and click my tongue in disappointment. "What would your superiors think?"

Even with his olive skin in the dim light, I can see the red hues of fury creeping across his face. "Fine," the Commander spouts.

Micah clears his throat, calling attention to himself. "I don't want to know about this, do I?"

I laugh, patting his shoulder. "Probably not, but we are pretty tired." I turn to look at the stairs. "Is the bedroom ok for tonight? We'll be leaving at first light."

"Of course, Darya." Micah leans in for a hug, backing away from Dax quickly as he releases me. "Take care of yourself."

He leaves through the side door that leads straight into his kitchen. I reach out to Tarq. "We'll be upstairs if you need us," I say as he slips his head in my hand.

Dax pulls me away from Tarq, hauling me up the stairs to the open loft. There's a large seating area and a comfortable king-size bed. Dax tows me straight to the bed and sits me down.

"Do you think he's gonna be ok down there?" I'm completely distracted. Since teaming up with the quirky wolf, we've only been apart for an hour when he went hunting. I don't remember having any issues with his being gone then, but I miss him now.

Dax jams my fingers in his waistband and pulls his shirt off. "Darya, you just convinced him to stay down there. He's fine." He kicks off his boots.

"How are Storm and Mason?" I don't know why I'm asking about them. They've never expressed interest in me, but here I am, giving a damn.

Dax scrunches his face, pulling my clothes off. "They're fine, Darya. They just took down a buck, so they're better than us since they have food." He flops on the bed with me.

I swirl my fingers over Dax's chest, resting my head on his shoulder.

"Tomorrow's going to be the hardest day. We have to cross the basin. It'll take the whole day. I've lost horses there." I just keep talking, completely lost in thought.

Dax mashes my hand flat against his skin. "We'll be fine, Darya. Go to sleep."

I look up at him. "But we're going —"

"Darya," Dax growls deeply. "I want you badly right now, but I can't with that godforsaken wolf in my head. Go to sleep!"

* * *

Before I met Dax, I don't remember dreaming. I can't recall the last time I remembered a dream when I woke up. However, my dreams have been so vivid since meeting him that they feel real. Tonight, I'm running down a path so fast that everything blurs. As I slow down, I recognize the trail from yesterday. I run around a bend, and the horses come into view. I watch myself and Dax dismount from the white mare.

My body is glowing. It's pulsing mainly gold with some red. I run straight to myself and bump into my brightly glowing hand.

"Tarq?" I mumble in my sleep.

The dream fades, and something bangs loudly.

"Darya, wake up," a voice calls out. Not out loud but somehow in my head.

The banging sounds again.

"Darya, I need you to wake up," the voice calls out again.

Why do I recognize that voice?

The banging is deafening this time. "Open up!" A voice shouts. "Inspection!"

"Darya!"

I bolt upright in the bed, suddenly realizing whose voice I hear. "Tarq!"

Dax jumps up, ready to defend me. He looks around the room and then settles his confused expression on me. "You heard him?" He grabs his shirt from the corner of the bed and pulls it on. "Never mind, let's go. Get dressed."

I quickly grab my clothes off the floor, pulling them on. I reach for my boots, and as I finish pulling them on, I notice that Dax and I aren't touching. I run my hand over the Blood Mark. *No pain.* We'd made a point not to stop touching for so long that this feels strange. *It feels lonely.*

"Dax," I call, following him across the room. "Do you feel anything?"

"What?" he asks, confused. He touches his Blood Mark, realizing he'd crossed the room without me. "No, but right now, that's a good thing."

He reaches for my hand, pulling me down the stairs. The banging sounds again just as we hit the Commander's stall. "You're on, Anthony," Dax says, crouching to remove the chains binding the man to the wall.

"Thank you," I whisper to Tarq as he curls around me, facing the barn's sliding door. He doesn't acknowledge me, making me question my sanity again.

Dax pulls the last chain off the Commander and offers him a hand. "Darya, get over here," he says, holding up the chains.

My eyes narrow, and I shake my head slightly. Tarq begins to growl. Looking down, I see he's aiming that growl at Dax.

"Knock it off, Tarq." Dax glares at the wolf before shifting his eyes to me. "We need to look like prisoners, Darya. Get over here."

"Darya, no," the voice pleads as Tarq looks up at me.

I cup his chin. "Why are you in my head?" I ask, tilting my head.

"I want to know the same thing," Dax growls. "But right now, I need you over here."

I look at all three in turn, not knowing what to do. I trust Dax, but he's asking me to trust the man who's hunted me for ten years. *And now I have a wolf in my head.*

"If you think you'll survive that inspection team on your own, go for it," the Commander says in his normal snarky tone. "I'd love to see you try."

He's right. The officers around here know who I am. "Don't make me regret this," I sneer.

I enter the stall and let Dax lock the chains. I wrap some around his wrists, ensuring they appear secure. Tarq remains by my side, watching closely.

"Tarq, come lay down behind us," I say, coaxing the wolf. "We'll lean against you. Just be still."

Tarq crawls behind Dax and slides in to put his shoulders behind me. He curls his neck around my hip. *I won't leave you,* he tells me, closing his eyes. *I can see through your eyes.*

I run my hand down the side of his head and tug his jaw. "Tarq, as comforting as you are, I'm gonna need you out of my head for a little bit."

He sighs, fluffing his lips. *Yes, Darya.*

The Commander crouches, looking us over. "This doesn't look believable," he says critically. He licks his teeth while staring Dax in the eye, reaches back, and punches me.

It takes a minute to register what happened. I see stars, and the pain has me holding my face as I lean back against Tarq. "What the hell, asshole?!" I yell out. The Commander stands quickly as Tarq jumps up, dumping me on the stall floor. I hear Dax yell, but I can't understand him over the roar of Tarq's snarl. "Tarq, get over here," I say through my pain. "We don't have time for this shit."

The Commander chuckles. "God, that felt good."

"Cross me again, and your family dies," Dax warns him.

Tarq is still growling as he slides back behind us.

"I don't see a problem," the Commander says, smirking. "No one would believe I'd nab her without hitting her at least once."

"Go open the door," Dax growls.

The Commander laughs, closing the stall door.

Dax grabs my chin. "You ok?" he asks, turning my head to check my eye.

I pull my face free, not interested in the attention. "He hits like a toddler," I grumble. Tarq lifts his head to survey the damage. "Head down, big guy," I whisper, scratching his chin. "You're supposed to be dead."

Tarq lays his head back down with a huff and closes his eyes.

"Storm's out back," Dax says quietly. "She says there's five of them."

I'm still blinking, trying to clear my vision, so I roll my eyes to him. "What the hell is he doing?" I hiss loudly. "He's supposed to be getting rid of them."

"Shush," Dax hisses. "They're coming." He slumps down, leaning on Tarq's hip.

Some heavy boots clunk down the aisle, and a man coughs out a laugh. "Can't believe you finally got the bitch," he says. "How'd she ride?"

Tarq twitches his paw and begins to pull away from my leg. I stretch my fingers out, finding his mouth. He opens his jaws slightly, allowing me to hook my middle finger around his fang to hold him still.

"Nah," the Commander scoffs. "There'd be no bounty if I split her in half."

"I suppose," the gruff voice replies. "Let me buy you a drink then."

There's a clapping noise, and then the stall door closes. The footsteps take a while to make it to the back door. I assume the other officer is looking over the horses as they go. Most of them would fetch an excellent price at the market.

"Storm says they are all leaving," Dax says.

I sit up slowly. Tarq slides his tongue over my finger before opening his mouth.

"Tarq wants to talk to you," Dax grumbles.

I run my hands down the sides of the wolf's face. "Not right now, honey," I say with a smile. "I'm gonna do one crazy thing at a time for now."

Dax pulls his chains off and turns to work on mine as a door nearby opens.

Micah peers over the stall door. "You ok?"

"Oh, Micah," I gush, sighing. "Where did the officers go?"

"That militia guy you were with said to tell you to leave the black horse and get out of town." Micah shakes his head, confused. "He said a she-wolf would tell you when to call it." He helps me up. "I'm getting too old for this crap, Darya."

"I'm sorry," I say, squeezing his arm. "Did he happen to say if we should leave through the front or back doors?"

"He said to go out the back way," Micah answers.

I look down at Tarq. "Can you go make sure he's not setting us up?"

"The door's open," Micah adds as he moves the horses' gear to the stall walls.

Tarq looks at Dax before darting through the door leading to the house.

I shake my head. "Oh sure, now he asks for your permission."

Dax pulls the last chain links off my ankle and piles it up with the rest. He rolls his eyes at me, clearly annoyed. "He asked me to call for him if you needed him." Dax frowns for a moment but then looks up at Micah. "Do you have an extra horse we could buy? It needs to be fit enough to keep up with my mares."

Dax saddles the Friesian to leave for the Commander and joins me to finish the white mare. Micah brings us a brown gelding. It's shorter but seems fit.

Dax lowers the stirrup once we've finished and cups my cheek. "Tarq says it's clear. We should go." It doesn't feel the same when Dax runs his hands down my arms and kisses my neck. Judging by his frown, he's noticed too.

I put my hand out to Micah. "Thank you," I whisper. "We will not forget this."

He shakes my hand with both of his. "Be safe."

I lead the mare through the side door. We carefully move through the kitchen and living room, finding Tarq waiting outside the front door. "Ok, now you can talk to me," I say.

"I'm good," Tarq's voice rings in my head again.

"Figures." I shake my head. "Alright then, Tarq. Let's run like hell."

Stepping into the white mare's stirrup, I sling myself into her saddle and hiss. She shoots forward with Tarq beside her. We stick to the back of the buildings as the sun rises. After about half a mile, we veer to the right, onto my regular trail out of town. It heads toward a creek where we can stop for water before crossing the basin.

When we hit a small area of shorter fir trees, I slow the mare and then stop her between a few trees to wait for Dax. Tarq has been quiet, just following my lead. When we stopped, he laid down directly under the mare's head. I try to think of my calmest horse. Not one would've allowed a wolf near them, never mind under them.

"*Dax is coming,*" Tarq announces.

"Why can I hear you?" I lie on the mare's neck, looking down at him.

He shifts around to look up at me. "*I don't know,*" he says thoughtfully. "*You have that colorful aura. I can't stand the thought of being away from you.*"

"What does it mean?"

Tarq's lips fluff. "*Ask Dax.*" He's a little less pleasant now. Almost angry. "*My parents always said we were different. Maybe that's why you can hear me. Ask him where they are.*"

When Dax arrives, his brown horse dances under him as it catches Tarq's scent. The grumpy wolf lays his head down.

"Where can we lay low while we wait for Anthony?" Dax asks.

It takes me a minute to think about it. I don't usually stop between town and the creek. "There's an abandoned manor a little over a mile to the north," I tell them. "It's out of the way, but the locals say it's haunted, so we should be safe there."

I lead them through the trees and down an overgrown road. The manor appears once we cut through a section of thick brush. I stop the mare, slide out of the saddle, and walk in front of her. Dax falls in step with me while Tarq jogs ahead to check the area for us.

"What happened to Tarq's parents?" I ask Dax as he puts his arm around my shoulders. Dax tenses and looks away. I slide my arm around his waist and hook my fingers into his waistband, hoping the familiar feeling will help. "What's going on? Tarq thinks his parents might know why I can hear him."

Dax stews long enough for us to reach the entrance's steps. He turns and sits on them. As he puts his head in his hands, I take a moment to look at the manor. It's not changed much over the years. All the glass is missing, so the windows are boarded up. It's two stories, but having been inside, I know the second floor has collapsed onto the first. It was probably grand before the bomb hit the basin.

"Tarq's parents had personal issues," Dax starts, pulling me out of my thoughts. "I don't know, maybe a bit defiant. I banished them from the lake a few years ago."

"Could we find them?" I use my sweetest voice. Rosalee says I "paint with honey" when I want to.

Tarq jogs up to my hip and stares at Dax, waiting for his answer.

Dax looks from me to Tarq. "What makes you think they have the answers?"

"They always said we had a higher purpose than serving an Alpha," Tarq tells us.

Dax raises his eyebrows. There's a mix of surprise and anger in his expression. "I'll see what I can do," he huffs. I turn around to sit on the step below Dax. He leans forward, wrapping his arms around my shoulders. "When did this start?"

"Hmm?" I'd completely lost focus staring at Tarq's head. "What?" The wolf lays at my feet, resting his jaw on his crossed paws.

Tarq looks up and catches me staring at him. He's so beautiful that all I can do is smile.

"Him," Dax says, pointing at Tarq.

I reach down, pulling at the fur under Tarq's throat. "Last night, I think. I'm pretty sure I was hearing him in my dream."

"I was thinking about what you look like to me," Tarq says shyly. *"I didn't know you were there until you said my name."*

"And how did you look?" Dax asks, sounding annoyed.

I scrunch my face up in thought and scratch Tarq's chin. "I was gold, or at least the air around me was," I say slowly, trying to remember. "There was some red, and it was pulsing." I smooth Tarq's fur back down. "I've never seen anything like it."

Dax sighs, putting his forehead on my shoulder. "Alright, we'll figure this out later. It's time to get moving."

Tarq stands up and jogs over to the white mare. He shakes his fur loose and leans back on his haunches. He lets out a howl that starts low and deep, almost sad. I'm frozen, watching this massive wolf sing. His second howl is much louder with a higher pitch and seems to never end. After finishing the long call, he jogs back to us and lies down.

Tarq looks up at me as I raise my eyebrows, confused.

He chuckles. *"The mare's on the way, Darya. Have faith in my skills."* His smile is unmistakable in his voice.

I smile back. "There you are." I tug his throat. "I was afraid you were lost forever."

"Stop encouraging him," Dax grumbles from my shoulder. He lifts his head, glaring at the wolf.

Tarq rolls his eyes and lays back down.

Dax begins to growl, making the brown horse jump. "Wolf!"

"Leave him alone!" I snap at Dax. I put my hands over my face, digging my fingers into my eyes. "I'm sorry, Dax. I didn't mean to yell. Can you two please just stop?"

They both sigh, and Dax puts his head back on my shoulder.

"Thank you," I whisper.

"You're welcome," Tarq says calmly.

Dax growls.

I throw my hands in the air. "For fuck's sake!"

9

I storm off, walking the length of the manor to sit in a small grassy area I saw when we arrived. I'm relieved when Tarq slides his head under my hand. It's easy to be around him. He simply falls in step with me until I flop in the grass when we reach the open yard.

Tarq sniffs at my cheek and neck.

"I'm sorry, Tarq," I whisper. "I just don't feel like myself lately."

He pushes his nose under my head until I lift it and allow him to slide under me. He shoves me enough that he ends up under my head and shoulders. I reach for the fur under his throat. *A wolf would normally feel loyalty to their Alpha, but I never knew where I belonged,* Tarq says quietly. *What I should feel for my Alpha, I feel for you, Darya.*

I can't remember ever being shy or bashful. I've never cared enough to be nervous. Yet, here I am, blushing like a little girl. "Why?"

I don't know, but I am here for you. I will always be here for you. Tarq lays his head down, trapping my hand between his neck and front legs.

I turn my eyes to the passing clouds. "Can you stop fighting with Dax? Please? For me?" The sound of galloping hooves begins to filter through the chirping birds and Tarq's breathing. He lifts his head to look behind him. "Tarq?"

He turns and nuzzles his nose into my neck, making me giggle.

"Can you at least try not to piss him off?"

For you, anything. Tarq sighs, putting his head back down.

Tugging his fur, I let my mind go blank and focus on the white and gray coloring of the clouds. The freedom of absolutely nothing on your mind is a fabulous feeling, and I tend to enjoy it a little too much sometimes. I suddenly want to nap in the morning sun, leaning on this wolf who makes me feel... *Well, I don't know how he makes me feel. I just know it's something good.*

Tarq growls, shifting under me. *"Darya,"* he says slowly. *"I need you to calmly get behind me, please."*

I try to move slowly but trip over my feet. The sisters are creeping toward us, their heads low and teeth bared.

"We're going to move to the right." Tarq leaves his eyes locked on the sisters. *"I can't reach Dax. I'm gonna need you to call out to him."*

We step to the right together. "Dax?" I whisper. Shaking my head, I roll my eyes.

The sisters' snarls grow louder, and we can't back up as fast as they advance.

"Dax!" I scream this time, continuing to move with Tarq.

I can tell by the sisters' reactions the exact moment that Dax rounds the corner of the manor. They lie down, hanging their heads. "What the hell is going on here?" Dax is at a level of fury that would scare an entire army away. He stares at the sisters, periodically shifting from one to the other.

Tarq and I stand together, watching the silent argument. He backs up to lean his shoulder against my hip, and I pull my fingernails through his fur to gently scratch his neck. Even Anthony joins in our confusion once the Friesian stops beside the manor. His bewilderment is comforting since he usually understands these wolves when I don't.

"They don't trust you," Dax says as he approaches us. "They didn't like Tarq alone with you." He peeks back at the sisters to ensure they're still where he left them. Dax snaps his fingers at Tarq and points at his nose. "And why can't I hear you?"

Tarq stands his ground and ignores Dax. His eyes haven't left the sisters.

"I'm sending them home," Dax announces. "They've never been disobedient, but you are making my wolves crazy."

Tarq looks up at me, and I voice my opinion before Dax can make a decision that I don't like. "He's not leaving me," I state firmly.

Dax rolls his eyes. "I don't mind him when he's quiet." He flicks Tarq's nose, and the wolf snaps at him. The sisters jump up, but without looking, Dax reaches a hand back and points to the ground, telling them to lie back down. "You somehow silenced him. I'd like to figure out how." He cups my cheek, steps closer, and puts his chest against me. "Go," he says quietly, staring into my eyes.

I almost don't hear the sisters leave. The rhythmic rustling of the leaves near the trees is the only sound. "I've asked Tarq to stop trying to piss you off," I whisper to Dax as he hovers an inch from my face. "He's agreed. I'd like the same promise from you."

Dax brushes his lips against mine, it sends a shiver down my spine, but the wave of fire and ice is gone. "I will try not to get pissed at him about everything," he says with a little smile before looking down at Tarq. "If I'm to tolerate you, you better do your damn job," Dax growls.

Tarq glares at him. *I will, Dax.* He curls his head under and runs his nose down the length of my leg. I get the feeling that this is his display of possession.

Dax closes his eyes and sighs with a smile. "I cannot describe just how wonderful the silence is." He opens his eyes and pushes my hair behind my ears. "He's your pain in the ass now." He presses one last kiss to my lips before turning away to retrieve the horses. "So, where are we heading today?"

I run my hand over Tarq's head and slide it down his neck to tug at the fur on his throat. "We're going straight through the center of the basin." I look down at Tarq. When he looks up, I run my hand up to his jaw. "This is gonna suck. Why don't we get some water?"

Tarq turns his head to lean it against my stomach and hums. I smile at him and pull at his jaw.

* * *

When we reach the creek, Dax brings me the brown horse and puts its reins in my hand. He winks as he takes the white mare from me. "Give me back my horse," he grumbles playfully.

Knowing this is another attempt to drive a wedge between Tarq and me, I look in the wolf's direction. His head is on his crossed front paws as he watches me. I sigh and turn back to the horse. *I don't even know what they are fighting about, but clearly, I'm a pawn since Dax gave me the one horse that's scared of Tarq.*

The Commander idles up and runs his hand under the gelding's mane as I adjust the stirrups. "You know," he says, flexing his jaw. "I understand that bad shit happens to everyone. It just seems to happen to you more often than anyone else."

I slap my stirrup leather down once it's adjusted to my length. Slowly turning toward the Commander, I narrow my eyes and tilt my head. He's not paying attention to my hand until my fist crashes into his nose.

"Shit, Darya!" He grabs his face, turning away from me. "Seriously?"

Nodding, I smile at him. "You were right. That does feel good." I turn back to the horse and hear Dax chuckling nearby.

"Shut up, Dax," the Commander grumbles. "You're rubbing off on her."

"Nah," he says from somewhere behind me. "Darya's always been a spitfire. You should probably stop pissing her off."

I shake my head and leave them to join Tarq under his shade tree. He lifts his head as I drop to my knee and puts his chin in my hand. "This is going to be a long run. Are you sure you can do this?"

He lifts his head to rub his muzzle gently along my cheek. *"I will do whatever you need me to."*

I pull back from him, raising my eyebrows. "What I need is for you to be honest with me."

"I promise."

"Is your wolf ok?" Dax asks condescendingly from behind me.

When I stand up to turn around, I see that he and the Commander have mounted up and are waiting. "He's fine," I say, smiling, ignoring Dax's tone. "Are you both ready?"

* * *

It's obvious when we hit the edge of the basin. It's essentially a barren wasteland. There are a few clumps of trees here and there but no water. When it rains, small pools form, but then the dirt cracks as it dries quickly. So, as we push hard over the dried cracks, dust kicks up behind the galloping horses. It's dangerous and lets everyone know where we are, but there is no way they can sneak up on us as long as we stay out in the open.

Tarq stays close to my horse's hind end, using its fear to push it forward, but its fatigue overpowers the fear just as the sun sets. I point to a small clump of trees to our right, and we all aim for it. Tarq eases off to allow the horse to slow his pace comfortably. The last rays of light fade out just as we hit the trees. I dismount and loosen my horse's cinch.

"Darya, I need some water."

I see Tarq slowly approaching me, watching the horse for any signs that he should stop. I can't help smiling at him. Even in the dark, barely visible, he's beautiful. "How are you holding up?" I lift my full canteen off the saddle horn and kneel. Tarq steps forward, opening his mouth for me. He closes his eyes and gulps all my water as it hits the back of his throat.

Tarq hums once he's done. He glances at the horse and narrows his eyes. *"Darya, was that all of your water?"* Tarq sounds gruffer than he's ever spoken to me before. I twist my face and wrinkle my nose, sure he can't see me in the dark. *"Darya, don't give me that look. I'm strong. I can handle dehydration. I won't survive losing you."*

*Ok, so maybe he **can** see me.*

Tarq looks up just as something brushes over my shoulder, and a canteen comes into view. "I bet he's scolding you right now," Dax says quietly.

I take the canteen from Dax and pull large gulps from it, leaving some for him. "You brought my grandmother's notebook, right?"

"Of course I did." He runs his hand down the length of my arm and hooks my fingers. "If we find someone who can help, they might want to look at it." Dax slides his lips over my wrist. "I miss being stuck to you."

I shiver a little from the cold but mostly from his short stubble tickling my skin. "Maybe they'll know why I can hear Tarq," I whisper. "Or what the Blood Mark is doing." I smile as Dax rests my arm on his shoulder and steps so close I can feel his breath on my lips. He brushes my neck where the Blood Mark resides and awakens some old sensations. "In the meantime, why don't you show me how much you miss me?" *Great. Here we go again. Why did I just say that?*

Dax lets out a deep breath as he growls. He slides his hands down my body and lifts me by my thighs. With my legs wrapped around his hips, Dax steps forward and pushes my back against a tree. Using his hips to hold me in place, he grabs the sides of my face and claims my lips. His hands glide down my neck as he pushes his chest into me, and something hungry for Dax takes over my body. I plunge my tongue into his mouth and moan as I grind my hips against his.

"Ahem," the Commander clears his throat behind Dax.

"Ignore him," I say as Dax slides his mouth down my jaw to my neck. He runs his tongue over the sensitive skin under my ear. "I plan to."

Wrapping my arms around his head, I slide my fingers through his hair and hold him firmly to my neck. He bites down, causing me to whimper for more.

"Look," the Commander starts, rather annoyed with us. "I know I'm just a passenger on this crazy train, but we need to get out of this wasteland."

I release an exasperated sigh and limply fall against Dax. "The asshat is right."

Dax slides his hands back down to my body and lifts me so he can put his forehead on my shoulder. "I'll need you to never put 'asshat' and 'right' in the same sentence again."

"Ok, first of all, fuck you very much," the Commander sneers. "And second, let's go."

"Darya, we need to go."

It's impossible to tell how close Tarq is, but this is the exact moment

I regret my current position. *He is so devoted to me. There is no way this little display didn't hurt him. I don't even know why I'm here. I didn't do this. I don't want this man between my legs. What am I doing?* I take a deep breath and let it out. *I'm panicking like a dumbass. That's what I'm doing. Get your shit together, Darya. Never let them see you falter. Just one more deep breath and listen to the wolf.*

I untwist my legs, dropping from Dax's grip. "Tarq says he's ready," I say, hiding my confusion. "We should go."

"Oh sure," the Commander says, throwing his hands in the air. "Listen to the damn wolf."

I step up to the Commander and put my hand on his chest. "Anthony?" I say slowly. "Can I call you Anthony? Your wagon's hitched to my caravan for a long time, so we should get comfortable, right?" I step into him and look up into his surprised eyes, gleaming in the moonlight. "Stop pouting. It's unbecoming." I shove him backward with a smile. He rolls his eyes and mounts his horse.

As I search for Tarq, Dax appears before me, holding his horse. He slides his arm across my lower back, leaning toward me. The glint in his eyes as they shine in the moonlight unsettles me. Dax is expecting something else. He's hoping to see the person he had against the tree a few minutes ago. *That wasn't me.*

I put my hand against his chest and push back. "We don't have time for this," I tell him as sweetly as possible. *My insanity isn't his fault.* "We'll continue this conversation later." I run my thumb over his lower lip. He growls, leaving me to mount his horse.

I turn away from him and find Tarq lying beside the gelding. The horse seems curious about him, wiggling its lips over his back. "Are you ready for the last leg?" I ask, kneeling to him.

"*Are you ok, Darya?*" Tarq tilts his head slightly to the side.

"I think so." I smile and reach straight for the fur on his throat. "I need a little favor from you, though."

He sits up, bumping the horse's nose. "*Anything.*"

I smile at Tarq's willingness. "You can see in the dark, right?" He nods, and I look up at the sky. The moon is shining now, but plenty of clouds are up there, blocking its light more often than not. "I'm gonna need your help spotting a landmark. We wasted too much time here, and if these clouds keep up, I won't be able to see it."

"What happened with Dax? You were acting strange." Tarq puts his muzzle on my cheek and sniffs at my neck. He's distracted, and I can't give him answers.

Sliding my hand up his muzzle, I hold him to my cheek and close my eyes. "This might be something for another time, but thank you for watching over me." I let him go. He pulls his head back to look me in the eye. "I need you to watch for one large tree before the basin's edge. We need to aim straight for it."

"I will find it for you," he says, standing up. *"But you'll tell me if there's something wrong?"*

I slide my fingers along his jaw, and he touches his nose to my forehead. "For you, anything." I run my thumb over his whiskers and stand up. "Alright, guys," I say to everyone, including Tarq. "Let's get this over with."

I step into my stirrup, and this time Tarq leads the charge, my horse willingly following him. I pat the horse's neck and lean forward to take my weight off his back. *I'd follow him too, little horse.*

Tarq leads the horses flat out for a few hours. As the tree comes into view, he begins to slow down and drops back to jog beside the trotting gelding. *"Ok, we made it to the tree,"* he says. *"Where to now?"*

I let the brown gelding slow to a walk. "There's a cave inside the tree line to the north. It's hard to see in the daylight, so it's impossible at night."

Tarq jogs off to scout for the cave. *"I'll find it. Cool the horses and be careful."*

Dax rides up beside me and runs his hand down my arm. "It's kinda hot watching you order my wolves around."

"Technically, I'm ordering my wolf around," I joke, attempting to change the tone. *I should probably talk to him about what's happening to me.*

Anthony pulls me out of my thoughts. "Darya," he says, sounding strange. "What the hell is that?" When I follow his gaze, he's looking at the tree line. There are, what looks like, hundreds of eyes shining out at us. Even Dax stops his horse.

"Those are reflectors," I tell them. "They're to scare the shit out of men like you, but they also mean someone is here that can help us."

"Darya, I found it," Tarq calls to me. *"These damn clouds. Can you see me?"*

He's right. The clouds had come back quickly, blocking out all hope of light. It's nearly pitch black, and I can't see any hint of Tarq along the tree line. I look over at Dax. "Tarq found the cave, but I can't see him. Can you?"

Dax shakes his head. I take a deep breath and cup my hands around my mouth to shout for him, but Dax puts his hand on my arm. "Even on a clear night, that wouldn't be a good idea, Darya."

"Do you have a way to call him back to us that isn't ridiculously loud, then?" I ask. Dax is right, but that doesn't mean I have to like it.

Dax cups his hands and blows into them, producing a low quail call. I lift my eyebrow. "He'll hear that?"

Dax chuckles. "Yeah. Give him a minute."

Something about his laughter unsettles me. I bite my lip and frown. "What did you do?"

Dax shrugs and looks away from me. "I only have one low call."

I hear Tarq before I can see him. He's hitting the ground so hard with his paws that they sound like distant thunder. His teeth glisten in the light as the moon peeks out, and his strides are so long that it doesn't even look like he's touching the ground. The clumps of dirt flying behind him tell a different story.

"You should've warned me." I jump off the gelding and run toward Tarq, trying to slow him down and get out of earshot of the men. I drop to my knees and hold my arms out as Tarq slides to a stop before me.

"What's wrong? Are you ok? Did something happen? Darya, answer me!" He's looking me over to find any hint of an emergency.

"Honey, I would if you'd let me talk," I say with a little smile.

"It's not funny, Darya." Tarq circles me. *"Are you ok?"* He sounds much calmer now.

"Please come here, Tarq," I say soothingly. "I'm not hiding an injury behind my back. I'm sorry. I didn't know."

Tarq steps forward into my arms. He slides his nose under my hair, taking a deep breath before dropping his head down my back. *"That's a panic call. It's a call only used in the worst of emergencies. All I could think was that I failed and couldn't protect you from everything."* I feel him momentarily lift his head off my back, then put it back. *"If he won't keep his word, why should I?"*

I push back on Tarq's chest and grab his jaw once he's in front of me. "Because you are better than that." He puts his head down, but I pick it back up. "Tarq, I've never had anyone want to guard me, and I'm going to guess you've never been a guard. We'll figure this out." I pull at his fur. "Thank you."

"I didn't do anything," Tarq grumbles.

"But you were willing to do whatever it took to protect me, and for that, I thank you."

"Then you're welcome."

Tarq curls around, allowing me to push myself back to my feet using his shoulders. Exhaustion is beginning to creep through my muscles. Tarq shakes his fur and jumps at a sound in the nearby woods. He begins to growl and steps to the side to move between me and the trees.

I reach out and run my fingers along Tarq's back between his hips. I let my nails trail up his spine. He stops growling and pushes his back up into my hand. "Come on. There's someone I want you to meet." I walk toward the woods ahead of him.

I hear Tarq shake and then jog after me. *"Hang on, do that again."*

I laugh at him as a figure emerges from the trees. One of my good friends and, ironically, the most book-smart person I know puts her hand out to me. "So now you talk to wolves?" Fray naturally has brown hair. I've seen her roots every once in a while, but she bleaches them white as snow. She calls it her signature look. Tonight, she is sporting two braids on the sides of her scalp that hide under the loose hair from the top.

I take her hand and give it a solid squeeze. "It's good to see you too, Fray."

Fray's eyes stay on Tarq as he jogs up to my side and puts his nose to my thigh.

I hear hooves behind me. "These two are Dax and Anthony," I say, jabbing a thumb over my shoulder without looking.

Fray pulls the crossbow strapped to her back and aims it at Anthony. "You're not welcome here, asshole."

I push her crossbow down as I look back at Anthony. "You just make friends everywhere you go, don't you?"

Dax ducks, trying to hide his chuckle.

Fray glares at me. "Did he do that to your face?"

I'd forgotten about the bruises I must still be sporting. I nod. "He did."

She tries to lift her crossbow to point it at Anthony again. "Did you at least do that to his face?"

"Some of it," I say, smiling. "Dax's guy did the rest of it."

"Then I like Dax."

Tarq rubs his head gently against my hip. *I like her.*

I run my hand down to his throat and tug his fur. "I thought you would."

Fray slings her crossbow over her shoulder. "I took down a buck this afternoon. Some steaks are cooking. Most of you are welcome to have some." She winks at Anthony.

Dax chuckles again. Anthony throws his canteen at him.

The men dismount before we all step into the trees and walk the rest of the way. Fray is her usual chatty self. I rarely actually listen to what she is saying. Tonight is no different. Tarq stays beside me as I absent-mindedly run my fingers over his jaw. He pushes and pulls me left and right to walk around things because I'm not paying attention.

"Darya!" Fray claps her hands in my face. "Girl, where are you?" I look at her, confused, as she looks down at Tarq. I follow her eyes. He's humming and guiding me, lost in his little world. "That is a huge bloody wolf, Darya. What's that about?"

Tarq sighs. "*No one ever comments on my eyes. It's always my size.*"

Giggling, I tug his fur. "I'm sorry. You do have gorgeous eyes."

Fray stops and raises her eyebrow.

Clearing my throat, I wiggle my face around to straighten it. "This is Tarq. You sort of hurt his feelings."

I push forward, and Fray silently follows us. I know she's watching Tarq and me. I would. Who wouldn't be fascinated by the idea of this enormous, sorry, beautiful wolf standing beside someone like they're best friends? *I'm fortunate to be the one walking with him.*

We climb a steep grassy hill to the mouth of the cave. The fire pit is pretty far inside this cave. We don't use it in the winter because you can't vent it properly. If you let the fire burn all night, it'll smoke you out or kill you. It has a large cavern where we had built makeshift stalls to keep the stolen horses overnight. Our horses enjoy the freedom and a good roll.

Once the horses are settled, we gather around the fire. I sit on the ground with Tarq and stretch my legs toward the burning wood, letting the heat ease some of my aching muscles. Tarq flops as far from the fire as possible while still laying his head on my lap. Dax slides in beside me and puts his arm around my shoulders. Anthony quietly studies Fray from a rock across the fire while she turns the meat that she's placed in iron skillets.

So this is what it feels like to be part of a family. It's not Rosalee's fault that I never felt part of something. She tried. But here with this wolf in my lap, the arm of a devoted man around me, a friend cooking up some meat, and then there's Anthony. I wrinkle my nose. Well, I'll come back to Anthony when I figure out his role. This is the closest I've ever felt to having a home.

10

Fray finishes cooking most of the meat while we silently sit around. Tarq catches a quick nap, and Dax trails his fingers across my back. Anthony stays perched on his rock. He pulls out a diamond stone, spits on it, and sharpens his dagger. When he finishes, Dax reaches for the stone, and Fray raises her eyebrow.

"I gotta admit it's strange seeing you travel with people," Fray says, tilting her head. She watches Dax reach into my boot to pull out my knife. *I have no secrets from this man.* "You usually prefer the hooved type of company."

I watch Dax unfold my 4-inch blade and test its sharpness. "We're heading across the Hollow," I say, flicking my eyes back in her direction. At the sound of my voice, Tarq opens his eyes and looks up at me. I smile at him and run my hand from his chin to his shoulder, leaving it there. He settles back on my legs and closes his eyes.

"Over by the O'Shea farm?" Fray asks. "I heard the old man's son started bounty hunting."

I heard about that a few months ago. I also heard Casey wasn't good at it, so I'm not concerned. "We found some information about what my grandmother wrote," I tell her. "We're hoping to find a relative of a hedge witch somewhere along the springs. The notebook says she was from around there."

Fray gasps and claps her hands. "Oh, Edith has her little ranch over there," she says, smiling broadly.

I had forgotten about Edith. She was only slightly older than us, young 30s at the most, but she ran a small yet successful cattle ranch. My favorite part about Edith, though, was her house. "That's right," I say, smiling back. "She has that little guest cottage that she lets us use." I'm used to roughing it, but having that little house to myself was always a treat. It's been nearly a year since I've been out that way.

Fray pulls the meat off the fire and sets it aside. Tarq lifts his head and sniffs at the air as the smell of cooked venison fills the cave. Fray notices and throws some of the scraps for him to catch. *Maybe it's just that humans fall under the spell of these wolves. We get close and can't help loving them. He's a beautiful wolf, a gorgeous man, and he's probably the closest thing I have to a best friend.*

Dax pulls me out of my thoughts when he leans over to whisper in my ear. "He's gonna need more than scraps, Darya," he says. He drapes his arm around my shoulders and points his finger at Tarq, who's licking his lips with his eyes locked on Fray's hands.

Pulling Tarq's chin up, I make him look me in the eye. "Do you need to go hunt?"

His entire body shifts so he can poke my cheek with his nose. *"No, Darya, I'm fine."* He rolls over onto his back, laying his head against my stomach, and his nose ends up against my chest. It's Tarq. In the back of my mind, I know he's a man, but all this time I've spent with him, he's been a wolf. He's sweet, kind, goofy, protective, and, above all, a wolf. I flash him a crooked smile and scratch him behind his whiskers. When he starts to hum, Dax growls.

The glare I give Dax could probably kill a mortal. "I thought we were past all this?"

Fray loudly drops her fork into a pan. Even Anthony looks up, startled. "You really can hear him!"

Across the fire, Anthony starts laughing. "The wolf and the idiot bicker like old ladies over her," he says, coughing through his laughter. "It's hilarious."

"But you can hear him, right?" Fray excitedly asks.

Tarq shifts around, setting his legs back underneath his body. Whether he likes her or not, he's preparing to kill her.

I rest my hand on the back of his head, and his ear flicks slightly in my direction. "I can, and he needs to eat. He'll need more than we're cooking, unfortunately."

Tarq doesn't take his eyes off Fray but lays his head beside me on his paws. *I'll not leave you again.*

"Oh, that's no problem," Fray says, getting up. "I've got the shoulder in the cooler box back here. I was gonna cure it tomorrow, but he can have it." She points to the back of the cave. "I'll grab it for you, big guy."

Tarq rolls over and taps his paw on my arm. *I like your friends.*

I wink at him. "They all seem to like you."

When Fray returns, she heaves the shoulder at Tarq, who lies beside me to eat his raw meat. She then passes around the plates, making a show of not wanting to give Anthony any but still feeding him. "You should remember this moment," Fray tells him. "This is when I could've let you starve but chose not to."

Dax keeps smirking at me as we pick off the same plate. The noise beside me begins turning my stomach. Now, I've never owned a dog. So I've never had the pleasure of hearing one rip meat off a bone. I imagine it's just a little quieter than Tarq is right now. The more I try not to pay attention, the louder it seems. It becomes clear that this is causing Dax to smirk when he takes the plate of meat from me and places it on a rock far away.

"What happened to your grandmother's notebook?" Fray asks, oblivious to my plight. "You got it with you?"

I nod and point my finger at Dax as I cover my mouth.

"Yes, my beautiful?" Dax asks, sounding about as innocent as a murderer. "How may I help you?"

I give him a look of desperation, which only makes him laugh.

"Tarq, get that thing away from Darya," Dax says, trying to make his laughter sound like a cough. "You're making her sick."

It's when the noise stops that finishes me off, and I jump up to run to the mouth of the cave. Once there, I throw up my venison. Anthony joins in the laughter as I lean against the wall trying to catch my breath.

The man has never seen me sweat, and here I am, undone by a wolf eating meat. I hate that he's enjoying this.

"Here, Fray, I have the notebook," I hear Dax say. His roaring laughter has died down to a chuckle.

When I rejoin the group, Tarq has taken his shoulder to the other side of the rocks and is lying closer to Anthony. I take a deep breath and walk over to him. I kneel, waiting for Tarq to finish chewing the chunk of meat he's just torn off the shoulder. I hold my hand out for his chin and try not to think about the little pieces of raw meat that have fallen off his fur and now sit on my skin.

"I'm sorry, Darya," Tarq apologizes so sweetly that I can't help but regret making him feel this way. *"You only had to tell me."*

I stick my jaw out in an exaggerated frown. "It's something I'll have to get used to, is all," I say, squeezing Tarq's jaw a little. I pull his muzzle down to put my forehead against his head. "I told you we'll figure this out together. Don't worry about them." I move our heads so we're both looking toward the men. "We'll show them."

Tarq chuckles, pulling back to put his nose to my cheek. The same nose with ground-up venison on it. *"Oh, sorry,"* he says. *"Let me get that."* He runs his tongue slowly over my cheek. Tarq closes his eyes and hums as he pulls away. *"Darya, please go sit with Dax before I do that again."* His tone sounds like he's talking through clenched teeth, almost as if the thought is causing him pain.

I stand up and take a step back, confused. "I'm sorry," I say slowly.

Tarq turns away and runs his tongue over the raw meat several times. *Is he cleaning his tongue off with raw meat?*

"Here it is!" Fray exclaims from over by the fire. "Darya, come here. I found the part I was looking for."

I look back at Tarq one more time. He has rolled his body and put his back to me, but I hear him still humming. *We're all struggling with this craziness. I hadn't realized how much this was affecting him too.* I back a few more steps before turning around and joining Fray by the fire. I let Dax slide his arm around my shoulders and thread our fingers, just looking for something familiar.

Fray turns the book toward us, points at something, and quickly turns it back to herself. "It's right here," she says, excitedly giddy. "We thought this was in some code, but it's not." She says "we", but she means "I". I've never understood anything in the damn notebook.

"Fray, what are you talking about?" I ask, more irritated than I mean.

She begins turning the book to read it from different angles. I know the section she's reading. Small notes are made in the margins, and there are pencil drawings of what we thought were dogs, but now it makes more sense that they are wolves. "We thought that 'Luna' referred to the moon, as it often does, but it's actually talking about a person."

Dax sits up and looks over my head to see Fray more clearly, paying attention now. Tarq steps around the rocks with his head held low. He seems embarrassed about how he acted earlier but wants to participate in our conversation. *Sweet wolf, you don't need to be ashamed.* I release Dax's hand and put my arm out for Tarq. He lifts his head and joins me by lying down and resting his head on my lap.

Fray isn't paying any attention to us. "So over here, it says, 'Luna be thy ruler to command over all.'" She turns the book again. "This says, 'thy Luna to sacrifice in honor of the Blood Mark.' I can't make the rest out, but there's a question mark after it. This last part is 'With thy Luna rebirth, her blood shall heal them all.'" Fray closes the book. "I'm trying to remember, but I think the Luna was the queen of all wolves."

"She sacrificed herself to remove the full moon curse from the wolves," Dax whispers.

Sitting in that cave, listening to them piece together my part in this curse, I remember Celeste talking about my sacrifice. I feel Dax's arm squeezing my shoulders. Tarq adjusts his body so he's cuddling up to my waist. I even catch Anthony frowning out of the corner of my eye.

I'm the Luna. The weight of my entire situation crashes down upon me at one time. *I have to die to free them. I was born to die for them.*

Dax leans his forehead against my temple. "Fray, is there anything in there that can help us?"

"Based on what I remember and what you said, the Luna was the Queen of wolves, and she sacrificed herself for them." She opens the book back up and starts frantically thumbing through it. "There's a part about being called upon again for the child of the Lunar Pack. I just can't find it now, but I know it's here. I've read it."

I wipe the tears running down my cheeks but not before a few fall on Tarq's fur. "Enough," I say firmly. "I've had enough for now." I stand up and brush the dirt off my shorts. Tarq jumps up beside me, staying at my hip. "I'm sorry, Fray," I say, apologizing for my sharpness. "I just can't handle any more of this right now."

I step around Tarq and hold my hand up, stopping Dax. *I'm not in the mood for more confusion right now.* I don't bother trying to stop Tarq. He won't listen anyway. I walk to the back of the cave, where the firelight barely reaches. I grab one of the blankets we have rolled back here and lay it next to the horse pen. I've always found their sneezes and stomping calming.

I flop onto the blanket with my arms out to my sides. Tarq slides up beside me. He leans his back against me and gently rolls his head and neck so that the top of his head is against my cheek.

"So, you're the Luna," Tarq says thoughtfully.

Sighing, I bend my arm around his neck and tug the fur on his shoulder. I bite my lip, trying to fight back the tears. *I don't want to die, but how could I leave this beautiful wolf cursed?*

"At least that explains why you can hear me," Tarq says, interrupting my pity party.

The tears start to drop from my eyes, and I have no hope of stopping them. "I just need a minute to feel sorry for myself, ok?" I let the tears freely flow for a few minutes while gently running my fingernails through Tarq's fur. *At least I got to experience this—Tarq's devotion and Dax's love. I even think Anthony has become something to me, though I'm still not sure what.*

"We'll find another way, Darya," Tarq says, pulling me out of my head. *"I won't let anything happen to you."*

I take a deep breath and let it out, trying to relax the tension that has built up in my chest. "I have to believe that the Luna would have done it some other way if there were one."

"I finally found my purpose," Tarq says rather firmly. *"I'm not letting you go that easily. You are my Queen, after all."*

Smiling through my tears, I scratch his shoulder. "I'll make you a deal," I say. "I'll try with you if you don't call me your Queen."

"Deal." Tarq rolls onto his belly and twists his body to give me the top of his shoulders to scratch. As soon as my nails land between his shoulder blades, he rolls into my hand and closes his eyes.

I giggle. "What does that feel like?"

Tarq relaxes onto his stomach and pushes his front paws under my arm. *"Like it does as a human. That spot between your shoulders is impossible to reach on your own."* He touches his nose to my cheek. *"Just don't scratch my butt or belly. Things might get awkward."*

Giggling, I slap his shoulder, but then I think about him and all he's lost, apparently waiting for me. "I think we should find your parents."

"I would like that."

The day's weight seems to crash over me as I calm down. I stretch out my limbs and yawn loudly.

"You should sleep, Darya," Tarq says, gently running his nose down my jaw. *"Leave the worrying to someone else tonight."*

I reach up for his head and tug on his ear. "You'll stay with me?"

"Always." Tarq leans his shoulders slightly and tucks his head in beside mine.

* * *

In the morning, I wake sandwiched between Dax and Tarq. Right now, their heat is overwhelming, but overnight, it probably kept me comfortable. Tarq has twisted a bit and curled his front legs neatly against his chest while his hips are still straight with his back legs underneath him. Dax has thrown his right arm over my waist, and his hand is resting on Tarq's ribs. *It seems these two don't hate each other as much as they let on.*

When I lift Dax's arm off me, he rolls away onto his back. *Ok, that was easier than I thought.* Tarq's head presses firmly against mine, so I can't turn toward him. I can only move my eyes. His neck is still over my arm, and his nose is to my throat. I slowly sit up, pulling my left arm from under Tarq.

The beautiful wolf is still asleep when I set his muzzle on the blanket. I breathe a sigh of relief. I haven't had a moment to myself since meeting this crazy pack. I don't even know what that feels like anymore. I quietly lift myself off the blanket and quickly make my way to the mouth of the cave.

When the sun hits my skin, I feel relief wash over me. I close my eyes and turn my face to its light. It's quiet without anyone bickering or telling me I'm some kind of queen and my only job is to die. Sighing, I crouch down with my head in my hands. *That's right. Hello, reality. I could've gone a little longer without you popping into my head.*

"It's nice out here," a voice I'm not interested in hearing says.

I open my eyes and turn toward it. Anthony is leaning against a boulder twisting a few sticks together.

His face skews in thought. "I didn't mean to scare you," he says, almost sincerely. "I just meant that I understand why you use this cave."

Raising my eyebrow, I tilt my head. "Did you forget how to be an asshole?"

Anthony snorts and jumps to sit on the boulder. "There's no sense in that," he says with a smirk. "Besides, I like to bask in my glory when I'm right."

"Right about what?" I sneer, standing to face him.

Anthony's grin says, "I'm happy that you are miserable," and he's wearing it right now. "I told you that they would get you killed."

I came out here to get away from these exact thoughts. Being surrounded by the men I was born to save was enough of a reminder. I didn't need to hear Anthony gloat about my fate like he had a hand in it. "You know, you could be something else, something better," I spit out, closer to tears than I'd like to admit. "These are good people who take care of their own."

His eyes squint into a glare. "And everyone else ends up scarred, broken, or dead."

"Then stop being everyone else, Anthony!" I can't help that my voice is rising. I'm mad. His pity party about being beaten up is too much for me right now. "You could be a part of this. You can't go back." I wave my arms in frustration. "You burned that bridge."

"I'm aware," Anthony snarls, throwing his twisted sticks toward the trees.

"Darya, are you ok?"

I glance around, finding Tarq at the mouth of the cave. It's only been five minutes, but my heart leaps like he's been away forever. When he shakes his coat out, I notice that not a single strand of fur comes loose. "Come here. I'm fine," I say, smiling. "Is Dax still asleep?"

As Tarq approaches me, he keeps his eyes on Anthony. *"He was up late with Fray,"* he says before looking at me. *"I think they were working on that notebook."*

I put my hand out for his head. "Let's take a walk then."

With my fingers curled around his jaw, we walk beside the cave and through the trees. We descend into a small open area with a stream across the edge of it. A low stone fence indicates a house might have been here long ago, but there's no hint of a dwelling now. I thought one day I would build a cabin up here, far away from people. *It doesn't look like that'll ever happen.* My thoughts cause me to frown.

"This is one of my favorite places," I say sadly. "The stream flows from a spring in the mountain, so it's freezing. No one ever comes up here."

Tarq slides out of my hand and steps into the water. He jumps back and shakes his paw out. *"You weren't kidding."* He chuckles as he jogs back to my side.

I bump his shoulder with my hip. "Is the big, bad wolf cold?"

He shakes his paw again, making sure to get a little of the water on me. *"Yes, he is."*

Smiling, I step over to the stone wall and sit with my back against it. "Next time, listen to me."

It's so easy to be with Tarq. I don't feel he will judge me for my thoughts or feelings when we talk. I also don't feel like I'm burdening him with them. *It doesn't hurt that he's so damn gorgeous, except for maybe right now.* I watch Tarq flop near my feet and roll. He twists several times to scratch his back and stretches his legs. I nudge his shoulder with my foot, giggling.

"I don't think I could do this without you," I admit.

Tarq looks at me upside down for a moment but then rights himself and crawls to lean against my leg. *"Well, you'll never have to find out because I'm not leaving you."*

I grab his jaw, pulling it until I can rest my forehead on his head.

"You are my Luna. I am here for you." Tarq pulls back, rubbing his nose against my cheek. He runs his tongue over his nose and closes his eyes. *"However you need me, you have me."*

I reach out to Tarq, and he doesn't hesitate to step into my arms. I don't know if it's his sincerity or that the world is suddenly crashing around me with a short timeline, but tears threaten my eyes again. I bury my face in his fur and let it all out.

After a while, my tears dry up, and I just hang onto Tarq, not wanting to let him go. I'm not a crier. It almost makes me mad that Tarq is seeing this, but I don't want to die. I don't even want to lead them. I just wanted a simple, quiet life where I could be happy and feel like I belonged.

"What's going on, Darya," Tarq says softly. *"You don't seem the type to fear death."*

I sniffle a little and gather my thoughts. "I feel like if I say that I don't want to die, then I'm saying that I don't want to help you," I say, realizing there is no way I could ever abandon these wolves. "That's not true. I will do whatever it takes to break your curse." I lift my head and look into his eyes. "But I don't want to die."

Tarq chuckles in the true form I've come to expect from him. *"Well, that's good. I'd be worried about you if you were fine with dying."* He bumps his nose to my cheek. *"Plus, saving you will be a little easier if you want to live."*

I tug at his fur. "You're a good friend."

"And you'll make a great Luna."

I shake my head. "Tarq, I was only born to die." I sniffle, wrinkling my nose. "I'm only a Luna to remove your curse, not to rule over you.

I'm just Darya, the girl who happened to be born into the family line created to save you."

"*You were born of the Luna line. Your blood runs through a Luna's heart.*" He taps my chest with his nose. "*You are our Luna in every sense of the word. You will unite us into a true wolf pack.*"

I look down at my chest where his nose had poked and then back up into his beautiful eyes. "I don't know anything about being a Luna," I say, frowning. "I don't even know how to be a part of your world."

"You'll learn. We will help you," Dax announces. He walks around the wall and sits beside me. His warmth is comforting as he drapes his arm around me.

Tarq doesn't look happy when Dax leans in to kiss my temple but nods his agreement and lies by my feet. He slaps his paw in a puddle and splashes water on his muzzle.

"Well, I'll help you," Dax says, laughing. "I don't know what he's gonna be doing."

I rub my boot over Tarq's shoulder, and he leans against it, humming. "You each have unique qualities and are both important to me."

Dax puts his forehead against my temple. "So, I've been thinking," he says quietly. "After we find the witch, we should find his folks." He turns away from me and looks at Tarq. There's a softness in his eyes that I've never seen when he looks at the young man or the wolf he becomes.

I run the back of my finger along his jaw to his chin and look at Tarq, smiling. "I think that's an excellent plan." Tarq sits up and winks at me. I take a moment to appreciate them for everything they have brought to my life. I take a deep breath when my heart feels like it might explode with pride and love for them. "Alright, boys, today we climb a mountain. Are you ready?"

I slap my hand on Dax's leg. He growls quietly as I stand up and reach for his hand.

"Come on, Alpha," I say merrily. "Get off your ass."

He smiles and accepts my hand. "Yes, my Luna."

I cringe at his words. "I know I started it, but I don't think I'm quite ready for titles."

Dax winks at me. "As you wish, my Luna." He presses his lips to my knuckles.

"Do you want me to bite him?"

I pull my hand away from Dax and make sure he understands my look of dismay before I smile and shake my head at Tarq. "That's enough out of you two," I say in my best Rosalee impression. "Let's go."

11

The cliff trail is relatively steep but does flatten out in a few places. The flat areas only have enough room for two of the three horses to rest. It wouldn't be horrible, but most of the trail is stone, and one slip could send us all over the edge. There is another way. A pass to the west slopes through some fields but takes much longer.

"How are you holding up?" I ask Tarq while the horses rest.

He's lying in the tiny sliver of shade beside some scratch brush. *"I'm fine, Darya,"* he says. *"I feel bad for the horses. I told Dax to quit putting shoes on them."*

I lean on my saddle horn as my horse rocks his hips. "You'll tell me if you need to stop, right?"

"Yes, Darya." I can hear his smile in his words.

"Are you about done?" Anthony grumbles. "It's hot as hell up here. We need to go."

This cliff trail takes about three hours without stopping. It takes us five with the few breaks we took, but it's completely worth it as we round a corner at the end of the rock wall. The spring fields are bursting with brightly colored wildflowers as far as the eye can see. The soft breeze causes them to sway and blend as no painting could ever capture.

I stop my horse and drop from my saddle beside Tarq. "Pretty great, right?"

The wolf closes his eyes and takes a deep breath, drawing in the scent. He then runs his nose over my leg, breathing me in. *"It smells almost as good as you,"* he says whimsically.

I turn my head to the side, and he tucks his nose toward his chest as if embarrassed. "Do I smell that good?"

Dax slides his arm around my waist, and Tarq steps away. "You smell good enough to eat." He growls, leaning down to lick my neck.

I know he's there and might even have feelings for me. *Why am I trying to apologize to Tarq with my eyes?* I shake my head. "The O'Shea farm is on the other side of the valley, but there's a small ranch to the east where we can stay tonight."

"Are you talking about Edith's place?" Anthony asks, stepping up beside us. "You've seen those bottles hanging in the trees, right? That woman is crazy."

"Those are just decorations, Anthony," I reply, laughing. "You have a problem with the woman because of her decor?"

Anthony raises his eyebrow. "How have you survived this long?" he asks. "Those are wards. That crazy lady has spelled crystals in them."

I smile broadly. "Well, maybe Edith can help more than we thought."

Dax shrugs. "It's worth a shot," he says. "We found nothing helpful in the notebook last night."

I wrap my arm around his waist as we walk toward the ranch. "I didn't think you would," I say. "Fray's been looking through that book since my father died. It's a miracle she was able to help us as much as she did just by finding out that I can hear Tarq."

Dax pulls me closer, resting his chin on my head. "They keep these fields pretty well hidden, don't they?"

"It's my secret gem." I reach out for Tarq and tug at the fur on his neck.

"It is beautiful here," he agrees.

We continue on foot for the rest of the day. The floral scents are intoxicating, and losing yourself in the beautiful blend is easy. I think about what could be if we figured out how to break the curse and save me—the home I could have where I felt like I belonged. I don't want to lead them, but I have grown to like the companionship these people provide. *Even Anthony, though I'm still not sure where he fits in. I'll come back to that.*

It's past sunset when we reach Edith's. The first thing I notice as we hit the edge of the house's grounds are the bottles hanging from the trees. I can't help smiling at Anthony's fears.

"Are you going to survive stepping over the threshold, Anthony?" I say, taunting him.

"Mark my words, woman, that's some crazy voodoo shit," he sneers.

Dax stops suddenly, interrupting my laughter, and tries to yank me back. "I think he's right."

I turn to face him and feel his fingers catch on my belt loop.

"Um, Darya?" *Wait. That voice wasn't in my head.*

I spin away from Dax to look where, just moments ago, Tarq had been walking under my hand. Everything from our first meeting comes crashing back like a runaway horse. I swallow hard, and my jaw relaxes to accommodate the extra air I need. My eyes mist up as they take in Tarq's human form. He's blushing and nervous and beautiful in every way.

Without thinking, I pull out of Dax's grip and close the distance between myself and Tarq. Relief washes over me as my arms wrap around his waist. My head rests against his chest with my ear to his heart, listening to it thump a strangely familiar beat. His arms fold around me, and he lays his cheek against my head. *This is where I belong.*

"I'm here," he whispers. "I'll always be here for you."

I've been listening to Tarq in my head, but his words mean so much more out loud. My arms tighten around him. His heartbeat remains steady. "I needed you," I whisper back.

Tarq wraps his hand around my head, holding me to his chest. "I know you did," he murmurs. "I'm sorry it took so long, but I'm here now."

Someone behind me clears their throat, reminding me we're not alone. Sighing, I relax completely against Tarq's body. "I just made this awkward, didn't I?"

Tarq sighs, raising his head for the first time since I latched onto him. "I'm fine," he says, resting his cheek back on my head. "But I think we might have some explaining to do."

I can't hold Tarq tighter, so I flex my arms and step into him. I'm not ready to let him go. *I don't really know what to do. My arms are around someone my heart wants, and just a short time ago, my body was demanding the man behind me. Is any of this real?*

I slide my hand over Tarq's back, feeling his muscles react. *It doesn't matter what my mind, body, or heart wants. I'm only here to save them.* I think about how furious Dax must be, silently standing behind me. He is just waiting for me to step aside so he can kill Tarq. I sigh and squeeze his waist one more time.

Leaning back, I look up into Tarq's eyes. I've been looking at them while he was a wolf, but my breath catches for a moment seeing them so closely now. They are gentle and caring, accented by his sandy blonde hair that falls into them as he looks down at me. I cup his cheeks, and he matches my movements by grabbing mine. I slowly let out a sigh, trying to prepare to face Dax.

Tarq closes his eyes, clenching his jaw. "Please don't ever do that again."

I raise my eyebrow, unsure of what he means. However, I know what I need to do, and I should do it before I climb back into Tarq's arms and never leave them. "I've got you," I tell him. "I'm the Luna, after all, right?"

Tarq opens his eyes and smiles down at me. "That you are, Darya."

I take a deep breath and turn to face Dax, keeping Tarq behind me. *He won't hurt me to kill him.* But when I see Dax, he's pacing just a few feet from us, right where I left him at the property line. He stops and faces me but doesn't approach us. His glare is one that he's reserved only for Tarq, but it's directed at me.

"Dax?"

"Looks like you've got yourself a werewolf problem, Darya," a familiar voice calls out. Edith is walking toward us with a shotgun aimed in our general direction. After a few more steps, she spots Anthony and settles her aim on him. She stops beside me and turns to run her eyes over Tarq's body. "Although this one is stunning." She bites her lip.

"This is Tarq." I step between them, blocking her view.

"We should probably find him some clothes, or I might have to take advantage of him," she says, arching her eyebrow. Tarq grabs my hips and keeps me between himself and Edith as she moves toward Dax. "And you must be immortal," she says calmly, as if these are every-day things.

"Why am I locked out?" Dax growls.

"Oh, honey," she replies, smiling. "If I can't kill you, you aren't get-ting past my wards." She looks past Dax at Anthony. "My wards can't stop you, but I'm pretty sure my shotgun will." She lifts her eyebrow as if asking him to test her theory.

"Good to see you too, Edith," Anthony sneers. He sidesteps to look at me. "Darya, I'm staying out here tonight."

Edith winks at him and turns back to me. "Why don't you two come with me?" She smiles, leaning around me to look at Tarq again. "I'd love to hear this story."

Edith has always had silver-gray hair. She leaves it loose to sway in the moonlight. Her arrogance makes me smile as she swaggers with the shotgun over her shoulder.

I reach back and put my hand on Tarq's chest. "Go with her," I tell him as he pushes against my hand, trying to get closer. "She'll have some clothes for you."

Tarq looks up at Dax and then back at me. He shakes his head. "I'll not leave you again."

I sigh and tilt my head a little. "Tarq," I say, pushing back against him. "You're naked."

He rolls his eyes. "Fine," he agrees. "I'll be right back then." Tarq jogs after Edith, catching up to her at the house's front door.

Taking a deep breath, I turn back toward Dax. The moment I cross the boundary, he snatches my arm and slings me away like it would claim me again if given a chance. "Dax, you're hurting me," I snap, yanking my arm out of his hand. "Don't ever do that again."

"Darya, I can't protect you if I can't get in there," he growls.

I step back, holding my hand out. "Hang on," I say, confused. "That's what you're pissed about?"

Dax sighs. He slides his hand down my arm, catching my fingers at the end. "Life has just thrown you into an impossible situation." He rolls his eyes and puts his hands on my shoulders. "That damn wolf pisses me off, but he's helping you." Dax slides his hands up my neck, and the Blood Mark tingles at his touch. "You are our Luna. I will not question you."

I sigh in relief, thankful that he won't be trying to kill Tarq. I close my eyes as Dax rests his forehead on mine. "I don't know what I'm doing, but I need to go in there and talk to Edith."

Dax leans back, shaking his head. "Absolutely not."

I grab him by the wrists, gently pulling his hands off my neck. "Tarq will be with me."

"I'll stay with her, Dax," Tarq says, walking up.

"That's Alpha," Dax snarls.

"See?" I say, ignoring his anger. "Safe."

Dax starts to growl as I back toward the barrier, pushing his hands further from my body.

"I'll send him back out here afterward," I promise him. "And look, the cottage is right there." I point to the small outbuilding that Edith uses as a guesthouse. "I'll be fine, Dax."

Tarq puts his hand on my shoulder as I cross the boundary, causing Dax's eyes to narrow and his growl to deepen. "You better be back out here tonight, wolf," he threatens.

I shake my head. "So grumpy."

I spin around and grab Tarq's arm. We quickly walk to Edith's, barging through the door. I let my eyes run down his body as he closes it. I probably missed the perfect chance to look at him earlier, but he's the most beautiful thing I've ever seen in clothes or fur. I'm not sure seeing him naked would be any better.

Edith has dressed Tarq in vintage jeans. There are a few holes in the legs, but they fit him perfectly and sit low on his hips. The dark blue button-up shirt is unbuttoned and open, showing some of his chest and abs. The sleeves are short, and a mark runs down his right arm that matches Dax's. I remember seeing the same thing on Nate.

Tarq approaches me slowly, leaving his eyes on the floor. I would imagine he feels strange about how I keep staring at him. I reach for his cheek and wait for him to look at me, feeling that this needs to be Tarq's decision.

When he finally does, I smile at him. "You are my guard and, more importantly, my friend. You have no reason to look down."

Tarq smiles, opening his arms. I am all too happy to step back into them. I slide my hands inside his shirt and wrap my arms around his waist. "I owe you so many of these," Tarq whispers. I don't think he does, but I'll take them anyway. My world feels complete or just somehow better in his arms. His heartbeat is the calmest thing I've ever encountered.

"I could stay like this forever," I whisper before I realize my thoughts are coming out of my mouth.

Sighing, Tarq runs his hand through my hair. "I can't stay like this," he says quietly. "I'm stronger as a wolf."

I step into him, erasing anything that could qualify as a distance between our bodies. "I know." *All I want to do is hold him.*

Edith clears her throat from beside us as she stops with a tray of tea cups. "If I had known he wasn't available, I wouldn't have dressed him so yummy." She arches her eyebrow and nods toward her couch. "Come on, you two. Time to tell me what's going on."

I pull away from Tarq. "He's my guard, Edith."

Tarq chuckles.

Edith sets her tray down on the coffee table and points at Tarq. "He knows what's going on." She winks at him, handing me a cup as I sit on the couch. Pointing to her neck and looking at me, she sits on the floor on the other side of the table. "This is new. You wanna talk about it?" She hands Tarq a cup of tea as he sits on the floor and leans against the couch beside me.

"A witch we talked to called it a Blood Mark," I say. "Dax has one too." I take a sip of the tea and feel my face heat up. I poke at my cheek with my fingertips.

"It's healing you, Darya," Edith says. "It's perfectly safe."

"Oh," I whisper, surprised. "Thank you."

Tarq looks back, and I run my fingers over his cheek.

"A Blood Mark is only present when breaking a curse," Edith says slowly, narrowing her eyes. "You're not cursed. Who is?"

My eyes flick down to Tarq, who's still staring at me. "They are."

Edith gasps. "They're descendants of the Lunar Pack?"

"How is it that everyone knows about this but me?" I scoff. "I haven't exactly been under a rock."

I'm grumbling to myself because no one is paying attention to me. Edith taps on planks over her fireplace hearth, looking for a loose board, while Tarq stares at her.

"One doesn't talk about such things openly, Darya," Edith says. "Not with the militia so close to us." There's a hollow thud when she hits a board just below the hung painting. "Ah, here it is!" She shimmies the board out of its spot and pulls an old, disheveled journal from a compartment.

When she places it on the table, Tarq leans forward. "What's that?"

Edith smiles. "Estrella is my ancestor," she says, opening the book. "We've been waiting for you for a long time, Darya. I didn't know it was you, but we have been waiting."

Tarq slides closer to me. "I won't let you hurt her." *He doesn't know we're here looking for help. How many ways can I fail this man?*

Edith winks. "My, you are delicious when you get angry." She smiles, letting her gaze wander to Tarq's chest. "But no, baby, I don't want to hurt her." She hums happily as she turns back to her book.

I lean down, putting my cheek against Tarq's head. "I'm sorry," I whisper. "I shouldn't have assumed Dax told you what we were doing."

Tarq puts his hand over mine on his shoulder, studying Edith.

"Estrella set the wheels in motion to break their curse," Edith says. Her fingers trail across the pages as she reads to us. "Only the blood that created it can break a blood curse."

"So that would be Olivia's blood?" I ask, sitting up.

Edith frowns and looks up. "If only it were that easy," she says sadly. "This would require both Olivia and Mira's blood since both activated this curse."

I close my eyes and open my fingers, threading them with Tarq's.

"My ancestors' spell book will guide us once we have the blood," Edith says softly. "We've had many years to work out how to save you, Darya."

I raise my eyes. "How on earth will we get blood from two women that have been dead for over a hundred years?"

Edith smiles. "Where there's a will, there's a way." She tosses her hair, looking down at her book. "If you can get their bones, you'd do well to bring them to my brother. He can help."

My face instantly cringes. "Jaxson?" I groan. "Isn't there anyone else?"

Edith is used to my dislike of her brother. "Sorry, honey, he has our mother's books."

Tarq looks up at me, confused. "What am I missing?"

I look down at him and frown as Edith giggles.

"My brother had this tiny little crush on her." She holds her fingers close together.

I fall against the back of the couch, pulling my hand away from Tarq. "He tried to make a love potion!" I shout.

Edith laughs as she stands and lifts the tray of cups. "Fine," she says. "I'll get the book from him." She retreats to the kitchen.

When Tarq crosses his arms over my legs, I slide my hand over his cheek. "We can do this together, right?"

Tarq hums, leaning on my hand with his eyes closed. "Always."

I'm sure I could conquer the world with this beautiful man. I wish I knew what the humming was, though.

Edith returns with a glass vial of purple liquid I've seen many times. "I grabbed this for you, Darya, in case you still have issues sleeping," Edith says, handing me the sleep aid and the key to the cottage. "I think it's about time we call it a night. Old man O'Shea died a few months ago. Heart attack, I think. Tell your men out there to be careful. His son's been sniffing around."

I roll my eyes and nod, standing up from the couch. "Thank you for everything." I lift the vial she made for me. "I'm not sure I'll need this, but I'll take it, just in case."

Edith's eyes travel over Tarq's body again. "I can think of a few ways to wear yourself out."

"Nice, Edith." I roll my eyes, pulling Tarq toward the front door. "Have a good night," I yell as we pull it open. "Thanks for everything!" I quickly close the door behind us.

"She's terrifying," Tarq says, grinning. He puts his arm around my shoulders and guides me to the guest cottage as I laugh at him. "No, seriously, never leave me alone with that woman."

I wrap my arm around his waist and bump my hip into him. "Stop. Edith is harmless."

Tarq frowns. "I feel dirty."

I burst out laughing.

"It's not funny, Darya," he tells me, laughing himself. "I'm a wolf. If I feel dirty, it's pretty bad!" He takes the keys from my hand and squeezes my shoulders.

"If it's not funny, then why are you laughing?" I look up, arching my eyebrow.

He shakes his head as we reach the cottage door. "I want to check the house before I leave you here, Darya." He leans down to my head, momentarily resting his cheek against me before pulling away. "Wait here."

"I need to talk to Dax," I tell him, handing him the vial. "Can you put that inside for me?"

Tarq nods and unlocks the door as I turn to face the fire burning beside the property barrier. I take a deep breath and ready myself as I walk steadily toward it.

Dax stands and wraps his arms around my shoulders when I cross the barrier. He tucks his face down into my hair and takes a deep breath. "You smell like that wolf," he sneers.

I push away from him, narrowing my eyes. "Then I'll take a bath." I pull him over to the fire and sit across from Anthony. "Sit down. We have things to discuss."

Dax lies beside me with a sigh, resting his head on his saddle. He holds his arm out, but I shake my head.

"Edith is who we've been looking for, and she's given me our first task." I pick up a stick to twist in my fingers. "We have to collect blood."

Dax grabs the stick out of my hand. "Whose blood?"

I sigh. "And that is where it instantly becomes more difficult." I look in his direction. "We need blood from Mira and Olivia."

Dax throws the stick into the fire and sighs, rubbing his fingers over his eyes. "That's problematic."

"Edith says we just need their bones," I say hopefully. "I assume you know where Olivia is."

"I do. It's Mira that's going to be a problem."

I shrug. "So let's deal with one problem at a time and start with Olivia's bones."

Dax sits up and reaches for my cheek. I let him move closer, leaning on his hand with my eyes closed.

"Old man O'Shea died, Dax," I tell him, relaxing into his touch. "His kid's been poking about."

"Never mind that," he whispers, coming closer. "You look tired, my beautiful."

He pulls me to his chest and slides his arms around me. His rain-soaked forest scent is now burnt wood and ash. I get the feeling that nothing in the past 175 years has been fair to Dax, but he is still trying to care for me. *I can't do this right now.*

I pull away from him. "I have to go," I announce. "Tarq is waiting for me."

Dax begins to growl.

"Don't start."

Anthony snickers across the fire.

Without looking back, I storm straight to the cottage. Tarq is leaning against the door's frame. He smiles as he sees me approach but stops when he notices my scowl. I fall into him, latch my arms around his waist, and push him back into the cottage. I kick the door closed, not stopping until we're in the small living room.

When we finally stop, my chest is heaving air, and my eyes burn from tears that won't come. Tarq holds my head to his chest, allowing me to hear his steady heartbeat. *I remember wanting to run my tongue all over Dax just a few days ago, but I can't remember why. Now I want to stay here in Tarq's arms like it's a happy place. I could never be satisfied anywhere else. This is what insanity feels like, right?*

I take a deep breath, sliding my hands down to his hips. "Everything is changing so fast. How am I supposed to do this?"

We sigh together. "You're strong, Darya," Tarq says. "You'll find a way."

I pull away from him and wipe my face. "I guess I should probably get my shit together, huh?"

"You can lose your shit around me anytime you need to," Tarq says, smiling. He reaches over to the coffee table and picks up the vial. Handing it to me, he gestures to the bedroom. "For now, though, I think you should get some sleep."

I'm surprised that Tarq follows me to the bedroom. "Thank you for checking the house," I say, placing the vial on the bedside table. When I turn around, he's standing in the doorway, looking like he's fighting his own battle. One hand is on the door frame, while the other is on the handle. Both have white knuckles, as if his grip on them is the only thing keeping him there. I step toward him, and he instantly wraps around me. "I want you to stay," I whisper.

Tarq's arms tighten around me. "Please don't ask me to. We both know I shouldn't."

I frown. "I know."

"Tomorrow, I'll return to being a wolf, and you'll still be the Alpha's Luna." He takes a deep breath before sliding out of my arms and leaving the cottage without looking back.

I fall onto the bed, rubbing my hand over my mouth. I find the Blood Mark lifted when my fingers slide over my jaw and down my neck. *What the hell?*

I jump up and lean over in front of the mirror. I've never really studied it before. My wolf is black with gray tips. Its white fangs are quite pronounced as it pulls its lips back in a snarl. Its eyes are red and glow so brightly that they could very well be gems embedded in my skin. *Why are you so angry, wolf?* Slowly, I run my fingers over the edges again, trying to remember if I've ever noticed the wolf raised before.

"Are you ok?" Tarq asks, back in my head.

I sigh, closing my eyes.

"I'm sorry," he says sadly.

I can't do this. I grab Edith's vial and chug its contents. Knowing this concoction well, I throw myself onto the bed.

12

In the dark, my bed begins to shake. I can't open my eyes. Something pulls on my wrists when I move my arms. As I turn my head, something brushes against my face, and my left arm feels ripped open. I'm unsure if my weakness is from the sleeping concoction or something else.

The more awake I become, the more I realize how screwed I am. My arms are stretched out and tied at the wrist, and my feet are tied down. The thing covering my face is very thick because it's pitch black, even when my eyes finally open.

"Darya? Where are you?" Tarq's voice is a false calm.

He's looking through my eyes. I try rubbing my chin against my left shoulder, but the searing pain from the crook of that arm stops me. I try the right shoulder, and light appears around my chest.

"Hey there," Tarq gushes, relieved. *"I need to see something around you, Darya. I'll come to get you."*

I stop to think for a minute. My captors have tied me so I can't move any of my limbs and put this enormous sack over my head. They've done something to my arm, and I don't have the strength to fight the ropes. *This has to be someone who knows me.*

I start to cough. Just a little in the beginning, and then it gradually gets worse on its own. Soon I'm coughing so hard I'm on the verge of throwing up. When the cover slides off my head, the brightest light I have ever seen flashes in my eyes.

"Shit, that's bright!" Tarq yells in my head.

I close my eyes, wincing in pain from the light and his shout. I slowly crack my eyes back open and try to take a breath, prompting me to start coughing again. I lean to the side in my coughing fit and see the large tree we used as a landmark two days ago.

"*I'm coming,*" Tarq shouts.

As my cough settles, I look around. I'm lying on a board over a wagon with my arms strapped to the sides. I squint, trying to focus my eyes as my vision blurs, but they roll closed.

"*Come on, Darya, I'm almost there.*"

His voice wakes me up a little, and my eyes fling open. They land on my left arm before closing again. It's sliced open with my blood draining into a bucket. *Well, that explains a lot.*

"*No, no, no. Darya, stay with me.*"

But I can't. I have nothing left to give. I'm so cold that my body starts to shake. I can hear voices but can't make out their words. Someone taps on my cheek a few times and then tries to pull open my eye.

Tarq, I need you.

There's suddenly a lot of yelling. A man's voice cries, "Look out!" and a horse screams. A gun goes off. Some more yelling, and then it's silent. I'm not sure I'm still alive until the wagon jolts, creaking loudly. I feel something slide over my arm where it's sliced open. It's comforting. Then whiskers rub against my cheek. *Tarq?*

"*Darya?*" He sounds so scared. "*Can you hear me?*"

I'm breathing in small bursts but not moving much air. I try to convince my lungs to slow down, but my chest is too heavy. I can't lift it. *Come on. It can't end like this.*

"*Stay with me. Help is on the way.*"

Tarq moves around my body, and his teeth slide over my skin as he frees me from the ropes. He nudges my body, and I fall like a dead weight onto the wagon floor. My chest heaves, and my body starts to shake. Tarq rocks the wagon as he moves around to lie against me. I can feel his body heat up, and he lays his head on my shoulder so that his cheek is against mine.

"*Please don't leave me.*" Tarq hums quietly, adjusting to put more of his body against me. I focus on my chest as it makes an attempt to pull air. Tarq lifts his head, and I feel his nose on my cheek. My chest draws one more shallow breath. *"I can't lose you, Darya. I love you."*

* * *

My last breath leaves my lungs, and I can't feel Tarq anymore. My world turns dark, cold, and unfriendly. There's no light, no beginning, no end. Just black. It's slightly comforting to see myself when I look down. I try to walk around, but are you moving when you can't tell if you've covered any distance? *I could see this being my hell. I'm not entirely sure that I deserve hell.*

"Oh, be dramatic, won't you?" an angry voice sneers.

I turn to see a beautiful woman barely dressed in furs standing nearby. She seems about my age or slightly younger and is definitely from another time. She has blonde hair that fades to blue at the tips, which lies over her shoulders. Her dark brown eyes match mine, but I could never pull off the evil smirk she's wearing.

"Why are you here?" I snap. "Let me die in peace. Whoever you are, you're ruining this for me."

She laughs, throwing her head back. "Oh, no," she says slowly. "I'm not going anywhere. I'm the Luna, and it's time we talked, little girl. Come with me."

I hold my hands out. "Come with you? You have another shade of black that we need to go see?" Rain hits my outstretched hand, and trees materialize around me. There are a few puddles, and the rain creates little dripping noises in the calm forest. I close my eyes, soaking in the peacefulness.

"I love the smell of the forest after a hard rain," Luna whispers.

I roll my eyes open. "Why am I here?"

"Impatient girl," she snaps. "You're here because you keep screwing up your only job."

I raise my eyebrows. "What job are you talking about?"

"You only need to die on the right damn day," she yells, jabbing her finger at me. "You need to stay out of my way so I can finish that mark and then kill yourself on the day of your birth. That is it!"

Wait. She needs to finish the mark? Luna shimmers when I touch my neck. I recall things feeling strange whenever Dax touches the Blood Mark.

"You're the one that wanted Dax!" I didn't mean to shout at her, but I'm justifiably angry. *She used my body to sleep with Dax!* I tilt my head. *That actually explains a lot.*

"Of course. Dax's the Alpha and the cursed immortal. Anyone lower would be an insult!" She lets a grin creep across her face. "And as I recall, you liked it too."

"Stop it, just stop. You can't just treat people like they're your playthings. You hurt Dax," I say, shaking my head. "And Tarq is a good man."

"Oh, you think so?" she says, sickeningly sweet. "Let me show you what your good man did when he found you."

Our surroundings change so fast that it makes me dizzy as she brings me back to the basin. I put my hands out to steady myself, but it doesn't help because she's making me watch through Tarq's eyes. Everything blurs at this speed, and his snarl is so loud that it overpowers my thoughts.

Tarq runs straight to the horse pulling the buckboard. He bites down and takes a chunk of its throat with him. The horse falls, sliding to a stop as it dies behind him. He spins around and aims for the driver.

As he gets closer, I see that it's Casey O'Shea. The man's mouth moves, but Tarq's snarl is too loud. He jumps down from the wagon and runs past another man I don't recognize. That man has a shotgun aimed at Tarq, but when Casey runs past him, he bumps the barrel, so it's aimed too high when it goes off.

Tarq grabs the gunman by the hip, slamming his torso against the ground. I hear his bones break and see blood spray from the enormous openings left by Tarq's large teeth as he's thrown through the air.

Tarq banks to the right and catches up to Casey like he was just casually strolling. The man didn't stand a chance. Tarq leaps in the air and wraps his jaws around Casey's neck. I close my eyes too late, and

Tarq rolls mid-jump, ripping the man's head from his shoulders. I fall to my knees and throw up in the pretend world, still somehow running around as Tarq.

Luna lets the surroundings fade back to the forest, and I throw up again in a puddle on the forest floor. She stands over me as I straighten myself, still on my knees.

"You just threw up in your head from seeing what he did," Luna barks. "You have no idea what you are doing, little girl. Your puppy love is over! Let me finish what I started!"

"I'm not dying?" is all I can manage to get out.

"No, Baby Luna. Being me has its perks. Do your job, or I'll do it for you."

* * *

My eyes snap open, and I pull a dry, raspy breath. I'm still on the wagon, and hooves are pounding the ground. Tarq comes into my view as he moves, realizing I'm awake. His front leg is lightly draped across me, holding me still. All I can smell is the metallic scent of the blood on his fur.

"Get off me!" I spout in a hoarse whisper. The wolf jumps up, and I roll to my side before I throw up.

"I thought I lost you," Tarq says sadly.

When the wagon slows, I hear Dax talking to the horse. *Oh, Dax. I have to tell him what she did to him.* "Tarq, get down," he says. "Let me get back there."

"I won't leave you." I hear his protective grit and know he means every word.

I can't handle him right now. *I need Dax and his calmness.* "Get out!"

Tarq hangs his head and jumps from the wagon. Dax slides behind the driver's seat and touches my cheek. I hadn't realized that Tarq was keeping me warm, so now the heat from Dax's hand is a welcome comfort as my body shivers. His smile makes tears leak from the corners of my eyes.

"Hey there, my beautiful," Dax says, wiping my tears. "I thought we were gonna lose you for sure." He takes my hand as I try to lift it. "Just stay there. We'll get you back to the lake and find some blood."

The gates open, and my tears freely flow as I pull on him. I can't let him go without telling him it wasn't me. I didn't want to hurt him. Instead, something else comes out. "You were right," I whisper before my eyes roll closed.

* * *

I'm lying on a bed when my eyes open again. I draw a deep breath and lick my dry lips. Mari appears in front of me, holding a cup. I pull my head away as she approaches. *I'm not sure I can bring myself to trust this woman.*

"Easy, it's just water," she assures me. "Just take a small sip for now." She puts the cup to my lips again and tips it slightly. The water hits my throat like the elixir of life.

"Thank you," I say with my scratchy throat.

She smiles as she twists her long black braid into a bun. "My pleasure, Luna."

Great, this again.

"Someone's been waiting to see you."

"Who?" I can't help myself. Despite everything, I still want it to be Tarq.

"Who would you be hoping to see besides me?" Edith asks, barging into the room.

I try to smile politely, but she sees right through it.

"That beautiful man has been sitting outside this room for days," she says. "Nothing could lure him away. Trust me, honey, I tried." Edith raises her eyebrow, giving me her wicked smile.

Mari hands her the cup of water as I begin coughing and bows before leaving the room. Edith holds the cup to my lips, letting me drink more to calm the cough.

I sink back into the pillows and look at her thoughtfully. "Edith, I talked to the Luna."

Edith backs up, falling onto an armchair beside the bed. Her brow furrows. "Like, in a dream?"

"Sort of like that. She threatened me." I clear my throat, trying to get rid of the scratching. "She said she needed to finish the mark, and my only job was to kill myself."

Edith shakes her head. "No, there's another way."

"Luna told me to stay away from Tarq," I whisper. "She showed me what he did in the field." I sigh and drop my eyes to my hands.

Edith gasps, covering her mouth. "That must have been hard to watch. I'm so sorry."

I look up when she moves to the bed and takes my hand. "It was horrible," I answer.

"Tarq was so afraid of losing you," she says slowly. "I'm sure he wasn't thinking about anything else, honey."

I take a deep breath, biting my cheek. "I need to see him."

"Oh, Darya," she says, shaking her head. "Dax left orders that he's not allowed in here."

I smile as genuinely as possible. "I will repeat myself, and your response had better change." I look straight into her eyes. "I need to see him."

Edith holds her hands up and smiles. "Alright, but you better tell Dax I said no first." She pulls open the door and whispers.

Moments later, Tarq steps into the room. My chest aches as I look at him. It could be how incredible he looks in his black button-up shirt. The sleeves are rolled to just below his elbows, the top three buttons undone. His jeans perfectly fit his body, with the shirt tucked behind the useless belt's buckle. It could also be how he's staring at the floor, too ashamed to look at me.

How could he be anything but proud? How do I help him? His rescue was brutal, but I know that bitch didn't show me everything.

"Come here," I say quietly.

Tarq takes a few steps but stops halfway across the room, still refusing to look up.

"Why must I repeat myself?"

Tarq smiles as he closes the distance. "You sound strong, Darya."

I push against the pillows, sitting up. I lean somewhat to grab Tarq's arm, pulling him to me. He sits gingerly at the edge of the bed beside me and holds my hand.

"I want to thank you for saving me." I smile, but he doesn't look up.

Tarq shakes his head slightly, his hair covering his eyes. "I should've never left you. It won't happen again."

I reach under his hair for his cheek. "I said thank you."

"You're welcome," Tarq whispers, closing his eyes.

"I saw what you did in that field," I say. "Can you show me the rest of it? What happened after?"

Tarq lifts his head and raises his eyebrows.

"I want to see it." I slide my thumb over his cheekbone.

"I've only done it when you were sleeping." He shakes his head slowly.

Moving across the bed, I lay the pillows down. "I guess it's good this has worn me out, huh?"

Tarq tries to stand up, but I catch his arm. "Darya, let me get Edith or Mari."

I shake my head. "They can't show me what I want to see." I pull his arm until he's moving toward me. "You're all I need right now."

I roll away, pulling on Tarq until he lies down and slides his arms around me. My eyes close as his body melts perfectly against mine. He buries his face in my hair and takes a deep breath, letting it out slowly.

"Darya?" Tarq whispers.

"Don't say it," I say, stopping him. "Just be here right now, ok?"

My hands move to find his, and I thread our fingers. Moments later, I feel him heat up, and I'm lulled into a light sleep.

The images he shows me are all jumbled up. When I see the horse die again, I know Tarq's trying to get past the attack for me. I can feel his heat on my back like a safety net. I lean against him and wait for him to reach something he wants to show me.

As the vision slows, Tarq approaches the buckboard. I remember the wagon jolting horribly, but he actually steps up very gently. Moving slowly, he sniffs me the entire way. Tarq surveys the wound and licks it when he reaches my arm. I watch the cut close as he pulls back. I'm not sure I could tear my eyes away if I had the choice. He licks my arm a few more times, cleaning it off thoroughly.

I'm unsure if my chest is aching in this dream or real life, but the pain is real. He sniffs my face and chest before moving to work on the ropes. As Tarq chews them loose, I realize I haven't heard anything he said this whole time. *He's trying to hide that he told me he loves me.*

Tarq finishes with the ropes and nudges me off the lifted board. I didn't notice it then, but he grabbed the plank I was on with his teeth and threw it off the wagon. He then slides up next to me as close as possible without crushing me. Tarq settles his head beside mine and lets me hear his hum again. I listen for a few minutes before I fall into a deep sleep, smiling.

* * *

It's dark outside by the time I wake. The moon lights the trees outside the patio doors, and a lantern burns low across the bedroom. I feel the bed behind me to find it empty and cold. *Why did I want to see that? Luna will never let me have him.*

Someone knocks on the door, and my heart races until my eyes fall on Edith instead of Tarq. "Hey, honey," she says softly, reflecting my frown. "How are you feeling?"

Without warning, tears begin streaming uncontrolled down my face, and I reach out to her. Edith quickly shuts the door, locking it. She sits on the bed and hangs onto me while I sob uncontrollably.

"Tarq told me you wanted to see what happened after the attack."

I ball my hands into fists. "Edith, I don't know where I end, and she begins." I take a few deep breaths. "When Dax is around, he's all I can think about, but when he's not —"

"It's Tarq." She finishes my sentence.

"What am I supposed to do? Luna said to stay away from Tarq." I look up at Edith. "She said the Blood Mark is unfinished, and I needed to let her complete it." I fall back into the pillows.

Edith sighs. "Well, she's right. It's not finished."

"I'm not interested in her being right," I sputter angrily. "I want her gone."

Edith smiles, making me feel horrible for getting angry. She rests her hand on my arm. "What is real is that both men love and respect you unconditionally, and they will wait for you to figure this out." She grabs a cup from the bedside table and offers it to me.

I eagerly accept it, taking a few sips and smiling at her. "Where is he?"

"Dax or Tarq?" Edith raises her eyebrow.

I wrinkle my nose. "I hate that you even have to ask that." I twist my face in thought. "Let's just go with both."

She smiles and nods. "Dax thought he'd have more time until you woke up, so he and Anthony went to get Olivia's bones. Tarq left sometime after you fell asleep. Mari said he goes to the lake to clear his head."

I kick the blankets off and push myself upright. Swinging out of bed, I find my boots on the floor.

Edith rushes around the bed. "I figured you'd want to see him. Let me help you."

I wipe the sweat that's formed on my forehead. "How long have I been out? Why am I so weak?"

Edith helps me out of bed and opens the patio doors. "You lost a lot of blood. We've been here a little over a week." The patio turns out to be a full deck, and Edith guides me down the length of the house to some stairs. "I'm sorry I had to keep you sedated for so long. There wasn't exactly a lot of blood lying around for you. It took a while to collect all that you needed."

We slowly work our way down the stairs. It felt like hundreds, but I only see ten when I look back. "Why did they want my blood?" I ask, trying to understand what happened.

"They must've found out you're the Luna, Darya." When I raise my eyebrow at Edith, she frowns. "Fray," she whispers. "I'm sorry, Darya. Anthony found her outside the cave."

Stopping, I inhale deeply and straighten my back. "Take me to Tarq."

She squeezes my arm and helps me walk to the lake. It's clear why it's called Moonlight Lake when I see its surface shimmering with the moon's light.

"This is beautiful," I whisper.

Edith groans and bites her lip. "He certainly is."

I follow her eyes to the bank, where Tarq emerges from the water. Wearing only a pair of shorts, his wet skin shines just like the lake from the moonlight. He shakes his head, slinging water everywhere. I hold it together until he runs his hand through his hair and looks up. Pressure builds in my chest, and I hang onto Edith, afraid I might fall. His eyes hold mine captive as he starts to climb the bank toward us.

Edith clears her throat. "I feel like I'm intruding," she says quietly. My fingers dig into her skin as my body tenses. "Ok, I'm just gonna go." She pulls out of my grip just as Tarq reaches us and slips his arms around me.

I relax into his embrace, letting my ear find his heartbeat. My hands start at his ribs and slowly slide around to his back. His heat has dried his skin, but his hair is still dripping as he lays his cheek on my head.

"You said you'd never leave me again." My voice is barely a murmur.

"I'm sorry," Tarq whispers. "I wanted to give you a choice." He cups my head and holds me against him. "Now that you know what happened, I will let you decide."

I bite my lip, wrinkling my nose. *I need to stall.* "What am I deciding?"

"If you want me," he whispers.

I thought he'd be too scared to ask me to make this decision. *Of course I want Tarq. I like this feeling of family, of belonging. The comfort that being in his arms gives me. His embrace is my happy place. Who wouldn't want him or this?* I nuzzle my face against his skin as he steps closer so that he's against me from head to toe. *This is not my path.*

I pull my head free of his hand and lean back, only pulling away what's necessary to hold his face. His eyes nearly melt my heart. "I will always want you," I say slowly, trying to find the right words. "You are my guard. You're my friend. I can't do this without you."

Tarq's face drops slightly, and he looks over my head. I've never loved anyone but my family, so I'm not sure how this is supposed to happen, but this is the exact moment that I realize I'm completely in love with this man. I want to take away all of his pain. *You are mine, and I can't have you.*

I take a deep breath and slowly trace his jawline until he looks back down at me. "I need my guard." I smile, trying to ease his pain. "I need him to focus on his job. Can you do that for me?"

"I will always protect you." His voice might have only whispered those five words, but I hear so much more behind them.

Unable to stop myself, I reach up on my toes and lightly brush my lips against his, instantly regretting it as the Blood Mark sears to life. I put my forehead on his chest. *I hate you, Luna.*

"Are you ok?" Tarq hooks his arm around the back of my knees and lifts me off my feet. He cradles me against his chest. "So, what did you think of my lake?"

I smile as I glide my fingers over his chest and watch his skin react where I touch. "So now you're claiming a lake."

He flashes a crooked grin as he turns to the woods, carrying me back to the house. "Well, you've taken my bed, so I need to move on to bigger and better things."

Great, Darya, wake up in another man's bed. That worked out so well last time.

Tarq stays quiet for the rest of the walk. I focus on my fingers gliding over his skin and think about Dax. I'm unsure how to explain what's been happening. *I'm not sure I understand it myself.*

"Darya," Tarq whispers. "We're home." He sets me on my feet.

I look up at the house, awestruck. It's another enormous two-story cabin. The second-floor porch wraps around the whole building, with doors leading into each room. The first-floor porch only goes part of the way because a six-stall stable extends to one side. The Friesian and white mare both look over their stall doors at us.

"This is gorgeous," I whisper as he guides me around back, which is built into the side of a hill. "And you get to live here?"

"Nate and Mari live here too," Tarq says, sliding his arm around my waist. "Dax wanted them to keep an eye on me, and I like them, so, what the hell, ya know?"

Tarq holds my left hip and braces my shoulder, helping me climb the stairs. We sit on the top step and take a break. Tarq keeps his arm around my back, and I lean against his shoulder. I can't help thinking about the story of Olivia waiting for Markus. *I would do that every night if I could.*

13

❦

I could've sat in Tarq's arms forever if we weren't interrupted by a loud crash. He slowly pulls me to my feet, keeping his body between me and the noise. Putting his finger to his lips, Tarq braces me against his chest and cautiously moves toward his door. I'm pretty useless in my current state, but I want to know what made that crash.

Turning the handle, Tarq opens the door and helps me into his room. I look around to find Dax sitting in the overstuffed chair beside Tarq's bed. Behind him, the door is wide open with the frame busted, and a large chunk is missing where the door would generally catch. *I forgot Edith locked the door.*

"Where have you been?" Dax growls.

Tarq steps around me, steadying me behind him by my hips. "Dax, calm down," he growls back. "She was with me."

Taking a deep breath, I walk around Tarq. "It's ok," I whisper. I place my hand on his chest.

Tarq glares at Dax. "I'm kinda tired of fixing the shit you break in my house, Dax."

Dax's growl intensifies as he stands. "That's Alpha to you, wolf!"

I reach for Tarq's jaw and run my finger along it until he looks down at me. "Tarq, can you give us a minute, please?"

He shakes his head. "Um, no," he says, cupping my cheeks. "Every time I leave you, something bad happens."

I cringe a little. "I can't deny that," I say with a little smile. "Let me talk to Dax. Just the other side of the glass, not out of sight."

Tarq stares at me for a painfully long time. He finally sighs, rolling his eyes. "I'll be right outside." He looks up and glares at Dax. "Alpha," he sneers before stepping outside and closing the doors behind him.

I watch Tarq walk to the railing and lean against it. He crosses his ankles and rests his palms on the top rail. His long smooth muscles seem highlighted by the moon. *Blink, Darya.*

I turn back to Dax and hold my hand out when he tries to approach me. "Sit down," I tell him as calmly as I can manage. "I have some things I need to say, and you are going to stay over there so I can."

Dax falls into the chair, resting his elbows on its arms and putting his fingertips together. He looks up at me and raises an eyebrow expectantly.

"First," I start, holding up one finger. "This thing with you two is over." I motion my finger out toward Tarq. Dax opens his mouth and leans forward, but I raise my other hand. "Stop," I snap. "I'm not done."

Dax sits back in the chair, waving his hand as if permitting me to continue.

I shake my head. "It's so cute that you think you're in charge of this shit show. Tarq is **my** guard, and you will leave him to me now."

Dax continues to stare, not moving.

"Second," I continue. "You'll not control me anymore. I don't know much about the hierarchy, but I'm on top from what I understand."

Smiling, Dax taps his finger against his lips.

"What the fuck are you smiling about?" I don't know why, but I'm furious at his smile.

He shakes his head. "I wondered when you'd assume your role."

"I'm not assuming anything," I huff as Dax stands up. "I'm trying to end an old feud."

Dax steps toward me. "Darya, come here," he says calmly. He reaches out for my neck, placing a hand on each side. The moment he touches my Blood Mark, my anger dissipates. "I know these marks had something to do with our feelings, Darya. I'm not going to force anything on you." He pulls me into his arms and holds me against his chest. "I'm just as confused as you are, so I will give you time."

I let my body relax into Dax, thankful to have him back. He has a calmness that soothes me. He makes me feel like we're all going to be ok somehow.

Dax doesn't linger, sliding out of my arms and opening the door for Tarq. "Get in here, wolf," he says, returning to his gruff voice. "This involves you too."

Tarq steps back through the door, leaving it open, and sits on the bed. "What? It's my bed," he says, laughing at Dax's glare.

Dax rolls his eyes as he reaches for my hand to help me move around the bed to sit between them. "I got a few of my mother's bones," he says, releasing my hand. "So that just leaves Mira's."

I tilt my head to the side and look over at Tarq. When he winks at me, I doubt he's even paying attention to the conversation, and I can't help smiling at him. I turn my eyes back to Dax. "How are we supposed to find Mira's body?"

Dax sighs, leaning forward. "Not we. You. I need you to go talk to Miles."

My smile's gone. "Your brother?" I sputter, coughing as the words come out.

Dax sighs as he leans back and flexes his jaw. "He's still no brother of mine, but yes, that Miles." He looks at me with pleading eyes. "I need you to go talk to him about his mother."

To say that I'm stunned would be an understatement. I let out my breath when my chest starts to hurt. My mouth opens and closes several times, but I can't find any words to say.

Tarq clears his throat. "Maybe you should tell her the story, Dax."

"ALPHA!" Dax booms.

Tarq clicks his tongue. "Is that important right now?" He reaches his hand out to me. "I'm technically not part of your pack now that our Luna is here, anyway."

I squeeze Tarq's thigh as I look back at Dax. "Tell me."

Dax mashes his lips together and lets out a deep breath. "So you probably figured out Miles is immortal too. I don't know if it was intentional, but it happened." He pauses, running his hand through his hair. "For a while, our packs fought, but it was pointless since neither of us could die. So we made a truce."

Dax leans his head back and stares at the ceiling.

I shake my head, confused. "A truce?"

"Each pack stays in its territory," Tarq says quietly. "Any crossing of the line is considered an act of war."

I stare at Dax, but he doesn't move. When I turn to Tarq, he shakes his head.

"You're not going," he says. Tarq's not offering his opinion. He's telling me no.

My eyes narrow. "What is it with you two? Is it a wolf thing? Oh no, it's a man thing, isn't it? Stop telling me what to do." I continue to glare at him.

Tarq's jaw drops a bit. "Darya," he starts, sighing.

"So help me, Tarq. If you're not about to say sorry, you better stop there," I spout angrily.

Tarq reaches out for my hand again. "If you go, I'll go, and that will start a war, Darya."

As I piece our conversation together, I place my hand in his. I half expect him to pull me to him, but Tarq just lays his hand on the bed and gently runs his thumb over my knuckles. I remember his own words and smile. "What happened to not being a part of his pack anymore?"

"Yes," Dax hisses, pointing at Tarq. "There is that." He leans over and pats my knee.

Tarq frowns and squeezes my hand. "I don't like it."

"You don't have to like it. You just need to trust me." He doesn't look happy, but he won't be able to let me walk into danger alone. "If I'm going to talk to Miles, you will get Tarq's parents," I add, turning back to Dax.

"Yeah, alright," Dax agrees, slightly less chipper. "I'll draw you up a map. It should take you about a week to get there." He gets up from the chair.

"I want Anthony to go with us," I quickly say before he can leave.

"Why?" Dax turns back to me with his eyebrow raised.

"He's the only person I trust to make good decisions in emotional situations."

Dax and I regard each other before we turn to Tarq, who rolls his eyes but doesn't argue. "I'll have him get ready," Dax says. "Anyone else?"

"We'll need Edith," Tarq speaks up.

"Whatever," Dax grumbles. He puts his hand on my cheek. "I'll have that map for you in the morning, my beautiful. Get some sleep." He runs his thumb along my cheekbone, then glares at Tarq. "Wolf," he growls. Dax releases my face and leaves the room.

I pull my hand away from Tarq and twist around to face him. "I suppose you're staying?"

He moves toward the center of the bed, wiggling into the pillows. "Well, this is my bed."

"Yes, but as the Luna, I'm claiming it tonight." I shift onto my hands and knees to move up the bed. "So big, bad wolf," I start as I crawl toward Tarq. My breath catches when our eyes meet. *This was a dumb idea.* I put my hand on the headboard to push myself away, but it's too late.

Tarq sits up, bringing his face so close to mine that we share air. Heat pulses over my body, even causing a bead of sweat to run down my spine.

I swallow hard. "I shouldn't have done that." I watch his eyes as he tips his head to gently rub his lips against mine.

Tarq's eyes roll as I exhale into his mouth. "Then I probably shouldn't do this." He grabs me, crashing onto my lips as he flips me over his body. I couldn't fight this if I wanted to. Every piece of me wants to be in his arms, letting him love me. Well, every part except my Blood Mark, which is burning at a dull roar. *No, Luna. I want this.*

Tarq slides his hand up the left side of my body. His tongue glides softly over mine as his hand pushes the center of my back. Luna was feral with Dax. All she wanted was his body. I want more than that from Tarq. I'll be the first to admit that how I feel is not normal, but it does feel organic. I crave his presence. I want to hear his words, his thoughts. I loved him from the moment I met him. If it wasn't for...

Suddenly I'm screaming at the top of my lungs. Tarq latches his hand over the left side of my neck and covers my Blood Mark. I shove him as hard as possible, and he lets go of my neck. His eyes search my body, looking for an injury, but I end up curled in a ball on his bed with my hands over the wolf.

He lies beside me, running his fingers gently through my hair. "Did I hurt you?" he asks. He sounds like he's afraid of the answer.

"Just wait," I whisper, grabbing his arm so he won't leave. I stay in my curled-up ball, one hand over the Blood Mark and the other holding onto Tarq. When Edith runs in to check on me, I wave her off. I look up into Tarq's worried eyes and pat my neck. "Luna doesn't like you very much."

"Well, I don't exactly like her either," Tarq grumbles. He lies back, pulling me onto his chest. His steady heartbeat helps me find a rhythm for my breathing, and I settle into him. "Is she ok with this?"

I smile as I stretch the rest of my body along his. "Maybe she just prefers me to be calm," I say, sighing. "Will you stay with me?"

Tarq rolls, nearly burying me under his chest. He binds me to him with his arms and heats up. My eyes close as he says, "I will never leave you."

* * *

When I wake in the morning, true to his word, Tarq is still with me. He's lifted off me slightly, so I can see the bright light of the midday sun. He runs his fingers slowly through my hair, staring out the door.

Tarq closes his eyes when my fingers twitch against his hip, and I lift my hand so it barely touches him. I slide it up his ribs and, turning it over, gently run the top of my nails down to his hip. When Tarq starts to hum, I smile and bite my lip.

"What is that?" I whisper.

He groans a little. "That's maybe a story for another day."

When I pull my head back, I can see the slightest tint of pink in his cheeks. Now I'm officially intrigued. "Does it have to do with what you were thinking about?" I ask with a mischievous grin.

Tarq rolls off me entirely and stretches out on his back. "I was thinking about you."

"That's a boring subject." I follow his lead and push against him, stretching my arms out. My body moves across the bed.

Tarq jumps toward me. "Darya, wait!"

Too late. I hit the edge of the bed, crashing to the floor. "Ow."

He peeks over the side, smiling at me. "You, Darya, are far from boring."

My butt hurts, my pride stings, and Tarq's making me laugh. *I'll kill myself, Luna, I promise. Can't I just have him while I'm still alive?* I stand up, rubbing my rear end. "Shut up," I say, laughing with him.

Tarq fakes a frown, reaching out to me. "Aw," he says in his fake pity tone. "Come here."

Reluctantly, I give him my hand, and he yanks me over his body to his right side. I squeal in surprise as Tarq effortlessly rolls me over his body and cradles me as if we've done this daily. His hand slides safely up the right side of my neck, and his thumb pulls at my bottom lip. His eyes ask for permission, but I can't find my words as my chest aches for him.

I lift myself and gently kiss his lips, testing Luna's anger. She only hits me with the tiniest warning, so I push harder. If this is all I get, I just want to experience it. I pull on Tarq and close my eyes, curling my legs over his hip. When our tongues meet, Luna's had enough of doing what I want. She sends a burning pulse over my neck, and I pull away.

Somehow, this beautiful man understands. I can see in Tarq's eyes that he wants so much more, but he simply slides his thumb over my cheekbone and smiles at me. He presses his lips to my forehead and lets out a deep sigh.

When he pulls away, Tarq flashes me his goofy grin and winks. "Let's go start a war."

* * *

A few hours later, we're readying the horses in front of Dax's house. I lean against the gelding's shoulder while Tarq secures my saddlebags.

"Why do I have to go on this suicide mission?" Anthony grumbles.

Tarq leans over the gelding's saddle to look at him. "The boss wanted you."

"I just got my kids settled."

I step near Tarq to test the cinch, and he slides his arm over my shoulders. "When the Luna asks you to do something, you do it." He looks down at me and smiles. "It's just better that way."

Anthony scoffs. "You do know I'm not a wolf, right?"

"Nobody's perfect, Anthony," Tarq answers, still staring into my eyes.

Edith's voice pulls Tarq's attention from me. "I'm not so sure about that," she says, examining every inch of Tarq.

Laughing, Tarq lifts his arm off my shoulders. He spins slowly with his arms out. "Take it all in, Edie," he tells her. "Darya needs her guard."

Edith bumps her hip into mine as we watch Tarq enter the house. "Ten minutes is all I need, Darya."

I turn back to my horse, shaking my head. "You know that it's not up to me, right?"

"Oh, honey," she says, lifting her eyebrow. "Look at that man." She turns me by my shoulders to face the house. "He is head over heels."

Nate is talking to him, but Tarq isn't paying attention. He's staring at me with an intensity that takes my breath away. Without thinking, I shrug Edith's hand off my shoulder and walk into the house.

Nate turns as my boots hit the wooden floor. "Hey, Luna, we're just going over some last-minute stuff."

I run my hand over his chest without looking at him and feel his muscles relax under my touch. I move around him, walking straight to Tarq.

Cupping my cheeks, Tarq searches my face. "Darya?"

I take one of his hands off my face and kiss its palm. "I need my wolf. Are you ready?"

Tarq pulls me into his arms. He ducks his head, tucking his face into my neck, and I hear him take a deep breath. "Darya?"

My arms tighten around him, trying to memorize how he feels. "Now you can say it."

Tarq moves toward my ear. "I love you."

* * *

We've been pushing the horses hard for a few hours when Tarq pulls off the main trail. He guides us to a small creek with lush grass and a few rose bushes. I drop off my horse and let it wander to the water with the mares. Tarq takes a drink and then flops in the shade.

"This is beautiful," I say, sitting beside him. "You seem to know all the best spots."

Tarq touches his nose to my cheek. *"When you're part of a pack you don't belong to, you find places that make you feel whole."* He nudges me until I lean on him. *"Now, I want to share them all with you."*

I roll over onto my back, leaning against his shoulder. "Have you thought about how we're gonna avoid a war?" I pull the fur on his throat.

"I was hoping Miles would abstain if the Luna asked him to."

I shake my head, laughing. "So you plan to flash your pretty new penny and hope he won't try to kill it?"

Tarq pokes my shoulder with his nose. *"Well, no,"* he says, chuckling. *"Not when you put it that way."*

I sit up, turning to face him. "We should come up with a different plan. Maybe one that doesn't get me killed before I can break the curse."

Tarq stands up and stretches. *"Probably,"* he says. *"I'm gonna go cool off. Can you get those two ready to go?"* He nods at Anthony and Edith before jumping in the water. He lays down in a shallow area and looks back to catch me staring at him with a smile. *"You know you want to join me,"* Tarq says, teasing me.

I shake my head and turn away. Edith is adjusting her saddlebags, but Anthony's brooding catches my attention. As I approach him, he closes the knife he had been cleaning his nails with and glares at me as he puts it away.

I stop a few feet from him, reaching for his hand. "Anthony, did anyone tell you why I asked for you?"

He stares at my hand. "You realize me and my family are stuck with these damn wolves because I saved your ass, right?" He's angry, and I can't say that I blame him.

"You are not here as a punishment or to get you killed," I say, stepping forward to put my hand on Anthony's chest. "You are here because I trust you to make smart decisions in the heat of the moment. You are here because I need you. You're one of us now."

Anthony looks surprised for a moment but then returns to glaring. "Yeah, well, you're still not at the tippy top of my list."

Smiling, I pat his chest and step back. "As long as I'm not at the bottom, I'll take it." My hand falls as I turn away from him. "Come on. It's time to get going."

Edith is holding my horse when I approach her. She hands me his reins and pulls a small velvet bag from her pocket. "I made this for you," she says, giving it to me.

"What's this?" I find a crystal encased in wire inside the bag. It's connected to a rather long strip of ribbon.

Edith pushes it back into the bag and pulls the strings to seal it. "When you want the thing you need the most, you'll know what to do. Until then, keep it safe." She pats my hand and waits for me to put it in my pocket before mounting her horse.

* * *

The next few days pass by uneventfully. We fall into a rhythm that works pretty well. Anthony helps me with the meat that Tarq brings back and is a good cook. Edith keeps Tarq busy while we rest by reading her family's journal with him. He makes me tell her things, but otherwise, he's distracted.

Tarq lies with me at night, and I curl against him for his heat. He likes to sleep with his nose under my hair or against my neck but waits until I fall asleep before he does it. Tarq doesn't seem to realize he wakes me up by humming after he moves. I'm starting to understand why he doesn't want me to know what that is. *It seems to have something to do with his feelings for me.*

On the third night, we find ourselves on a beautiful quiet beach. Our fire is the only light source since it's a cloudy night, but Tarq says he doesn't smell any rain, so we should stay dry. We have turkey for dinner while Tarq keeps the one duck he caught for himself. Apparently, he likes duck meat. It's too tempting to leave him alone to eat it in peace, so we make a game of him snapping at me when I try to steal it.

Anthony sits beside me, opening Dax's map to show me where we are. "According to this map, we're at the edge of Miles' territory," he tells me. "Once we reach the end of this beach, we'll be on enemy land."

I raise my eyebrows. "That's a bit dramatic, don't you think?"

"Their pack is not like ours, Darya." Tarq stops eating and looks up at me.

I frown. "So what are we expecting?"

Tarq turns back to what's left of his duck and doesn't answer me. I look at Edith, who holds her head down, paying attention to whatever she's brewing. When I turn back to Anthony, he's wearing a smirk. It's the look he uses when he's about to tell me bad news. Ten years of this man's expressions, and this was my least favorite.

"Darya," Anthony starts with a chuckle. "If the wolf isn't talking and the witch is brewing her healing tea, I'd say we're expecting the worst."

I turn to Tarq and Edith again, but neither will look me in the eye. I shake my head. "Tell me now, or I'll leave all of you here and go on without you," I say, coming close to a growl of my own.

Tarq sighs, fluffing his lips. *"I only know the legends, Darya. They are said to be brutal and unforgiving. You will not be going without me."*

I turn to Edith. "And you?"

Edith puts her hands up. "I only know what Dax and Tarq have told me about their brutality. I'm brewing tea just in case." She removes the pot from the fire and splits the tea between six vials. Edith reaches over to tug Tarq's ear. "This only works on humans, not wolves, so you need to be careful. Life wouldn't be worth living if I couldn't stare at your beautiful body." She holds a rag out to him.

This has become something of a routine for us. It seems to mean a lot to Tarq, but I'm not sure he's ready to discuss it. He brings me the rag, and I run it carefully over his muzzle, cleaning off the bits of meat and bone. Tarq sits quietly in front of me with his eyes closed, and I get to spend that time appreciating how beautiful he is. Maybe it's just about the kiss he gets when I've finished.

"Edith's right," I tell him after I kiss his nose. "You need to be careful."

Tarq rubs his whiskers against my cheek. "*I promise that I will protect you.*"

"You know that's not what I said," I reply, frowning.

"*You should sleep.*" Tarq ignores my dismay. "*I fear we may not sleep well once we cross the border.*"

I roll down onto my side, holding my arms out for him. Tarq usually crawls up beside me and puts as much of his body against me as possible, but tonight he simply flops beside me. His nose nearly touches mine, and he's blowing so much air that it's taking my breath away.

I grab Tarq's muzzle, pulling it to the side to kiss him behind his whiskers. "You are something else sometimes." I shake my head as I stretch my legs out over his body. "Good night, Tarq."

He chuckles and lays his muzzle over my eyes to block the fire's light. "*Good night, Darya.*"

14

The following day, we ride along the beach to the trees that mark the territory line. Tarq jogs directly to my horse's right side. With Anthony in the lead and Edith behind me, I quietly accept that my new role makes people want to protect me. *At least this protection comes with a beautiful wolf.*

I push my horse past Anthony when he stops at the trees. The bushes at the line are thick and create a curtain, blocking our view. Once I ride through them, my eyes adjust to the lower light, and the dark greens and browns of the forest come alive.

I dismount, joining Tarq in front of my horse. Anthony and Edith come through the brush and follow my lead without question. Tarq takes slow, deliberate steps toward a clump of trees to our left. As we draw closer, men begin to filter out. Tarq starts to back up, and I run into his hip.

Some of the men continue to advance. The rest move to flank us— all of them except one. The single man hangs back, leaning against a tree with his ankles crossed. He's tall with tan skin. His hair is black but peppered with gray or white and cut short. His black pants and green plaid shirt are in better condition than the other men's clothing, although his white undershirt has seen better days.

"I'm not here to fight," I call out, putting my hand on Tarq's hips. "I'm only here to talk to Miles."

"Then talk," says the man against the tree. He flicks his eyes up to me, and my breath catches. Even at this distance, I know he's Miles. In the dark gloom of the forest, Miles' eyes stand out like blue beacons, just like Dax's. Miles pushes off the tree and begins walking toward us. "I suggest you start with who you are and why you brought a Lunar wolf onto my land."

"Tarq is my guard," I say, smiling. "He's no longer part of the Lunar Pack."

Miles tilts his head slightly, arching his eyebrow. "And who the hell are you?"

I step forward and place my hand in front of Tarq's nose. He remains where he is as I move away. "I am the Luna," I say, sounding as proud as I can now that he's making me nervous. "I'm here to break your curse."

Miles raises his hand, and things move so fast that I can't react.

"Darya, run!" Tarq slams into me, knocking me over. When he falls to the ground, there's a spear in his chest. Miles signaled for someone to throw that spear at me, and Tarq saved my life before I even realized I was in danger.

In my mind, time is standing still. I stare at Tarq lying motionless on the forest floor. The spear enters his chest, and the tip sticks out his right side, just behind his elbow. "Tarq!" I scream.

I try crawling toward him, but Miles steps in my way. "Get up," he growls.

I can't because my eyes are stuck on Tarq's body. A movement of any kind would tell me that he's still alive. I become aware that the rest of my group is not beside me as Miles hauls me off the ground and firmly holds my arm. I turn to see Edith and Anthony still at the brush line.

"You humans can leave," Miles barks. "I better not see you on my land again."

Anthony bows and backs away quickly, pulling Edith with him. She's fighting him, but he makes a motion I've seen him do every time he found me for the past ten years. He touches the side of his eye and moves his finger forward slightly. It's the smallest of movements, but he did it every time he said, "I will always find you."

I have tears running down my face and can hardly breathe. Miles' grip on my arm hurts like hell, but that does not compare to the pain in my chest. My beautiful wolf, the man I love, is dead or dying on the forest floor.

"Move," Miles orders, jerking me forward. He nods at his men, and a horse-drawn wagon emerges from the trees. A few men grab Tarq's legs and sling him onto the wagon.

I've heard a lot of things in my life. However, the cry that Tarq lets out will never have an equal. It's loud and high-pitched, much like a horse's, but it hits me like a punch in the chest and physically knocks me back.

I clutch my chest and choke for air, pulling against Miles' hand. He hurls me forward, and I land beside the wagon on my hands and knees. Tarq's head hangs off the side, but I'm close enough now to see his ribs moving. I should feel relief that he's alive, but that scream means he's in tremendous pain.

Miles stomps his boot into my ribs, knocking me over. "Some Luna you are," he sneers as I cry. He hauls me back to my feet and grabs my face, digging his fingers into my jaw. "Tie her to the wagon. She can walk to the compound." Miles drops my jaw, and I stumble forward a few steps. His man ties my wrists with a length of rope and secures me to the wagon. "Better keep up, Luna." Miles laughs.

"You have to help him!" There is no way I look like I should have any authority. I have been openly sobbing this whole time. I can feel the swelling around my eyes, and I've been wiping my nose, so it has to be red. Miles' grip on my jaw definitely left a mark, and my breathing is labored. But I stand up as straight as I can and look him in the eye, acting like I'm giving him an order.

Miles grins. "Oh yeah," he says happily. "I'll take care of that." He steps over to Tarq and firmly grips the spear. Miles turns to me, flashing a sickeningly broad smile before he gives it a quick, violent jerk. Tarq jumps to life, his body rigid as he lets out another high-pitched scream. I try to run to him, but the wagon lurches forward, and Miles catches me by the neck. He puts his lips to my ear. "If you touch him, I will slit his throat."

He waits until the rope yanks on my wrists before letting me go. The bindings waste no time digging into my skin as I jog to create slack. My eyes dart around as I walk, looking at the men surrounding me. These men look like hardened, scarred criminals. Tarq was right when he said Miles' pack was nothing like the Lunar Pack.

After a while, we step onto a road. Miles appears next to me as a few wolves drop out of the woods, flanking the wagon. A woman steps from behind a tree and hooks her arm around his, handing him a canteen.

Miles looks at me and winks. "You look thirsty, Luna," he says, smiling. I watch him drain the whole canteen. Licking my lips, I lose focus just long enough for the rope to run out of slack and yank me again. Miles laughs as I hiss through my teeth from the pain.

The woman with Miles distracts him, making him walk faster so I can watch them from behind. She has long brown hair and is close to my height. She seems more interested in Miles than he is in her, but I can use this. *Hopefully, he has a type.* I wrinkle my nose as my eyes trail down her body. *However, I'd never wear shorts that didn't cover my entire ass.*

I turn away from them and focus back on Tarq. I try to move closer since Miles is distracted but back off when he pulls out his knife. He slows after that and makes sure to stay beside me. Now that we're on the smooth dirt of the road, even at a distance, I can see Tarq's ribs moving as he breathes.

"You guys have the same eyes," I tell Miles, hoping to get him to engage.

The woman steps around him. "Don't talk to him, you stupid bitch," she sneers.

Miles shoves her away. "Have some respect," he barks. "That's the Luna you're talking to." He's looking away from me but must be glaring at her based on her frightened expression. The woman slinks back and disappears into the woods. *Maybe we're not his type, but there's a new angle. Perhaps he respects the hierarchy in his own weird way.*

"Miles?" I start, but I stop short when he turns back to me.

"Shut up," he growls. "Learn your place."

Ok. I'm out of angles. I have no idea what my place is.

We walk for the rest of the day, not stopping until the sun sets. Miles unties my rope from the wagon and pulls me to a nearby tree. He expertly throws the rope over a high branch and pulls on it until my hands are above my head. I can move enough to lean against the tree but must remain standing. I'm slightly optimistic that I might have a chance to get out of this until he throws the rope over the branch of a nearby tree, tying it there.

Miles returns to the wagon and grabs a large pack from the other side of Tarq's body. He cringes as he looks at the spear. "Damn, Luna, that looks like it hurts, right?" Tarq is only ten feet away from me, but he might as well be ten miles away with as useless as I am, tied to this damn tree. Miles approaches me with a smile, but he seems different. *He looks tired.*

Miles grabs my jaw and pushes me against the tree. I smell earth and leather as he steps up to me, barely putting his body against mine. His jaw appears clenched, and all of his muscles are tense. Despite everything, I just want to put my hands on him. I want to cup Miles' cheeks and tell him it will all be okay. *He's my wolf. I'm his Luna. Every inch of me knows if I could just get my hands on him, this would all be over.*

Miles twists my head out of the way and puts his face down by my neck. He takes a deep breath, as only Dax and Tarq have dared. When he pulls away, his eyes are closed. Miles slowly breathes out, licking his lips. "You smell amazing," he says as he opens his eyes. "Now, behave yourself so I don't have to kill you." This time he gently releases my jaw and steps away.

I watch his men, wolves, and the woman gather around a fire they build down the road from me. They're far enough away that I can't enjoy any heat from the fire but close enough that they can keep an eye on me. Miles sits with his back against a tree away from his men. He keeps his eyes on me as he's given food and another canteen.

I'm not going to figure him out tonight. I turn my attention back to Tarq. I haven't heard him since he told me to run. There isn't enough light to see if his ribs are moving. I try to move closer, but the ropes cut further into my skin. I lean against the tree and await any sign that I haven't lost my wolf.

I spend hours staring at Tarq. My exhaustion gets the best of me a few times, but the ropes wake me as I fall over. Miles and his wolves have fallen asleep. Only one man stands guard at a time, and they have changed a few times that I've seen.

"Darya?"

My heart jumps out of my chest at Tarq's voice, and I fall against the ropes as my knees weaken. It's dark, and I can't see him very well. I swallow some spit to lubricate my throat to whisper, but when I try, I just cough.

"I don't think I can last much longer, Darya, but I want to show you something."

I can't stop myself. I pull against the rope, trying to get it to give. I lean against the tree and try to steady myself enough to kick my feet up to my hands, but every time I try, I swing away. I revert to pulling against the rope.

"Be still. If I can hear you, so can Miles."

I look up and see blood trickling from under the ropes. *Tarq's right, and I'm not doing myself any favors.* Leaning against the tree, I clear my throat and try talking to Tarq again.

"Tarq?" I whisper.

"I want to show you something, Darya. I need you to relax for me. I mean, really relax, ok?" Even in my head, his voice is almost a whisper. *"Close your eyes and let your mind go blank. Tell me when you see it."*

I close my eyes, but my mind won't go blank. I can't help panicking, thinking about Tarq's words. *How long does he have? How am I going to save him? Is Anthony actually coming for us?* I take a few deep breaths, slowly letting them out, and focus back on Tarq. When I do, his image filters in, and I'm watching myself again.

I'm in Tarq's bedroom. I can even smell his scent, which I overlooked then. I gasp loudly at how vivid it is.

"Good. Just watch, Darya."

I watch myself talk to Dax. That bright aura around me is all red.

I can't see any gold, but the pulsing rhythm looks familiar. I see Dax look up at Tarq and leave, but my eyes don't move. Tarq never looked away from me this whole time. I watch as I turn around to talk to him and then crawl up the bed. I notice a small spot on my neck when I lift away from him. There's a small area of gold where the Blood Mark is. *She's losing control! My color is red, and I'm beating her.*

He lets the vision fade. I try to keep it together, but the tears leak through my best efforts as my chest begins aching.

"Darya?"

I wipe my face on my arm. "Please don't leave me," I whisper.

"I don't think I'm gonna have a choice. I just wanted you to know how strong you are." I hear him take a deep, raspy breath.

My chest starts to heave as I panic. "I can't do this without you. Please try to hold on." He's silent. The sun is rising, and I can see his ribs moving slightly. "Tarq?"

"I love you, Darya."

These wolves are making me soft. I've cried more since meeting them than I have in my entire life. "I love you too," I whisper as fresh tears stream.

"I only had to die to hear you say that." Tarq's thoughts fade to nearly silent by the end of his sentence.

I sniffle, wiping my face on my arm. "Please don't," I beg, as if it's his choice. Tarq doesn't answer me. I push off the tree and move as close as the rope allows. I feel fresh blood run down my arm as I pull against it. "Tarq?" I hiss louder than my whisper.

"You want me to check on him for you, Luna?" Miles' voice takes my breath away.

I turn and crash right into him as he walks up. His face is calm, his smile borders on pleasant, and all I can do is panic over his words. "No," I squeak. "Please, Miles, I haven't done anything." I take a deep breath and step back, but he grabs my arm. "Miles, please don't hurt him anymore."

Miles' eyes haven't left mine. He's a few inches taller than Dax, easily towering above me. "I'm gonna like having you around, Luna." He licks his lips, moving his gaze to the blood that has run down my arms from under the ropes. Some of it is dried, but plenty is still fresh. Miles glances down at me before putting his mouth on my forearm. His eyes roll closed, and he starts to hum.

"Calm down," Tarq says. He sounds frail, but he's still trying to protect me. *"Miles knows more about the hierarchy than any of us. He will honor it. Just don't piss him off."*

I take a deep breath, tilting my head as I watch Miles.

He smiles as he looks down at me and slowly licks the rest of my blood off his lips. "You taste even better than you smell. I'm gonna enjoy closing those wounds." Miles runs his tongue up my arm again before pushing me away. He unties the rope from the other tree and ties me back to the wagon.

Tarq's right. Miles knew that wolves' saliva heals me. What else does he know?

* * *

They dragged me behind that wagon for the entire day. Without food or water, I'm lucky I'm still on my feet when we finally stop a few hours past sunset. They drive the wagon between a few dilapidated wooden buildings. I was doing fine while moving but fell to my knees when the wagon stopped. Miles seems to be drawn to every moment of weakness I have because he is on me in a flash.

"Get up," he barks.

I sigh. "Miles," I say, pushing myself upright to look at him.

He grabs my arm and hauls me to my feet. "Come on, Little One. It's time to watch your guard die."

I wish I was shocked by his statement, but I'm not sure I have the energy for such things. Miles tries to lead me into one of the buildings. My feet won't stay under me, and I keep tripping, so he flings me over his shoulder. I'm so exhausted that I'm thankful for the ride.

It's dark in the room he brings me until someone walks in behind him with a lantern. Miles throws me against a wall and lifts my bound wrists above my head. I hear him moving chains around, but my eyes are on the men carrying Tarq. They throw him down on the floor. He's silent, but his ribs are still moving. Barely, but a little is better than not at all.

I look up at Miles. "I need water," I tell him, trying to sound stronger than I feel. "I don't know your plan, Miles, but I'm pretty sure you're not trying to kill me."

Miles locks a chain around my ropes. "Hmm, Little One," he says, cupping my cheeks. "I definitely want you alive." He lets go of me and turns to Tarq. "Let me make your dog a little more comfortable." He yanks the spear out, and I watch Tarq's blood spill from his wounds. "I'll leave the lantern. I wouldn't want you to miss this." He leaves the room, locking the door behind him.

Miles' footsteps fade across a wooden floor, and there is no other noise besides Tarq's fast breathing. This room is full of trash and broken furniture. Nothing in here could help Tarq.

I lean down on the ropes, kicking my feet up to my hands. The ropes open my wrists back up, but I get my knife out of my boot. As I drop my legs down, I hear footsteps outside the door. I palm the knife just as the door opens.

Miles walks in, looks at my arms, and shakes his head. "Luna, you're gonna have to stop fighting those ropes." He holds a cup to my lips. I'm thankful it's just water, but I'm so thirsty that I would've drank anything. Miles lowers it, letting me take a breath. "I'm not taking them off until you calm down." He puts the cup back to my lips, and I drink the rest of it.

I look up at Miles. I would probably enjoy his company if he weren't hanging onto the chain that binds me and torturing the man I love. "Miles, where's your mother?"

He narrows his eyes quizzically. "The Westend Cathedral. Why?"

"She caused all of this, Miles."

He pushes the chains, jerking me away, and throws the cup across the room. "I don't need a history lesson from you, little girl. I was there." Miles storms from the room, locking the door.

I open my knife and start working on the ropes right away.

Thankfully Miles only wrapped the chains around the ropes, and Dax is good at sharpening blades. It only takes a few minutes to cut the bindings. I jam my knife back into my boot and kneel beside Tarq.

I lift his head and slide my legs under it. Tarq's eye is glazed over when I pry it open. My wrist trickles blood onto him as I run my hand over his fur. I reach into my pocket for the vials of tea. The velvet pouch brushes against my fingers. I had completely forgotten it was there.

When I finish the tea, I pull the crystal out and turn it over in my hand. *It's just a crystal. Damn you, witch.* I look in the bag hoping for instructions and then laugh at myself for even trying. *What was it that she said?* "When you want the thing you need the most." I look at the ribbon. It's long. If I wore this, it would hang down nearly to my waistline.

The thing I need the most? I look down at Tarq. *I want and need you more than anything.* I reach under him, tying the ribbon around his neck. I hold my breath as I look him over, waiting for anything to happen. *Tarq's what I need the most. Why isn't he healing?* Just as I begin panicking, he shifts right in front of me.

I have no idea what I was expecting, but a seamless transition from wolf to man was not it. I gasp, staring at Tarq for a moment. He's naked, beautiful, and wounded. His breathing is shallow and ragged as he groans and grits his teeth. The vials clink together when I jam the velvet bag into my pocket. *It only works on humans.* I pull the full vial out and look down at Tarq. *Please let this work.*

Tipping his head toward me, I carefully pour the tea into the corner of his mouth. I keep my eyes on Tarq's wounds while running my fingers through his hair. My wrists have nearly healed, so I should see some results soon if it works on him.

Tears drip onto Tarq's cheek as I trace my fingertips along his forehead. "Come back to me," I whisper.

Tarq slides his hand over mine and squeezes my fingers. "I will never leave you," he says hoarsely.

Relief washes over me at the sound of his voice. "Please tell me it's working."

Tarq winces as he tries to move his arm. "That spear did a lot of damage. It's gonna take a little while."

I kick the debris away and help him lean against the wall. Sitting beside him, I drape my legs over his lap to cover him up.

"I'm sorry it took me so long."

"For what?" Tarq whispers.

I sigh. "Everything."

"It feels more like you have perfect timing." Tarq presses his lips to mine in a sweet, gentle kiss.

I expect the Blood Mark to burn, but it doesn't. I hook my fingers on his jaw and pull him to my lips again. I smile at the lack of pain and push against him, deepening the kiss. All I feel is him and the need for more.

Tarq pulls away, wincing. "Ah, woman," he hisses. "Watch the hole in my chest."

"I'm sorry," I whisper. I run my fingers over the area I'd accidentally brushed with my elbow. "Is it healing?"

Taking my hand, Tarq puts his lips on my palm. "Yes," he says, sighing. "We need to talk. I want you to know everything this time. I want this to be your choice."

I pull away from him, confused. "What?"

"I see those colors around your body because you are my mate, Darya." His eyes search my face as he speaks. "We see the 'color of our heart,' whatever that means. It will fade once we've bonded."

"Tarq, I'm not a wolf," I say slowly, furrowing my brow. "I can't be your mate. My grandmother's book says I have to bond to the cursed Alpha."

He kisses my forehead. "Edie's book explains that," Tarq says, smiling. "The ancient Luna bonded with Dax. I don't see her anymore. I only see you. I didn't understand until we learned you're the Luna." My eyes are on his wound, watching it heal as I try to absorb his words. He pushes my chin up to look into his eyes. "We will bond the first time we are together. From that moment, we will no longer desire anyone else's touch. I will be yours forever." He bites his lower lip, looking nervous. "And you will be mine."

Admittedly, I'm more confused than anything right now, but the one thing I am crystal clear about is that I want him. I love Tarq. Mate or not, whatever this crazy wolf crap is, I love him. *But I need to be honest and upfront with everyone.*

I take a deep breath and smile. "I love you," I tell Tarq and watch him completely relax. "I have to talk to Dax first, though. None of this has been fair to him, and I want to be honest with him." I press my lips to Tarq's and then lay my head on his shoulder. "Thank you for telling me."

Sighing, Tarq lays his cheek on my forehead. "I've waited my whole life for you. I'll wait for as long as you need me to."

15

Spending time with Tarq transports me to another place where things are calm, and I love every minute. His heart steadily thumps against my ear as I run through everything that has happened. When I get to the visions he had shared with me, I sit up suddenly and knock my head into his jaw.

"I'm so sorry!" I laugh through my apology. "Your heartbeat. That's the rhythm that the aura is pulsing at, isn't it?" Tarq's face flushes. It's not easy to see with only the lantern lighting the room, but he seems nervous. "What's wrong?"

Tarq leans back against the wall, looking down at me. "Darya, you're not just anyone," he says slowly. "You're the Luna. How could I ever be enough to be your mate?"

I run my fingers over his lips and smile. "I love you as you are."

His eyebrows furrow. "Do you smell that?" Tarq sits up and lifts my legs off his lap. "I smell smoke." He stands up, pulling me to my feet. "Someone will be coming. Miles wouldn't let anything happen to you. I need to shift." He rolls his shoulder and swings his arm as we move across the room.

I pull Tarq's jaw toward me when he stops at the door. "Tarq, look at me," I say, waiting for his eyes to meet mine. "I love you. You will always be enough."

Tarq crashes onto my lips, wrapping his arms around my back. I let our bodies melt together and slide my tongue over his. He pulls back and smiles, kissing the tip of my nose. "I love you too," he whispers. "Now take this necklace and stay behind me. I hear footsteps."

I lift the ribbon from his neck as he steps back. Tarq shifts back into the sandy wolf and shakes his fur out. He lifts his right leg and bounces down on his front legs a few times before swinging around to put his hip against me.

"They're nearly here."

He rocks back onto his haunches, and things happen so fast I'm glad I didn't blink. The door crashes as it's kicked open. Miles steps through and is taken by surprise as Tarq grabs him by the hip and slams him onto the floor. I hear bones break, and Tarq throws him across the room.

"Do you think he'll be ok?" I gasp. Despite everything Miles has done, I don't want him to suffer.

"What? He's fine. Dax always healed when I trained with him. Come on," Tarq says, darting to the doorway. We run down the hallway and find a back door. I pull it open to find the air thick with smoke. *"Grab my fur,"* Tarq tells me. *"I'll get you out of here."*

I step into the smoke, grabbing a handful of fur on his neck. There's yelling all around us, but Tarq leads me in a straight line. Soon we're walking past trees and stepping over logs. Someone grabs me and puts something wet over my mouth. I spin around and find Anthony no more than an inch from my face.

"I told you I'll always find you," he says, smiling.

For the first time, I am genuinely thrilled to see this man. I release Tarq's fur and throw my arms around Anthony's neck. "You set the fire?"

He pulls me off him and spins me back around. "Thank me later if we survive."

He hands me the rag, grabs my arm, and leads me further into the woods. As the sun rises, we reach where Anthony's tied our horses. I notice Edith's absence, but I don't get to ask about her with our rushed pace.

I pull the rag off my face and look down at Tarq. "Northwest," I say, coughing. "Miles said she's at the Westend Cathedral." Westend was a monastery the militia burned down a few years ago. They left the church.

Tarq nods as I step into the gelding's stirrup and throw my leg over him. He darts into the woods, and both horses take off after him. It's not long before we clear the smoke completely at this speed.

"How are you holding up?" Anthony rides alongside my horse to hand me a canteen.

After a quick drink, I raise my eyebrow. "I'll survive," I say. "Where's Edith?"

"I got tired of hearing her whine about that damn wolf," Anthony scoffs. "She said her brother lives around here. I sent her for the book you need."

"How is she supposed to find us, Anthony?" My irritation only gets worse when he shrugs.

"*I can call her horse,*" Tarq reminds me. "*Let me have some of that.*" He jogs to the other side of my horse, where I can lean over to pour water into his mouth. Tarq licks his lips and bumps my hand with his nose. "*Thank you, My Love.*"

I lay on the horse's neck to run my hand over his muzzle and rub his ears between my fingers. "Are you doing ok?" I whisper. "That was a lot of smoke."

Tarq only hums in response.

I smile when he closes his eyes. "You still need to tell me what that is."

"Are you two done?" Anthony barks. "I just burned down an entire werewolf village. We should be leaving the country, never mind the area."

"*He's right, Darya,*" Tarq says.

"I never thought I'd hear you say that," I say, laughing.

Anthony blows out his lips. "The wolf just agreed with me, didn't he?"

Tarq growls. "*Tarq. My fucking name is Tarq. Darya, tell him my name!*"

I sit up, looking from one to the other. "Are you two kidding me right now? Tarq, he knows your name. I can't do this with either of you. Just... the church, please."

Tarq resumes leading the horses through the woods. *"I'm sorry,"* he says. *"He knows how to push my buttons."*

I giggle. "You can hit him when we get home."

We're not following a trail, so I don't have much time to think as we weave through the trees and dodge limbs, but I can't help smiling at the thought of home. I'd lived with Rosalee for years but always called it her house. I don't even have a place at the lake, but it's still the closest I've ever felt to having a home.

Tarq leads us through the gates of the church grounds around midday. The church is in disrepair, but the militia couldn't figure out how to knock it down. I step down from my saddle and tug Tarq's fur.

"So this is where the old bat's bones are?" Anthony asks, joining us.

I tilt my head. "That's what Miles said."

Anthony throws his reins over the saddle horn. "Alright, let's go look for her. I'll take the wolf with me."

Tarq growls.

I glare at Anthony. "Do you see a void that needs filling?" I snap. "Leave him alone. We don't need another Dax."

Anthony chuckles as he walks to the far side of the cemetery grounds.

Tarq stretches out to call Edith's horse. His call is clear and beautiful. Once he finishes, he shakes out his coat and tilts his head. *"What?"*

"You are so beautiful." I kneel and put my arms out to him.

Tarq pushes past my arms, knocking me over backward. He chuckles as he lies on me.

"Has anyone ever told you that you're heavy?" I say, coughing under his weight.

"Are you calling me fat? I thought you said I was beautiful." Tarq laughs again as he rolls off me, leaving his legs to hold me down.

Bending my arm, I push his head closer so his muzzle lies across my throat. "You know you're beautiful," I tell him, leaning my cheek on his head. "To be fair, I think all my wolves are beautiful. You just happen to be my favorite." I pinch the tip of his nose, making him sneeze. When he does, his leg jerks, catching my attention. "Let me see your paw, Tarq."

He places his paw in my hand. It's large with rough pads. I would guess that would be for traction. His claws are long but dull.

"I thought these would be sharper," I say.

"*Nah, we use them too much.*" He adjusts his head so that his nose is against my skin. "*It's the back claws you have to watch out for.*"

He hums as I move his pads around to inspect his claws. "Are you going to tell me what that is now?" I lean my cheek on his head. "Miles did it when he tasted my blood."

Tarq snaps his head up. "*When he did what?*"

"If you two can wrap up play time, I found something." Anthony's sudden appearance makes us both jump.

"Give us a minute, Anthony," I request, smiling at his scowl.

"Hurry up," he barks as he stomps away.

I lean my cheek back against Tarq. "Tell me."

He sighs deeply. "*It's a low growl, like a cat's purr.*"

"So it's something you do when you're happy?"

"*No,*" he says thoughtfully. "*It's stronger than that.*"

"TARQ!" We both jump as Anthony's voice echoes across the grounds.

"*Holy shit,*" Tarq shouts, popping his head up. "*Did he just call me by my name?*"

"Tarq?" I know I'm whining, but I really want to know, and he's finally trying to tell me.

Tarq rolls over and stands up. "*Another time, Darya.*" He nuzzles his nose against my neck. "*Mmm, you smell so good.*" His breath tickles my skin. "*Edith is nearly here. I'm gonna go dig up some bones.*"

I watch him run in Anthony's direction. As he drops from my sight, horse hooves ring in my ears. I turn toward the woods to see the white mare coming through the trees. Edith looks exhausted, but at least she's on the horse. She nearly falls when she dismounts.

"I am never getting on that horse again," she says, panting. "Never, ever again." She drops down to her hands and knees and crawls to me.

I giggle. "I'm just glad you were on her." She rolls over and sprawls out beside me. "It was Tarq," I tell her, rolling to face her. "He howls, and it calls them to him."

She grabs my hand and smiles. "I knew you'd figure out the gem ward."

"Edith, I don't understand this thing with Tarq." I narrow my eyes and sit up. "I was with Dax because I was under Luna's control. How do I know that I'm the one who wants Tarq?"

"Darya, that boy loves you," she says, smiling as she sits up. "He will give you the time you need, but you won't need much. He's yours, and you are his."

Tarq appears in the gateway to the cemetery. We both watch him and sigh.

"I wish it weren't true," Edith tells me sadly. "That boy is a delicious cake locked in a case." She looks back at me, smiling. "I really like cake."

I giggle and pull grass to throw at her. "What should I do about Dax?"

Edith sucks air between her teeth. "I think that man knows more than he's telling us."

For some reason, what she says triggers a memory. I think about when we were sitting in front of the manor, and Dax asked me how I looked in my dream. *He knew I was Tarq's mate.*

I watch my wolf jog toward us. "Tarq?" I squint, slowly piecing my words together. "Is that an arm?"

"*Complete with hand,*" he replies cheerfully. "*Wanna shake it?*"

"Here he is, Edith, the man that I love." I gesture toward Tarq. "How about that cake now?"

Tarq drops the bones in Edith's lap. "*Wait. There's cake?*"

"I do love cake." Edith arches her eyebrow, sliding her hand over his head.

I throw my hands in the air. "How the hell do we get anything done?"

Tarq rubs his face in the grass, knocking the dirt out of his fur. "*I've gotten plenty done. I just dug up a dead bitch.*" He stands, shaking out his coat. "*Am I supposed to turn down cake?*"

I look at him and sigh. "Yes, Tarq. You are when you're the damn cake."

Edith starts laughing as Tarq walks around us.

"*Oh*," he says in realization. "*Edie was drooling over me again.*" He knocks me down with his head and crouches over me. "*Eat your heart out, Edie. I'm off the market.*" Tarq turns to me, putting his nose in my face. "*Mine.*"

I grab his muzzle and pull him to look into my eyes. "You're lucky I love you," I say, smiling at his playfulness. "Now go find out what's keeping Anthony. We need to leave."

Tarq jumps up and runs toward the cemetery as I sit upright.

Edith flashes me a crooked smile. "Anthony's right," she says, laughing. "You two are quite entertaining."

I roll my eyes. "Did you get your mother's spell book?"

"I had to steal it," she answers, frowning. "Jaxson wasn't interested in helping you."

"Well, I wasn't interested in his help," I reply. "So, thank you for not bringing him."

Edith stands up, offering me her hand.

"We need to put some distance between Miles and us," I tell her. "Anthony burned down their village, and Tarq sort of broke an immortal man."

Edith laughs. "That sounds intriguing."

"Maybe some other time." I point toward Anthony and Tarq. "Here they come."

Edith helps me prepare the horses while Anthony tosses a few salted steaks to Tarq to make room for Mira's bones in his saddlebags. I stop and lean against a tree to watch my group. Anthony had given food to Tarq, a wolf he pretends to despise. Now he's whispering with Edith, and she giggles, bumping her hip into him playfully. *This is my family*. I smile at the thought.

"Let's go," I tell them, swinging into my saddle. "I don't want to be near Miles when he heals." Edith and Anthony follow my lead while Tarq noisily finishes the last of his steak. "Anthony, it's a straight shot from here to the lake with a stop at Rosalee's, right?"

Anthony groans. "Darya, that woman will shoot me on sight."

A rifle sounds nearby as if conjured by his words, and a bullet hits a tree beside us.

"Woman," Anthony growls. "Bad shit follows you everywhere."

We turn the horses and push them into the woods.

"Shut up, Anthony," I yell.

Tarq shoots past us to take the lead. *I think the man has a valid point, Darya.*

My horse lunges forward, staying right behind Tarq. "Stop agreeing with him!"

Unsure if anyone is following us, we run the horses hard most of the day. By late afternoon, we hit the trail that will take us straight to Rosalee's. The moss-covered terrain will hide our tracks, but it's slippery from the rain that started a few hours before.

Rosalee steps onto her front porch as we arrive. "I had hoped you'd make it back to us," she says, smiling broadly.

We quickly join her out of the rain as she opens the door for us.

"Come and warm yourselves by the fire," she says, ushering us inside. When Anthony reaches the door, she puts her arm out. "Not you, Commander. You're not welcome here."

I grab Anthony's arm and pull him through the door. "Please, Rosalee," I say, smiling. "He's helping me."

Luckily the next one through the door is Tarq. "And a wolf, Darya?" Rosalee is quickly reaching her limit with me as Tarq zips past her. "That thing is huge!"

Tarq sighs, lying down by the fire. *It's always about my size.*

"But he is a beautiful wolf, Rosalee," I say, laughing. "Look at his shoulders and chest."

Tarq chuckles, and Edith adds, "And he's got a great ass, too." She leans into me to whisper in my ear. "Can I borrow that necklace?"

I dig in my pocket, pulling it out for her. "Rosalee, you remember Edith, right?" Edith takes the necklace and joins Tarq by the fire to dig in her bag. I turn back to Rosalee as she closes the door. "It's great to see you," I say, guiding her to the long couch facing her fireplace. "Where's Stanley?"

Rosalee sits and scans her guests. "He's in Silverton for the night," she says, watching Edith try to sneak into the hallway with Tarq. "And where are you going with that wolf?"

Edith stops in the doorway but points around the corner for Tarq to keep going. "I'm just going to change, Rosalee," she says. "The wolf follows me everywhere." She winks and disappears around the corner.

Rosalee gives me a confused look, but I only shrug as I stretch out on the couch. We make small talk, and she asks about where I've been. She's never been a fan of how I make a living and is convinced it will kill me. I'm not sure I can tell her I'm traveling around with wolves, and I should probably avoid the fact that this **will** kill me. I'm relieved to have someone help me skirt the conversation when Edith comes back to join me on the couch. She pats my leg excitedly, but Rosalee notices Tarq is missing.

"Where's that wolf?" she asks, looking around.

Edith smiles. "He went to get someone for me," she says. "He'll be gone for the night."

"Good," Rosalee replies. "I never liked dogs. Wolves are probably worse."

Edith pats my leg again. Looking up to glare at her, I catch movement across the room. My breath catches in my throat, and my eyes blur with tears as Tarq leans against the door frame with his arms crossed over his chest.

He smiles. "Hi."

I barely notice my body's movements as I close the distance between us. Tarq slides his arms around me as I fall onto his chest. I hate myself for questioning my feelings for him earlier. There is no doubt in my mind now. I've been waiting for him my whole life too, and this is where I belong.

"I didn't know I needed this," I whisper.

Behind me, Edith clears her throat. "Rosalee, I'd like to introduce Tarq. He's —"

"Darya's mate." Rosalee finishes Edith's sentence with a frown. "I guess that family history finally caught up to us."

I spin around to face her. "You knew!" I've never really been angry with Rosalee until this very moment. Tarq holds my shoulder to stop me from moving forward momentarily. I take a few deep breaths and shake my head. "I think it's time for you to be honest with me."

Rosalee pats the couch cushion next to her. "Come, you two. Sit down and warm up," she says, smiling sweetly. "You're still soaked, Darya."

Tarq slides his arms around me from behind. "I think I can help with that, Miss Rosalee." Tarq lets his body heat up, and my eyes close as I lean against him.

"Oh, and he's polite. I like him, Darya."

Tarq breathes a quiet laugh and kisses the top of my head as he lets me go. I sit on the couch facing Rosalee while Tarq sits on the floor, leaning against my leg. He threads his fingers with mine on his shoulder.

"I suppose we should start at the beginning with the last Luna," Rosalee starts. Anthony and Edith turn away from the fire, joining our conversation. "The Luna was human. She was a queen, for lack of a better word. She would rule and calm them, and she was their protector. Throughout history, the Luna would lead; her mate was the Alpha. He would rule in her absence. The Luna would bear one child, a daughter, the next Luna.

"In 1835, the Luna sacrificed herself to remove the full moon curse. She released her people from the curse, but due to losing the leadership of a Luna, the wolves fought and eventually divided into many different packs ruled by men."

Rosalee pauses to watch as Tarq kisses my hand and holds it to his cheek.

"In 1910, a pack war came down to the meddling of women, and they called upon the Luna again. The spell created our family line to produce the next Luna to sacrifice herself when the time came to free the Lunar Pack from its curse. The ancient Luna must bond with the cursed Alpha, and the new Luna must pair with the next in line to lead in her stead." Her eyes move from me to Tarq. "Which must be you, young man."

Tarq shakes his head. "No, ma'am," he says. "I'm not interested in a life without Darya. She's our Luna. She will lead us."

"I'm afraid you don't have much choice if you want to lift that curse."

Tarq squeezes my hand. "We'll stay cursed then. We've dealt with it this long. I'm not losing her."

I put my lips to his ear. "I love you too," I whisper. I look up at Rosalee. "The ancient Luna has been fighting me about Tarq."

Rosalee nods. "Once she finishes that mark, she will calm," she says. "You will have him to yourself until it's time."

"Until I have to die," I say, frowning.

Rosalee frowns too. "I'm sorry, Darya. I wish there were another way."

Tarq hops onto the couch and puts his arms around me. I twist into his chest and grab a handful of his shirt. I recognize the fabric of his T-shirt. Edith trades meat for cloth with the militia, and she must have made this shirt for him. She wouldn't let us down. She adores him too much to watch him suffer.

"We're working on another way, Rosalee," Edith says as if she knows I'm thinking about her. "We still have time. We aren't letting her go that easily."

Tarq ducks down to put his cheek against my forehead. "We all believe in you, Darya. You are so strong, and that strength comes from those that stand with you." He twists his body slightly so I can see the others without moving away from him. "Look at them. We're all here for you."

Edith beams at me, and even Anthony is grinning. Sighing, I smile at them. *Ok. I can do this.*

Rosalee clears her throat, calling our attention back to her. "That's all I know, but if I can help in any way, please let me know."

I stand up with her and pull her into a hug. "Thank you, Rosalee," I say, rubbing her back. "We just need a place to stay for the night."

Rosalee pulls back and looks around at everyone. "You're welcome to the living room. There's enough wood to keep the fire going through the night." She says a quick good night and retreats up the stairs.

My room is upstairs too, but I pull Tarq to his feet and lead him toward the back door. "Make yourselves comfortable. We'll be out back." I open the door to the covered back porch and usher Tarq to the rocking chair in the corner. I sigh, sliding over the arm of the chair and into his lap.

Tarq cradles me against his chest. "What's on your mind, My Love?"

"I just want some time to be us. No wolves, no curse, no interruptions," I tell him, running my fingers down his neck.

He puts his feet up on the railing and rocks the chair. "I don't mind being a wolf, but I miss putting my arms around you."

Tarq quietly rocks the chair, rubbing his lips gently over my forehead and tickling my thigh with his fingers. Every movement causes my nerves to fire under his touch, and my resolve fails with every swipe. *I've got to do something.*

"Dax knew, didn't he?"

"Yeah." Tarq sighs, leaning his head against the back of the chair.

"Why didn't you say anything?"

"Darya, he's my Alpha. I'm not allowed to challenge him." Tarq kisses my forehead. "I wanted this to be your choice."

I reach up, sliding my finger over his lips. "What if I didn't choose you?"

"Then I would spend the rest of my life wishing you would."

Oh, to hell with this.

I pull him to me, plunging my tongue between his lips. Tarq lifts me off his lap and sits me on the railing. Clothes fly in a frenzy as I cannot get him naked fast enough. Mate or bond or whatever, I need this man. He runs his tongue over my neck so slowly that time seems to stand still as he finally enjoys an unrestricted taste of me. He holds his breath and licks his lips before letting it out.

"Are you sure about this, Darya?" Tarq says, resting his forehead against mine. "There's no taking this back." His eyes are burning into mine.

My whole body is alive with firing nerves calling for his attention. This man is all that I need. I want those eyes to look at me like I'm everything for the rest of my life. "You are mine," I whisper, wrapping my legs around his hips.

Tarq closes his eyes and excites my body as it finally becomes acquainted with his touch. He pulls me off the railing and pins me to the house's wall with his hips. Nerves fire under Tarq's touch and miss him when he leaves. His growl and hum mix into a beautiful song as I rub my hands over his skin, committing as much to memory as possible.

Tarq's growl intensifies as my moans urge him on. I bite down on his neck as my body releases a full-out celebration, and I do my best not to announce my enjoyment to everyone in town.

Pushing past my muscles, Tarq moans through his release with less emphasis on being quiet. I stay latched onto his neck, my nerves still very aware of his presence and not interested in him stopping or leaving. Tarq nuzzles his face into my neck, taking a deep breath. My eyes roll closed as my body heats up again.

He licks my ear lobe and breathes out. "Now I am yours."

16

Our clothes are still on the porch in the morning, and someone has covered me with a blanket. Tarq's body is blazing hot as he cradles me, making me sweat, but I don't care. I woke up unsure if last night had happened. Our lack of clothes and my body's need for him confirm that it had.

Tarq wakes as I pull my arm from the blanket. He kisses my forehead and takes a deep breath. "Good morning, My Love." He stretches his legs, pushing against the railing to rock the chair. "Rosalee didn't want you to get cold." Tarq pulls the blanket off my legs. The rush of cool air feels refreshing on my skin.

"Oh, that must have been a conversation," I say, smiling broadly.

He chuckles. "It was a sweet gesture, but controlling my temperature when I'm asleep is difficult." He squeezes my thigh. "I kept trying to cook you."

I shake my head. "Why didn't you just take it off?"

Tarq shrugs. "Seemed rude."

"As opposed to cooking me?"

"I'm sorry, who are we cooking?" Edith asks, popping her head out the back door. She sees our clothes strewn about and smiles. "I was going to tell you Rosalee is cooking breakfast, but you've been snacking on my cake, Darya." She wags her eyebrows and grins as she closes the door, leaving us staring after her.

Leaning back, I look up at Tarq. "I did have some cake, right?" I ask, smiling. "That wasn't a dream?"

He smiles and moves his hand from my thigh to my cheek. My leg instantly misses his touch, but my cheek rejoices. "I am yours now and forever, Darya," he whispers.

Tarq's lips are so soft against mine, and they excite every nerve around my mouth. I feel like nerves are reaching for him everywhere he touches, stroking the underside of my skin. The simplest of touches now feels like the most erotic.

"I love my cake," I murmur.

Tarq smiles and growls. "You're making me hungry." He ducks for another kiss.

"I assume you'll be dressing for breakfast." We turn to see Rosalee standing in the doorway. She's wearing her typical disapproving expression.

Since I can only snicker, Tarq answers for both of us. "Yes, ma'am. We'll be right in."

She nods, slipping back inside.

"Come on, My Love," Tarq says, lifting me from his lap. "She's pan-frying ham, and I'm starving." He pulls his pants on before helping me dress. Tarq takes every opportunity to put my body in his mouth, starting with my thigh and ending with my wrist. By the time my clothes are on, I'm out of breath, and he's humming. "I am so glad I get to do that for the rest of my life."

"Ok, but I'm going to need you to stop, or we'll need to take these clothes back off," I say, laughing.

Tarq grabs his shirt and pulls me to his chest. He cups my head, putting my ear to his heart. Its beat is just as steady and comforting as it always is. I melt into his body, feeling my nerves reach for him. "This feels amazing," Tarq whispers before pushing me away and sliding his shirt over his head. "But stop touching me, or I'll have to eat you."

Images of the Red Riding Hood fairytale flood in, and I can't help laughing as Tarq drags me into the house. Rosalee's kitchen and living room are in one big open area. She's walking toward Anthony with a plate of food when we enter.

"Don't you ever feed these people?" Rosalee asks, stopping beside me so I can kiss her cheek.

I wink at her as I take a roll off the plate. "Not normally."

Anthony takes the plate from Rosalee. "Woman," he growls at me. "Give me my damn food."

I bite into his roll as I watch Tarq sneak into the kitchen and lift the lids off the pans. I hand Anthony his food with a smile.

"I hate you," he grumbles.

"Oh, Anthony," I laugh. "That's not true."

"It's a little true." He takes a bite of his roll and throws it at me as I escape to the kitchen.

"Hey!" Rosalee yells. "Let's try to act grown in my house, please!"

Anthony hangs his head. "Yes, ma'am."

Rosalee walks back to the kitchen, and Tarq quickly swallows the sausage he pulled out of the pan. She stops beside him and stares expectantly.

"Ma'am?" Tarq squeaks, turning red.

She steps up to him with her arms outstretched, and Tarq smiles as he accepts her embrace.

Rosalee whispers to him as I lean over the island counter. "You look after our girl and make sure I see her again." She groans, squeezing him tightly.

Tarq's smile broadens. "Yes, ma'am." He winks at me.

Then Rosalee pops him on the back of the head and lets him go. "And quit stealing food out of my pans."

"Yes, ma'am," Tarq says, jumping away before she can swat him again.

* * *

We'd said our goodbyes an hour later, and Tarq was, once again, my wolf. Rosalee even grabbed his chin and kissed his muzzle before giving him another sausage link. Tarq promised we would be home in six hours. *I know I'm being selfish, but I can't wait to be alone with Tarq. I wish that I had known what was happening in the very beginning.* I duck as a branch nearly takes my head off. *Maybe I should pay attention.*

Tarq leads us up to the lake in the early afternoon. The horses slide to a stop while Tarq leaps into the water, shifting mid-dive. I dismount and watch the water, waiting for him to surface.

Edith steps beside me, hooking our arms. "Ten minutes, honey," she says. "All I need is ten minutes with that man."

We watch as Tarq surfaces in the water and begins swimming toward shore.

Edith holds out a pair of shorts, still watching Tarq. "You better take these," she whispers. "I'm not strong enough." She places them in my hand and backs away.

I walk down to the bank to meet Tarq since he's never appeared interested in modesty. He reaches a shallow area and begins to rise out of the water. Walking straight to me with justifiable confidence, he wraps his arms around my waist.

"Hello, My Love," Tarq whispers into my neck before deeply inhaling my scent.

I can't explain what that does to me, but I want to remove my clothes. Holding up the shorts, I shake my head and pull away from him. "Put these on, please," I say, smiling. "You are being very distracting."

Tarq takes them and smiles down at me. "You're just being mean to Edie." He puts on the shorts and threads his fingers with mine to pull me up the bank. When we reach the others, he kisses Edith's cheek. "Let's go home, guys," he says, turning toward the woods.

We only take a few steps when we hear rustling ahead. Tarq tries to push me behind him, but I step to the side to see Dax coming out of the trees. He's covered in blood and looks genuinely surprised to see us. He scans our group and then looks down at my hand, which still holds Tarq's.

"Darya?" he says, stepping toward me.

Pulling free from Tarq, I rush to Dax. I run my hands over his face and bare chest. "What happened?" I ask, looking for wounds. "Are you hurt?"

Dax grabs my wrists. "Darya, I'm immortal," he says, shaking his head. He sighs and purses his lips as he looks from me to Tarq. "It would seem that we need to talk." He looks down at me, lets go of my wrists, and holds my chin. "Let me clean this off."

Dax slides his thumb over my jaw before releasing me and stepping away. His growl starts as Tarq glares at him when he walks past. Tarq's eyes follow him before turning back to me.

I reach my hand out to him as I look at the others. "He's talking about us," I say. "You two should go home. Thank you for all your help." Tarq steps beside me, taking my outstretched hand as I grab Anthony with my other. "I mean it, Anthony. I don't think we could've escaped without you."

Anthony nods. "You're welcome." He slides his arm out of my grip and joins Edith to leave us.

Tarq slides his arm around my lower back and turns me to him. He cups my cheek, tipping my face. "You are perfect," he whispers, lowering his lips to mine.

"Oh, I like where this is going," I say, smiling. "Do go on."

Tarq gently presses his lips to mine in an innocent, light kiss that doesn't entirely satisfy me. I push up into him and part his lips, sliding my tongue over his. Tarq tightens his grip on my waist, pulling me against him as my fingers thread through his hair.

"Ahem." Dax clears his throat, announcing he's back from washing up at the lake.

I try to pull back, but Tarq holds me firmly in place. He rubs his lips against mine and gently kisses me before letting me go.

"Tarq, give us a minute." Dax keeps his eyes on me as he speaks.

Tarq looks at Dax and then back at me, shaking his head.

I place my hands on his chest. "Hey, it's ok. I'll be fine."

He narrows his eyes and looks back up at Dax. "He's kept us apart long enough, Darya."

Running my finger under his jaw has become my way of requesting that he look down at me. "I can't deny that, My Love, but I would like this time with him. Will you allow me a moment alone with Dax, please?"

"Fine," Tarq replies, softening his expression. "Come here." As requested, I step back into him, and he presses his lips to mine as he glares at Dax. Tarq pulls away and winks at Dax before disappearing into the woods.

Dax motions toward the grassy area near us and sits down, patting the ground. "I owe you an apology."

My anger instantly flares. "Did you want me to call Tarq back? You owe us both an apology."

Dax rolls his eyes and winces. "Maybe you could just pass it along."

"Why did you do it?" In many situations, these actions would be unforgivable, but my circle of loved ones is small, and it's Dax. He's endured so much more than the rest of us. Besides, he's one of my wolves, and I still love him.

Dax sighs. The strongest man I have ever met looks broken. "You were mine, Darya." He looks up at me. "I loved you. I still do, but it's different now."

I sit down beside him, patting my Blood Mark. "Your bond is with her," I tell him. "I'm sorry, Dax. I don't want to see you hurt."

"Are you happy?"

I nod my head. "I think I am."

Dax stretches his legs out before him and leans back on his hands. "Can you at least admit that he's a pain in the ass?"

I throw some grass at him. "Yes, I can," I say, laughing. "But he's my pain in the ass which somehow makes it better."

Dax chuckles slightly. "If you say so."

I bump my shoulder into his and feel his muscles instantly relax. "Dax, I want to try something." I turn toward him, holding my hands up. After laying my hands on Nate and Tarq and how Miles refused to touch them, I want to see if I'm genuinely calming these wolves. "Your bond with Luna may have blocked this." I place one hand on his shoulder and the other on his chest.

Dax's eyes roll as his muscles begin to relax. "What is that?"

"I think it's a Luna thing because my wolves seem to relax when I touch them." I frown, thinking about Tarq. "It doesn't work as much on Tarq, though."

"It's probably the bond," Dax says, falling back, stretched out and relaxed. "He's missing out." He puts his arm out for me, and I don't hesitate to roll down onto it. "It's good to have you home."

I lie quietly with Dax as the afternoon turns into evening, allowing him to enjoy my touch. The clouds slip by, and the trees blow in the breeze. When the shadows are long enough to reach us, I roll onto his chest and wait for his eyes to open. "Dax, whose blood was that?"

"Things didn't go so well with Miles, huh?" Dax asks instead of answering my question.

"Not really," I reply slowly. "Why?"

He tucks my hair behind my ear. "Because he's here."

I push off him. "Hang on. He's here? Where?"

Dax runs his hand over my arm. "He's in the barn. Says you burned down his village."

"That was Anthony." I sigh, shaking my head. "Dax, why do you have him here?"

Dax licks his lips, tucking his arm behind his head. "I didn't know what else to do with him. I can't kill him, and he's not gonna stop coming for you."

"What does he want with me?" I'm so confused. Dax only answers the questions that he wants to. He is better at hiding things than I will ever be.

"Because he's crazy, Darya." Dax sits up and stretches. "He's locked up. He can't hurt you."

He's not being honest with me. "Dax?" My plea lands on deaf ears.

"You look tired," he says, standing up. "Some people are waiting for you at the house, and then you should get some rest." Dax reaches his hand out, but when I don't take it, he rolls his eyes. "Come on, Darya, that wolf will be looking for you soon."

I take his hand. "Tarq," I mumble, glaring at him. "His name is Tarq." *Now I sound like him. Maybe I should lie down.*

Dax holds his arm out. "We're gonna be ok, right? You and I?" His eyes seem tired again, like when we returned from the cabin.

I link my arm with Dax's. "I love you, Dax," I say, smiling. "You're my wolf, and I will need you to teach me how to help the pack."

"You'll make a wonderful Luna." He lifts my hand to kiss my knuckles, then returns it to his arm.

"I'm only this strong because of those who stand with me," I say, quoting Tarq with a smile. I lean against Dax's shoulder and let him lead me to Tarq's house. We're not far, so it's a quick walk. The sun dips behind the trees as we leave the woods. "So this is really his house, huh?"

"His family's, yeah." Dax leads me toward a door on the first floor. "They own this land and the acreage the lake sits on."

Laughing, I step up onto the porch. "Oh shit, he actually does own the lake."

Dax raises his eyebrow as he reaches for the door. He opens it to reveal a grand room with tall ceilings and overstuffed green chairs. Behind the large couch is a narrow staircase leading to the bedrooms. There are handcrafted tables with woven carpets underneath them. The fireplace is large enough to stand in, and the painting above it is enormous. The castle cast in oil paints has a presence all on its own.

"This is gorgeous," I whisper to Dax as I cling to his arm. "I can see why he gets pissed when you break shit."

Sighing, Dax leans against the door as he closes it. "Yeah, we don't need to bring that up, Darya." Footsteps behind me attract his attention. "And here, Luna, are your other guards."

Dax links our arms again as he introduces them. Bruce is Tarq's father. He's tall but not quite as tall as Tarq. His dark brown hair is cut short, and his brown eyes are warm as they look upon me. He shakes my hand confidently but appears disconnected from Dax and the woman beside him. He steps aside and pours himself a drink the moment he finishes introducing himself.

"This is Amelia, Tarq's mother." There's a definite change in Dax's tone. It's calmer. Amelia has blonde hair, and her eyes match her husband's. Her smile is grand, and she rushes at me with her arms outstretched.

"I am so happy to meet you, Luna," she says excitedly. "I hear you've captured my son's heart." She steps back, holding my arms out before pulling me back for another hug. My eyes follow Dax to the kitchen, and I spot Tarq over Amelia's shoulder, smiling at me as he leans against the counter. "Gosh, you are beautiful," Amelia gushes, reminding me she's there.

I can't take my eyes off Tarq. He's too far away from me. He must feel the same way because he pushes off the counter and strides into the room, wearing a grin that takes my breath away.

"Give us a minute, Mom," Tarq says, putting his hand out for mine. Amelia steps aside as he slides his arms around my lower back, leaning close to my lips. "She's right."

I reach up on my toes and rub my lips against his. "Kiss me, you fool."

Tarq smiles and cups my cheek to pull my lips to his. I open my mouth, allowing him to run his tongue over mine. My chest instantly tightens, and my body heats up. As my nerves fire, begging for him, I lean my forehead against his and groan quietly.

Taking a deep breath, Tarq stares at me with a twinkle in his eye. "I want to do inappropriate things to you right now."

I breathe out a laugh. "And I want to let you, but let's go be appropriate with your parents first, ok?"

He growls with a smile and leads me to where they sit on the couches.

"So, we hear our son's been doing his best in our absence," Bruce says as we approach them.

Tarq directs me to a chair opposite them. He sits on the arm and holds my hand.

"He has," I say, looking up at him proudly. "He's had to save my life twice. Apparently, I attract trouble." I wink at him before turning to his parents. "You should be proud of him."

Amelia is smiling broadly, but Bruce hasn't smiled once. "I'm not," he says coldly.

I'm not sure what to say to this. Amelia takes a sip of her drink, frowning slightly. Bruce leans back in his chair and looks into his glass. I turn to Tarq, looking for guidance.

"It's ok, Darya." He winks at me. "It would be a miracle if I ever did anything right in his eyes."

"Oh no, you managed to land the Luna. That's a damn miracle in itself," Bruce scoffs.

I'm not sure I'm thankful I met the previous Luna, but I borrow some of her anger now. My eyes narrow as I stand up. "That's enough," I shout. Amelia freezes as Bruce looks up at me. Even Dax leans over to watch through the kitchen doorway. "Tarq is my guard and my mate. You can keep your mouth shut if you can't respect him."

Bruce's face drops and flushes red. "I'm sorry, Luna."

There's no stopping this flood now. "I know you are," I shout. "What you should be doing is apologizing to Tarq."

Bruce stares at me for a moment before turning his eyes toward Tarq. "I apologize for my comment, Son," he mumbles, looking like he'd swallowed a pine cone.

Tarq nods his head and looks down at his hands.

Oh! Now I see why I'm dealing with his insecurity. I turn to face him and lift his chin with my finger. "You look down for no one, My Love." I run my thumb over his cheek. "I am proud of you." I brush Tarq's hair away from his eyes and kiss him before retaking my seat.

Amelia smiles. "We are thrilled to have you in our home, Luna," she says.

Tarq's mother continues, carrying the conversation despite her sour husband. She talks about where they had gone over the past few years and what they had seen. I can't help my pang of jealousy as she describes their time by the ocean. Amelia also tells us about a mountain range called the Rockies and the size of the elk they hunted. The most intriguing fact was that there didn't seem to be a militia presence in the Rockies.

"You should see it someday, Luna," Amelia gushes.

I glance up at Tarq, who is uncomfortably eyeing his father. "It's been a very long week for us," I announce. "I think we're going to turn in early." Tarq smiles, clearly appreciating the exit I've given us. "It was a pleasure meeting you."

Amelia stands and hugs us both while Bruce walks outside. "It will be an honor to serve you, Luna." She brushes her hand over my face before turning toward the kitchen and leaving us.

Tarq takes my hand and leads me upstairs. There's no hallway, only the balcony. We pass the first door, which, when I look in, appears to be the bedroom I've already seen. He leads me through the second door, closing it behind us. With the grand scale of the room, it is clearly the master bedroom. The bed is against an entire wall of windows. The fireplace is smaller than the one downstairs but still larger than average. Two oversized rocking chairs are in front of it, shrouded with bulky quilts.

I walk to the bed, running my hand over the pillows with floral embroidery and lace accents. The bed posts stick up from the frame, and the mahogany wood has carvings of small wolf heads. I've seen carved wood, but never with so much detail or covered with whatever made this smooth and almost shiny.

Tarq slides his finger under my chin, turning my eyes to his. He smiles and steps closer to me. "Are you happy?"

I hold his hair back from his eyes. "You make me very happy, My Love."

Tarq leans to kiss me gently and nips at my lips. His hands press down my back, and his fingers curl under the bottom of my vest, heating my core as my nerves call out to him. I breathe a soft moan as his fingers trace the waistline of my shorts. Tarq groans and breaks my belt, allowing my shorts to easily fall from my hips.

I pull away from him and look down at the broken leather. "Tarq?" I whine, giggling.

"No, no," he says, pulling my face back to his. He rubs his lips against mine as he whispers, "I'll make you another one." He smiles and licks my top lip.

I open my mouth to exhale, and Tarq comes entirely undone. He pulls my vest open, sending brass buttons flying, and slides his hands over my skin. I push his shirt up, and he grabs it from me, yanking it over his head. My body begins to burn up, and I feel like I'm starting to sweat from my heat. When I pull my hair off my neck to find relief, Tarq steps back to remove his jeans.

His eyes travel over me in a way that might have made me nervous with anyone else, but with Tarq, I feel overdressed in my underwear. Stepping back to me, he helps me remove the rest of my clothing. Tarq's hands move slowly over my skin, allowing me to feel each nerve fire. I return the favor as I figure he must feel similar sensations.

Tarq takes a deep breath along my neck. "I love you," he whispers.

My body is tired of the delay. "Show me," I whisper back.

Growling, Tarq grabs my thighs to lift me to his hips. He rolls us onto the bed, claiming me and causing a flash of light as I close my eyes. I smell thick salt, and there is water lapping against something. As my vision clears, I see beautiful waves roll onto a beach. It looks just like the pictures I've seen.

Tarq gently rolls me over to lay me on the sand, and I feel its warmth against my skin. The waves touch me, causing me to shiver before retreating to the sea. It's stunning, but when Tarq slides his hand up my thigh, he grabs my full attention. I tip my hips, letting him know I'm ready for him. He smiles and claims my mouth, plunging his tongue between my lips.

With each thrust, all my nerves reach for Tarq. Every part of me wants his touch. His tongue slides over mine, and my neck wants to experience it. My chest wants to feel his teeth. My cheeks ache for his lips.

I slide my hands along Tarq's sides and dig my fingers into his hips. My body relishes every moment of attention he gives it. We call to each other in our enjoyment until, finally, the beach fades away, and we roll onto our sides on the bed.

Tarq nudges my face with his and presses his lips to mine. "So that was a pretty good beach, right?"

I laugh, biting my tongue. "Tarq, I do not want to talk about the beach."

He frowns. "Why not?"

I don't know what makes him so perfect, but I can't get enough of him. "I love you."

Tarq laughs. "I know you do." He licks his lips. "Get over here," he says, rolling me over him.

We spend the rest of the night enjoying how our bodies call out for each other. When the lantern beside the bed runs out of oil, we use our hands to feel our way around, and I memorize how every inch of him feels. Tarq takes advantage of my exhaustion by the night's end, running his tongue over my whole body. I've never been so tired and so happy at the same time.

17

B y morning, Tarq has rolled to bury me under his shoulder and chest. I nuzzle into him, trying to get closer, and he tightens his grip on me. Tarq sighs happily, ducking to kiss the top of my head.

Someone clears their throat, and we both tense. I want to see who it is, but Tarq tucks me further under his shoulder. I'm unsure how to handle protection, but I'm nearly positive I'm not supposed to be giggling. Tarq lifts his head to look around and lets me go.

"He's not here for me," he says, smiling as he closes his eyes.

I sit up as Dax leans against the fireplace, stoking a small fire that looks like it's been burning for a while. I stare silently at the back of his head before looking down at Tarq, who is now pretending to sleep beside me. My eyes flick to the trees, hoping to borrow a little of their peacefulness because my anger flares as these men test my patience.

"Dax," I say, breathing out slowly. "We've discussed how much I hate waking up to random people in the room."

Turning to look at me, he leans against the hearth and flexes his jaw, trying to hide his grin. "I know we did," he says. "I was there."

Tarq chuckles in his pretend slumber.

I hit Tarq in the head with a pillow. "Are you two kidding me right now?"

Dax circles his finger around his face. "Do I look like I give a shit?" Tarq bursts out laughing, covering his head with his arm as Dax throws some clothes at me. "Get dressed. I need your help with something."

My eyes follow Dax as he leaves. I look down at Tarq, who's giggling and getting louder the longer I'm silent. I pull on the T-shirt Dax threw at me. "I'm taking my bond back."

Tarq latches onto my waist, pulling me beside him. He smiles and cups my cheek. "That's not how that works." He kisses me and growls when I push him away.

I jump off the bed, looking for my shorts. "Well, it should," I grumble. "Why don't you make me something to eat, Chuckles?" I pull my shorts up and walk to the door. When I turn around, Tarq is snuggled back into the pillows. "Tarq?"

He stretches out, gesturing at his body. "I'll have to cover all of this up, Darya."

I wink at him. "I promise to picture you naked."

"I can work with that."

***

I don't find anyone downstairs, but the front door is open. I step onto the porch and find Dax leaning against a tree beside the trail to the pond. When he sees me, he pushes off the tree to head in my direction.

"Alright, I'm here," I announce. "What do you want?"

"Miles got out last night."

I hold my hand out, intending to stop him from coming closer. "What the fuck, Dax?"

Dax continues to advance on me. "Edith's packing. You need to go back to her house."

"How could you let this happen?" I shout, backing away from him.

Catching my arm, Dax holds it firmly as only Miles has dared. "Let's go. You need to leave now," he growls.

I stand my ground as Dax tries to pull me. "I may not be able to kill you, but you will regret not taking your hand off me right now."

There's a loud bang from the house. I catch Tarq jumping over the rail and shifting out of his clothes. He snarls, barreling straight at us. Dax releases my arm just before Tarq slams into him, knocking him down the hill. Tarq positions himself between Dax and me with his legs squared, prepared to defend me.

Smirking, I watch Dax brush off his clothes. "I did warn you."

"Are you ok?" Tarq asks, continuing to snarl at Dax.

I reach for his hip. "Dax was just leaving."

"I'm not leaving without you." Sighing, Dax runs his hands through his hair. "You need to leave, Darya. You're not safe here."

Tarq stops snarling. *"What's he talking about?"*

I roll my eyes. "It's not important."

"Darya, what is he talking about?" Tarq steps back where he can see me while keeping an eye on Dax. *"Tell me."*

"Fine," I say, sighing. "Can we at least do this inside? I'm starving." I gesture toward the house and lift my eyebrows at Dax. "Yes, you," I say, annoyed. "To the house." I turn toward the porch, but Tarq stops me. "Tarq, I'm hungry," I whine.

"Just let him go ahead so I can keep an eye on him, Darya," Tarq grumbles.

I motion for Dax to go ahead of us while looking at the bits of fabric strewn about the yard. Tarq had been wearing the black shirt I saw him in after the attack. It fit him perfectly, and I loved how it looked on him just as much as I wanted to remove it. "I liked that shirt," I say, frowning.

"I did look pretty good in it, huh?"

"You really did," I agree, laughing.

Dax glares at us. "Can you two take anything seriously? This is important."

I arch my eyebrow, grinning at him. "I think I fell into some serious the other day. I brushed that shit off, though. Worst five minutes of my life."

"Aw, Baby," Tarq gushes, licking my arm. *"You make me so proud."*

"Well, I'm honored to learn from the master," I tell him, tugging his fur.

Dax opens the front door and barges in. He walks straight through the living room, disappearing into the kitchen. I close the door behind us and lean against it, looking down at Tarq as he blocks my path.

"I need you to wait here while I grab some pants." He pauses, and I look up toward the kitchen. *"Darya, stay here."*

I look down and smile, running my hand over his head. "Mm-hmm, I'll be here."

He runs upstairs and shifts just before entering the bedroom.

"He's the only one who can do that," Dax calls out from the kitchen.

Looking through the doorway, I see Dax leaning over the counter, watching me. I push off the door. "Do what?"

Dax uses a knife to point at the stool across the counter from him. "Sit," he orders. "Food's almost ready." He slides the blade through a slab of pork, expertly cutting strips of bacon. Once I sit, he slides a coffee cup to me.

I watch him over my cup. "Enough with your half-truths, Dax. Tell me."

Dax looks up from his food prep and sighs. "The shifting."

My fingers dig into the coffee cup. "Dax, they're wolves. They all shift," I snap. "What the hell are you talking about?"

Tarq slides his hand over my hip, startling me. "I'm the only one that can shift within the confines of the curse," he says before kissing my cheek. "Didn't I ask you to wait for me?"

I look at him from the corner of my eye. "What in our history made you think I would listen?" Tarq takes my cup and stares at me as he drains it. "That was mine," I whine.

"I'll get you some more," Tarq says, laughing. He bounces around the counter and dips my cup in the boiling pot. Dax has the only towel, so Tarq grabs Dax's shirt to dry the outside of my cup.

Dax points his knife at Tarq. "You are not immortal," he warns. "You need to tell her the rest."

Tarq slides the cup into my hands and leans down on the counter, smiling at me. He turns to Dax with his eyebrow lifted. "What we discuss is not your business."

Dax narrows his eyes, growling.

"Knock it off, you two," I snap. "Tarq, Dax had Miles locked up in the barn."

Everything rewinds to the day I met Tarq as his fingers dig into the counter and his face flashes a level of anger I will never understand. He turns to Dax. "Why is that psychopath here?"

Dax grabs a handful of meat and throws it into the pan on the stove behind him. "He came for her." He points his knife at me. "Killed thirteen of his wolves before I got him. I didn't know what to do with him, so I put him in the barn."

There's a deafening silence in the kitchen.

After a few minutes, Tarq's eyes grow wide. "You said 'had.'" He slowly looks from me to Dax. "Where the fuck is he?"

Dax leans on his elbows, looking at Tarq. "And the plot thickens."

Tarq looks at the ceiling and mashes his fists to his forehead. He looks down at me as I hide behind my coffee cup. "I would like to formally apologize for any time I have left you wholly or partially in the dark about anything."

I move my cup and smile broadly. "I accept your apology."

"You two speak your own language," Dax grumbles, shaking his head.

Tarq raises his eyebrow. "Then, in a language I understand, one of you better tell me where that psychopath extraordinaire is!"

I cringe a little. "I don't know," I tell Tarq. "Dax said he escaped last night."

Tarq snaps his head toward Dax. "What the fuck, Dax?"

"That's what I said!" I shout, laughing.

Tarq points at me. "Get your shit. We're leaving."

Carefully placing my cup on the counter, I smile up at him. "Excuse me?"

"He's right," he says, sighing loudly. "And Darya, you know how much I hate to admit that, but you aren't safe here." He leans toward Dax and glares. "However, you tried to take her away from me again. That I cannot forgive."

Dax stands upright, looking unimpressed. "I don't care." He returns to the stove and dumps some eggs onto a plate before sliding it to me. "Maybe if you told her everything, she'd be willing to leave."

Tarq flips his hand dismissively as he pulls the bacon from the pan.

Dax rolls his eyes. "It's not just that he can shift, Darya. It's infinitely easier for him."

"Why?"

"Darya, if I knew the answer, I'd help my other wolves," Dax grumbles.

If only I could strangle these two with their partial information.

Tarq takes my hand. "He's saying that if we are here when Miles returns with the rest of his pack, it could be just the two of us against a hundred of them."

My eyes wander from one man to the other. *They are the strongest men I have ever known. How could they fail at anything? They wouldn't push me to leave if they thought they could protect me. But I can't just leave my pack. Sure, I've only met a few of them, but they are all mine, and I need to protect them.*

"I'll go," I say thoughtfully. "I can draw Miles away from here."

Tarq releases my hand, backing away. "What? No, Darya. You need to hide."

Getting up from my stool, I calmly walk around the counter and put my hand on his chest. "No, My Love," I say, smiling. "I will draw Miles away so he'll spare the pack." I can feel the tension radiating off Dax, so I place my hand on his forearm. "To survive this, I will need you both. Will you help me?"

* * *

The guys finally agreed that my plan was better than theirs, and we started our journey west. I requested that Anthony join us again and was pleasantly surprised when he accepted the invitation. He and Edith are riding behind me while Dax leads the way. I made Bruce stay behind and patrol the pack territory, mostly because I didn't want to deal with his attitude, but I did need someone to alert us of any trouble.

"Are you doing ok?" Tarq asks.

I look down at him. "I'm fine," I answer, slowing my horse. "You remember the way?"

"*Of course I do,*" he scoffs. "*I'd never forget where we spent our first night together.*"

I shake my head, laughing. "That's not how I remember it, but I'm gonna let you live in your little world."

"*Everyone should live in my world. It's so much better here.*"

"Yes, My Love. I agree," I say. "We're getting close. Would you mind grabbing us some dinner?"

Amelia jogs up to join us. "*I can go, Luna.*"

I smile down at her. Her blonde coat matches her hair, and she is beyond stunning. "Thank you, Amelia, but your son knows where we're going tonight."

"*I got it, Mom. Keep my woman safe.*" Tarq darts toward the river.

"*It's fun watching him be happy.*" Just like Tarq, I can hear her smile. Tarq's smile sounds like he's laughing, but Amelia's smiling voice sounds like love or admiration.

I step down from my saddle to walk beside her. "Amelia, can I ask about the mate and bonding stuff?"

"*You are the Luna. You may do as you wish.*" She slips her muzzle into my hand as Tarq does.

"I love him," I say, trying to put my thoughts into words. "I'm pretty sure he loves me, but is that only because we're mates or the bonding? Is it our choice?"

"*Your mate is what you need them to be, Luna,*" Amelia says. "*They will be your protector, caretaker, guardian, or maybe just a companion. Feelings are purely voluntary.*"

I think back to my first encounter with Bruce. "How is your relationship with Bruce?"

Amelia hangs her head. "*We're not all blessed with a love like you have.*"

I don't like Bruce, but he's one of my wolves. I love him just as much as Amelia and wish I could give them happiness. "I'm sorry."

"*Watching my son love you is enough for me.*" Amelia's smile returns to her voice. "*I'm glad that he makes you happy.*"

Feeling overwhelmed with sorrow, I blink back the threatening tears and mount my horse. I push the group a bit faster until we reach the cave. We work together to light the fire and secure the horses. My chest feels tight until Tarq announces that he's on his way with dinner.

"I feel like a superhero coming to save the day," Tarq announces.

I burst out laughing in my relief. Three pairs of eyes are instantly on me as if I've lost my mind. Amelia just snorts and lays her head down.

"He's melted your brain," Dax says, poking the wood in the fire.

Anthony scoffs. "It's not fair that we can't hear what he's saying," he grumbles. "I mean, the she-wolf gets to hear him."

Amelia growls. *"My name is Amelia!"*

I sigh, rubbing my forehead. "Here we go again."

"Hang on!" Tarq chimes. *"Is Anthony starting shit again? Tell him to wait for me!"*

As if I've lost the ability to filter my words, I look at Anthony and open my mouth. "Tarq says to wait for him."

Anthony laughs, clapping his hands loudly. "That same shit pisses the she-wolf off? That's perfect!"

"A little help, please, Dax?" I beg as Edith joins in the argument.

Dax has been quietly sitting on the ground beside me since he set this whole exchange in motion. He leans back against the rock I'm sitting on and looks up at me, unamused. "What do you want me to do?" He swings his hand around, gesturing to our group. "Not one of these fools is part of my pack."

I lean down, putting my head in my hands. "How am I ever gonna do this?"

"It takes time to learn to lead," Dax says, sliding his hand over my knee. "Much of the wolf leadership is coming naturally to you, but those," he pauses to point across the fire, "are not wolves."

I peek from behind my hands. "How do you do it?"

Dax grins. "Fear and sarcasm." When he sees me frown, he continues. "That's not your style, Darya. You show these wolves love and compassion." He runs his hand over Amelia's muzzle. "You bring them honor and dignity." He smiles at her before turning his eyes back to me. "Wolves only need to meet you to love you. I believe your human leadership should be the same."

"He's right," Tarq says, making me jump. I find him standing behind me with four geese at his feet. *"And you know how much I hate to admit that."* Tarq puts his chin on my shoulder.

I lean my cheek on his muzzle and grab Dax's hand. "I don't know what I would do without you two."

"Probably sleep peacefully at night," Dax says, returning to the fire.

Tarq chuckles, nudging my cheek with his nose. *"After having boring sex."*

"Ok," I say, giggling. "That's enough out of you two." I look up at Anthony and Edith, who are now arguing over the usefulness of the wolves. Amelia is chiming in as if they can hear her. "Food's here!" I shout.

Like an act of pure magic, the bickering stops. Amelia takes the geese to Anthony, who begins plucking the feathers. Edith fashions a spit for one of the birds and sets a pan out to heat for some smaller cuts. They compare the birds and decide which to cut up and which to roast whole.

Amelia lies beside me as I slide off the rock to sit with Dax. She gently places her head on my leg and looks up. *"You are a true Luna."*

I rub my hand over her shoulder, feeling her relax under my fingers. "Thank you, Amelia."

* * *

When I wake in the morning, the sun is just beginning to rise. Amelia had taken over standing watch at some point, and Tarq now sleeps beside me.

"Did you sleep well, Luna?"

I spot Amelia sitting near the cave opening and nod to her. My movement disturbs Tarq, who rolls over, flopping his head across my hips. Smiling, I slip my fingers through his fur.

"He's just a big, dopey dog, isn't he?"

I turn toward Dax's whisper and see him watching Tarq. I reach my other hand out to him. "You want some of this?" I whisper.

Dax smiles, taking my hand. He relaxes with a deep sigh but notices my frown. "What's on your mind?"

"We're running out of time, and I'm too busy hiding from Miles to accomplish anything."

He squeezes my hand. "Darya, you found some impossible-to-find bones. You came back from the dead. You also managed to tame the wild beast."

"*I am not a beast,*" Tarq mumbles.

Dax continues, unaware that Tarq's woken up. "You've accomplished quite a bit in a month, and we have another month to finish the rest."

I tug Tarq's fur. "But you are wild," I whisper, smiling.

He rolls upright and lays his head across my chest, facing Dax. "*And why, My Love, are you holding that man's hand?*"

I drape my arm over his shoulder. "Is my wild wolf jealous?"

Tarq mashes his nose against mine. "*Yes.*"

I giggle, turning toward Dax.

"You're good for him," he says, grinning. "I didn't think he'd ever calm down."

Tarq lays his head back down on my chest. "*Mm-hmm,*" he grumbles. "*The love of a good woman. Blah, blah, blah. I've always been calm.*"

Smiling, I shake my head. "Somehow, I doubt that's completely true."

"*It's kind of true,*" Tarq says, tucking his nose in my hair.

"See?" Dax says, raising his eyebrow. "A month ago, he'd have bitten me by now."

"You bit Dax?" I scoff and tug a handful of fur, but Tarq doesn't respond.

Dax laughs. "He broke my leg one summer 'cause I called him a shit hunter."

"Tarq!" I turn my head so my cheek is lying on his muzzle. "You said you trained with Dax. That doesn't sound like training!"

Tarq stays tucked in my hair. "*Training, fighting,*" he grumbles. "*I feel like we're splitting hairs.*" Tarq chuckles as I roll over to tightly wrap my arms around his neck. "*Woman, don't make me lick your face.*"

"I thought you weren't a beast?" I giggle.

Tarq jumps from my arms and braces to attack. *"Them's fightin' words, Luna."* He adds a snarl for effect.

I laugh, tugging the fur on his throat.

"See? Good for him," I hear Dax say behind me.

"Is everything ok over there?" Anthony calls from across the fire.

I sit up and smile at him. "Doesn't everyone wake up to a snarling wolf?" I kiss Tarq behind his whiskers. "Come on, let's get going."

* * *

We're skirting part of the basin instead of running straight through like last time. Tarq and Amelia scout the woods ahead, freeing me to speak with Edith privately. Once they leave, I drop back to the rear.

Edith looks at me curiously as I fall in beside her. "What's up, honey?"

"I need to talk to Luna," I tell her.

She shakes her head slowly. "Oh honey, I don't think that's a good idea."

"She needs to finish the Blood Mark, Edith," I whisper. "It hasn't changed, so I need to know what she wants."

"I don't like it," she whispers back, still shaking her head.

I roll my eyes. "She's the only one that can finish this thing, Edith," I hiss. "And I need this to stay between us."

Before she can agree, Tarq bounds toward us, soaking wet. He shakes, spraying water everywhere.

I hold my hand up, blocking the water. "And what do you have to say for yourself?"

"My mother pushed me in the damn creek." He sounds angry, but there's something else there.

I can't contain my laughter. "I'm sorry, she what?"

Tarq looks up at me with his ears tucked. *"Why are you laughing?"*

"Why did your mother push you into the creek?" I giggle at his pitiful expression.

Edith joins in the laughter. "Oh, is that what happened?"

I look down at Tarq, raising my eyebrow. "Where's your mother?"

He tucks his ears again. *"How should I know?"* he asks, his smile ringing in his voice now. *"I was telling you about how she pushed me in the creek."*

"He tried to push me off a log and fell on his ass!" Amelia chimes in, jogging up.

"Oh, there we go," I say, smiling. "The truth."

Tarq chuckles and bumps his shoulder into his mother's as she joins us. *"That is not how this event will be remembered."*

Amelia looks up at me as Tarq darts in Dax's direction. *"You're good for my son."*

I sigh. "So I keep hearing."

* * *

By nightfall, Tarq and Amelia pick up a strange scent and begin following it. After a while, it becomes clear to Dax that it's Miles' scent.

"Amelia and I will track him," Dax says. "You need to keep moving." He looks down at Tarq. "Straight to the cave. No detours."

I groan. "Dax, we're all tired. How is he always one step ahead of us?" I ask, staring at him as he grabs my face.

"Listen to me," Dax says, kissing my forehead. "I will protect you from him. Just keep moving." He slides from my hands and mounts the white mare. He nods, and Amelia leads him away from us, deeper into the woods.

I turn to Tarq, who's been patiently waiting. "How are you holding up?" I ask him.

"My Love," he starts. He sounds tired, but I know he's about to tell me something about being okay. *"I am everything you need me to be. I will carry us through the next day to keep you safe because that is what you need."*

And how do you argue with that? I slide my hand under his jaw, kissing him behind his whiskers. "I love you."

* * *

I'm alone when I wake a day and a half later in the cave. I had an exhausted wolf in my arms when I went to sleep. There's barely any light outside when I sit up, so I know it's not morning. Anthony is awake, sitting by a small fire. He nods at me and waves for me to join him.

"Tarq went hunting," he whispers. "Said your stomach woke him up." He looks over where Edith is sleeping before grabbing his lantern. "Come on, Darya. I want to show you something."

He offers his arm, and I smile as I take it. I don't know what Anthony and I are now, but we trust each other. We leave the cave and walk toward the creek I had taken Tarq to.

Anthony slows as we reach the stone wall, holding the lantern up. "I thought you'd want to see this."

Along the wall, by the creek, is a grave marker. Fray's name is etched in large letters across the top with smaller writing under it. I hold my chest as I remember the first casualty of my fate.

"We stopped here when we went to get the bones," Anthony says, helping me move closer. "It took Dax two days to carve them damn words."

I lean closer to try to read it in the low light. My foot snags on a lifted root, and I start to fall. "Oh shit, Anthony!" I yell.

He catches my arm, stopping me just short of falling into the creek. "You clumsy shit," he says, smirking.

I recognize the distinct growl that erupts behind him. Pulling against Anthony, I lift myself with his help. "No, My Love, it's ok," I say as Tarq steps around the wall.

"You've got the wrong idea, wolf," Anthony says, trying to keep me behind him. He puts his arm out to shove me aside and triggers Tarq.

"Tarq, stop!" I jump forward to get between them.

Tarq's jaw latches onto my arms with an excruciating amount of pressure. His body knocks me into the freezing water, and his elbow presses down on my ribs, only allowing short bursts of air. Tarq slings his body around to snarl at Anthony. It takes his weight off my ribs and lets me take one deep breath before he steps on my shoulder, pushing me underwater.

Tarq's back claws rip through my skin as I flail. Anthony yells something, and suddenly I'm released. I sit up, gasping and coughing.

Anthony scoops me out of the water, putting my shoulder against his body so I can't see it. As he carries me back to the cave, I look over his shoulder and watch Tarq step out of the water to lie down. My chest aches for him.

18

Edith gasps, rushing toward us with a blanket as Anthony places me beside the fire. She pulls my shirt away from my skin, and we both hiss, although I'm positive it hurts me more. After wrapping the blanket around my shoulders, Edith leaves me to rummage in her bag. "What happened?"

Anthony throws another log into the pit. "That damn wolf nearly killed her," he sneers.

"What wolf?" Edith asks, pulling out a pot and placing it near the fire.

"Tarq," I answer. "He thought Anthony was attacking me. I tried to stop him." I carefully pull my arms out of the blanket, scanning the unblemished skin. *His teeth should've shredded my arms, right?* I look up at Anthony. "Go get Tarq."

Anthony glares at me. "No," he says defiantly. "He can stay out there and think about what he's done."

"Tarq's not a dog. Please stop treating him like one," I say, wincing from my shoulder's throbbing.

Anthony stares at me for a moment before standing up. "Fuck!" he yells, stomping out of the cave.

After a few minutes, he returns and helps Edith measure items to put in the pot. I turn toward the cave's mouth and see Tarq sitting just inside, hanging his head.

"Come here," I tell him.

I see him flinch, but he doesn't stand. *I almost killed you. I'll stay here.*

I roll my eyes, clenching my jaw. "I am your Luna, and I told you to come here."

Tarq stands, clearly startled. *"Darya, please?"*

I've had enough. "I will not ask you again, Tarq."

Tarq's breaking my heart but cannot abandon me when he thinks he's hurt me. He slowly walks toward me with his head hung low. Once he's close enough, I hold out my arm.

Tarq lifts his head and studies my skin. *"How?"*

"I guess wolves can't bite the Luna," I tell him. "I could use a little help, though." Allowing the blanket to fall from my back, I show him the blood-soaked shirt.

Stepping forward, Tarq touches his nose to my cheek. *"Take it off,"* he says.

I try, but Edith has to help me. "I have my tea brewing," she tells me. "It should take care of whatever he can't heal."

Tarq steps around me and watches my face as he gently slides his tongue over my wounds. He only manages two swipes before his eyes roll closed, and he starts to hum. His limbs weaken, and he sits down. I hold his head up and direct him around to the open areas as he continues to lick my blood in a euphoric daze.

Once he's closed up the wounds, I let his head lower to my leg. He lays down, licking his lips. *"You taste amazing,"* Tarq says dreamily.

Edith shakes her head and brings a rag to finish cleaning the blood. She eyes Tarq as she pours water from a canteen on it. "I'm sure he would love to do this, but I think he's had enough," she says, chuckling.

"Have you thought about my request?" I ask as she helps me into one of Tarq's shirts.

"That Luna has brought you nothing but misery." Anthony's angry words echo down the cave. "Why would you want to talk to her?"

Tarq instantly snaps out of his daze. *"What?"*

"Edith!" I shout as she tries to slink away.

She sits down next to Anthony, who's stirring her tea. "He's the voice of reason among us, Darya," Edith says as if I should've expected her to tell him. She pours the tea into a cup and reaches across the fire to hand it to me. "When you tell me you want to do dangerous things, I will need help."

"*Darya, no.*" Tarq puts his paw in my lap.

Downing the hot tea, I take his paw and rub his pads as I talk. "Listen, all of you," I speak slowly and clearly for them, pointing to my Blood Mark. "This is not done and hasn't changed in weeks. Luna said she needs to finish it. She obviously wants something. Unless you know what that is, I need to talk to her."

I look at each of them, one at a time. None of them have anything to offer.

"Then we're all in agreement," I say, standing up. "I need to talk to Luna."

Dropping the blanket, I leave them in the cave. The sun is rising gloriously, and its light filters through the trees. I look up at the boulder Anthony sat on the last time we were here. I still had a level of ignorant bliss then. Now every day gives me a new opportunity to screw it all up. I feel something gently touching my arm and blink my eyes back into focus.

Tarq steps in front of me, sliding his hand down my arm. "Come with me," he says.

He leads me further up the hill to a quiet part of the creek against the cliffside. I've come up here to hunt. He probably smelled deer in this direction this morning. I release his hand and walk to the center of the clearing. Sighing, I drop into the tall grass. Tarq lies beside me, pulling at the tips of my hair. Aside from a quiet sigh, he stays silent until I'm ready to talk.

"I need to do this," I whisper. "I need you to support me." I lean toward him until my forehead is on his chest.

Tarq pushes my hair from my face. "I will always do what's needed to protect you." He stops to consider his words. "If I have an opinion, My Love, I will give it. But I will always support your decision. Regardless of whether I like your choices, I will stand beside you."

"I love you," I say, sighing.

Tarq pulls on my neck. "Come here, My Love." He guides me to his chest and firmly runs his hand down the center of my back, pushing me against him. He pulls up the bottom of my T-shirt and lightly trails his fingers over my back and hip. When Tarq puts his lips to my forehead and breathes out, he sends a wave of heat down my entire body.

I hum a sigh and smile. "That feels good."

Reaching across his chest, Tarq slides his hand over my cheek and jaw, letting his fingers trail down my neck. His thumb pushes my chin up so he can claim my lips. I roll over, straddling him and pushing my tongue into his mouth. Tarq slides his hand up my shirt, asking for more.

"Um, so, the food's ready," Edith says, sounding more intrigued than uncomfortable considering what she's just interrupted.

I pull my tongue out of Tarq's mouth and rest my forehead against his, taking a moment to catch my breath. "Thank you. We'll be there in a minute."

Tarq smiles and nips at my lips, trying to convince me to return to him. I latch my teeth onto Tarq's lower lip and run my tongue over it. As I let it go, I rest my forehead on his again.

"What did you get for breakfast?" I ask, smiling.

Tarq's eyebrows raise. "What?" he asks, nearly panicked. "Fish, Darya. I'm really good at fishing. Now come here." Tarq pulls me to him and plunges his tongue into my mouth.

I understand how he feels. I always need him, but when we're touching, it's overwhelming. I just want to pull every stitch off and let him have me. I bet this would suck if I hated him, but I love and crave this man.

Tarq drops his hands from my face and yanks his shirt off. Coming back to me, he reclaims my mouth and rubs his hands across my back. He slides his tongue underneath mine, exciting every nerve in one motion.

"Luna, we have a problem." Amelia's voice causes me to jerk away from Tarq.

"Fuck!" I shout.

Tarq's eyes open wide. He grabs my face again, scanning it as if it'll tell him what's wrong.

I sigh, frowning at him. "I need you to talk to your mother."

He arches his eyebrow and tries to pull me back to him. "I don't think you want my mother to know what I want to do to you right now."

Giving in to Tarq would be much easier than fighting this. My entire body desires him.

I shake my head to clear my thoughts. "I'm sorry, baby. It's your mother. She's trying to talk to me."

"So?" He's growing more desperate, and I'm a heartbeat away from giving in.

"She says there's a problem," I whisper against his lips.

Tarq releases me. "Back up."

I roll off him as he pulls the crystal's ribbon over his head. I barely clear his paws as he shifts. "Wasn't that the only outfit we brought?"

"*I'm sure Edie has more,*" Tarq says, flipping over and shaking out his fur. "*Besides, I look better without them.*"

I grin as he approaches me and runs his nose along my neck. "I can't deny that."

"*Mom, what's up?*" he asks Amelia as he tickles my neck and shoulder with his whiskers.

"*Is the Luna safe?*"

Tarq slides his nose up my neck and along my jawline. He closes his eyes as my breath catches in my throat. "*Of course she is. What's wrong, Mom?*"

She doesn't answer right away. Tarq begins to hum as he slides his muzzle along my cheek.

"Please tell me that I didn't pass on sex just so we could exchange pleasantries with your mother," I grumble, running my hand over Tarq's jaw to hold him against my cheek.

He pushes past my hand to bury his nose in my hair against my neck. "*Mother, spit it out. If you are ruining my chance to get laid just to see if she's ok, I will never forgive you.*"

I laugh and swat at Tarq's shoulder. "I know I'm the Luna and all, but please don't ever say that to your mother again!"

"I don't know. She's my mother. That trumps what the Luna wants." He pushes his nose into my skin and takes a deep breath of my scent. *"God, you smell good."*

My entire body heats up straight to my core. My face flushes from the effect Tarq has on me. Of course he notices everything that happens with my body and can feel the heat.

"See, I'm not the only one thinking about it," Tarq says, humming. He pushes his muzzle down the front of my shirt and licks my chest, making me gasp. *"You just slip that necklace on me, and I'll be naked, hard, and ready."*

"SON!" Amelia shouts.

"Holy hell," I grumble, pushing Tarq back. "Get off me." He steps back, and I stand up, moving away from him.

"What?" Tarq chuckles.

"Miles was leading us in circles," Amelia says. *"He knew we were tracking him. He's long gone."*

Tarq stops laughing and looks up at me. *"Ok, I'm back."*

I throw my hands in the air. "Why can't anything go right? Just one thing. Is that too much to ask?"

"What does Dax say?"

"He still wants you to go to Edith's," Amelia tells us. *"Miles can't get past the wards. It's the safest place."*

"Tell her to meet us there," I tell Tarq. I walk to the creek's edge and momentarily stare at the water. As everything begins to bubble to the surface, I feel like I'm about to burst. "FUCK!" I scream. My shout bounces off the cliff and echoes through the woods, making the trees voice the same opinion about our current situation.

It's not long before my outburst attracts Edith and Anthony. "What's wrong?" Edith asks, out of breath from running.

I rub my forehead. "Everything that can go wrong is going wrong."

"Are you pregnant?" Edith smiles, clapping childishly.

Tarq tilts his head. *"Why would she instantly jump to you being pregnant?"*

"I'm gonna be a grandmother?" a very excited Amelia exclaims.

"What?" I am so damn confused right now.

"No," Tarq says, then looks back at me. *"Wait. Are you pregnant?"*

"Oh, I needed some good news today," says Amelia, still very excited.

"Fuck. Tarq, stop thinking!" I shout at him.

Tarq tucks his nose into his chest and glares at me. *"Well, excuse the hell out of me."*

I sigh, hanging my head. Even as a wolf, I can tell I've offended him and everyone in his family tree in four words. "That's not what I meant. Please just tell your mother that I'm not pregnant."

"It's gonna break her heart," he says sadly.

"I'm aware, My Love." I slide my hand along his muzzle. "However, I'm not the one that broadcasted my confused thoughts to her."

Tarq sighs, fluffing out his lips. *"Fine."*

I shake my head, watching him lie by the creek to talk privately with his mother. I turn my eyes back to Edith. "As for you, no, I'm not pregnant, but Miles has outwitted Dax, and we need to go."

Edith frowns. "I bet that man makes some beautiful babies."

Anthony scoffs, pushing us back toward the cave.

* * *

After a quick meal, we brave the trail up the cliff and along the wall, finally arriving at the flower fields. Tarq runs ahead of us, bounding through the flowers. We step down from our saddles, but Edith and Anthony stay back, letting me walk alone. It's been a while since I've had quiet time to think things through.

Miles knew Dax was tracking him. He could've let me suffer without water. Why did he bring it to me? Why not have someone else do it? Miles had someone else tie me but handled all my care once I started bleeding. I try to remember every detail of my exchanges with him. *He got angry when I brought up his mother.*

"Tarq?" I call out, looking up from the flowers.

My beautiful wolf is chasing butterflies around the field. He's mid-jump when he looks over and falls on his face upon landing.

I shake my head. *Let me proudly introduce the man I love, my mighty protector. May his greatness be known far and wide.*

Tarq bounces back to his feet and shakes off the flower petals before running to me.

"That was," I pause, searching for the right word, "graceful."

"*Moving on,*" Tarq grumbles.

"Did Dax ever talk to you about Miles?" I ask.

"*I only remember him telling me that Miles lost his shift when the curse was activated.*" He runs his head under my hand. "*There was something about his inability to have a family, but I don't remember why.*"

That brings up another thought—Amelia's excitement about a grandchild. *If Edith's family is wrong, Amelia will never have a baby to celebrate. Even Tarq seemed excited when asking if Edith was right.* I slide my hand down his neck and tug his fur.

"*Are you ok?*"

I look down and smile. "I think I'm just scared. Maybe I could borrow a little bit of your strength?"

"*What's mine is yours, My Love.*" He rubs his head against my hip.

"Come on, let's get going," I say, stepping back into my saddle. I turn back to Tarq and smile. "Butterflies?"

"*I was bored,*" he answers without looking at me.

I raise my eyebrow and wait for him to notice.

"*I have a lot of pent-up energy. How would you like me to get rid of it?*" Tarq chuckles.

I scoff. "And I'm just supposed to suffer in silence?"

"*Well, Darya, you're not a wolf strong enough to break immortals, so yes.*"

I giggle. "Butterflies?"

Tarq laughs. "*Not another word, woman.*"

I shake my head, still laughing, and urge my horse forward.

* * *

It's past sunset when we arrive at Edith's. Tarq slows my horse and stops just before crossing the barrier. Edith and Anthony ride past me, but Tarq doesn't move.

"What's up?" I ask him.

"*I made a deal with Anthony,*" he tells me. "*I have to wait for Edie to bring me clothes.*"

I sigh. "A deal?"

"*He promised to stop calling me 'wolf' if I stopped showing up naked around him all the time.*"

"But why am I here?" I don't mean to sound selfish, but I don't become a beautifully naked man when I cross the boundary. *And I happen to enjoy seeing him naked.*

"*Because I'd have to break a promise to protect you in there. So, you will stay out here until I can go in there,*" Tarq says in a way that makes me think I should've known his answer.

I watch the others walk into the house and lean on my horse's neck. "How'd Amelia take the news?"

"*She's alright,*" Tarq says, looking up at me. "*She was pretty excited, though. I never took her for the grandmother type.*"

I reach my hand down, and he slides his head under it. "Maybe we could curb the whole 'breaking Amelia's heart' thing."

I look up as Edith's footsteps approach. "Alright, beautiful, get dressed," she says, holding out an armful of clothes. "We have work to do."

I dismount and walk across the line with Tarq. Taking the clothes from Edith, I hand them to him as he dresses.

"I think we found a way for you to talk to Luna," Edith tells me, leaving her eyes on Tarq's body. She sucks on her lower lip and hangs onto my arm to steady herself. "I have never been jealous of anyone before. Are you sure I can't borrow him for just a few minutes?"

Tarq shakes his head and pulls on the shirt. "You know, I'm standing right here."

"Yes, but I don't care if I have your permission, beautiful one." Edith smiles wickedly as she bites her tongue and runs her finger from his chest to his waistband. She sighs and drops her hand. "Anyway, let's go talk to a dead bitch."

Tarq tucks me under his arm as Edith turns away from us. "Please don't loan me out to anyone."

I laugh. "Baby, you're my brand of crazy." I wrap my arms around him. "No one else could handle you."

Edith leads us into the living room. She motions toward the couch and sits opposite us. "I looked through my mother's book," she says. "I can use a variation of the mixture I used to keep you sedated after your kidnapping. The goal would be to knock out your body but only relax your mind."

Anthony emerges from the kitchen with a tray of tea cups. He sets the tray on the table and looks up at me as he sits on the floor with Edith. "Are you sure about this?"

I nod to him. "I'm pretty sure she's the only one with the answers I need."

Edith mixes something into one of the cups and gives it to me before handing out the rest. "Ok then, bottoms up," she says, smiling. "We'll be here with you the whole time."

I test the tea before gulping it down. Sliding my legs on the couch, I lean onto Tarq's chest.

"Are you ok?" he asks, tightly wrapping his arms around me and kissing my head. "Do you want to lie down?"

The room starts to spin, and I grab onto his arm. "I love you," I whisper as my eyes roll closed.

* * *

I know it worked when I find myself standing in my black hell again. I reach my arms out to be sure there's nothing to grab. *Come on, Luna. Where the hell are you?*

"It's about fucking time you showed up," Luna growls, appearing before me.

"What are you talking about?" I try to step back, but we remain the same distance apart. "Luna, you're the one that has stayed away," I yell back. "I thought you were happy."

Her eyes narrow. "Is that mark finished? Are you still banging that mongrel guard?" She raises her eyebrows. "Then no, Baby Luna, I'm not happy."

I don't know why her words shock me, but my jaw drops. "That guard is not a mongrel," I shout back. "He is my mate and the next Alpha."

Luna purses her lips as her face reddens. Her hand comes out of nowhere and smacks my cheek harder than anyone has dared.

Even in this dream world, it hurts like hell. I grab my face and glare at her. "What the fuck?"

Luna matches my glare. "You will not subject me to any more shameful acts with that cur dog!"

I am starting to think she says these things to get a rise out of me. "Enough of the name-calling, Luna," I say. "Can we talk like we have a common goal? And can you please do something about this?" I gesture to the endless darkness that surrounds us.

"Whatever," she grumbles, and our surroundings change.

I realize I'm not actually here in this world, but that slap really hurt, so it makes sense that I'm freezing when we suddenly stand in a blizzard. "Luna, neither of us is dressed for a blizzard," I shout. "What are you doing?"

"There's no making you happy," Luna scoffs, changing our surroundings to an old, rundown room. There are piles of dust and dirt covering broken furniture. An old chaise and table in the center of the room have many layers of cobwebs extending from them.

"I give up," I say, rolling my eyes.

Luna raises her eyebrows, surprised. "You don't like my home? Where I killed myself for my wolves?"

"Is this what it looks like now?" I ask, taking another look.

"No," she grins. "It's a pile of rubble now. I assume it would look like this if it were still standing."

Why the hell do I even bother with her?

I shake my head and sigh. "Luna, I came to ask you to finish the mark."

"You've got some stones," she yells, glaring at me again. "If you had just done as you were told, it would already be done." She sits on the chaise, and dust plumes around her. "I bet no one told you who has to kill you, did they?"

"What are you talking about?" I'm exhausted by Luna's cruelty and nearly uninterested in the answer.

"The curse, Baby Luna. For you to survive, you must be stabbed in the heart by the love that resides there." She smiles proudly.

I turn and twist her words, but they keep meaning the same thing. "Tarq has to kill me," I whisper.

"That's correct, little girl," she says in a sickeningly sweet tone. "That mangy beast must end your life. But first, you will give me what I want to finish that Blood Mark." She grins with a twinkle in her eye.

"Luna, no," I plead, shaking my head. Her look says it all. I don't need her to tell me what she's craving. *She wants Dax.*

She scowls. "I don't want your dog. I want my wolf!"

I continue to shake my head. "Luna, please?"

"You will give me what I want, or they will stay cursed, and I will see to the end of the Luna line!" She marches to me, stopping a few inches from my face. "I'm done talking to you. Get out!"

* * *

She shoves me, and I wake up, flailing in Edith's living room. I sit up, gasping for air. Tarq's arms attempt to grab me, but I jump up before he can latch on. I dart toward the front door and pull it open, needing fresh air after that dirty room. I cross the yard and fall into the grass near the guest house.

Tarq kneels beside me just as my stomach begins ejecting its contents. Although the tea should be the only thing in there, it takes a while to stop. When I finally feel like I've finished throwing up, I fall over onto Tarq, thankful he stayed.

"What happened?" he quietly asks as he holds me to his chest, running his fingers through my hair.

His loving touch and caring words prove too much for me, and my emotions flood out. I grab his shirt and cry as he rocks me in his arms. I press my ear to his chest and let his heartbeat calm me.

Tarq pushes my hair away from my face. "Please talk to me."

"Can we just have tonight?" I ask, unsure how to tell him what Luna wants. "We can talk in the morning."

Tarq's brow furrows as he studies my face. "Are you sure? You don't seem ok, Darya."

I muster up a smile and force my tears back. "I'm sure," I say. "That just took a lot out of me."

Tarq doesn't smile back. *He knows I'm lying.* "If you're sure." He lifts me and holds me against his chest. Walking straight to the cottage, he carries me to the little kitchen and sits me on the counter. I watch Tarq pull some rags, wetting one with water from the cooler box. He returns to me and rubs it gently over my face.

I close my eyes, letting him soothe my fevered skin. "Is there any chance you could be less perfect right now?" I whisper.

Tarq kisses my cheek. "No."

He dries my skin off before picking me up. When I open my eyes, he's taken me to the bedroom. He lays me on the bed and pulls my boots off. As Tarq carefully removes my clothes, I notice his touch is different. When he touches my skin, my nerves aren't responding. Tonight, he's my caretaker, and I love him even more for it.

Tarq undresses but leaves on his shorts. He leans onto the bed and stops. "Is this ok?" he asks.

Fresh tears run from my eyes as I grab Tarq's arm, pulling him to me. "Come here, my perfect man."

He slides beside me and gathers me up in his arms. I snuggle as close as possible, placing my hands and cheek against his chest.

"I wish I knew how to help you," Tarq whispers.

"Just love me," I reply.

"Done."

19

Whether I sleep with Tarq as a wolf or a man, I've always slept soundly. So, when I jump awake to Luna slapping me, I know I'm alone in bed. My eyes fling open to find him standing in the doorway to the balcony. Tarq's leaning against the frame of the French doors and staring into the distance. His preoccupation allows me a moment to appreciate his beauty.

Catching my movement, Tarq smiles. "Good morning."

I raise my eyebrow. "It could be," I reply, smirking.

Tarq growls, quickly crossing the room to join me. I hold his face and run my thumbs over his cheekbones. He closes his eyes and leans into my touch. I try to pull him toward me, but he doesn't budge.

"Darya, marry me," Tarq says, opening his eyes.

"What?" I drop limply onto the bed.

"I don't want to wait to see if this works," he says, sitting beside me. "I want to marry you."

I sit up and put my hand on his chest. My conversation with Luna floods back in. "We need to talk about last night first."

Tarq puts his hand on my cheek. "Whatever it is, Darya, we'll get through it together."

He's right. We need to do this together. "Get dressed. We need to talk to Edith."

I'm unsure what I did to deserve him, but Tarq doesn't question me. He pulls his clothes on and even helps me dress. Then without a word, he escorts me to the main house.

Edith meets us in the living room and ushers us toward her dining room, where Anthony is piling food on the table. There are pancakes, ham, sausage, eggs, and some kind of bread covered in egg and cinnamon. I sit next to Tarq and watch him load his plate. *This explains why I had no issues getting him here.*

When Edith sits down, she notices I'm watching Anthony with a confused look. "He is proving most useful," she says with a wink as Anthony sits down. "Alright, we're all here. What's up?"

"Luna told me what she wants to finish the mark." I keep my eyes on Tarq as he pops a rolled-up pancake in his mouth. He looks up at me, and I reach out for his hand. He offers it willingly, threading his fingers with mine. "She wants to sleep with Dax."

Something flips inside Tarq. His face runs through emotions, starting with hurt and despair and quickly changing to rage. He closes his eyes and begins to shake. The scariest part is that Tarq isn't even growling.

I cup his cheek with my free hand and run my thumb over his eyelid. "Talk to me."

Even when he opens his eyes, his rage makes him unrecognizable. "I'll just fucking kill him!" he yells. "Then that bitch will have to deal with me!"

He's so close to me that his spit lands on my face, mixing with my tears. I want to wipe my face, but I'm terrified that he will do something he'll regret if I move.

Anthony clears his throat. "I don't think that's the answer, mate."

Tarq turns away from me. "What the hell do you know?" he yells at Anthony.

"I know that Darya loves you, and Edith will do anything to protect you both. I know you better calm down because I've done some shitty things to that woman," he points at me, "and I have never seen her scared until now."

Tarq sighs and puts his forehead to mine. The room remains still as Tarq takes this time to calm down. I try rubbing my hands over his skin, but I don't think it helps. *Dax might be correct, but I can't believe there's no way for a Luna to calm her Alpha.*

When I see Tarq lick his lips, I pull away and push his head up with my thumbs. "Are you ready?"

He nods sadly.

"I begged Luna for another option, but she threw me out. She threatened to end the Luna line." I notice Edith wiping a tear from her eye. "I'm not interested in your pity. I'm telling you this because I'd like your help."

Tarq rests his forehead on my shoulder, clearly unable to suggest anything. Edith pulls her family's journal off a shelf behind her while Anthony reaches his hand across the table.

I smile, accepting it. "You keep sneaking up on me, Anthony."

"Here it is," Edith interjects. "So Luna is bonded to Dax." She slides her fingers over the page. "According to this, Darya, she's right. She is the only one who can finish it." She stops and taps her lips. "There might be a way to knock you out and let her drive."

Tarq's eyes widen as he shakes his head. "What if you don't come back, Darya?"

I rest my hand on his cheek and turn to Edith. "Is Dax here?" I ask, standing up. "Somehow, she ended up being his mate. He should have a say in this."

Tarq stops me. "Darya, you need to eat something."

My stomach lurches as I look at the food. "No, my stomach is still upset from last night."

"I'll bring you to him," Edith says. She puts her book away before leading us outside. We walk to the other side of the guest cottage, where a small grove of trees offers shade from the afternoon sun.

We find Dax lying with his eyes closed under one of the trees. His head rests on his saddle, and Amelia lies with her head splayed across his chest. He's running his hand through her fur absentmindedly.

"Why are you petting my wolf?" I ask Dax playfully.

Amelia jumps up, backing away from Dax. *"Oh Luna, I just..."* she stammers. *"I mean, I was… I'm sorry."* She hangs her head and approaches my side.

I tug the fur on her neck. "It's just a joke between Dax and me, Amelia. It's ok." I smile down at her as she looks up.

Dax opens his eyes and yawns. "What brings you all out to my slice of paradise?"

"I talked to Luna," I tell him, sitting down. "She told me what she wants." I pause and turn to Amelia as she lies beside me. "Amelia, this is going to get uncomfortable. You're welcome to use the guest house if you want to take a bath and grab some clothes." I run my hand over her head.

"If this has to do with you and my son, Luna, I'd like to stay," she says.

I nod and return my attention to the relaxed Alpha. "Luna's bonded to you, Dax," I tell him. "She wants you."

Dax lifts his eyebrow and turns to me, confused.

"I know you're not that dense, Dax," I bark, rolling my eyes. "After feeling my bond, I can't blame her. She wants to sleep with you."

Dax bolts upright and puts his hands out to Tarq. "What the fuck, Darya?" he shouts. "A little warning next time." His eyes narrow at Tarq. "I didn't say it, wolf. It was the damn Luna."

Tarq rolls his eyes. "She was smart enough to tell me away from you."

It was nice of him to give me credit, but that's not what happened. I forgot about his temper and hadn't expected him to get angry. *I'm not exactly excelling in my new position.*

"I love you, Darya," Dax starts slowly. "You know I do, but my bond is with her, not you." He lays back down in a huff. "I can't do that to either of you. There has to be another way."

"Luna, may I suggest something?" Amelia says, lifting her head. *"Tarq told me that he can show you images or memories."*

I nod. "He can."

She tilts her head. *"What if he could alter your whole reality?"*

I shake my head. "I don't think I understand, Amelia."

"What is she saying?" Edith asks.

"She's talking about how Tarq can show me images," I say. "She's wondering if he might be able to alter reality or something."

Edith taps her chin. "You might be onto something there, Amelia," she says, climbing to her feet. She walks toward the house, waving her hand dismissively. "I need to go look something up."

Anthony stares after Edith. "I think I'm gonna go with her." He rises and jogs after her.

Dax watches him leave, shaking his head. Tarq lays beside me and pulls at the ends of my hair. I stare at both of them, thinking about their strengths. Dax is a competent leader, keeping everyone in order, even at a distance. Tarq is so powerful that he throws himself into any danger to protect me. Now there's another player in the game who is outmaneuvering them.

"Dax, how did Miles get away from you?" I ask.

Dax reaches out to me. Smiling, I move to sit between him and Tarq. I grab both of their hands and fix my eyes on Dax, waiting for his answer.

He purses his lips. "Miles is a strategist, Darya," he finally says. "He's the kind of person who knows how things will end before they even start. When you think you're ahead, you're actually eight steps behind him."

Tarq scoffs beside me, reminding me of another issue.

"I need your help with Tarq."

Tarq narrows his eyes. "Don't talk about me like I'm not here. What do you need his help with?"

Sighing, I release his hand and hover mine in a circle over his narrowed eyes, clenched jaw, and tight chest. "This, Tarq," I say. "This is what I need help with."

Dax chuckles, sitting up. "That I can help with." He reaches behind his saddle and pulls his bow from the tall grass. "Come on, kid. Let's go play ball."

Tarq jumps up, pulling his shirt off. "Now you're talking." He lifts me to my feet and pushes his pants down. "Here, baby, hang onto this for me." He pulls the crystal's ribbon over his head and drops it in my hand as he shifts. Shaking out his fur, Tarq bounces in place. *"Bring it, old man!"*

"Come on, Darya," Dax says, throwing his pack over his shoulder. "Let's go wear your wolf out."

Dax leads me to the flat cattle fields covered in tall timothy grass. He releases me and steps away before dropping his bag. Dax pulls an arrow from his pack, jamming it into the ground. He produces a rubber ball from his pocket and stands still, grinning as the wolves line up on either side of him.

Amelia stands still, watching Dax. Tarq completely loses his ability to control himself. He's bounding in place and throwing his head around, saying things I'm glad Dax can't hear.

"Knock it off," Dax shouts. "You know the rules."

Tarq settles down and stands, ready to pounce.

Dax launches the ball with incredible power, and my wolves take off. Clumps of dirt fly as they dig into the ground for traction. I shield my face with my arm until they are far enough away. The ball is still in the air, and both wolves are running at an unbelievable speed.

Dax nocks his arrow, drawing back on his bow, and lets it loose after the ball. He puts his arm out and slings it over my shoulders as I join him. "That, my beautiful, is how you run the aggression out of that wolf."

The arrow somehow beats them to the ball, knocking it out of the air. Tarq slides as he grabs it off the ground and flips over. He gets back up and runs to us, effortlessly passing his mother.

I kneel as Tarq approaches. "I guess I'm gonna have to learn archery, huh?"

"I have no idea why this is so fun," Tarq says. He runs his muzzle across my cheek, pushes his nose against my neck, and takes a deep breath. *"If he made that ball smell like you, there's no way he'd beat me."*

"You about ready, slowpoke?" Dax goads Tarq.

Tarq growls as he joins them. Dax hurls another ball, and they both take off. As he's aiming his arrow, I pick up an extra ball lying by his feet. I rub it over my neck and through my hair. I breathe on the ball for good measure and return it to him.

Dax lets his arrow loose and smirks at me. "That's cheating," he says.

As Amelia gives Dax the speared ball, Tarq lines back up. "Last one, guys," Dax tells them. "It's too dangerous to have Darya out here." He picks up the scent-covered ball and jams a new arrow in the dirt. Amelia sets up, ready to run, but Tarq's nose goes straight into the air. I hear him sniff a few times, and then he follows the ball's movements.

"*Good God, woman,*" he says, mesmerized. "*What are you doing to me?*"

Dax hurls the ball as hard as he can, and Tarq takes off before his mother even flinches a muscle. I duck behind Dax as Tarq pelts us with clumps of dirt. As soon as it stops, Dax nocks the arrow and lets it loose, but Tarq has already caught up to the ball. He catches it in his mouth and rolls onto his shoulder to allow the arrow to sail over him.

"*Are you ok?*" Amelia asks Tarq.

"*Mm-hmm,*" is his only reply, but I see his paws in the air a moment later.

Dax crouches to collect the equipment. "What is that fool doing?"

I smile and shake my head. "I have no idea."

Everything about what just happened has me craving Tarq. I can feel him breathing me in and his lips over my neck just before he opens his mouth. I begin sweating as I close my eyes, remembering his tongue tasting my skin.

"You coming?" Dax's voice pulls me away from my thoughts.

I turn to him and smile. "I think I'm gonna wait for Tarq. You guys go ahead. We'll be ok." I slide my hand over Amelia's head as she passes me to walk back to the trees with Dax.

"*That was mean,*" Tarq says.

Scanning the tall grass, I spot him over where he was rolling. I can just barely see the ball in his mouth. "You said you could beat him if the ball smelled like me," I call out, smiling. "I was simply testing your theory."

"*It would appear I was right.*" Tarq approaches me and rubs his head over my hip.

"Come on, crazy man," I say, laughing. "Dax won't be happy if we stay out here too long."

Tarq leans against me, aiming me so I'll walk toward the back of Edith's house instead of where Dax is. *"Let's go for a walk."*

Tarq leads me to a cluster of trees beside the creek that supplies the whole property with water. He twists his jaw out of my hand and drops the ball.

"Take off your shirt," Tarq says, circling me.

I stay still too long, and he runs his tongue up the back of my leg. I gasp and pull the shirt over my head.

"Boots."

I want to see how he'll reprimand me, so I wait. Humming, Tarq slides his tongue across my stomach at my waistband. I breathe out a moan as a need settles deep within me. I slide out of my boots and kick them to the side. Tarq circles me one more time. He keeps his nose so close to my waistband that I can feel his whiskers on my skin.

Tarq turns to face me. *"Where's my crystal?"*

I pull it from my pocket and hold it with trembling hands. Sliding his neck through the ribbon, Tarq shifts right into my arms. He reaches for my belt, but I push his hands away to undo it before he can break it. He breathes out a laugh and pushes my shorts down.

I wrap my legs around Tarq's hips as he lifts me by my thighs. He puts me against a tree to push my lips to his and slides his tongue into my mouth. Tarq's growl starts as he claims my body, urged on by my quiet moans.

I open my eyes and look around when Tarq moves to slide his tongue over my neck. I freeze as they land on Miles. He's leaning against a tree right across the creek, staring at me.

"Tarq," I squeak, slapping at his shoulder. "Stop, stop, stop, stop."

Tarq pulls back and sighs when he sees I'm not looking at him. "Miles is behind me, isn't he?"

I nod.

"Fuck me," he grumbles.

I raise my eyebrow. *There's no need to waste a perfect opportunity.* "I believe that is how we find ourselves in this predicament."

Tarq smiles. "I love you." He claims my mouth in a deep kiss that I happily return. I thread my fingers through his hair and hold him to me.

"Should I just come back later?" Miles snaps.

Tarq leans his forehead against mine and groans quietly. "That would be great, Miles," he says. "I don't get a lot of time with my woman."

Miles stays where he is, but I can tell our playing is grinding his nerves by how he's flexing his jaw. "Are you shitting me?" he growls.

Tarq rolls his eyes. "Yes, Miles, I'm shitting you." He gives me a soft kiss. "Give me a minute to put her down, and we'll have round three."

Miles' eyes widen as he realizes that Tarq is the wolf he's gone up against twice.

Tarq sets me down against the tree. "You're gonna pull this off me," he whispers, moving my hands to the ribbon. "I want you to grab your clothes and run."

"He doesn't want to kill me, Tarq," I say, shaking my head. "Let me talk to him."

Tarq ignores me, using my hands to lift the ribbon as he steps back to shift. He spins around to snarl at Miles. But the Alpha isn't interested in him. He's watching me dress with a curious expression.

I finish dressing and lean against a tree. "Miles, why do you keep trying to stop me?"

He rolls his eyes. "Dax didn't tell you, did he?" He shakes his head. "You'll kill us, woman. This curse is the only thing keeping us alive."

My breath catches, making my chest ache. As I step forward, I slide my hand over Tarq's back. "I didn't know," I whisper.

"You wouldn't help my pack if you knew," Dax says from behind me. I turn to find him approaching us with Amelia and a nearly white wolf I've never seen before. "Found one of your strays, Miles."

Miles snaps his fingers. "Get over here, you fool."

The wolf jogs to sit beside the Alpha.

Dax crosses the creek and hops onto an old cart. "Watch the sandy one. He's different."

Miles scoffs, crossing his ankles. "I coulda used that warning a while ago." He studies Tarq and then looks at Dax. "Why aren't you stopping this?"

"Why are you fighting it?" Dax asks. "Everyone you loved is dead. Your mate died a long time ago."

"Don't talk about her," Miles growls.

I watch this exchange between the Alphas with wide eyes. I should be used to Dax's relaxed demeanor by now. He seems to have pleasant conversations with everyone. But these two talk as if they converse daily and know each other well.

"You need some Luna in your life, Miles," Dax mumbles, lying back on the cart. He lifts his arm, and Amelia looks up at me. I noticed that they spend most of their time together. *I'm not entirely oblivious that something is happening with them, but Miles needs my attention.* I nod to Amelia, and she runs to the cart, leaping up with Dax and sliding under his arm.

When I turn back to Miles, he's glaring at me. Even from here, I can feel the power of his emotions. They aren't the hate or anger I would have assumed. Miles is sad. I cross the creek with Tarq by my side, growling at the Alpha.

Miles flicks his eyes at Tarq. "Why are you growling at me?" he sneers. "I didn't ask her to come near me."

I reach out and catch Miles' arm. I slide my fingers down to his hand and step forward until my other hand holds onto his neck. As I rub my fingers over his skin, he slowly relaxes. Miles ducks his head down, and I put my forehead against his.

"I forgive you, Miles," I whisper.

Pulling away from me, Miles gently holds my face. "You might be onto something here, little brother," he says, smiling.

"Don't call me that," Dax grumbles from the cart.

Miles and I move to the side of the tree and lie down. Tarq lays behind me, so I can lean against him. When I reach out for Miles' hand, he doesn't hesitate to give it to me. With the stress of the past few days, I don't mind the hours we waste lying in the grove while the Alpha relaxes.

After a few hours, I try to see if Miles is ready to talk. "Who is this wolf with you, Miles?" I hold my hand out to the wolf. He eyes me nervously, lowering his head and tipping his ears back.

Miles nods his head, and the wolf slowly crawls forward. "That's Chase," he says. "He's yours if you want him."

"That's not how I work, Miles." I wink at the wolf. "If he chooses to come with me, he can." Chase reaches my hand, and I let him rub his muzzle against it. "My wolves are free, and I love them that way." As he steps closer, I slide my hand up to his ear and down his neck. "Hi, Chase," I say, smiling.

He gently rubs his nose against my cheek. *"Hello, Luna,"* Chase says quietly.

Amelia lifts her head, and Tarq rubs his ear against my leg. *"Why is that fool's voice in my head?"* he grumbles.

"I guess Chase has decided to join us." I can feel Chase taking deep breaths of my scent. His whiskers tickle me, but it's different from Tarq's touch. *I don't mind how this feels, but I wouldn't desire it. What they say about bonding is true, I guess.*

When Chase pulls away and lies against my leg, I turn to the Alpha. "Miles, did you do any research on the curse?" I ask.

"For years, my wife tried to find a way to get my shift back," Miles says, sighing. "I loved being a wolf. I wasn't an enjoyable person once I lost that."

"Being a wolf is pretty great," Tarq agrees. *"He's right about that."*

"He's also right about not being an enjoyable person," Chase adds.

I giggle at my wolves. "Miles, we're not always the best version of ourselves," I say, turning back to the Alpha. "But that does not need to define us."

I watch Miles for a while, but he stays quiet.

"Some scars are just too deep to heal, Luna," Amelia says as she watches over us from the cart.

I relax back into Tarq's fur and think about everything again. *Miles had over 150 years to become the man he is today. What happened to him? What made him this way?* I try to picture what could have happened when Tarq begins quietly snoring.

Distracted, I turn my head back to the Alpha. "Miles, will you help us?"

He rolls toward me. "No," he says.

"Miles, we can't keep fighting," I say, frowning. "I'm not trying to hurt you."

"I said I wouldn't help you, but I won't stand in your way."

Sighing, I squeeze his hand. "I wish I knew how to help you."

Miles squints his eyes at Tarq, hearing his quiet snore. "Is that mutant sleeping?"

"He's tired. Please don't do anything," I beg as his eyes twinkle with mischief.

"Luna, why would I do anything?" He grins, lifting his eyebrow. "I feel like we're pretty even. I tried to kill him. He tried to kill me." Miles adjusts for a quick getaway.

"Oh, Miles, please don't." *I don't know why I even bother. These men find ways to keep themselves entertained.*

Miles jerks on my hand, shifting me against Tarq's shoulder. My sleeping wolf jumps into action, lunging toward Miles. The Alpha rolls away, and Tarq slams into the tree. He jumps back toward Miles and stops to snarl an inch from his face.

I run my hand over his hips. "I'm sorry, Tarq. I know you're tired."

Tarq snaps his teeth at Miles and comes back to circle me. He slides his muzzle under my hair and drags his nose around my neck, breathing me in. I close my eyes, enjoying his attention.

Once he emerges, I reach for his jaw. "Did you have your fill?"

"Never," Tarq says.

I lift his nose and gently blow into it. His head becomes heavy as he starts to hum.

"Woman, what are you doing to me?"

"There you are," Anthony says, approaching us from the house. His eyes wander around the group, ending at Miles and Chase. "You're just making new friends, Darya?"

I turn toward Anthony, releasing Tarq. "Miles stopped by for a chat." I smile and hold out my hand for my new wolf. Chase slides his chin into it. "He was kind enough to drop off a new guard."

Anthony lifts his eyebrow. "You do live in your own little world, don't you?" He shakes his head. "Edith needs to talk to you."

"We'll be right in," I say as Anthony walks away. I scratch the sides of my wolves' muzzles while I wait for Miles to look at me. "Miles, will you be staying?"

He shakes his head. "I can't. If I do, I'll try to stop you."

I frown and push myself off the ground. I reach out to Miles and pull him up to me. He looks confused, but I step into him and wrap my arms around his waist. Miles closes his arms over my shoulders and leans his cheek on my head. "Don't let this be goodbye, Miles," I tell him. "This is not how our story ends."

Miles squeezes me one more time before leaning back and cupping my cheeks. "Dax was right," he says, sliding his thumbs under my eyes to wipe my tears away. "You are a true Luna. I will come if you call for me." He kisses my forehead, slides out of my arms, and walks away.

20

My world remains still until Miles disappears into the trees beside the fields. Tarq slides his head under my hand, but my legs buckle. Dax jumps off the cart and catches me before I fall. He holds me to his chest, resting his chin on my head.

Dax swats at Tarq when he growls. "Knock it off. You're not what she needs right now." He begins a slight rocking motion and keeps a tight grip on me. "I told you a wolf that doesn't love you is a wolf that hasn't met you, but you can't save them all." He kisses the top of my head. "Miles hasn't been whole for a long time."

I grab his hips and push away from him. "Would it be ok with you if I keep trying?"

Dax breathes a laugh. "That would be fine with me, Darya."

"He is, after all, one of my wolves, and he deserves to feel at peace like everyone else," I say, winking.

"Alright, you better see what Edith has for you." Dax looks down at Tarq. "I brought your clothes." He looks over at Chase, who's lying down near the water. "I think that guy could use a good meal."

Chase sits up, noticeably cheerier. *"Would that be ok, Luna?"* he asks.

I pull out Tarq's crystal, sliding it over his head so he can get dressed. Kneeling to Chase, I pass Tarq his clothes. "You can stay out here with Dax and Amelia if you'd like," I tell him. "There should be good hunting at dusk. You listen to Dax, though, ok?"

Chase touches his nose to my cheek. *"Yes, Luna,"* he says, bowing his head. He nods to Tarq and jogs to catch up to Dax as he heads back to his small grove on the other side of the boundary.

Tarq helps me back to my feet and holds my cheeks as he searches my eyes. "You really wanted him to stay, didn't you?" he asks. "Even after everything he's done?"

Sighing, I purse my lips. "We can't define someone by their past if they are willing to learn from it." I reach up on my toes and lightly press my lips to his. "Just because Miles' past is so much longer than others shouldn't mean he doesn't deserve the same chance."

Tarq smiles down at me and kisses me again. "You truly are amazing."

"Well, let's see how Edith is gonna get me out of my new Luna mess." I slide my arm around Tarq's back and let him escort me to the house.

He opens the door, and his hand trails down my back as I walk past him. Tarq digs his fingers into my hip and swings me around to face him. I reach up to run my finger along his jaw and kiss his lips.

"Hey, you two," Edith says as she enters the room, pulling me out of the moment. "I heard Miles is here."

I slide my hand down Tarq's chest and squeeze his hip before stepping past him and frowning at Edith. "He left," I tell her.

Edith's eyebrows knit together. "Darya, honey, that's not something to frown about."

Tarq closes the door and steps up behind me. "That's not what she wanted," he tells her, holding my hips as his chest presses against my back. "She has it in her mind that she can help him find peace."

Edith stands before me and places her hands on my shoulders. "I know you are working hard at learning to be the Luna, but I need you to focus on this and let that go for now."

Sliding her arm around my shoulder, she guides me into the dining room, where Anthony is surrounded by books. There are pictures of plants and measuring charts in the texts. Tarq takes over, ushering me across the table from the others.

Anthony looks up as we join him. "How did it go?" he asks, smiling.

Tarq rubs my arm as he pulls a chair out. "Not as well as she hoped," he says sadly.

Anthony frowns. "I'm sorry to hear that. Are you ok, Darya?"

This man keeps sneaking up on me. It surprises me that, although Tarq and Dax wanted to comfort me, neither asked if I was ok. I smile at Anthony's sincerity even though I want to cry. "I will be," I say. "Thank you for asking."

Anthony waits for everyone to sit before setting the tone for our conversation. "I'm afraid this isn't going to be much better," he announces.

I attempt to stand up, but Tarq stops me.

"No, My Love," I tell him. "I've had my fill of disappointments today."

He gently guides me back down to the chair and cups my cheeks. "It's time to lean on us," he says. "You are only the Luna because you have wolves to lead, wolves who love you." He grins and tucks my hair behind my ear. "Let those who love you carry some of your burdens."

I grab his face and pull his forehead to mine. "You make it so easy to love you," I say, feeling some of my stress leave as I exhale a deep sigh.

"It's part of my charm." He tips his lips to mine and sweetly kisses me as he smiles. With a sigh, he pulls away and turns to Anthony. "We're ready now."

"Ok, first of all, we will only get one shot at this." The look he gives us reads as a warning. "Edie only has enough of this herb," he points to a picture in one of his books, "to make one dose. It's aged a certain way and takes years."

So, don't screw this up. I get it.

"Second," Edith says, almost apologetically. "This will only shut off part of your mind, Darya. You'll lose control of your body but still be able to feel it."

I let the information turn around in my head for a while. I repeat the words. I twist them. I just can't get them to make sense. "I don't understand," I finally say. "Will she be able to finish the mark?"

Edith and Anthony look at each other before answering. "Yes," Edith says.

"Then what's the problem?" I ask, holding my hands out.

Anthony takes a deep breath. "Darya, you're going to feel everything she does," he explains. "You'll feel everything done to her, but you won't be able to control your body."

Edith and Anthony are staring at me. Tarq puts his forehead on the table, and I let my eyes dart around the room. I need to look at things that don't have eyes right now. *I'm supposed to have an opinion, or maybe I'm supposed to stop them. No. They're waiting for my permission. I don't have the answers. I'm not even sure I'm thinking straight, but I only have one question.*

I can feel the emotion drain from my face as I look at them. "Is this the only way?"

Edith frowns. "I've been looking since Amelia gave us the idea. Nothing else has even come close."

"Was there anything else you wanted to tell us?" I sigh as I rub my forehead.

"No," Anthony answers.

I take a deep breath and let it out as I run my hand up Tarq's back. He looks up with an expression of defeat. "Give us the night," I tell them. "I'll have an answer for you tomorrow." I slide my finger along Tarq's jaw.

"Darya, we don't have much time," Anthony tries to warn me.

"I said I need the night," I bark, glaring at him. Anthony leans back and raises his eyebrows. "I'm sorry. I didn't —" I start, softening my eyes and taking a deep breath. "I'm sorry, Anthony. Please just give us the night."

I stand up and take Tarq by the arm, marching straight out of the house. Once the front door closes, I clutch my chest and struggle to breathe. My chest hurts so much that it doesn't even want air.

Tarq grabs my face and forces me to look up at him. "What's wrong?"

"I can't breathe. I can't be here. I need to get out of here." My words come out in quick bursts.

"Ok," Tarq whispers. "Hang on." He slides his arm around my waist and blows a shrill whistle.

Within moments, the Friesian is sliding to a stop beside us. He gives me a leg up onto her back and jumps up behind me. Wrapping his arms around me, he grabs onto her mane before hissing at her, sending her running toward the woods. Tarq must feel my desperation because he continues to urge her forward as we ride further away from the little ranch. He keeps one arm wrapped tightly around my waist and the other extended to the mare's mane. It's past sunset by the time he lets her slow down to a walk.

I look around in the dark. "Where are we?"

Tarq slides off the horse's back and breathes out a laugh. "I have no idea, but we're not at Edith's." He reaches up for me.

I drop into his arms and hang tightly to his neck. "Thank you for this," I whisper. "I feel like it's one thing after another, and we are never gonna get a break."

He runs his hands over my hair and ducks down to kiss my neck. "You're not alone anymore, Darya," he whispers back. "Lay some of that on me."

I let him go, sighing, and hook my arm with his. "I have a better idea," I say, smiling. "Why don't we just be regular people taking a walk tonight?"

Tarq lifts his eyebrow and grins. "Sounds crazy," he says, laughing. "Let's try it!"

We stroll quietly with the mare following us. The only sounds come from the occasional cricket and our feet. As we walk, Tarq pats my hand. I love that he knows when to give me time to think because my mind is racing. *Dax never agreed to be with Luna. I'm making this decision for both of us. How do I know he'll go along with it?* I look up at Tarq. *Can Tarq ever forgive me if I do it? Will he understand that it isn't me? That I won't be the one wanting to be with Dax?*

I love my bond with Tarq. It makes his touch comforting and exhilarating at the same time. I always want him around, touching me and gracing me with his words. I love that his arms around me make me feel so safe that I could sleep forever. That's my bond, and I love it. I hate Luna's bond. *I need to stop being unfair to her. It's not their fault they bonded. Neither of them asked for this.* I sigh and roll my eyes. *I have to let them do this.*

I step on top of a fallen tree that Tarq leads me up to, and he stops. "You never gave me your answer," he says, looking up at me.

"Baby, I haven't answered a lot of things. I'm going to need specifics." I smile at his innocence.

He frowns. "Marrying me."

My heart hurts a little bit. "Tarq, I love you. I didn't know I could love anyone as much as I love you." I look down at him and slide my hands along his jaw to latch onto his neck. "If it's a question of do I want to marry you, the answer is yes. More than anything, I want us. Beyond that, I can't answer you. We need to get past what I need to let Luna do." I pull him to me, and he lays his head on my chest. "I need to know you'll still want me."

Tarq pushes against my hips and grabs my face. His eyes have a fierceness I've never seen before. "I will always want you, Darya. That will never change."

I lean down to kiss him. "It would make me feel better."

"Fine," he says, winking. "I've waited this long. I can wait a few more days." He pulls me off the log and slips his arm around my waist. "Come on. We need to find some water for the mare."

We walk in silence for hours until we leave the woods, stepping onto the sand of a small beach beside a lake. The mare walks past us, straight into the water, dragging her nose and drinking her fill. Watching her, I take in some landmarks, and even in the dark, I recognize where we are.

"This is Brown Lake," I say, turning to Tarq. "I didn't realize we'd gone so far."

"I don't know, Darya. This water looks blue to me." He grins and licks his lips, distracting me a little.

Giggling, I shake my head at him. "When the militia took this land during the uprising, it belonged to Old Man Brown," I tell him. "The name just stuck. There's an old militia base a few miles that way, but they haven't used it in years." I point down the bank.

Tarq leads me closer to the water and sits in the sand, pulling me to his lap. I sink into him and stare across the water as he envelops me in his arms. He lets his body heat up, ensuring I don't feel any night-time chill.

"When it's just you and me, I feel like nothing can touch us." I run my fingers over his arm absentmindedly.

Tarq chuckles. "Funny," he says. "I spend the whole time worried that I won't be enough to protect you."

I look back at him. "I didn't think you were afraid of anything."

He tightens his grip on me and kisses my forehead. "I will always be afraid of losing you."

I lean back to lay my head on Tarq's arm and run my finger over his jaw. "Then I promise you will never lose me," I say, smiling. "I will forever be at your side."

Tarq smiles in return, leaning down to press his lips to mine. "That's not a promise you can make, but I appreciate the attempt." We look out over the lake as a flash of lightning cuts across the sky. "Looks like a storm is trying to chase us out of here. Are you ready to head back to reality?" he asks, pushing me back to my feet.

I stick my lip out and pout as he stands up beside me. "I don't really have a choice, do I?"

Tarq laughs and puts his hands on my hips. "So what you're saying is that it's like when you make a decision, and I say no, but you do it anyway?"

I frown. "Yes."

"Oh, well, then I know exactly how you feel."

He laughs as he leans down to kiss me. I tangle my fingers in his hair and pull him away from me after just a peck. I run my teeth along his jaw, sliding my tongue over the skin under his ear and pulling his ear lobe with my lips. "I love you," I whisper.

Tarq groans through his teeth. "You pick the most inappropriate times to make me want to tear off your clothes."

I back away from him and pull the white cotton shirt off. I spin around, waving it above my head. Moving toward the trees, I kick off my boots and slide my bottoms down my legs. As I reach the trees, I do one final spin wearing my cockiest grin.

"There," I say triumphantly. "No tearing necessary."

Tarq stands frozen exactly where I left him. His eyes glint in the disappearing moonlight as he watches me. I swing around a thinner tree and then lean my back against it. He licks his lips as I trail my finger from my mouth to my belly button. When I swing my hips away from the tree, Tarq reaches his limit.

He marches to me and slides his hands over my body. Laying his face against my neck, he takes a deep breath. "Woman, what are you doing to me?" he whispers.

I pull Tarq's shirt over his head as he presses his body against mine. His hands wander over my skin, spreading the enjoyment as I push his pants over his hips. My nerves reach out to him with such force they feel like they might burst through my skin.

Lifting me to him, Tarq takes what I've offered and sighs in relief as he finally gets what he needs. No matter what is happening around us, nothing else exists when I'm with Tarq. I love that it feels like we are the only people that matter when our bodies come together. Time stands still until my furthest nerves receive his attention, and I'm pushed over the edge.

Tarq growls at me and pushes against the muscles trying to force him out, moaning loudly with me. Neither of us bothers to hide our enjoyment of each other. Our voices echo into the forest until he pulls me away from the tree and collapses to his knees. Tarq settles me in his lap and rests his forehead on my shoulder. I cradle his head and slide my fingers over his crystal's ribbon.

I take a deep breath and prepare myself for what I'm about to say. "I'm gonna let Luna have Dax."

Tarq doesn't respond. He stays still in my arms, but I hear him sigh.

"I love our bond. I love how it feels to be with you. I understand why Luna wants that, but mostly I want to do it for Dax." I run my fingers through his hair and wait for him to process my words.

Lifting himself from my shoulder, Tarq rests his forehead against mine. He kisses my lips, then slides to my neck, pulling me close. "For Dax," he says, sighing.

Needing a distraction, I look out at the water and try remembering the last time I went swimming. *It's probably been years.* "Do you think that water's warm?"

Tarq chuckles and stands up, holding me to his hips. "Let's find out." He calmly walks into the water, so I'm shocked when it's freezing. I gasp and try to climb up his body as he walks further into the deeper water. "Darya, wait. Hang on. Come here, My Love." He moves me so I'm back against his chest with my legs wrapped around him. "Wait for it," he whispers, holding me close.

I bury my face into his neck, and my teeth uncontrollably chatter as he steps further into the water. "This is not getting any better," I say in a broken whisper through my chattering teeth. My entire body starts to shake, and then I feel something warm. Tarq's heating up, but so is the water around us. My body stops convulsing, and I smile into his neck. "Nuh-uh, seriously? You can heat that much?"

Tarq leans his cheek against mine. "For you, My Love, I would turn this lake into a bubble bath if that's what you wanted."

I pull back to giggle at him. "Well, now that you mention it..." Tarq scoffs and pulls me off of him. He cradles me in his arms, kisses my forehead, and hurls me over the water. I squeal as I hit the water, expecting it to be freezing, but it's only slightly cooler than the water Tarq had heated. I swim back up to the surface and smooth my hair back. "I was just taking you up on your offer." I laugh as I swim back to him.

Lightning cuts through the sky close to us. "I forgot about the storm," Tarq says, reaching his arms out for me. "Come on, Luna. It's not time to die yet."

When I reach him, he slings me around to his back. Tarq walks straight for my trail of clothes. He lowers me to the ground and hands me the T-shirt. Thunder rumbles, indicating the storm is moving closer, so we dress quickly. Tarq tosses me up onto the mare and jumps up behind me.

"Maybe we don't have to rush back." I lean against his chest and look up at him.

Tarq kisses my temple, and I barely see his smile. "We can take it slow if you'd like," he whispers. He clicks to the mare, sending her walking into the forest, returning the way we came.

Allowing the horse to stroll through the woods makes our return trip take hours. We ride into the yard as the sun peeks over the horizon. I slide off the mare with Tarq and allow her to walk back to the barn alone. Tarq lifts and cradles me against his chest. I open the door for him, and he kicks it closed. We barely reach the bedroom and fall into bed in an exhausted heap. He doesn't even have the chance to heat up before I drift off.

* * *

"Where the hell have you two been?" Anthony shouts, waking us up with a jolt.

Tarq tightens his grip on me and pulls me further under his chest, grumbling.

"Are you serious?" Anthony's so angry that he's talking through his teeth. "You are so lucky Dax can't get in here." He stomps out of the cottage and slams the door behind him.

I stretch my arms and yawn. "So, Dad's pissed." Tarq chuckles and runs his hand over my hair. "I bet we'll have to have the sex talk next," I say, tucking my arm back under his chest.

"He'll probably send Mom in for that," Tarq grumbles.

"Yes, he did!" Amelia shouts, making us jump again.

Tarq rubs his face against the pillows. "Calm down, Mom. We went for a ride."

"No, Son," Amelia responds, irritated. "You took off for an entire evening with the Luna. The Luna, Tarq!" she yells.

Tarq sighs. "She was with me and perfectly safe. Now, please, we're tired, Mom," he whines.

I stick my arm up and wave it around. "The Luna is right here... alive. It was my idea."

Amelia scoffs. "Then you're both at fault. What if something happened?" she asks, changing tactics. "What if you needed us and we were too far away?"

"I feel like a teenager," Tarq mumbles.

I giggle. "Rosalee used to yell at me until I stole her a big gray gelding," I say. "Amelia, would you like a horse?"

"That would smooth everything over," Tarq joins in.

"Dax is right about you two," Amelia shouts, exasperated. "I just can't with you." She huffs before stomping out just like Anthony and slamming the door.

"Nice teamwork," I say, turning my face back into Tarq's chest.

He rolls his shoulder, trapping me under him. "Great working with you." His body heats up as he falls back to sleep. I manage to let out a sigh before joining him.

* * *

It's dark when we wake back up. Tarq runs his fingers through my hair when I wiggle under him. "That's the best sleep I've had in a long time," he whispers.

I slide my finger under his shirt and smile as he groans. "Thank you for last night," I tell him.

Tarq opens his arms and releases me from his cocoon. "You should know by now that I will do anything for you, including, but not limited to, pissing my mother off." He smiles as he traces my jaw with his fingers.

"She was pretty mad." I frown.

Tarq breathes out a laugh. "I'm a little more nervous about Dax's reaction," he says, cringing. "We should avoid him."

I roll my eyes. "Agreed."

"Well, you wanted to feel normal. Did you get your fill?" Tarq pushes my hair behind my ears as I sit up. "Ready to go back to being the Luna?"

Luckily Tarq is easily distracted. I straddle his hips and lean over him, letting my hair fall over his face. He takes a deep breath of my scent and gives me a moment to recall our evening.

We were so carefree. There were no voices in my head. *Wait. Where were the wolves? They were panicking, and I couldn't hear them.* I think back to a conversation I had with Dax. *He said he had to concentrate on the specific wolf when they were further away. Great. One more thing I have to learn.*

Tarq is scraping his teeth along my neck. *Now I'm distracted.* I smile and tuck into his neck, biting down on his skin. Tarq pushes me over, hooking my leg over his hip. He growls, slides his tongue past my lips, and lightly tickles my thigh with his fingers.

I push against his chest and pull away from him. "I love you, but I need to go sleep with Dax," I say with an exaggerated frown.

"Seriously?" Tarq sighs and looks down at his shorts. "Well, that's cured." He rolls off me onto his back. "We could hide a little longer."

I run my hand over the side of his face. "No, My Love," I whisper, kissing his cheek. "I need to get this over with." I roll over and sit up at the edge of the bed. After pulling my boots on, I look back at Tarq, still lying with his arm over his forehead. "Are you coming? I'm sure Edith has some dinner set out."

He bolts upright. "You had me at food."

21

We walk together to the main house and find Anthony and Edith sitting across the dining room table from an angry-looking Amelia. They had been talking but fell silent when we entered the room. Anthony is grinning, which means someone is angrier at us than he is.

Tarq's eyes widen as he looks over the table covered in platters of food. "Is this what heaven looks like?" he whispers.

Amelia glares at him. "Heaven's not full of people pissed at you, Son."

Tarq pulls a chair out for me. "People are always pissed at me, Mom," he says, laughing. "At least there's food here." He grabs some of everything on the table and offers me each one. He stops and furrows his brow when I decline all of it. "Are you ok?" he asks, rubbing my back.

My stomach growls, but my throat threatens to reject anything I dare to feed it. I nod to Tarq with a smile as I grab a roll off his plate.

Edith clears her throat. "We're running out of time, guys," she announces. "I've nearly finished making the blood, and then we'll need to head to the mountains for the..." Her voice trails off.

Frowning, I take a bite of the biscuit and force it down my throat. Tarq told me on the ride back why we'll be going to the mountains. They've planned to set up an area in a field for the sacrifice. He also told me he knew he had to be the one to kill me. I rode the whole time in silence, hiding my emotions. Something about his love is amazingly pure, and knowing what he'll have to do is almost too much for me.

I run my hand down Tarq's arm before turning to Edith. "I've decided to let Luna have her time with Dax," I tell her. My stomach rumbles loudly.

"Darya, you need to eat," Tarq says.

I hold up my roll. "I am, My Love. I promise," I say, taking another bite.

I slowly place the bread on the table as my stomach objects. It feels like sandpaper going down my throat. Jumping up, I bolt for the door, barely making it outside for my stomach to heave its contents. I fall to my knees, sniffling and trying to catch my breath.

Tarq kneels beside me and hands me a glass of something only Edith could concoct. "Edith says this will help your stomach," he whispers.

I wipe my face and take the glass from him. "Thank you."

"When's the last time you ate, Darya?" Tarq asks. "Because I can't remember."

I try to think back as I sip on whatever this drink is. So much has happened in such a short time. *I haven't eaten since Luna told me she wanted to sleep with Dax. I woke up and got sick. What did I eat before then?* "The fish," I tell him, finally remembering. "When we were at the cave."

"Darya, it's been days." Tarq frowns.

"I'm fine." I force a smile. "I'm just stressed, My Love. Once we finish the Blood Marks, I'll feel better."

He kisses my forehead. "I'm taking you to the healer if you don't. No arguments." Tarq rocks back off his knees to pull me into his lap, cradling me against his chest.

I let him hold me as I sip the rest of Edith's drink. He rubs his lips over my forehead and whispers that he loves me. His presence is soothing. I'm unsure if I feel better from his love or the drink, but I'm thankful for both.

"Luna, are you ok?" Chase asks.

He must be at the barrier. I stick my hand up, waving it around as an acknowledgment.

"Dax thinks you're sick."

Sighing, I stand up and pull Tarq with me. "Let's get this over with before everybody climbs into my business."

Once through the front door, Edith ushers us to the couch in the living room. "I hope it helped," she says, taking the glass from me.

"It did. Thank you," I say. "So, how are we doing this?"

Tarq sits at one end of the couch, and Edith guides me to lie down, leaning against his chest. "I've adjusted the blend to be more organic," she tells us. "It will relax your mind enough that Luna should be able to take over, and you will be free to go somewhere with Tarq." Edith hands me a teacup as I settle in.

"Where are we going?" I ask, smiling up at Tarq.

"I thought I'd take you to some of my favorite waterfalls." He brushes his hand over my cheek.

"I'll see you there?" I'm nervous, but hoping it doesn't show.

"I wouldn't miss it for the world," Tarq says, leaning to kiss my lips.

I raise my cup in a toast and gulp it down quickly. My eyes widen as I remember we hadn't told Dax we were doing this tonight. "Amelia, tell Chase to go somewhere, plea—"

* * *

The tea kicks in fast, and I'm suddenly standing in the black nothingness again. *This can't be right.* I look around and hold my arms out, trying to find something to grab. *Where's Tarq?*

"I told you not to subject me to any more of your shameful acts, didn't I?" a furious Luna shouts.

"Luna?" I am so confused. Edith has never been wrong.

Appearing right before me, Luna shoves me. "When I speak, you listen! Now you'll face the consequences."

I sigh. "What consequences, Luna? I'm sorry."

She giggles. "No, you're not. Not yet. But you will be." Luna smiles broadly.

My chest tightens. "What are you doing?"

Winking, Luna puts her finger to her lips. "Shh, lover boy is coming." She opens my eyes and turns my head toward Tarq as she sits up. His head has flopped back. Edith is shaking him, and Anthony slaps his face.

"Darya, is that Luna?"

I slowly turn and see Tarq standing in the black abyss with me.

"Oh good, we're all here," Luna says excitedly. "Come on, class, let's go fuck a real wolf."

My hand clutches my chest as it painfully heaves air. I stare at Tarq as he watches Luna leave Edith's house through my eyes. "Luna, please don't do this," I beg. "I'm giving you the time with Dax. You have me. Please let him go." My words fall on deaf ears.

Amelia smiles as we approach. "Is everything ok, Luna?"

"Do not address me, wolf," Luna snaps back.

Amelia's jaw drops as she stops to watch my body walk past.

I've never felt so helpless. I try moving to Tarq but can't progress through the blackness.

"*No, no, Baby Luna,*" Luna's voice booms in my head. "*You'll be watching from your own corners. If you behave, maybe I'll give you snacks.*"

"Darya, I don't understand," Tarq says, turning to me. "I can still see what she's doing with my eyes closed."

He's forcibly closing his eyes and rubbing them. Luna also controls our vision so much that we still look through her eyes no matter what direction we turn. Tears are running freely down my face. I am about to pay the ultimate price for ignoring her orders.

"I'm so sorry," I cry out. "This is my fault. This is what Luna does when she gets mad."

Tarq turns to face me, wearing every emotion imaginable. I fall to my knees and stare at him as my body rocks, still heaving deep breaths in my panic. I see that Luna has made it to the edge of the barrier.

"Please don't," I beg her again.

She spots Dax lying under a tree, throwing a ball in the air and catching it. Tarq turns away from me as Dax looks in our direction.

"What are you doing out so late?" Dax puts the ball down and smiles.

Luna walks my body straight to him without a word. She straddles his hips and locks onto his mouth. Dax responds instantly by twisting his fingers in her hair and wrapping his arm around her back, pulling her closer. Tarq falls to his knees and throws up.

"Tarq, look at me," I yell. "Focus on my face. Don't watch what she's doing. Just look right at my face."

Dax pushes Luna up and rips my shirt off her.

My heart breaks when Tarq turns to me. My sweet man is gone. The only emotion left on his face is anger, and I barely recognize him. "He thinks he's fucking you!" he screams.

Luna stands up, pulls Dax's clothes off, and slides out of my shorts. She ensures we get a good look at how ready he is for her. I haven't been able to take my eyes off Tarq. I'm sure I'm watching the man I love as he begins to hate me.

"Go get him, Darya," Tarq snarls. "He's ready for you!"

"He can feel her, Tarq," I say through my heaving breaths. "He knows it's her. He doesn't know we're here."

Tarq slams his palms on his forehead. "FUCK!" he screams, his face turning beet red.

Luna looks down, showing us Dax sliding into my body. That must have been for Tarq because I can feel everything they do. I gasp, falling forward and covering my head with my hands.

Tarq's growling so fiercely that I'm close to appreciating Luna keeping us apart. I'm not sure I'd survive this night if he could reach me.

Dax pulls Luna's wrist to his mouth and slides his lips over the inside of her arm. He hooks his thumbs in the crease between her hips and legs, pushing her against him. Dax counters her movements and sets off my nerves now that they are under his mate's control. Luna moans loudly, and I grit my teeth, refusing to make this experience worse for Tarq.

Dax knows what I like. He hits all the right spots, unknowingly forcing me into a release in front of Tarq. Luna laughs and licks his chest as I shake uncontrollably through my tears and rage. She continues to enjoy Dax until he finally releases himself deep within me. Luna sighs contentedly and flops onto his chest.

I roll to my side and curl into a ball. I can't see what she's looking at through my tears anymore. I can barely breathe as I lay frozen on the black floor. I can't look at Tarq. I can't face the hatred he must be feeling toward me. I want to throw up, but Luna won't let me. I think she prefers it to look more like I'm enjoying myself.

"*I hope you liked the show, Mutt,*" Luna's voice booms. "*Now run along.*"

It takes me a moment to realize what she said, but I snap my head up as soon as I do. Tarq's gone. I should feel relief that he no longer has to deal with her, but I know I've just lost the man I love.

Luna closes her eyes and allows me to lie in the dark. I tighten the ball I'm curled into and cry until I have nothing left. *I don't want to feel this anymore. I would rather die of my broken heart.*

When I'm about to give up, Dax speaks, and Luna opens her eyes. "Is there something you can do to save me?" Dax asks.

Luna snorts. "Why would I do that?"

"Because I'm asking you, as your mate, for help." He slides his fingers over her back. It feels like a memory versus something happening right now.

Luna sighs, looking up at him. "There might be something I can do with the original full moon curse, but I can't stop you from dying, Dax. That's not why your mother called on me."

Dax lays back with his arm under his head. "Could you do the same for Miles?"

"I'll think about it." Luna nestles her head back onto Dax's chest, and I watch my fingers trace small circles on his skin. His reaction slowly diminishes to nearly nothing. "I don't have much longer. There's something wrong with this body. It's weak."

Dax runs his fingers over my face, moving my hair behind my ear. "Are the marks done?"

Luna lifts herself and braces a hand on his chest. "They are. You'll not see me again until the curse has lifted."

Dax grabs the back of my neck, pulling me to his lips. His kiss is passionate, and Luna matches his affection. Dax's eyes are so gentle when he pulls back from her. I hate that he's bonded to such a horrible person. "Shouldn't you be taking her inside before she wakes up?" he asks, still believing she is the good person I was to him.

Luna laughs, and Dax sits up, looking confused. "She's already here,"

Luna announces triumphantly. "She's been here the whole time. She and that stupid dog of hers have been along for the ride. I let him go a while ago, though. He's probably long gone by now."

Dax begins frantically feeling around for his clothes. "Luna, why would you do that?"

"She disobeyed me," Luna states plainly.

Dax jumps up and pulls his pants on. "CHASE!" he screams. Luna turns her head to see the wolf running in from the fields. "You need to shift. Your Luna will need you soon."

Luna sinks back onto my elbow. She keeps her eyes on Chase, and I lay in the blackness, watching him change painfully into his human form. It was slow and horrible in every way. She lets out a quiet laugh, and her hold on me diminishes. Unfortunately, I cannot leave my broken heart behind.

"Can she hear me?" Dax asks, crouching beside me. He runs his hand down my arm.

I collapse as Luna leaves altogether. "Please don't touch me," I whisper.

Dax pulls his hand away. "I'm sorry, Darya," he says. I don't doubt it, but his sorry won't heal me. "Chase, take her to Edith."

Chase hasn't had time to dress, so he picks me up and cradles me against his bare chest. He puts his cheek to my forehead as he runs across Edith's yard. Shifting me around, he tries to work the doorknob but gives up and kicks the door. "Open up!" Chase yells. "The Luna needs help!"

The door opens, and something forcibly turns my face away from Chase. I open my eyes and see Anthony. "What the hell happened?" he growls as he lets go of my jaw.

"I don't know," Chase answers. "Dax just told me to shift and take her to Edith."

"Where's Tarq?" I manage to mumble.

"I don't know," Anthony whispers, grabbing me from Chase. I grasp his shirt and hold it tightly in my fists as I sob uncontrollably.

"I saw him shift and run across the fields a few hours ago," Chase says as Anthony walks away.

I close my eyes. I don't want to hear anymore. I can feel my tears soaking through Anthony's shirt, and Edith's voice filters in from the background. I don't even care if she's trying to talk to me. At least now they can kill me, and I won't want to return. Edith wrenches my head and tries to pour something into my mouth. Most of it ends up on Anthony.

After carrying me through the house, Anthony lays me on something soft. A thick blanket is thrown on top of me, and I pull it over my head. I curl up and put my forehead against my knees. *She won. He's gone.*

* * *

There's a breeze on my face when I open my eyes. I find myself lying in bed back in the cottage. I look at the open doorway to the balcony and remember Tarq leaning against it so comfortably. *That was the morning he asked me to marry him.* I roll over and stick my head under the pillows. *Why would they move me in here? I don't want to see any of these reminders.*

Fresh tears leak out as Tarq's words echo in my head. He was disgusted watching Dax have me as if I had anything to do with it. I don't blame him. I remember Luna distorting the details of the attack in the field to make Tarq look worse. I also remember believing it at first. The pain in his eyes when I yelled at him on the buckboard is forever etched in my memory.

I hear the bedroom door open and take a few deep breaths, trying to calm myself down. I find Anthony standing in the doorway when I lift the pillow off my head. I don't care that I look like a child. My arms reach for him, and I'm overwhelmed by my emotions. He slides onto the bed and wraps his arms around my shoulders while I cling to his shirt, sobbing.

Anthony runs his fingers through my hair. "I'm so sorry, Darya," he whispers. I let everything out completely unashamed. I know I had no idea what Anthony was to me just a short time ago, and I'm sorry that it took us so long to reach this point. At this moment, in this bed, he is everything to me. He is holding my pieces together so I don't fall completely apart.

The room is dark by the time I've drained myself of energy. Anthony stayed with me the whole time, letting me soak through his shirt. He never said a word. There really wasn't anything he could say. So Anthony just let me wear myself out and spend everything I had bottled up until I had nothing left. I close my eyes, knowing he isn't judging me for my heartache.

* * *

It's still dark when I wake back up. Amelia is sitting on the bed next to me, rubbing my back. I roll onto my side and curl my arms under my head. Amelia tucks my hair behind my ear and slides it through her hand a few times before lying beside me.

"Have you heard from him?" I ask her as I sniffle.

She frowns and holds onto my shoulder. "I'm sorry," Amelia says, shaking her head. "But I think he can hear us."

I sigh, closing my eyes. "I should've never ignored Luna," I tell her. "He was so angry."

Amelia runs her fingers over the side of my face. "My son loves you, Luna," she whispers. "He would never just walk away."

"You didn't see what she did to us," I whisper back. "The way he looked at me... He meant the things he said." Fresh tears drain from the corners of my eyes. "Next time you try to talk to him, will you tell him I love him?"

"He needs to hear that from you, Luna."

That would be great. If Tarq were here, I would have no reason to miss him. I would tell him that I love him every minute of every day. I would never give him a chance to forget or doubt my love. I would hear him in my head.

I bolt upright. *Hear him in my head. I can talk to him!* "Where's Dax?"

"Oh, Luna," Amelia says, shaking her head. "He's not to blame. He's been worried sick about you."

I pull the blanket out of the way and move to the edge of the bed. "No, I need his help." I stand up, looking back at her. "Amelia, where is he?"

"He's in the grove. He's been waiting for you to wake up." She grabs my blanket and follows me out of the bedroom.

"How long has it been?" I ask as I pull open the front door.

She jogs after me, trying to cover me up. "It's been five days."

I march straight to the tree grove. Dax stands at the boundary's edge, waiting for me. I collide with his chest and let him envelop me in the safety of his arms. It would be easy to blame him. But we share this pain. I know he feels something about Tarq being gone. He cares for Amelia, and she is upset that her son has left and refuses to talk to her.

Amelia throws the blanket to Dax, and he wraps it around me. Someone had dressed me in shorts and a tank top.

"Let's cover you until I don't feel so weird about seeing you nearly naked." Dax scoops me up, carries me over to his tree, and sits down. "She doesn't look good," he calls out to Amelia. "When's the last time she ate?"

"We've gotten a few spoonfuls of soup in her," Amelia says. "Otherwise, it's been over a week."

"Have Edith boil some chicken and soak bread in the broth," he says. Amelia doesn't answer, but I hear her boots on the gravel as she leaves.

"I'm not hungry," I tell him. "I need your help."

Dax sighs. "You need to eat, Darya."

I shake my head, trying to sit up. "No, Dax, I need to —"

"Darya, you're pregnant," he interrupts me.

I stare at him. "What?" I say, confused. "No, I've been sick, Dax. I don't want to eat."

Dax tightens his grip on me. "I can smell you, Darya," he says, sighing. "I could smell you that night. You only get one shot at this as the Luna, and that baby needs food."

My chest starts to tighten again. "I can't do this," I say, my voice rising with every word. "How am I going to do this?" Panic begins flooding throughout my body. I pull at Dax's shirt, trying to claw my way out of his arms. My legs kick around, attempting to reach the ground. "I need to get out of here. I had everything, and she took it all away. This is what she wanted."

Dax slumps against the tree, pulling me to his chest. "I know it's not exactly like his, but listen to my heartbeat." He cups my head and waits for me to stop fighting him. "Listen to how steady it is, my beautiful. Try to match it."

I lie against him, listening to his heart until Chase arrives with the requested food. When Dax reaches for the bowls, my limbs have relaxed, and I'm breathing normally again. I let my eyes travel up to Chase's face and smile weakly.

"It's good to see you awake, Luna," he says. Chase blindly followed orders that night. He had no idea what had happened, but he did what was necessary to get me the help I needed.

"Thank you for helping me, Chase." I reach for him and squeeze his hand when he gives it to me. Dax lifts his chin and looks toward the house, signaling Chase to leave us. He bows and backs away.

Dax pulls a chunk of chicken from one of the bowls and hands it to me. "Edith boiled this chicken. The flavoring is very light, so it shouldn't upset the munchkin," he says as I take it from him. "It's still packed with healthy things that you need."

I take a small bite of the chicken. My mouth and throat don't complain, and my stomach stays settled. I take a few more small bites before popping the rest of it into my mouth.

"There," Dax says, smiling. "That's better, right?" He hands me a few more chicken pieces before switching to the bread. My stomach growls in response, making him chuckle. "That little wolf tamer in there sounds happy. Here's some bread that's soaked in broth. It's easier to swallow and will help give you some fluids."

"How do you know how to take care of pregnant women?" I ask as I take the food from him. I bite the bread, relishing its soft texture and how easily it hits my stomach.

Dax pushes my hair behind my ear. "Amelia," he says. "She had trouble with Tarq. Maybe it runs in the family."

"How do you know it's his?" I ask. My stomach clenches just thinking about it. "It could be yours."

Dax cringes slightly, rubbing the back of his neck. "I refuse to believe it's anything but his, Darya." He tightens his arm around me and hands me some more bread.

"I need you to teach me how to talk to him, Dax." I pop the whole piece of bread into my mouth. My stomach likes the meal he ordered, so there's no need to be careful.

Dax sighs as he relaxes back against the tree. "I think you should eat and rest before we try anything like that, Darya."

"Does anyone else know about the baby?"

He hands me some chicken. "Not that I know of."

"Can we keep it that way?" I look up at Dax as I chew the chicken.

He looks tired when he tips his head down to me. "He has a right to know, Darya."

"Please, Dax?"

"If that's what you wish, but you know my opinion." Dax hands me the last piece of chicken and stacks the bowls. "How does your stomach feel?"

I smile and yawn loudly. "Nearly full for the first time in weeks." I take the few more bites needed to finish off the chicken. "Thank you for helping me." My eyelids have become heavy, and I snuggle into Dax's chest, listening to his heart. He's right, it's not entirely like Tarq's, but it's close enough to relax my mind.

"Thank you for not holding what Luna did against me," Dax says. He ducks to kiss my forehead. "Get some sleep, my beautiful. We'll try to reach your wolf in the morning."

22

Birds are merrily chirping when I wake in the morning. Chase is leaning against a tree with his feet propped on a stump, and Amelia lies under my legs. I can feel the heat radiating from the person cradling me, and I snuggle into it. I know it's not Tarq's warmth, but I take a moment to pretend and hope to heal some of my broken heart before leaning back to look up at Dax.

"Hey there. Are you hungry?" Dax asks, opening his eyes. He looks at Chase and nods his head toward the house. "Let's get you some food, and then we'll work on finding your wolf, ok?" Dax shifts me off his lap and puts me on the ground between his legs.

Amelia sits up, turning toward me. She has wet streaks in her fur under her eyes. *"He won't talk to me,"* she says. *"What did she do to him?"*

I pull her jaw to my shoulder and lean onto her head. "I'll find him, Amelia," I tell her. "I promise I won't stop trying until I do."

She stays on my shoulder until Chase arrives with my food. He hands Dax the bowls and passes me a glass of water. Dax takes it from me just as I'm about to drink some and gives me a chunk of bread.

"Your stomach will need this first," he says, smiling.

We spend the next few hours relaxing under the trees. I share my chicken and bread with Dax, but he won't take any egg whites, saying I need them more. I'm allowed to drink the water when Chase brings a second helping of chicken.

Once I'm stuffed, Dax suggests that my wolves go for a hunt. "This might be easier with some privacy," Dax says.

I reach for Amelia's muzzle and nod at Chase. "Go ahead. I'll be fine."

As they leave, Dax gives me an enormous gray sweater to cover up with and takes me to where they had played ball. "You can only talk to him as a wolf," he explains. "You'll have to picture him as a wolf. Remember him running around out here."

I think of him nuzzling me after the first throw. I remember his nose sliding under my hair and his whiskers tickling me. I brush my hand over my neck, and tears run down my face.

"Darya, I'm not saying that it's not ok to feel something," Dax says, pulling me around to face him. "But I need you to focus on him, not yourself."

The memory of him following the ball I'd coated with my scent comes to me. *It was like watching him crave me.* I roll my eyes and sigh. "Dax, I'm not short on memories. I see him everywhere." I let out a shaky breath. "I need to talk to him."

Dax grabs my shoulders. "This is going to take time, Darya."

"We don't have time. We've wasted so much already."

Dax shakes his head. "This isn't working." He sits down and motions for me to join him. "Can you tell me your favorite memory of him as a wolf?"

Sitting with Dax, I think of my wolf. Tarq's been perfect. He made me laugh when I needed it and supported me when I wanted to fall. "He made me believe in myself," I say as tears fall. "He made me love him." I ball my fist over my heart. It hurts so much as it aches for him.

"Darya, a piece of you is missing," Dax says softly. "He feels the same pain, only he's stronger and more destructive. We need to find him."

I focus on our conversation beside the manor. We talked about how Tarq felt. Smiling, I remember him sneaking sniffs of my scent before I knew what he was doing. *Tarq? Can you hear me?* I wait with my eyes closed. After a few minutes, I open them and shake my head at Dax.

"Why don't we take a break?" he suggests.

"No!" My eyes narrow. "I can do this." I'm speaking sharper than he deserves. I have no excuse. I'm desperate.

I close my eyes again, seeing Tarq lay his head on my chest in the cave. His sandy patterns are vivid in my memory. He playfully told me he was jealous that I held Dax's hand. Given what happened to us, it may not be the best memory, but he was so beautiful and happy. *Tarq? Please answer me.*

I try to will his voice into my head, but I only hear the wind blowing through the tall grass. I stand and begin walking across the field. The pressure in my chest builds as anger and panic take hold. "TARQ!" I scream. My useless tears start to fall again as I collapse.

Dax scoops me off the ground. He carries me straight to the trees and wraps me in my blanket. I waste more time crying out my emotions while he rocks me like a child. Everything inside me says I'm wasting time, but I can't stop.

"Why can't I stop crying?" I ask Dax between exhausting sobs.

Dax squeezes me, leaning to my ear. "It's the hormones," he whispers. "That baby's gonna make you a little crazy. You just need rest." He moves to recline against the tree and shifts me so my ear is over his heart.

Dax's heartbeat is close enough to Tarq's to make my chest ache again. "He asked me to marry him, you know?" I whisper, running my fingers over the creases in Dax's shirt. "It was the morning after I talked to Luna."

Dax scoffs. "That kid always did have horrible timing."

"He didn't know," I say, frowning.

"That didn't change his mind, though, did it?" Dax rests his chin on my head.

I smile, letting out a small giggle. "He asked me again the night we took off." I sigh, and my frown returns. "Why didn't I say yes?"

"I think we make the best decisions we can," Dax says thoughtfully. "All we can hope is that if we're wrong, we get the chance to make it right." He kisses the top of my head.

Thinking about Tarq and our time together, I remember that Dax has always been around. He seemed to have a hand in shaping Tarq into the man he's become. "Dax?" I look up at him. "What was Tarq like before me?"

Dax snorts. "That boy was a mess." He looks down with a grin. "One day after his parents left, I took him hunting. He was so mad at me that he spent the whole day chasing off the game. I finally had a deer in my sights. I lined up my arrow, and he came out of nowhere, chasing that beautiful buck away. I was so mad I shot him." Dax chuckles.

"You shot Tarq?" I say, surprised.

Dax grins. "He was fine," he says, still chuckling. "That's the little scar on his shoulder. You know the rest. I called him a shit hunter, and he broke my leg. We were out there all night waiting for my leg to heal. I got to pull the arrow out of him, so, silver linings and all."

I smile, slapping his chest playfully. "I feel like I'm missing something with you two. You fight all the time but keep coming back for more."

"That's what you do for the people you love, Darya," Edith says as she approaches. "You come back." She crouches, handing Dax a bowl of boiled goose and a plate of soaked bread. "I hear you're feeling better."

"I'll feel a lot better when I find Tarq," I say, colder than I intend. "Thank you for the food, Edith." She nods and backs away, realizing I'm dismissing her. I turn to Dax. "Sharing this with me cannot be enough food for you."

Dax chuckles. "I don't understand how you keep forgetting, but I am immortal, Darya. I don't actually need food."

"Fine," I say, smirking at him. "But you still want some, don't you?"

He laughs. "Yeah, I kinda do."

I lay against Dax and share the fowl, but he feeds me all the bread. With my stomach full, I sigh and rest my ear against his chest. "Dax?" I whisper. "I do love you."

Dax sighs and kisses my forehead. "I love you too, my beautiful. Get some rest, and we'll try again." He reclines back, and with his heartbeat so close to Tarq's, I drift off to sleep when his body heats up.

* * *

The attack in the field plagues my dreams. I can feel Tarq's muscles as he steps onto the wagon. My heart hurts when I look at myself. Then I take a deep breath and catch jasmine, lavender, and honeysuckle scents. I feel my chest vibrate as he hums and then tells me he loves me.

Our cheeks touch, and my chest swells like he thought his love would heal me.

I love you too.

"Darya?"

I jump awake, slinging my arms and scaring Dax. I try to free myself from the tangles of the blanket. "He heard me!" I shout in Dax's face. "He answered me, Dax! You need to help me! How do I do that again?"

Dax sits up, grabbing my wrists. He puts my hands on his chest and cups my cheeks. "Calm down. Are you sure it wasn't a dream?"

I scowl at him. "I **was** dreaming," I scoff, trying to remember the details. "I heard him say I love you. I told him I loved him too, and he said my name. He sounded surprised that he could hear me!" I'm back to panicking. "Why would I dream that he was surprised?"

Dax sighs. "You need to calm down, Darya," he says, looking down at my stomach. "We just got you feeling better."

I narrow my eyes. "I am calm!" I shout.

"Darya, this is closer to explosive anger than calm."

I giggle. "You're right. I'm sorry." I put my forehead to his chin. "He talked to me, though."

Dax shifts my body to cradle me in his arms again. "Tell me about the dream."

I concentrate on the whole experience. I'm sure I was feeling Tarq's body move. *Is that what I smell like to him?* "It was the attack in the field," I tell Dax. "The first time he said he loved me."

Dax sighs and stands up with me. "Let's take a walk," he suggests, keeping my arm hooked in his. He guides me to the flower fields, where we walk awhile. It's nice just to take a moment to enjoy his company and forget all the horrible things happening.

Breathing in the floral scents brings up another part of the dream. "Dax, what do I smell like?"

Dax points to some level ground in front of us. "Let's lay down here for a while," he says. "Before the bombs, there was a city called New York. It was like a town but so much bigger." Dax settles in the middle of the flowers and waits for me to join him.

I roll onto my back and lay my head on his shoulder.

"There were districts of different things, but one was the flower district. You could walk down the street and buy any flower you wanted. Even though it was the city and dirty, all you could smell were flowers. If you walked in the shops, though, it was like heaven." Dax rubs his fingers over my forehead. "You smell like the inside of those shops."

"I think I felt what Tarq was feeling in my dream," I say slowly, squinting at the clouds. "I'm pretty sure I smelled myself because I smelled flowers."

"Did you smell any fruit? Peach, in particular?" Dax asks.

I turn my head to look up at him. "No, just flowers. Why?"

He reaches to run his fingers over my stomach. "Then you weren't pregnant then," he tells me. "So that means that munchkin is, in fact, his. It also explains why your scent has had a stronger effect on him." He threads his fingers with mine. "It won't be long before he figures it out, Darya."

"Until then?" I ask.

Dax sighs. "I will keep your secret."

"I want him to come back because he wants to," I tell him. "Not because of a child." My eyes widen when I think about the curse. I roll onto Dax's chest and look down at him. "Dax, I have to die soon. He has to kill me. How could this child survive my sacrifice?"

Dax licks his lips and takes a deep breath. "Edith's book says the spell will rejuvenate all cells." He tucks my hair behind my ear. "I would assume the munchkin will be part of your cells."

I chew on my lip. "Do you think the spell will work?"

Dax chuckles. "I think that boy loves you so much that he will force it to work."

I smile, knowing he's probably right. "Well, help me find the munchkin's father so he can kill us."

Dax chokes on his laughter. "Always the festive one, aren't you?" He pushes my head down onto his chest so I'm listening to his heartbeat. I feel his body heat up a little and relax into him. "So, you found him in the dream where Tarq first told you he loved you. How about when you first told Tarq?"

I frown. "When he nearly died."

"Why can't you two do anything normal?"

"It's not a happy memory," I say, snuggling closer to Dax. His heat feels good on my abdomen. The baby probably likes it. *It's one of my favorite wolf traits, so I can't blame her. She's gonna love her Daddy. Ok. I need to find that crazy man, and I bet Dax is onto something.*

"Remember I told you this wasn't about you." Dax runs his fingers through my hair. "Look at it from his point of view. He knew you were his mate and was waiting for you to want him. He wouldn't have cared that he was dying. All he could hear was you... loving him." He pauses, giving me time to process his words. "Why don't you tell me about it?"

I close my eyes. "Tarq had just shown me that I was overpowering Luna," I recall. "I begged him not to die, and he told me he loved me." I feel a tear roll from my eye.

"You made me love you," I call out to Tarq. *"Please don't leave me."*

"I love you too," he answers.

"Where are you?" I ask. *"Please come home to me."*

Tarq pauses for a moment. *"How are you talking to me?"*

"Dax is teaching me." I cringe. I didn't think that answer through. *"He didn't know, Tarq. Luna told him just before she left. It was hours after she let you go."* Tarq remains silent, and I'm on the verge of tears when a waterfall appears. The water is clear, and the beach around it is sandy. *"Is that where you are?"*

"It's where I wanted to marry you," Tarq says sadly.

"It's beautiful." I smile and tip my chin out, feeling the mist on my face.

The image moves as Tarq lays his head down. *"It seemed like a good place to face my shame."* The scene becomes blurry for a moment. *"The things I said to you were unforgivable."*

This is my first real test as his Luna. We worked together as a team until Luna drove this wedge between us. Now Tarq needs me to be his

Luna and put us back together. *"What of my shame? What will you see when you look at me?"* I ask him. *"Will you see Luna and Dax?"*

"When I close my eyes, I see you," he starts immediately. *"I see the person who holds my heart, my dreams, my future, and above all, Darya, I see you loving me."*

I draw in a deep, shaky breath, clutching my chest. *"Come home to me, my beautiful man, where you belong."*

The image jumps as he stands up quickly. *"You better find a white dress, woman,"* he announces. *"I'm not taking no for an answer this time."*

The image fades, and I bolt upright. My smile is all Dax needs to see to know what happened.

"Where is he?" he asks.

"He's at the waterfall where he wanted to marry me," I say, frowning. "He said it was a good place to face his shame."

Dax scoffs, sliding his arm under his head. "What shame could he have? She used us. He was just there."

"He didn't understand what was happening. He got angry." I stop myself, replaying the words Dax just said. I realize that throughout all of this, I never asked Dax if he was ok. I didn't think about how this had affected him. I made that decision without giving him all the facts and played a role in his experience.

Dax shoots upright and grabs my face. His muscles are tense, and his arms shake. "He didn't hurt you, did he?"

I smile and run my hands over his arms, feeling him relax. "No, Dax," I say calmly. "He only said some things." I reach for his cheek. "Are you ok, Dax? You went through this too, and you've only been helping me. I want to know how you're doing."

Dax reaches for the bottom of the sweater and pulls it over my head. He wraps his arms around me and holds the back of my head as I rest my chin on his shoulder. Dax has required me to cover up since I asked him for help. At times, I had to sweat in silence because I knew he needed it. I take this action as a step toward his healing.

"I love you, Dax," I whisper.

Dax sighs and melts into me. "I love you too, Darya."

Being a Luna is an emotional role. I've realized I absorb the wolves' feelings, easing their effects. *They love and trust me, so I can't be selfish anymore.* Dax has been waiting for me to help him, and I was selfishly thinking of myself. Judging by the tears running from my eyes, Dax was in immense pain. *I need to do better.*

"Tarq said he's not taking no for an answer again, Dax," I say, pulling away from his shoulder once my tears stop.

Dax grabs my face and wipes my cheeks. "So, we have a wedding to plan then?"

"If I expect him to kill me, I should probably give him something he wants in return."

Dax chuckles and shakes his head, but his eyes flick over my shoulder. "He must've told his mother."

I turn around to see Amelia bounding toward us like a joyful puppy. *"Tarq's coming home!"* she shouts in my head, practically singing. *"He said he talked to you!"* Dax and I reach our hands out to her. She ducks under them and rubs her muzzle against my cheek before sliding her jaw down my back. *"Thank you, Luna."*

"I love your son, Amelia," I tell her. As she steps back, I catch her muzzle. "I will make sure it doesn't happen again. That is my promise to you."

She leans forward to put her muzzle to my cheek again and hums. *"I love you, Luna."*

"Oh, I love you too, Amelia," I tell her.

She touches her nose to Dax's cheek and runs toward the house. Dax shrugs when I narrow my eyes at him. *I'm positive he's the reason Amelia and Bruce have a miserable marriage.*

"That's the first time I've heard her hum in a long time," Dax tells me.

I switch gears. "Dax, tell me what the humming means."

Dax smiles. "Alright, but then we have to talk about the wedding." He lays down and puts his arm out. I lie with my head on his shoulder, turning to him. "It's sort of like a cat, Darya. It's involuntary, but it comes with emotional pleasure."

"So, you do it when you're happy?"

Dax sighs as he thinks. "Happy, relaxed, or comfortable. It could be any good feeling." He kisses my forehead. "I would guess your wolf hums when he's with you simply because he loves you so much."

"Thank you for telling me." I slide my hand under his shirt and lay it on his chest, letting him enjoy my touch.

Dax chuckles as he starts to hum. "You're welcome," he says. "And yes, I like to feel calm. It's been a while." He rubs his hand over my back, enjoying the Luna effects for a few minutes. "So, a pack wedding has some requirements. We'll need an elder, and Jules is the only one around."

"We'll just have the wedding at the cabin," I tell him. "We have to go there anyway."

"Sure," Dax replies. "We're lucky to have an elder still around. They aren't part of any pack and can live where they please."

"That's why the curse doesn't affect her." I begin to put some pieces together. He probably let her stay in the cabin, hoping it would stop her from leaving. "Dax, will you give me away?"

"I can't, my beautiful." Dax runs his fingers over my face. "I have to bless the union as the Alpha. Anthony can officiate the ceremony, though. I have no idea who thought he should be ordained, but it works for us." His face matches my frown. "What's wrong?"

"I can't think of anyone to walk me down the aisle but you and Anthony," I say sadly.

Dax groans as he gets to his feet, pulling me up. "Why don't you talk to Edith about the dress?" he says, wrapping his arm around my shoulders. "As for the rest, let your wolves take care of the wedding for you. You'd be surprised what a blend of love and wolves can do in a short time." He squeezes my shoulders and walks me back to the boundary.

* * *

Edith's house is quiet when I walk through the front door.

"Hello?" I call out.

"Look at that smile!" Edith exclaims, emerging from the kitchen. "Did you find Tarq?"

I release a contented sigh. "I did, and I heard you could help me with a white dress."

Edith hops to me, clapping childishly. "Oh, that perfect man!" she practically sings. "I have missed him! When is he coming back to me?"

I shake my head. "You realize he's marrying me, right?"

Edith laughs and curls her finger, beckoning me to follow her. She leads me down a short hallway to her bedroom. She opens the door just as Anthony pulls on his shirt. He blushes when he sees me.

"Hey, Darya," he says, shimmying past me in the doorway. "Good to see you're feeling better."

I watch him hurrying to the kitchen and lift an eyebrow at Edith. "Something you'd like to share?"

Edith looks confused. "I told you he was proving quite useful." She chuckles, disappearing into her closet. I sit and watch as yards of fabric land on the bed beside me. There are a few white dresses among the assortment of colors. "Amelia will probably want something special to wear, too," she calls out. "I think she would look amazing in midnight blue." Edith emerges with a dark blue silk dress.

"I believe she would appreciate that very much," I tell her. "You'll be able to make a necklace for her?"

"I'll make a few, but the groom's mother will definitely get one," Edith says, smiling. "I'll have Anthony boil water for a bath while we feed mini Tarq."

I roll my eyes. "Do I have any secrets?"

"Not from me, love," she winks. "Does Tarq know?"

"No," I admit. "What if he refuses to lift the curse?"

Edith takes my hand. "My ancestors were on point, Darya." She rubs her hand over my belly. "As long as you come back, so will she. He knows that. Let him be excited." She claps her hands happily. "Beautiful little Tarq baby!"

* * *

After I eat and soak in a bath, Edith helps me dress in a short flowy skirt and tank top she'd picked out. The sun is setting when I finally return to the cottage. I find Chase in the living room, stretched out on the couch. He puts his book down and carries the lantern to the bedroom to light my way. The doors to the balcony are closed with their curtains drawn.

"Alpha wanted me to stand watch until Tarq got back," Chase tells me.

Smiling, I slide my hand over his cheek. I stare at the freshly made bed as he bows and returns to the living room. *This is going to be the longest night ever.*

Falling onto the blankets, I smash my face into the pillows. I try using the memory of the night before we met Miles to reach Tarq again. He had laid down with his nose in my face. He was so playful and happy. I didn't know Tarq was my mate, but I loved him with all my heart.

I reach beside me, wanting to feel his fur. *"I wish you were here,"* I call out to him.

"I miss you too, My Love," Tarq answers.

I smile and relax into the bed. *"Dax told me about the hunting trip when you broke his leg."*

"I'm sure he told you how much he enjoyed pulling the arrow from my shoulder, too." I can hear his smile.

I sigh, smiling back at him. *"How much longer?"*

"I'll be there by morning, My Love," Tarq tells me. *"You should try to sleep."*

"That would be easier if you were with me," I whine.

Tarq's quiet for a moment. *"Are you in bed?"*

"Yes," I answer apprehensively.

"Put a pillow behind your back," he orders.

I raise an eyebrow but do as instructed. *"Done."*

"Now, I just want you to listen to me."

I relax onto the pillow and listen to Tarq describe how he sleeps with me. He tells me how he heats up and wraps his arms around my body. Tarq admits that he buries his face in my hair so I'm the only thing he can smell. He describes how my scent relaxes his mind and lets him sleep peacefully. I fall asleep listening to how he expresses his love for me.

23

Hot waves are blowing over the nape of my neck when I wake. Something pressed against my back radiates heat, and pressure on my thigh has awakened my nerves. My body is tense, wanting more. I know who's behind me, but this won't be real until I see him.

Moving slowly, I turn around to face Tarq. I curl my legs onto his hip, and his hand slides down my thigh. Tarq will soon notice his face isn't against my neck, but I want to stare at him in the low lantern light for now. I've missed his beauty. He even has a little grin on his face.

Tarq tips his chin forward and kisses the tip of my nose. *That explains the grin.* "Are you watching me sleep?" he asks, his eyes still closed.

I smile, putting my hand on his cheek. "Did you watch me sleep?"

Tarq arches his eyebrow. "Yes, I did."

"Then we're even."

His arms tighten around me, pulling me against his body. "I'm sorry for what I said."

Resting my hands on his chest, I reach my fingertips to his jaw. "Sweet man, I will say I forgive you because I know you need to hear it, but I am not angry at you."

Tarq presses his lips to my forehead. "You seem to be feeling better."

Sighing, I roll onto my back. "I've been receiving good care here."

Tarq slides his fingers over my shoulder and down my arm. He licks his lips and tucks his face into my neck. There are many things Tarq enjoys about our life together, but one of his favorite things is

266

memorizing how I feel. Every few days, he wants to run his hands over my body. It's been a week. He needs this.

I close my eyes and lie still, letting him explore my body uninterrupted. Tarq's fingers spread along my ribs. His hand slides over my hip and reaches for my thigh, pulling my leg to twist it toward him. Tarq opens his mouth, exhaling onto my neck as his hand glides to my hip. Heat pulses in a wave over my body, and I moan as air heaves from my lungs.

Tarq pushes my leg down and slides his hand back up my body. Dipping his fingers under my waistband, he starts from my left hip and moves across my stomach. Tarq stops and spreads his fingers.

"Darya?" he says from under my hair. "Is there something you may have forgotten to tell me?"

"Edith is sleeping with Anthony." I was much better at this before I met these wolves. Now I just say the first thing that comes to mind, sounding like a damn idiot. *Just tell me I'm not blushing. At least give me that.*

Tarq props himself on his elbow, raising his eyebrow at me while I acknowledge my shame. He leaves his hand low on my abdomen and gently slides his thumb over it. "And we'll discuss that later, but for now, I'll point out that I know your body very well, Darya."

"I'm sorry," I say, sighing. "I just found out a few days ago."

Tarq bites his lip. He does that when he wants to ask a question but is afraid of the answer. Dax told me I needed to learn my wolves to understand what each one required from me. Tarq is no exception. I run the back of my fingers over his cheek and wait for him to be ready.

He takes a deep breath. "Is it mine?"

I slide my thumb over his cheekbone, gently smiling. "When I first found you, I was reliving the attack in the field," I tell him. "Do you remember what I smelled like when you found me?"

Tarq sighs as he closes his eyes with a hum. "Heaven," he answers.

Grinning, I shake my head. "Close," I say. "I smelled flowers when you were near me."

"Lavender, honeysuckle, and jasmine, to be exact. Why?" He opens his eyes and nips at my hand.

I pull it away from him. "What do you smell now?"

"You mean besides heaven?" Tarq tucks his face back into my neck and takes a deep breath. I close my eyes and let my body appreciate his attention. "Fruit," he answers from under my hair. "What is that? Peaches?" Tarq props himself up again and looks down at me curiously.

"That is the munchkin, as Dax calls her," I tell him. "And, My Love, she is your munchkin."

Tarq smiles and gently kisses my lips but pulls back with a frown. "My mother doesn't know, does she?"

I raise my eyebrow. "No."

"Good." Tarq breathes a sigh of relief. "Let's keep this quiet. If she finds out, she'll never let me kill you."

"I can't believe you just said that!" I hold his face in my hands, laughing at him.

"It's true!" Chuckling, Tarq pulls me into his arms. "Now come here, woman." He rolls onto me, burying me under his chest.

I wrap my arm around him and slide my fingers down his back. "I don't have anyone to walk me down the aisle," I say, tangling our legs.

Tarq kisses the top of my head and lets his body heat up. "That sounds like a daytime problem, Darya."

* * *

Tarq wakes me in the morning with two steaming mugs of coffee. Little Luna does not like coffee. When my stomach turns, I wrinkle my nose and grimace. Tarq turns around, leaving with the cups, and returns empty-handed. He opens the balcony doors to air out the coffee scent before sitting on the bed.

"So, no coffee, but are you hungry?" He rubs my thigh.

I don't want to talk about my bland diet. "What are you doing up so early?"

"It's late, My Love," he tells me, leaning down to bite my leg. "We let you sleep while we packed. Dax said you needed it."

I frown. I'm pretty sure there's something I'd want to pack. "What about me? I need to pack too," I whine.

Tarq grins. "The only thing you need is me," he says. "And I'm packed. So let's go." He leans down to kiss me, and I latch onto his neck as I plunge my tongue between his lips. Tarq lifts me onto his lap, tangling his fingers in my hair. I pull the bottom of his shirt up. *Would this be considered unpacking?*

The front door opens, and Tarq pushes his forehead against mine, taking a few deep breaths. I stare into his eyes and rub my lower lip against his. He starts growling, causing me to smile.

"We need to get going, you two," Edith calls from the kitchen.

I'm running the tip of my tongue along Tarq's top lip, and he is too captivated to respond to her.

"Don't make me come in there," she yells. "I'm getting ten minutes with your man if you make me come get you."

Tarq pushes me back. "I'm pretty sure she's serious."

"I think you're right," I say, laughing. "Let's go."

* * *

Dax silently leads our group throughout the afternoon. We're skirting the basin, moving away from the cabin. Chase, Amelia, and Tarq are sticking to the shade and taking turns walking beside me. Edith and Anthony are bringing up the rear with a pack horse. If I didn't know Edith was bringing half of her wardrobe, I'd think the mound tied to the pack horse was a dead body.

"Where are we going?" I ask, jogging my horse to catch Dax.

"Just a little detour, Darya," Dax says, smiling. "We need to pick something up for the wedding."

"What do we need to pick up?" He's acting cryptic, and I don't like it. "Dax, we don't have time for detours."

Tarq joins us. *"We have time for this detour, My Love,"* he says.

Dax still picks up the pace to stop me from complaining. The wolves stay closer to me as we canter through the trails. We gallop across a cornfield before dropping back into the woods. I'm watching Amelia try to trip Tarq when I notice Dax has stopped at a sharp bend in the trail.

"Darya, come here," Dax calls out.

I slowly ride to where Dax stopped. He points ahead, and I cover my mouth when my eyes land on Miles walking toward us. The Alpha stretches his arms out, and I step off my horse, my vision blurred from tears. With Tarq beside me, I run to him, falling into his arms. He holds me to his chest and rests his cheek on my head.

"A little bird told me you needed someone to walk you down the aisle," Miles whispers. "I told you I would come if you called."

I love all my wolves from the moment I meet them, but there is a special place for Miles and Dax. I'm beyond happy to see Miles even after he tried to kill me and nearly killed Tarq. These damn Alphas have me wrapped around their fingers.

I look down as Tarq runs his nose along my leg. *"Mom told me about your little problem, and I ran into him on my way back,"* Tarq says. *"I should've asked you, but I couldn't think of anyone better to give you away."*

Pulling back from Miles, I cup his cheek. "I can't think of anyone I'd want by my side more than you, Miles."

"You don't have that bar set very high, do you?" Miles raises his eyebrow, grinning.

I pull him down to kiss his cheek and link my arm with his to return to the group. "You don't have anything against horses, do you?" I ask. "We need to move faster than a wander if we're gonna make it there in time."

Miles clicks his tongue but laughs. "It's not my preference, but I'll do what I must when the occasion calls for it."

I laugh with him as we swing onto the little gelding. Miles settles in behind me as Edith approaches us.

"Darya, you skipped breakfast," she says, holding a container out.

Miles takes the bowl from her and sniffs its contents with a raised eyebrow. "So, this is why he's so protective of you?"

"Mind your business, Miles," Edith warns. She stays behind to wait for Anthony as we ride ahead.

"Not another word about it, Miles," I say while we're still alone.

"Alright," he agrees. "But she's right. If you didn't eat this morning, you need to now." Miles lifts the cover and hands me a piece of soaked bread. "This food is the reason Dax first reached out to me. You might say it started our understanding of each other."

I look over my shoulder as I pop the bread into my mouth. "So, Dax asked you what to feed someone in this condition?"

Miles shrugs. "He had a wolf that was having trouble with her pregnancy."

I hook my leg over my saddle horn to turn toward him more. "Over a hundred years and no one ever had problems?"

Miles pulls out a chuck of chicken, feeding it to me. "Nah, I think this one was special to him."

I look at the wolves for a moment. Chase calmly walks behind Dax's horse, but Amelia and Tarq are playing around as they jog beside Dax. Amelia is biting at Tarq's legs. Tarq dives for her front legs and slides underneath Dax's horse, causing the Alpha to yell at them.

I turn back to Miles. "When was this?"

Miles sighs. "When you've lived this long, Luna, the years blur." He holds the bowl out to me. "Maybe twenty or thirty years ago."

I grab some chicken and turn back to my new family. Dax said he knew how to care for pregnant women because of Amelia. *He swallowed his pride for her.*

"Darya, come here." Dax pulls me out of my thoughts. He shows me that we've reached the basin's edge. "Nate and Marianna have been out here all day. There's been some movement over by the base, but that's it."

Sliding from the saddle, I look at the sky. "It'll be dark soon," I say, frowning. "I don't like going through at night."

"The wolves can guide us, Darya," Dax says. "Miles, what do you think?"

Miles rolls his eyes and raises an eyebrow. "This isn't my territory. Why the hell are you asking me?"

Laughing, I bump my hip into him and kneel to Tarq. "What are your thoughts, My Love?"

Tarq slides his nose under my hair. He rests his chin on my shoulder and hums. *Hmm, you smell good,* he says dreamily, closing his eyes.

"You can't trust a damn thing he says," Dax barks. "You're like a bloody drug to him." He grabs my arm, pulling me beside him. "We'll cross after dark. You need to talk to your wolf."

I run my hand over Tarq's muzzle. "Come here, My Love," I say, distracting him by sticking my fingers under his lip. "Let's go for a walk." I hear Dax telling Amelia to take Chase hunting, and I nod to her, giving her permission. We grab some clothes from Edith before returning to the woods.

Tarq walks with my fingers in his mouth until we're far enough away that I stop, putting the clothes on a rock. I pull the crystal out and slide it over his head. Picking up the pants, I hold them out as he shifts, but he ignores them. He grabs the sides of my face, pulling my lips to his. Tarq rubs his teeth over my jaw, and his hand slides down my back to reach under my skirt.

Taking a deep breath, Tarq inhales my scent. "That is nothing short of amazing," he says, humming.

Tilting my head, I allow him more access to my neck as he pushes my skirt and bottoms down. They slide to the ground when I kick my boots off. I look into his eyes expecting to see hunger or need, but instead, I find a fierce passion and love.

"How is it possible to love you this much?" I whisper, running my hands up to his chest.

Tarq smiles and rubs his lips against mine. "I don't remember how it felt before I loved you. My whole body craves you."

I push him down to the ground and straddle his hips. Tarq allows me to hold him down and give his nerves the attention they need. He threads his fingers in my hair to hold my mouth to his but permits me to control our movements. His moans urge me on, and soon his pleasure overwhelms me into a release.

Tarq pushes my hips against him until he joins me. When he's finally spent, I exhaustedly fall onto his chest. I relax into him and listen to his heartbeat mixed with his hum. Tarq brushes his fingers along my side, tickling my skin and exciting those nerves.

"Is Dax right?" I whisper. "Do I cloud your judgment?"

Tarq's hum stops as he takes a deep breath. "You are my judgment, My Love," he answers, running his fingers through my hair. "Every decision I make is with your safety and well-being in mind. You don't cloud my judgment. You clarify it."

I push off his chest. "Your safety is important to me," I tell him. "Why don't we try making decisions together?"

"Darya, you're the Luna," he starts.

"And you are my Alpha," I interject. I stand up, pulling my clothes back on. Tarq groans when I hold out his pants. "Come on, My Love. We still have to talk."

He stands and jumps into the jeans before grabbing the shirt. Tarq steps to me, but I hold my hand to his chest, stopping his advance. I take a few steps backward and find myself pressed against a tree.

Tarq smiles. "You won't listen to me anyway," he says, licking his lips.

"Tarq, focus," I say, trying not to giggle.

"I am focused, woman. Kiss me."

I lower my hand and let him come to me. Tarq gently kisses me, and I smile as he licks my lower lip. "I love you more than I can ever tell you, but I need your thoughts on the basin, Tarq, please."

Tarq chuckles. "If I weren't traveling with a bunch of wanted criminals, I'd prefer to go through during the day, but y'all are multiplying." He claims my lips and plunges his tongue into my mouth. I press my body against him, letting it call to him and losing myself in his touch.

Tarq pulls away from me when I moan into his mouth. He pushes his forehead into mine and brushes his thumb over my lower lip.

"We only have nine days left, Tarq," I remind him. "I need you present."

"You're right. I'm here. Let's get some food and head out at dusk." He takes my hand, leading me back to camp.

We find Edith and Anthony working together to prepare some meat by a small fire. I stop Tarq and point to Dax and Miles. The Alphas sit together, laughing while stripping sticks for skewers. They match each other's movements with their knives on the wood.

"They would've been an unstoppable force together," I whisper, frowning.

Tarq squeezes my shoulders and kisses my temple. "Instead, you'll be the unstoppable force bringing them together."

"I know the little bit that Dax has told me." I squint my eyes in thought, watching the Alphas. "I wish I knew the whole story. The feud between their mothers should not have caused so much harm."

Tarq tucks me under his arm and puts his chin on my head. "Darya, there's Mom, but where's Chase?"

I look around, but then, as if conjured up by Tarq's words, his voice rings in my head.

"Fuck! Luna, I'm coming in hot!" Chase yells. *"It's one of Dax's wolves. I don't wanna kill him!"*

Chase barrels toward us from the woods, followed by a wolf I recognize. He happens to be the first wolf I met.

"Nate! Stop!" I yell.

I try to run to him, but Tarq grabs me around the waist. Chase darts safely off to my side, but seeing me takes Nate by surprise. His back legs slide from underneath him, and he's headed straight for me.

Tarq stands between us to protect me, but it won't be enough. I slide my hand down his chest, grabbing the ribbon holding his crystal. "I'm sorry," I say as I yank it off his neck.

He shifts, knocking me back and crouching to take the full force of the impact. I roll over and crawl to him. Tarq lifts his head, checking me as I run my hands over his body. Next, I move on to Nate.

"He's not moving, Darya," Tarq says.

He stays still, letting me move around him in case Nate is hurt. I run my hands over his legs and his shoulder. I'm feeling down to his hips when Dax speaks up.

"He's fine," Dax growls. "Get your hands off him."

Nate jumps up, shaking the dirt out of his fur. He rubs his muzzle against my cheek and rests his chin on my shoulder. Nate closes his eyes when I lean onto him, scratching his chest. I pull away from him when he starts to growl.

"He's growling at me," Dax says. "He better do as he's told, though."

I frown. "Leave Nate alone, Dax. He's finally getting his scratches." I hold my arms out to Nate. "When he's had enough, you can have him back."

Nate steps into me, sliding his chin down my back. I wrap my arms around his neck and feel tears trying to leak, but after a few deep breaths, my body settles into a calm peace. Nate steps back and snuggles up to my cheek before Tarq approaches to hook necks with him.

I run my hand down Tarq's leg and kiss Nate behind his whiskers. "Go on, Nate," I say, smiling. "I need you to work with Dax tonight. And don't eat my guards." Nate moves away, eyeing Chase and Miles.

"I think you're rubbing off on me," Tarq says. *"Why the hell did I feel the need to hug that wolf?"*

"Our job is to lead them, My Love," I tell him. "Dax told me that every leader is different. Rosalee said that the Luna protected and calmed her wolves. I love them." I run my hand over his muzzle and pull his chin to my shoulder. "Since you love me, maybe it's natural to love my wolves too."

"Well, I do love you," Tarq says, humming.

"And I love you," I say, relaxing against his shoulder and rechecking him for injuries.

Amelia's small stature allows her to squeeze into the shallow rabbit burrows, and she has brought back enough for everyone. We move to a log near the fire as Anthony passes around the meat he had prepared. Tarq asked to have his meat cooked, but Anthony called him a spoiled brat and threw a raw carcass at him. Tarq chuckles and lies near me with the other wolves.

"Your pack is growing," Miles says, resting his hand on my shoulder as he sits with me. "Dax said that Luna can't save us." I cup his cheek and frown. "He also told me what she did to you. I'm sorry." Miles leans on my hand as he reaches to scratch Tarq's shoulder.

Tarq freezes mid-chew. *"What in the name of all things sacred? Tell that fool to get his fucking hand off me before I eat him."*

"Miles, Tarq's not ok with that." With Tarq's temper, I know he means what he's saying, but it doesn't stop me from laughing.

Miles looks down and chuckles. "Just trying to show the mutant some support."

Tarq sighs. *"Great. I finally got one to stop calling me 'wolf.' Now, this."*

"Never you mind. You are My Love, and that's the only nickname that matters." I slide my hand over Tarq's muzzle, wiping the bits of rabbit meat off that his tongue had missed. He jumps up, rubs his muzzle over my cheek, and tucks into my neck to take a deep breath.

"The last Luna had a very different way of ruling the wolves," Miles says, watching us. "Legend says she was ruthless and cruel." Miles pauses as our group begins to move around. The wolves turn to face him, and Amelia leans against Dax's legs when he sits beside Miles. "The story starts with her finding her mate at 15," he continues. "She rushed the ceremony and then poisoned her mother."

I frown. "Was that so she could be the Luna?"

"Actually, according to the legend, it was because of her father," Dax says. "History recorded him as a violent wolf, but killing a wolf is against pack law."

"As the Luna is technically not a wolf... It was just speculation anyway," Miles says. "So here Luna is, young, married, and in charge. The next thing would be to carry on the Luna line. With life expectancy being low, the sooner, the better."

"Only she couldn't get pregnant," Dax continues when Miles focuses on me. "She tried for a few years. The story says she blamed her mate."

I reach for my stomach, but Tarq gets there first. He lays his head in my lap and nudges my belly, so I settle for holding his jaw.

Miles rubs my back in a show of support. "He was her first attempt at a sacrifice," Miles tells us. "She killed him in a ritual that was supposed to grant her a child."

I pull Tarq up to my lips and kiss his muzzle. "I promise not to kill you."

He chuckles. *"And I promise to only kill you once."*

"I'm gonna hold you to that," I tell him, kissing the tip of his nose.

"Now let me go so I can cuddle with my kid," Tarq demands. I shake my head and let him drop back into my lap.

Dax rolls his eyes at us. "Anyway, thankfully, it didn't work because after meeting her, I'm sure she would've been a terrible mother."

"But she killed a wolf," I interject. "That couldn't have gone over well."

"It did not," Dax says.

"She was imprisoned in her tower to await the birth," Miles continues. "When they realized there wouldn't be one, she was given a choice. Being sentenced to death, she could either be beheaded or sacrifice herself to remove the curse."

"She's not the type to care about others. Why would she do it?" I ask, raising my eyebrow.

"Pack historians believed she did it to change history's image of her," Miles answers. "She would be the Luna who ended the curse, not the one who ended the line."

"What were the other Lunas like?" I ask.

"The elders don't have anything written on them," Dax says. "In the days of the Lunas, the elders were historians and didn't need books. They inherited the position from their parents, and the young historian would gain all the knowledge of the past upon the elder's death."

"They just knew it all," Miles adds. He puts his arms around me and squeezes. Tarq snaps his head up and growls at him. "Calm down, mutant. I'm just being comforting."

"Tarq! My fucking name is Tarq!" he snarls, lifting his lips. *"How fucking hard is that?"*

Miles rolls his eyes, and I pull Tarq's head back. "You do have an unusual name," I say, trying to distract him. "Where does it come from?"

"Tarq was my grandfather's name," Miles answers.

"So, you do know his name!" I shout, laughing.

Miles shakes his head as he stands to stretch. He looks to the west at the fading sun. "We'll need to be leaving soon." He nods to Dax, and they leave to ready the horses.

I slide to the ground, sitting with the wolves. "We're going to rely on your eyes," I tell them. "It's nearly a new moon, so it's gonna be too dark for us out there."

"*We're going straight to the cabin,*" Tarq says, taking over. "*That's to the east of here. The militia base is to the west. Above all, we must keep the Luna safe.*" He looks straight at Chase. "*You stay by her side at all times. If you leave her side, I will kill you myself.*"

Chase bows to Tarq. "*I will guard her with my life.*"

24

We gallop across the basin shortly after sunset with Dax in the lead. Miles and the wolves are with me while Edith and Anthony bring up the rear. We're cutting across the side of the basin, so it should be four hours of hard riding.

"Luna, I see movement to the south," Amelia says.

"What is it?" I yell over the hoof beats.

"There's a lot of dust. Maybe a herd moving," Chase answers.

"A herd?" I say, leaning back. "Miles, they see lots of dust getting kicked up."

"Move!" Miles whistles shrilly, and my horse shoots forward, pulling the ground under his hooves. "That's a brigade. They don't ask questions, Luna," he shouts over the thundering hooves. "Take her. I'll slow them down," Miles yells back to Anthony.

I grab Miles' arm. "What are you doing?" He tries to slide his arm around me, but I fling my arms around, stopping him. "No, Miles. We're not leaving you."

"Darya, they're too close. We're not all gonna make it," Tarq tells me.

I know he's right, but giving up one of my wolves doesn't feel right. "There has to be another way!" I cry.

Miles sits up, causing my horse to slow so Anthony's horse can match its speed. He wraps his arm around my waist and puts his head beside mine. "I love you, Luna. We will see each other again."

Before I can object, Anthony yanks me onto his horse and holds me in front of him. Over his shoulder, I watch Miles slow my horse and turn it toward the brigade. My wolves circle Anthony, abandoning Miles.

Tarq drops behind the Friesian and snarls ferociously. The horse jumps forward at a speed that takes my breath away. *"He's nearly reached them,"* Tarq tells me. *"They're slowing down. We'll be at the tree line soon."*

Dax jumps off the white mare once we're within the trees and starts barking orders, splitting us up. "Nate, go with Edith. Amelia, you're with Anthony. Give me Darya, and you two are with us," he says, pointing to Chase and Tarq.

Anthony lets me slide to the ground, and I find Tarq at the edge of the woods. *"They're arresting him,"* he tells me as I run my fingers through his fur. *"They don't seem to be coming this way."*

"If they're arresting him, we can go get him," I say, smiling.

"What? No, Darya," Tarq says, confused. *"Miles is immortal. He'll be fine."*

I frown. "But he was gonna walk me down the aisle."

Tarq sighs loudly. *"So, we're gonna go get him then?"*

"I love that you know me so well," I say, grinning.

"That doesn't mean I agree with you, Darya," Tarq grumbles, standing up and pushing me back toward Dax.

"Did they take him?" Dax asks as we approach.

"They arrested him," I answer.

As I move beside him, Dax looks down at Tarq. My beautiful wolf is lying with his head resting on crossed paws, looking away from me.

"You wanna go after him, don't you?" Dax asks. "That's why he's pouting?"

"He was only here for me," I whine. "I can't just leave him behind, Dax."

"Darya, he'll be fine. He's immortal."

"Why does everyone keep saying that?" I shout. "Just because Miles will survive doesn't mean we should leave him there."

Dax sighs, grabbing the side of my neck. "Fine, but we'll have to wait for them to kill him. That'll take days, and we only have eight left. What about the wedding?"

Kneeling beside Tarq, I patiently wait for him to acknowledge me.

"I will marry you," I promise him once he does. "We just need to get Miles first."

"If you insist we do this, we are doing it my way," he replies defiantly.

"Tarq, I know the militia. I can get him out of there."

"My way or..." He stops to think. *"I'll tell my mother about the baby."*

"Oh, we're going with blackmail now?" I smirk at his tactic. "You're lucky you're cute."

"I prefer ruggedly handsome, but will take whatever stops you from running into swords." Tarq sits up, bumping his nose into mine.

I rub my nose. "I don't do that."

Dax leans against his mare's shoulder, chuckling. "It's great that you keep each other in check now, so I don't have to. What's the plan?"

"We're going to Rosalee's," Tarq answers.

"What? No, Tarq," I say, surprised. "That's a day and a half away."

Tarq's eyes shine in the dim moonlight as he stares at me. *"Hey, Mom, you doing ok?"*

"How is the Luna? Is she ok?" Amelia shouts fearfully in our heads.

I scowl at Tarq. "Fine," I grumble. "Rosalee's it is."

Tarq chuckles. *"She's fine, Mother. She was just asking about you. Stay safe."*

"You're mean," I tell him, sighing.

Tarq jumps up. *"I know."* He leaves to celebrate his victory.

"That's out of the way," Dax says, adjusting his saddlebags. "What's he thinking?"

I roll my eyes. "I have no idea."

Dax ushers me to the side of the mare. "What's he got on you?" he asks, bracing my hips to help me into the saddle.

"He's threatening to tell his mother." I rub my belly.

"Mama Wolf would never let him kill you," Dax says, chuckling. He pulls my foot from the stirrup and uses it to fling himself behind me. "One of his better ideas. You have to admit that." He hisses at the mare, sending her galloping along the basin's edge.

* * *

Dax pushed everyone until well past sunrise. He let the horse and wolves stop to drink whenever we came across water but ran them hard otherwise. Exhaustion begins taking over as the sun hits its highest point at midday. When I lean against Dax's chest, my eyes close and refuse to open.

"Fuck me! Is that a duck?" Tarq yells, jolting me awake. I open my eyes to see we've reached a small stream. *"Get out of my way! I'm having me some duck today!"* Tarq barrels past us like he hadn't just been running for twelve hours. *"Here, ducky, ducky, ducky!"*

Dax stops the mare and drops from her back. After helping me dismount, he slides his arm around my waist to guide me near the stream. He slows my fall as I collapse beside the trunk of an oak tree.

"Get some rest, Darya," Dax whispers. "I'll see about some food."

"Come here, duck!" My eyes fling open as Tarq yells again. *"I promise I'll make it quick. Chase, go that way. Head him off!"*

"Tarq!" Dax's voice might not be in my head, but it's just as loud. "Knock it off and get over here!"

"Darya!" Tarq slides in the mud. He jumps into the deeper water to clean his fur and runs to us as my eyes close again.

"Dry off and stay with her," Dax says. "Quit playing around."

Tarq's dry fur rubs against my skin as he pushes under my arm. He lays against my hip, placing his head on my lap.

"Is that how you acted with the geese before I could hear you?" I mumble.

"Nah," Tarq says. *"I don't like goose meat. I just like chasing them. Duck, on the other hand... I'm so hungry."* He sighs as he hooks his leg around me, pulling me onto his ribs.

I groan quietly. "Dax will get you something to eat." I tuck my arms against my chest behind his front legs.

Tarq curls his head around and settles his nose against my hip. *"Sleep, Darya."*

* * *

When I wake, the sun is shining on my face. Tarq is still sound asleep.

I move my head slowly, trying not to wake him. Dax is sitting near the stream with Chase and appears to be cooking something over a small fire. Tarq's earthy scent overwhelms me, but my stomach still growls.

Dax glances in my direction and sees that I'm awake. He holds up some meat, mouthing the word: goose. I slowly pick my hand up, giving him a thumbs-up. I point to Tarq and change to a thumbs-down. Dax holds up a duck carcass, and I return to a thumbs-up. Dax smiles, shaking his head.

"Please tell me he got me a duck. 'Cause right now, I'm so hungry I might eat you."

I spit as I laugh at Tarq.

"Woman, you think I'm joking?" He lifts his head and wraps his jaws around my leg.

"Don't you dare," I warn him, smiling.

"You smell great," Tarq says, gently sliding his teeth over my skin. *"I bet you taste amazing. Just one leg. You have two."*

"Tarq!" Dax growls. "Get your mouth off the Luna!"

"Aren't we in charge?" Tarq whines, lifting off my leg. *"Why do I feel like we're always in trouble with the parentals?"* He takes a long lick of my leg. *"You do taste delicious, though."*

Giggling, I reach between his front legs and rub his chest. "Did you sleep well?"

Tarq rolls onto his back, sliding me to his stomach, and stretches his legs in the air. *"I always sleep better when you're with me."*

I scratch his chin as he looks at me with his head upside down. "Dax has a duck for you."

"Holy shit!" Tarq shouts. *"God love that man!"* He flips over, dumping me on the ground. *"I'm sorry. Are you ok? It's a duck!"* He watches as I sit up and shake my head at him. *"Unless you're offering."* Tarq steps up to me, licking his lips. He opens his jaws to put my shoulder into his mouth.

"TARQ!" Dax yells.

Tarq growls and closes his jaw. He curls around to look Dax in the eye as he slides his tongue along my arm.

"Wolf," Dax threateningly growls.

Tarq chuckles and bounds up to Dax, snatching the duck from his hand.

I watch him settle across the stream with his duck carcass before leaving for the fire. Sitting down next to Dax, I accept the meat he offers. Goose is greasy meat. I take a bite and grimace as I slowly chew. *Goose meat was much easier boiled.*

"Eat up," Dax says, throwing another chunk to Chase. "We lost a lot of time letting your wolf get his beauty sleep." Dax sees my face and grabs the extra piece of meat from my hand. "I'm sorry, my beautiful. I don't have any pans to boil the meat for you." He holds up the skewer he had used. "Did the best I could."

I swallow hard and grin at him. "I appreciate the food, Dax." True, it's hard to eat, but I'm grateful because he stayed awake and prepared it.

Dax leans over, kissing my forehead. "I know it's not easy, but eat what you can. I'll boil you something when we get to Rosalee's." Dax notices I'm watching Tarq pluck his bird clean. "He didn't hurt you, did he?" he asks.

I shake my head. "He was just playing. His teeth can't puncture my skin."

"He should treat you as the Luna, Darya," Dax says. "Others will see and think that they can disrespect you." He tries to hand me another piece of meat, but I shake my head.

"I wouldn't have him any other way," I tell Dax, smiling at Tarq. "You can't fall in love with someone and expect them to change." Tarq lifts his head with a feather stuck to his nose. He sneezes, and they plume through the air around him, making me giggle. I turn to Chase. "What about you, Chase? Do you think less of me?"

Chase is lying beside the fire, humming. I figure it must be from having a full stomach. *I love you as you are, Luna,* is his response.

My brow furrows, and I turn my eyes slowly toward Dax. "Well, that just turned weird."

Dax snorts. "The art of conversation eludes this one, but at least he's not a shit hunter."

Tarq lifts his head. *I'll hunt your ass when I'm done with this duck.*

I roll my eyes. "If this was the nonsense you were listening to, I understand how he drove you nuts," I tell Dax.

"Thank you," he whispers, kissing my temple.

"*Traitor,*" Tarq grumbles.

* * *

Once Tarq had eaten, Dax had us back on the trail. He pushed everyone hard, running straight through the rest of the day and all night. The wolves guide us to Rosalee's just before daybreak. Judging by the wolves' thoughts, they aren't faring well. If they aren't bickering, they're talking nonsense.

"I need to let them shift," I tell Dax as we approach the house. "They can't go inside like this."

Tarq and Chase jump on the front porch, trying to escape the rain. Chase accidentally bumps into Tarq. Snarling, Tarq snaps at Chase. The young wolf isn't interested in backing down to Tarq and lunges at him, catching his face.

"Oh shit." I sling my leg over the mare's neck and drop into the mud. The wolves are on their hind legs when I make it around the horse. They blur into a jumble of legs, paws, and teeth. Their snarls are loud, and their bodies colliding sounds like thunder. As I move closer, my irritation seems to transfer to my hands, making them feel hot.

"Darya, get away from them," Dax warns.

The wolves tumble down the stairs and jump back up to resume their fight. As they rear up at each other, I reach my left hand out, and one of them yelps loudly when I grab their leg. I pull my right hand back with my fist balled and swing it forward, connecting with the side of Tarq's face.

"ENOUGH!" I scream at them as they both fall back. "We are all tired. Chase, in a few days, Tarq will be your Alpha. Get your shit straight!" I turn to Tarq as I continue. "My Alpha, this is not good leadership, and I'll not have it." Tarq lowers his head as I turn to Dax and jab a finger in his direction. "And you will never run my wolves into a straight-up stupid oblivion again!"

All three look at me with a mixture of fear and pride. Even the horse is staring at me.

"Feel better?" Dax asks, cracking a smile.

"NO!" I scream at him and collapse into the mud.

"Darya?" Rosalee calls out from the porch. "Is that you yelling, girl?"

Tarq slowly approaches, rubbing his blood and mud-soaked muzzle against my cheek before poking at my pocket with his nose. Too tired to argue, I pull out the necklace Edith had made for his mother and slide it over his head. I rest my cheek against his chest as he lifts me off the ground and carries me onto the porch.

"I'm sorry, My Love," Tarq whispers.

* * *

I'm woken back up as Tarq lowers me into the tub in my bedroom. The water startles me, and I jump, practically falling out of Tarq's arms.

"I've got you, My Love," he says gently. I slide my fingertips over the cuts on his face. "I'm ok," he says, smiling. "You should see the other guy."

I move up in the tub and pull Tarq's arm until he steps behind me, sliding into the water. Sighing, I lean back against his chest.

"Dax is boiling you some chicken," he whispers. "It should be ready soon. Oh, and Rosalee made me promise I'd find some clothes after this."

Snickering, I picture Rosalee looking at Tarq's beautiful naked body. I watch his hand glide a soapy rag over my skin. "I'm sorry I hit you," I whisper. "I shouldn't have yelled at you either."

"Darya, your response was justified," Tarq tells me. "We are large, dangerous animals when we lose control. We could've hurt you or my baby, and I thank you for stopping us."

"I'd prefer that we avoid the situation entirely." I look back, lifting my eyebrow. "And I'm pretty sure she's my baby too."

Tarq shrugs. "I might share her with you occasionally."

I giggle. "Where's Chase?"

"He's resting. Dax wants him to ride to the base to find out where Miles is."

I roll over and rest my ear on his chest, letting his heartbeat soothe me. "It's always my wolves."

"We're all your wolves, Darya." Tarq rubs the rag over my back. "Everything we do is because we love you."

There's a knock at the door, and Dax appears with food. "Your chicken is done. You feeling hungry?"

I look at him but refuse to take my head off Tarq. I'm not ready to take my ear away from his heartbeat yet. I don't need food to listen to its beautiful steadiness.

"Give it here," Tarq says. "Whether she's hungry or not, she needs to eat."

Dax steps forward, handing it to him. "You sure you don't want some of that tea?"

"Nah, they'll heal," Tarq answers, shifting me slightly. "Give it to Chase. He needs it more."

"Alright, let me know if you need anything." He backs toward the door. "Rosalee is making some bread for us to soak later." He ducks out the door, closing it behind him.

Tarq pulls a chunk of chicken from the bowl and holds it out to me. He sighs when I don't take it. "My Love, you have to eat something." He moves it closer. "Just a little bit, and then I'll let you sleep."

I take the chicken and pop it into my mouth. "It turns out making a Luna is hard work," I whisper after swallowing the food. "Miles is gonna be ok, right?"

"Yes, My Love, he'll be just fine," Tarq says, handing me another piece of chicken.

After a few more bites, my eyes become too tired to keep open. Tarq lifts me from the tub and uses his heat to dry us off. He moves onto the bed and lies with me, wrapping a sheet around our lower bodies. He pulls me to his chest but doesn't roll over me as usual.

I reach for his cheek. "Don't go anywhere."

"I won't leave your side," Tarq whispers.

* * *

When I open my eyes, it's dark outside. Tarq's behind me, breathing on my neck. His arm drapes over my waist, and his fingertips brush lightly over my skin, awakening my sleeping nerves. I don't even care that he's now fully clothed, as requested by Rosalee. I can remedy that rather quickly.

"Hey," Tarq says, sighing. "I didn't think you'd ever wake up."

I turn over, and his lips crash into mine like he's been waiting for days to kiss me. I try to hook my leg over his hip, but I'm wrapped in the sheet like a cocoon. I pull away from him and look down. "What the hell is this?"

Tarq snickers. "It was the only idea I had. Rosalee made me promise we wouldn't do anything in her house." He tugs at the sheets to demonstrate how secure they are. "I can't say no to you, so I'm gonna need this to be a team effort."

I roll my eyes. "How long have I been asleep?"

Tarq rolls to his back, pulling me onto his chest. "A day," he answers. "Before you get upset, there was nothing better to do. We've only been waiting."

My stomach growls as I snuggle into him. "So tell me what's been going on."

"Or we could get you some food and then fill you in." Tarq reaches over our heads and bangs on the wall. He grins as a loud clattering rings on the staircase.

Chase loudly crashes through the door. "Sorry, Luna," he says, flushed. "I'm just so happy to see that you're awake." He straightens his shirt. "Luna, I would like to apologize for my behavior yesterday. I shouldn't have challenged Alpha." He shakes his arm and pulls it behind his back, but not before I notice a scar.

I jump up and reach my hand out. "Give me that," I tell Chase. He's hesitant but still offers me his arm slowly. I push his sleeve out of the way and look at his wrist. I slide my hand over the raised scar in my fingers' shape. *It was his leg that I grabbed.* "I am so sorry, Chase," I whisper. I kiss his wrist before reaching to his cheek. He kneels beside the bed. "I don't know what that was, but I never meant to hurt you."

Tarq clears his throat. "Edie's book has a passage that says 'there is fire in her touch.'"

"So we need to make sure I don't get pissed again until we figure out the rest of my abilities," I say, sighing. My fingers brush over Chase's scar again, and I look into his eyes. "What's going on with Miles?"

Tarq narrows his eyes when Chase turns to him. "No," Tarq tells him. "Your Luna is awake. I'm not doing her job anymore."

"The militia brought him here," Chase says, looking back at me. "They built gallows in town, and he's to hang today at noon."

"Thank you," I say, smiling. "I know that this is different from how you grew up. I am your Luna, and you are a Luna's guard. As my Alpha, Tarq is second in command to help me and take over if I need him to." I push his chin up so he'll look at me. "When I tell you to do something..." I lead.

"I won't question it," Chase finishes.

"Thank you, Chase." I sit back and smile. "Now, I am naked and hungry. Please take care of one of these issues."

"Yes, Luna." Chase bows before leaving.

I raise my eyebrow at Tarq. "What did you do to him?"

"In my defense, I'm pretty sure you did it when you punched me into him," Tarq says, grinning as I stare at him expectantly. "He broke his shoulder and had to shift for the tea to work. It hurt like hell. I think it scared him."

"Wait," I say, confused. "He drank the tea, and that burn didn't heal?"

"Well, it did, but it left the scar." Tarq pulls me back to his chest. "I'm gonna need you to always be around. He asked permission to do everything Dax told him to do."

I know he's trying to change the subject, and I don't want him to, but I can't stop giggling. "For me, it was the bowing."

There's a knock on the door, and Chase enters with a platter of boiled turkey and a bowl of broth-soaked bread. I sit up, leaning over Tarq for the dishes.

"Oh, turkey!" Tarq shouts excitedly. "You're sharing that, right?" He reaches for the plate but frowns when I move it away.

"Thank you, Chase," I say, smiling.

Chase bows and exits the room.

I turn back to Tarq. "I think I should just hang out naked all the time since nobody seems to notice."

Tarq calmly takes the dishes, placing them on the bedside table before returning to me with a sly smile. "Trust me, I noticed." I shriek as he lunges for me and pulls me over his body, slipping me out of his sheet cocoon. Tarq playfully nips at my neck, and his hand slides over my leg, pulling it to his hip. He growls as his fingers dig into my thigh. Resting his head against mine, Tarq exhales in my ear. "Yeah, I noticed."

I'm unsure how I survived nearly 25 years without my bond with this man, but my life sucked until we bonded. My ache for him is by far the best feeling in the world. My heart is pounding as he pulls back.

"Darya?" Tarq whispers.

"Ah ha," I reply, closing my eyes, expecting him to take me right here.

"I'm gonna need you to put clothes on."

I fling my eyes open, feeling him roll out from under me. Tarq slides off the bed and grabs my clothes from a table. He holds them out to me with a grin.

"What? No," I whine. "Come here. I have a better idea."

"I told you I needed your help with my promise, Darya," he says, chuckling. "This is not helping."

I wrinkle my nose and reach for the clothes. "Fine," I scoff. "Give me the chastity devices."

Tarq laughs as I pout while putting on the clothes and then pulls me downstairs. When we join her, Rosalee is sitting on the couch sewing a button on some pants. She smiles, taking the plates from Tarq as he ushers me onto the chaise lounge.

"I'm glad to see you up and about, Darya," she says, returning the dishes to Tarq. "I was starting to think this one wasn't taking care of you."

I accept the bowl of bread and a strip of turkey from Tarq. "He's annoyingly good at his job, Rosalee."

"She doesn't make it easy," Tarq adds, winking at me.

Rosalee snorts. "Just get her a horse," she says.

Tarq perks up. "I heard she got you a big gray gelding."

"I bet she didn't tell you why she did, though," Rosalee says.

A mischievous grin slides across Tarq's face. "No, Miss Rosalee, she did not tell me why she got you a horse."

"Darya's always been an enigma. She'd disappear and show back up as if no time had passed," Rosalee tells him. "I never knew what she was up to or where she'd gone. I'd just find her asleep in her bed. After she'd been gone for six months, I woke up to eight damn horses in my living room." She motions her hand to the room. "Just hanging out down here. Shitting all over. Scared the hell out of those horses screaming at her."

I giggle. "Rosalee scared more shit out of them." Tarq pulls my hip to play at spanking me but laughs with me.

"Yes, well, she took those horses away and returned with Old Blue. She finally told me what she'd been doing for the past few years." Rosalee turns back to her sewing.

"So if I just get her a horse, she'll behave?" Tarq asks, smirking.

Dax walks through the front door and sits on the couch beside Rosalee. "Nah," he grumbles. "She'll settle down once she has a family of her own." He winks at me, stealing some of my turkey.

I blow my lips out and snuggle into Tarq's chest. "I don't need to be here while you plan how to tame me."

As Rosalee recalls a few more stories from my childhood, I continue to pop pieces of bread into my mouth. Hearing my wolves laughing freely after everything they've endured lately is refreshing. When my stomach is full, my eyes begin to droop. Tarq reclines in the chaise with me and lets his body heat up. I blissfully sigh as I drift off to sleep in his arms.

25

The militia built their gallows right outside of Rosalee's café. They might have put them there because it's nearly the center of town or for the abundant space, but I'm betting it was to intimidate me if I ever came back. The militia is motivated by hate. I'd been stealing from them for two years before I pissed them off enough to send their top tracker after me. I met Anthony two weeks later.

"Luna, come here," Chase whispers. "People are looking at you." He pulls me to his chest and adjusts my cloak. Chase is shorter than Tarq, so resting my head on his shoulder with my forehead against his neck is easy. "You've got some nosy people in your town," he hisses.

"Why are they even here?" I ask, irritated.

"There aren't even snacks," Chase says, annoyed. "What kind of shit town doesn't have snacks for a hanging?"

I'm not even sure what to say. I've never been to a hanging. Why would there be snacks? *Hang the hell on.* "Just how many hangings have you been to?" I ask.

Chase peeks into my cloak, smiling. "I don't know. They've hung Miles six or seven times, so at least that many. You'd think they hung him for fun."

I raise my eyebrow. "You disturb me."

"That'll pass," Chase says, laughing.

I look down at my hands. They are against Chase's skin, and he's as relaxed as possible. He is happy and content with his arm around his

Luna, waiting for his old Alpha to be hung. I could see Chase being someone I'd team up with in my criminal life.

"Here they come, Luna," Chase says, pulling my attention back.

I watch soldiers lead Miles out with two other men. His hands are bound behind him, and blood runs from the corner of his mouth. *I wonder what's already healed.* Chase seems to know my thoughts aren't pleasant because he squeezes my shoulder, leaning his chin against my forehead.

One soldier announces the death sentence, as another slips the nooses over their heads. They pull the first lever, and my chest tightens as the man hits the end of his rope. Miles is the last of the three men, and I'm already panicking after the first one. Chase begins to growl as the soldier approaches the second lever. Looking up at him, I notice my hands are hot.

Tarq rushes toward us, pulling me off Chase and wrapping me in his arms. "Put them on me," he whispers. He angles me against his chest, so I can still see Miles. I don't want to burn him, but Miles nods, and something in me knows they're right. My hands slip under Tarq's shirt. As the soldier pulls the second lever, Tarq begins to hum.

I can't look away. My wolf is about to have his neck broken for the crime of riding with me, and all I can do is stand here and watch. Miles winks at me before they pull his lever. Right after it happens, Tarq pulls me through an alley and straight out of town.

"That was horrible," I say, pushing my hood off. I pull Tarq's shirt up. "Are you ok? We should get you some tea." He lets me inspect his skin thoroughly before grabbing my chin and looking into my eyes.

"Darya," Tarq says. "It doesn't hurt me." He cups my cheeks and smiles. "It actually feels pretty good." He pulls me to his chest and looks around. "Hey, is that your schoolhouse? Come on. Show me."

I want to talk about how I didn't burn the man I love, but that's not his style. He's done and wants to have some fun. *I wouldn't have him any other way.* Maybe we'll talk about it someday, but today, we're going to school. I smile as he steps away and leads me to the steepled building behind me.

"Aw, it's cute," Tarq says, ushering me into the one-room educational prison.

I step forward as he closes the door. "Sure, if your teacher didn't smack you with a ruler any time you stepped out of line," I tell him quietly. I run my fingers over the desks as I step through the center of the building. Untying the cloak, I sling it over the desk in the front row.

My fingers slide over the clean chalkboard before I turn back to Tarq. He's leaning against the door, watching me. His grin tells me he's not thinking child-appropriate thoughts. I walk to the other side of the room, watching his eyes follow me.

"Who taught you?" I ask him.

"Dax was my teacher," Tarq answers without missing a beat.

Sitting on the corner of the teacher's desk, I cross my legs and lean back to rest on my hands. "I bet you weren't a perfect student," I say, grinning.

Tarq licks his lips. "It's hard to get me to focus on things that don't interest me." His knuckles are white as he grips the door handle.

I slide to the desk's center, facing Tarq, and slowly let my knees spread. "You probably just needed different study material." His eyes leave mine to watch my fingers slide up my thighs, pulling my skirt.

"Yep, that's what it was," he says, locking the door and marching toward me.

Tarq's on me so fast I barely have time to react. He pulls me to him by the back of my head and hip. I attempt to remove his clothes as he slowly massages his tongue over mine, and he backs away once his pants are out of my way.

"My study material is overdressed," Tarq growls as he pulls my shirt over my head. He slides his hands up my thighs and under my skirt, lifting me enough to remove my underpants before releasing me. Nuzzling into my neck, Tarq takes a deep breath and grabs my hips, pulling me onto him.

My teacher always told me to speak up. He'd be proud as I call out to Tarq while he satisfies my nerves' cravings. He's a perfect fit, and it's like he's coming home. My body celebrates his attention as his hands gently roam over my skin. His fingers pull at my hips, and his tongue matches his body's movements in my mouth.

I grab onto the desk as Tarq uses his weight to put more pressure on my hips, making them tip just right. I cry out as my muscles clamp down on him. He leans back down on me, joining in my release. The walls shake from his deep growl until he's spent.

Tarq pulls me upright, allowing me to hang breathlessly from him. He tucks into my neck and takes a deep breath before slowly sliding his tongue over my skin. I don't need Tarq to tell me that he loves me. I feel it in every way he appreciates me, including when he enjoys how I taste.

"I don't believe there's anything more I could teach you today," I whisper, smiling.

He groans quietly. "You can school me any time you want."

"Luna, I need Tarq's help," Chase says, surprising me. *"There were too many to risk stopping them. They buried Miles."*

Pulling away from Tarq, I look into his eyes and smile. I know he has an eternal craving for me, but it never shows in his eyes. He always looks upon me with a peaceful love that makes my core ache for him.

"There are no words I could use to describe how much I love you," I whisper.

Tarq wets his lips and smiles, kissing me softly. "Do you love me?"

"Yes," I answer, slightly offended that he'd ask while still inside me.

"That's all I need to hear," he says, holding my jaw. "The rest I can feel."

Groaning, I wrap my arms tightly around his neck and nibble on his earlobe. "That's good, My Love, because I need to get you out of those pants."

Tarq pulls back and smiles as he slides his tongue over the edge of his teeth. "Have another lesson for me, teacher?"

He leans forward for my lips, but I catch his face before I get lost in his kisses. "Chase needs your help digging up Miles."

"Seriously?" Tarq frowns.

"I'm sorry." I flash him some pouting lips. "The sooner we get him out, the sooner he'll heal, and we can get out of here."

Tarq steps back, pulling his pants off. "You are gonna owe me for this."

"I look forward to paying that debt," I say, jumping off the desk to pull my clothes on. I lean against the desk as Tarq collects the clothes I had thrown around the room. Watching him do things is generally enjoyable but considerably more exciting when he's naked.

I accept the clothes with a smile as he drops them in my hands. Tarq kisses me one last time before I pull the necklace off his neck. He steps back as he shifts and then puts his front paws on the desk. Tucking his nose under my hair, Tarq rests his chin on my shoulder.

I watch his eyes close as he takes a deep breath of my scent. "So, My Love, will we be going to get Miles?"

Tarq takes one more deep breath. *"Yeah, I guess. Let's go do that,"* he grumbles. He drops to the floor and shakes out his fur. *"Come get the door. It'd probably be rude to break it down after we defiled their schoolhouse."*

Laughing, I follow him to the door and open it enough to ensure no one is around before letting him out. "Where are you headed?"

Tarq tilts his head. *"Me? Oh no, My Love. This little trip is a 'we' thing."* He chuckles, heading toward the trees. *"Come on, Darya. We need a lookout."*

I walk with him along the edge of the woods to the town's cemetery. We see Chase lying on top of a fresh pile of dirt from the hill overlooking the grounds. "This is a good vantage point," I tell Tarq. "I'll be able to see if anyone is coming from any direction."

Tarq looks down the hill but then turns back to me. He pushes my shirt up with his nose and slides his tongue over my belly.

I raise my eyebrow. "You're getting weird."

"And you're getting more delicious." Tarq jogs away, chuckling.

I sit on a large rock and watch over the graveyard while Tarq and Chase quickly dig up the grave. This town has never cared about the dead, so no one disrupts their grave robbing.

Once they have Miles, Tarq calls to me. *"Are we still good? I'm gonna need to shift to carry him."*

I focus on Tarq, and my chest tightens as it does every time I look at him. *"Can you hear me? It's still clear."*

"I will always hear you," Tarq says. *"Your voice starts my day, catches my breath, and eases my ache. It makes me need your touch, want your body, and desire your mind."* He sits calmly by the grave, covered in dirt, as I grab my chest.

"You know I can hear you, right?" Chase asks, ruining our moment.

Tarq chuckles and jogs up the hill.

* * *

Later that evening, Chase gives Rosalee a hand in the kitchen while Dax sits beside me. He's reclined with his head back, running his fingers through my hair. Tarq is lying with his head in my lap, humming.

"How long will it take to get to the cabin from here?" I look from Tarq to Dax.

"If you let me push everyone, half a day," Dax answers. "If not, it'll be a full day."

Looking down at Tarq, I trace the cuts still on his face. "No," I tell him. "You'll not be pushing them like that again."

Tarq catches my hand as it sweeps over his cheek and kisses it. "We will do as you wish, My Love."

"I wish you to be safe, so we'll not be pushing you again," I answer him firmly, but look to Dax so he knows my response is directed at him also.

Dax rolls his eyes. "Then the earliest we'll be able to do the wedding is the 28th. The day before the... the thing, but it'll give you time to consider your vows."

"My vows?" I spout louder than I intend. "I have to write my own vows?"

Tarq smiles. "It's pack custom, Darya."

I frown. "So you've already written yours?"

"I've known what I would say to you on our wedding day since I knew you were mine."

"So they should be good then?" I raise my eyebrow, challenging him.

Tarq's cheeks turn pink. "I think they are."

I laugh and tug on his hair. "Honey, you could say, 'Get over here and get naked,' and I'd be happy!"

Rosalee has left us alone until now. She bangs her spoon loudly against her pan and turns to me, looking quite cross. "That is not how we talk in this house, young lady!"

"Rosalee, there's a dead immortal in my bed upstairs. I think we've taken this house in a new direction today," I say, giggling.

"That is no excuse." She continues to glare at me until I drop my eyes.

"Yes, ma'am," I mumble.

She returns to her cooking, and Chase brings me some soaked bread.

"Thank you, Chase," I say as he hands it to me. He bows and returns to the kitchen.

Tarq opens his mouth and begs for some of my bread. I shake my head at him. "Bottomless pit." I still feed him a piece because I have yet to learn how to say no to him.

"I could always try something a little heartier," Tarq says, rolling over. He bites down on my thigh, making me gasp.

"Wolf," Dax growls.

Tarq stares back at Dax as he slides his tongue up my thigh.

"TARQ!" Rosalee yells, making him jump off me.

"Yes, ma'am?" he squeaks, sounding scared.

Rosalee is red in the face. "Get your tongue off my great niece," she snarls.

"Yes, ma'am," Tarq says, crawling to put his head on my shoulder. "Save me," he whispers. "She's scary."

"There, there, my monstrous wolf. I will protect you from the little old lady." I laugh, wrapping my arms around him and noisily kissing his head.

Sighing, Tarq relaxes into me. "My hero," he whispers. He snuggles into my neck and takes a deep breath, triggering his hum. Tarq wraps his arms around my shoulders and slides his teeth along my neck. I quietly groan as I tilt my head, allowing him more access.

"What did I tell you?" Rosalee shouts from across the room.

Tarq jumps off the couch, pulling his shirt off. "Yes, ma'am. I was just going for a run." He hands me his shirt and leans down for a kiss. "I'll be back soon, My Love."

I slide my fingers over his jaw as he pulls away. "Please don't go far."

"Yes, My Love." Tarq smiles before darting for the back door. Moments after I hear the door close, he calls back out to me. *"You taste so damn good."* I shake my head and turn back to my bread.

I spend the next few hours watching Chase learn to make a few dishes from Rosalee. I rub Dax's hands as I usually rub Tarq's pads when we stop for the night on the trail. Being the Alpha for so long, Dax seemed off-limits for most. It's nice to see him enjoying simple pleasures just as much as Tarq.

True to his word, Tarq isn't gone long. He returns with a peace offering of catfish from the pond. I grab the crystal from the post he'd hung it on, but he declines it. *"It makes it easier to follow Rosalee's rules this way,"* Tarq says, then starts chuckling. *"And she won't be able to hear all the naughty things I want to say to you."*

"You have to kill me in four days," I say, frowning. "Maybe you could whisper sweet nothings instead."

"I'll consider your suggestion."

Tarq jogs to the living room, leaving me to deliver the fish. As I walk by, he jumps on the couch and lays his head on a pillow.

"Uh-uh, Tarq," Rosalee says, brandishing her knife. "No wolves on the couch."

Tarq slides his ears back and hangs his head. *"Oh,"* he whines.

Stopping, I lean on the counter to watch his display with a smile. Dax smacks his shoulder.

Rosalee sighs. "Alright, just this one time." She points her knife at him. "You better behave."

Tarq pushes Dax with his paw, sending him halfway across the couch.

He moves to take over the extra cushion and rolls onto his back, trying to catch Dax's arm in his mouth. Dax looks down at him, annoyed.

"Tarq," I say, giggling.

Tarq flips over and moves away from Dax. *"He was checking my teeth."*

"I could've told you that they work just fine, My Love," I tell him, grinning. *"Now quit testing Rosalee before you get us kicked out of here."*

"You know she loves me," Tarq says, letting me hear his smile.

"Tarq brought these for you as a peace offering for his behavior earlier." I wink at him and turn to Rosalee, holding up the fish.

She pulls out a large, flat pan and takes them from me. "He kept his promise and brought you home," she says, smiling. "He can get in trouble a few more times before he'll need to apologize."

"He's a good man," I say, grinning.

Rosalee stops her food prep and sighs. "They tell me you should survive the sacrifice," she says. "Dax told me that Tarq has to be the one to kill you. He must truly believe it will work."

"He does," I reply, turning to watch him lounge on the couch.

"And you don't?" she whispers.

I turn back to Rosalee and pat her hand. "I believe that man loves me so much that he will make it work even if it doesn't want to."

Rosalee sets a plate in front of me with bread smothered in cheese and nods toward the men.

"I wish you could come to the wedding." I take the rag she used to hold the hot plate.

"Only the officiant is allowed at a pack wedding, Darya," she says with an understanding smile. "You are a part of their world now, and they are your life. You'll be in good company."

I frown as she pushes me toward the couch where Tarq is trying to behave, but Dax is annoying him by messing with his paws. I place the plate on the table and sit between them, glaring at Dax.

"What?" he snaps. "There's nothing else to do." He grabs a chunk of bread and throws his arm around me.

Tarq sighs, fluffing his lips. *"Well, that's not gonna feed me,"* he grumbles.

As if she can hear him, Rosalee holds up a de-feathered duck carcass and calls Tarq's name. "I would like a deer, please, before you leave."

Tarq lifts his head. *What the fuck? Is that...? Holy shit!*

Rosalee lifts her eyebrow. "Not on my couch."

"Yes, ma'am!" Tarq jumps off the couch, licking his lips to catch the drool trying to sneak out. *"Darya, please tell her to give me the duck."* He's tip-toeing toward Rosalee with his head high and ears pricked forward.

"Rosalee, he'll get you a deer," I tell her, giggling. "He really likes duck, though."

Rosalee tosses the duck to Tarq, and I walk with him to the back door. I sit on the rocking chair while he eats, pondering my vows. *How will I come up with words that are good enough in two days?* I scrunch my face and look down at Tarq.

This man is perfect and beautiful at everything he does. I raise my eyebrow—*everything but eating duck.* The size difference is almost comical. Tarq could eat the duck in two bites, but he's taking his time. He spits out some of the bones while others are pulverized with his teeth. I grin when I see his nose covered with mashed duck meat. *Ok. Maybe not perfect, but he's close enough for me.*

He deserves flawless vows. I can't remember ever being as happy as I am when I wake beside Tarq's furry muzzle or underneath his chest. He's supported me since the moment we met. It's been nothing short of miraculous. He's mine, and I need him.

Tarq slides his nose over my arm as my chest starts to ache. His head is wet from rinsing in the rain barrel.

"You seem lost in thought," he says, licking my arm. *"What's going on in there?"*

I smile and scratch his neck. "I was just thinking about you and my vows."

"It's just words, Darya. No one is gonna write them in a book." He sits down, putting his paw in my lap.

"You deserve so much more than just an I love you." I sigh as I rub his pads, ready to admit my feelings. "With everything we've been through, you deserve more than me."

Tarq snatches his paw from my hand and sticks his nose to my pocket. *"Give me that."* I pull the crystal out and slide the ribbon over his head. "You are so much more than you'll ever know," he says, pulling me from the rocking chair and holding me to his chest. "You're my reason for being. You are all the parts of me that were missing." He steps back and holds my face, making me look into his eyes. "I deserve you. Nothing more, nothing less. I deserve you because you are all I want and need."

I cup his cheeks and pull his forehead to mine. "You are so much better at this than I am."

Tarq smiles, breathing out a laugh. "It's easier for me, Darya. I've been waiting for you since the day I was born. You've always been in my heart." He reaches back for the pants he'd left out here earlier. He pulls them on and then scoops me into his arms. Tarq sits on the rocking chair, putting his feet on the railing to rock me. "You know, there's only one thing I want to hear."

I nuzzle into his shoulder and look up at him. "What's that?"

Tarq frowns. "I want to hear you breathe again after I kill you."

His answer takes my breath away. No response to that will ever be good enough. He leans down to rest his forehead on mine and moves his hand to my belly.

"I love you. Both of you," Tarq whispers.

I slide my hand over his face. "I love you too."

* * *

The sun is just rising when Dax slams the backdoor into the railing, waking us. "Let's go, you two," he growls. "Miles is up."

Tarq takes his legs off the railing. "Yeah, we're coming," he says. "I need to get Rosalee her deer." He looks down at me as Dax closes the door.

I nuzzle my face into his chest. "I'll write you a note to get out of class." I snicker when I feel him growing against my hip. "Too soon for schoolhouse humor?"

Tarq lifts me off his lap and carries me to the railing. He growls, cupping my cheeks and lifting my face to kiss me deeply. "Yes," he whispers, leaning his forehead against mine.

"Now!" Dax bellows, making us jump. He leaves without closing the door.

Tarq smiles. "I feel like we just got caught by the teacher."

"He was your teacher," I say against his lips. "Not mine." I slide my teeth along his jaw. Tarq's fingers dig into my hip as I run my tongue down his neck. He gasps when I bite down on his collarbone.

"DARYA!" Dax leans against the door frame, crossing his arms.

I peek over Tarq's shoulder and see Dax's glare. "I think we're both in trouble now," I whisper.

Tarq kisses me as he steps back to pull off his pants. He lifts the ribbon over his head, dropping it in my hand as he shifts. *You're on your own.* He steps on the railing and runs his nose under my hair. *It was great knowing you.* Tarq launches off the deck and disappears into the woods.

Scoffing, I turn to face Dax as Miles appears in the doorway. When I first met Miles, he was incredibly relaxed, and I thought it was because we were in his element or territory. But on Rosalee's back porch, Miles is calmly standing between Dax and me, eating a turkey leg like we're at his house. It's clear that Miles just doesn't give a shit, and I love him for it.

"Hey, Luna," he says between bites. "You ready to go?" Miles wraps his arm around me, holding me close. He ducks to my ear. "You're in trouble, aren't you?"

"Yeah, a little bit," I whisper.

He takes another bite of turkey. "Alright. I'll get you past him. Act sad." Miles ushers me past Dax as I dramatically frown, cuddling up to his chest. "There you go. Easy as pie."

"Oh, I like pie," Chase says from across the room. Miles and I stop to watch him collect the horses' gear from the hall and leave the house.

"You heard that, right?" Miles asks, raising his eyebrow.

"I just blame it on the fact that he was your wolf," I say, shrugging.

Miles shoves me onto the couch. "Shut up," he says, laughing. "Hey, they stole my horse," he reminds Dax. "You know if they got another around here?"

I frown. "I liked that gelding. I'll just go steal him back."

"No, you will not." Dax, Miles, and Tarq all respond simultaneously, but one voice has a growl.

I turn toward the door where Tarq is standing. There's blood and mud matted into his fur. "What happened? Are you ok?" I rush to him, and he backs out onto the porch. Tarq walks into the yard so I can sit on the steps to face him. I run my hand over his fur and show him the blood.

"*Deer, Darya,*" he tells me. "*I got Rosalee the deer she wanted. As for you, you are not running into swords.*"

My nose wrinkles. "Ok, you might be a little right about that."

"*I am all the way right about that. You will borrow a horse, ride up that mountain and marry me.*" Tarq's grumbling, but I've never felt more loved.

I lift my eyebrow. "If I do, do you promise not to growl at me?"

"*No.*"

26

I ride back to the cabin with Dax and Miles, freeing Tarq and Chase to race through the trees and grab snacks. This is the perfect time to press the Alphas for information. *Miles will talk, but Dax might be a problem.* When I lean against Dax, he automatically reaches around my waist and hooks his thumb over my hip. I place my hand on his arm, letting him relax first.

"Were you guys ever friends?" I ask after some time. I feel Dax look down, but he doesn't respond.

As predicted, Miles is willing to talk. "No," he says from beside us.

"That's a long time to hate each other over something someone else did," I say, looking up at Dax.

"It didn't start like that," Miles responds.

"It was never like that for me," Dax adds, sighing. "I felt bad for Mira until she cursed me."

"Growing up, I knew about Dax," Miles says. "It wasn't a big deal until our father refused to name me his successor."

"Then your mother went bat shit crazy," Dax scoffs.

"Yeah, she kinda did," Miles agrees. "Over the next few years, it was impossible not to pick up her hatred for Dax and Olivia. She convinced me I needed to kill my father to take over as Alpha. She said it was the way of our pack and my right." Miles sighs. "So I fought him. I had him beat. My sword was to his throat, but I couldn't do it. He was my father, and I loved him."

We stare at Miles as he looks down at his horse, waiting for him to continue.

"I didn't see my mother until it was too late. She stabbed him in the back." Miles takes a deep breath. "He died in my arms."

"I'm so sorry," I whisper, reaching for Miles. "That must have been horrible."

Miles moves his horse closer and takes my hand.

Dax's growl builds. "Your mother caused all this," he says through his teeth. "The curse, our hatred for each other, and my father's death."

"Our father, Dax," Miles says.

Dax hisses at the white mare, and Miles slides out of my hand as the horse shoots up the mountain. I look up at Dax when he slows her, but he shakes his head and wraps his arms around me.

"Is he gonna be ok?" Tarq asks.

"Maybe one day," I tell him. *"Can you stay with Miles?"*

"Yes, My Love."

* * *

We continue in silence, stopping every few hours for rest and water. The brothers refuse to talk again, but I haven't given up on them. Their relationship is worth saving. Tarq stays with Miles, even playing with him by pushing him into the water when Miles is filling his canteen. Tarq let him pour a canteen of water over his head as payback.

When Dax leads our group to the cabin at sunrise, he rides around to the back. My jaw drops, and I slide from the saddle. There's a white gazebo decorated with vines and roses. The white chairs that lead up to it have bows and ribbons accented with more roses. There's fabric covering the center aisle in the same color as the pink petals.

I walk down the aisle, running my fingers over the chairs and cupping the delicate blooms. "How did you do this?" I whisper, knowing Tarq isn't far.

"It's not every day that the Luna gets married," he replies, rubbing his muzzle against my hip.

I slide my fingers along his jaw. "It's your wedding too, my Alpha."

Tarq opens his mouth to taste my fingers. *"None of us will be there for me, My Love."*

I reach the gazebo and turn around. Tarq straddles my legs when I sit, pushing me onto my back with his chest. Miles sits beside me as Tarq begins rubbing his muzzle over the sides of my face and pushing my chin up to lick my neck.

"I miss being a wolf," Miles grumbles, lying back.

I giggle at Miles and scratch Tarq's shoulders. "What are you doing, my Alpha?"

"It's your last day as a free woman. What do you want to do?" he asks.

"I want to go somewhere with you," I tell him. "Where do you want to take me?"

Tarq jams his nose beside my neck, breathing deeply. *"To the nearest bed,"* he says whimsically.

I grab his nose and pull him away from my neck. "Go get dressed and take me somewhere better than a bed," I tell him.

"Fine, have it your way." He jumps off the gazebo.

I sit up, watching him bound to the house. When he disappears through an open door, I turn back to Miles. He holds his arm out, and I lay back on his shoulder. Miles calmly trails his fingers over my arm as I search for the right words.

"Miles?" I start.

"Luna, it's ok," he says. "I forgave myself a long time ago. I just wish I'd told Dax the truth." I thread my fingers with his and turn to lay my head on his chest. "All these years, I could've had a brother instead of an enemy."

"Oh, Miles, you two haven't been enemies for a long time." I prop myself up and cup his cheek to turn his eyes to mine. "I wish we had more time."

"We do, Luna," Miles says. "But right now, you need to get out of here and let us plan the perfect wedding for you." He smiles and wipes his thumb over my cheek, catching a tear.

"I love you, Miles," I say, trying to smile.

"I love you too, Luna." Miles takes my hand and lifts me as he sits up. "One more thing, Luna. My pack will be a problem for you once I'm gone." He puts his head down, and I wait for him to continue. "When Anthony burned our village, they scattered. I was tracking them down, but it's not easy with that lot."

I run my fingers along his clenched jaw. "Miles, they'll come around, just like everyone else."

He lifts his head. "They don't see you as the Luna. You'll be Darya, the woman who killed their Alpha." He cups my cheeks almost roughly. "You'll not be safe with them on the loose."

I lean against him until he lets me put my head on his shoulder. "Any suggestions?"

"Kill them."

Surprised, I bolt up. "I'll not kill my wolves, Miles."

"Luna, they are my wolves. If you could get your hands on them, you could calm them." He holds my hand to his face. "The problem is going to be getting your hands on them."

A door bangs at the cabin, and I take a deep breath, forcing a smile. "Let's keep this between us for now."

"As you wish, Luna." Miles kisses my cheek.

"Why are your lips on my woman, Miles?" Tarq says, grinning as he approaches.

Miles snorts. "Just hoping she'll realize I'm better than you." He helps me up and kisses my hand. "Enjoy your day, Luna. I'll see you tonight."

Tarq pulls me to him, and I watch Miles walk away, listening to his heartbeat. "I'm going to miss him," I tell Tarq.

"I know you will, My Love," he says, kissing my head.

He gives me a moment to collect myself. When I'm ready, I pull away and look up at him. "Ok, my Alpha, where are we going?"

Tarq smiles. "You'll like it. Come on."

He leads me to the side of the cabin where the Friesian is tied. She's tacked up and carrying front and rear packs. Tarq helps me into the saddle, hops up behind me, and hisses at the mare.

We canter down a well-traveled trail for a few hours before he slows her. Tarq leans to my ear and whispers, "Close your eyes." I turn my head to the side and lay it against his chest. After a few minutes, I feel a breeze against my skin, and he stops the horse. "Open them."

My eyes widen as they open. Tarq's taken me to a small grassy opening at the edge of a cliff. It's overlooking miles of forest and fields that appear untouched. Once Tarq helps me slide down, I step toward the ledge and stare in awe at its perfection.

"How did I not know this was here?" I ask as Tarq sits on a rock by the edge.

"Not everyone has the abundance of extra time that I have." Tarq smiles at me. "Plus, it doesn't hurt that I'm pretty fast." He stands, wrapping his arms around me.

I focus my eyes on his hand, seeing the mark that starts behind his shoulder and winds lazily down his arm. It ends beside the knuckle of his pinky.

"What is this?" I ask, tracing the visible part.

Tarq twists his arm, pulling his sleeve up. "It's the pack's marking," he tells me. "Our pack members are the descendants of the original pack who remained loyal to the Luna even after her reign had ended. That's why we're called the Lunar Pack."

Upon closer inspection, I notice symbols and markings, almost like little pictures between two thick lines. "Is it something that is put on you when you're young?" I imagine it would hurt and think about my unborn child enduring that pain.

Tarq shrugs. "I don't think it hurts, Darya. We're born with it."

I rub my fingers over his mark and look up into his eyes. "Tell me a story."

Laughing, Tarq releases me. "Tell you a story?" He whistles to the Friesian and pulls things out of her packs when she stops beside him. "What do you want to hear about?"

I help him lay out a blanket, thinking about his question. "Well, Dax told me about the time he shot you. Did you guys ever do anything fun together?"

Tarq blows his lips out. "The time?" He laughs heartily. "Darya, that man shoots me every chance he gets!"

"I don't believe that." I laugh along with him.

Tarq stops unloading the saddlebags and leans against the mare. He grins, watching me sprawl on the blanket. "I guess I can tell you about the first time he shot me. I was 15 years old." Tarq untacks the horse, setting her saddle at the edge of the blanket and laying his head on it. "If I'm going to share my food with you, you'll need to take my side on this."

I prop myself up on my elbow. "Your food?" I look around at the piles of containers. "There's a lot of food here, Tarq."

"I know," he says thoughtfully. "But I didn't bring any for you."

I frown. "You're mean."

Laughing, he feeds me some watermelon. "My parents got married when I was five," Tarq says, placing the fruit container on his stomach. "My father wasn't my biggest fan even then, so it wasn't a good time for me. After the wedding, my mother sent me to stay with Dax for a few weeks. I hardly knew him as anything other than our Alpha."

I feed Tarq a grape, letting him quietly reflect on his childhood.

"He tried to find something for us to do together, but I liked being a wolf, and he couldn't shift." A small smile plays across Tarq's face. "At age 5, I was about the size of a dog, and Dax got the idea to play fetch. Looking back, it kinda pisses me off, but it was fun. As I got older, I tried to catch it before it hit the ground. We did it so much that my mother joined in. Dax began to shoot arrows to race us to the ball when it got too easy.

"Right after I turned 15, I was so pissed at my father that Dax ran me for hours. That day was the first time I caught the ball before he could shoot it. I was so damn proud that I forgot about the arrow. Until it hit my ass, that is. I learned to roll out of the way after that." Tarq looks at me as I smile up at him from his chest. He kisses my forehead. "Forever known as the day Dax shot me in the ass."

"But it's a very nice ass," I say, giggling.

"I know it is, but I couldn't sit for a week." He moves the fruit and produces a container of boiled chicken. "My mother tried to forbid us from playing anymore, but she was joining in again as soon as I healed." He feeds me a chunk of chicken.

Tarq shifts his eyes up to the clouds. I slide closer to him and run my fingers over his face. I've done my best to get to know Tarq as much as possible in our short time together. I know I've never seen him not eat when surrounded by food.

"When you left, Dax told me something." I trace his jaw. "He said that it's ok to feel things." I lift myself back up so that I can look down at him. "I'm scared, Tarq," I admit. "I'm afraid this won't work. I'm scared that Luna won't allow it. I'm most fearful I'll leave you alone for the rest of your life."

Tarq wraps his arms around my neck. He pulls me against his chest, tucking down into my hair. From the beginning, Tarq has always made me feel like I could share my feelings without judgment. It's my turn to provide him the same support. I hang onto him, feeling the moment.

After a while, Tarq starts to giggle. "Luna must be so happy." His giggle turns into all-out laughter. "I'm marrying the woman I love with every inch of my body tomorrow, and I'm spending the day terrified of what she'll do to us because of it."

I'm afraid too, but I'm his Luna. "Do you still want to marry me?" I ask, still against his chest.

Releasing me, Tarq looks down. "Of course."

"Then meet me at the altar and let me handle Luna." I smile sweetly, doubting I'll ever be able to "handle" Luna.

Tarq smiles as we fall back into our conversation and tells me a few more stories involving Dax. My favorite was when Dax tried to teach him to fish, and it took too long to sit with a pole and bait. Tarq said he figured wolves could do it better, so he jumped in and grabbed them with his mouth. After that, Dax refused to go fishing with him but sent him to the pond anytime Amelia said she wanted fish for dinner.

Tarq looks toward the sun. "We need to get back to the cabin, My Love," he tells me, kissing my forehead.

"We don't have to," I say, frowning. "We can just stay here tonight if you want."

Tarq shakes his head. "No, I want you to experience this at least once."

I raise my eyebrow, but he refuses to tell me anymore. We collect the food and wake the mare for the return trip. The sun is already beginning to set, so Tarq pushes her. I feel he's talked out and needs to lighten up a bit. The mare and I are exhausted when she stops at the cabin, but Tarq bounces around like he stole our energy.

"It'll take a few minutes to set up," Tarq says, ushering me toward the porch.

I'm about to grill him for details when a voice stops me.

"Luna, may I have a word?" Bruce asks from somewhere I can't see.

I haven't heard his voice in so long that it startles me. "Give me a minute, My Love," I tell Tarq, reaching up for his chest. "I need to go talk to someone."

"Is everything ok?" Tarq asks, raising his eyebrow. "Should we call my mother or Chase?"

"No, My Love, I'll be fine." I smile, patting his chest. "If you get worried, you can send Miles. He always seems to know where to find me."

He nods and leans down to kiss me before climbing the stairs. I turn to look around the yard.

"I'm right here," Bruce says, popping his head out at the edge of the woods.

I join him in the forest and find a trail that skirts the property. We turn and follow it together. "There are so many conversations that we could have, Bruce," I tell him, slightly crosser than I intend. "Which one would you like to have?"

Bruce's ears sink back as he looks up at me. *"I'm sure you've realized our family is not normal by now. Amelia and I have a different kind of relationship."*

I narrow my eyes. "Bruce, Amelia would never be so forthcoming with details about your relationship."

Bruce's lips fluff. *"As your guard, I feel a duty to be at your wedding, but I won't be going."*

"You may not have ever gotten along, but you're Tarq's father," I snarl.

Bruce stops and sits down. *"I'm not."*

"You're not what?" I glare at him.

"*I'm not his father,*" Bruce says, hanging his head. "*Amelia was three months pregnant when I met her.*"

"Oh," I whisper, sinking beside him.

Bruce lies down and crosses his front paws. "*A mate is what you need them to be. Amelia needed a father for her child.*"

I think back to Tarq's description of what would happen when we bonded. It happened just like he said it would. *However, he downplayed the intensity... a lot.* I know what Amelia said, and Bruce seems to feel the same way, but something is off.

"Bruce, I don't think that's quite right. Did you two bond?"

He looks away from me, laying his head down. *That explains some of this.*

"You didn't have to be so hard on him. You were the only father Tarq knew."

Bruce picks his head back up. "*I know it's difficult to understand, but he wasn't always like he is now. He was different.*"

I shake my head. "I'm aware of his strength."

Bruce bumps my hands with his nose. "*Luna, it's much more than that. With his strength and temper, he hurt a lot of wolves when he was younger.*"

I look down, reaching for his muzzle. "He said some things to me out of anger and exiled himself." I slide my fingers over his whiskers. "That could not have been easy on him."

"*It wasn't,*" Bruce says, closing his eyes and leaning on my hand. "*He was so angry and scared that it only made things worse. So I made a decision. He would try to earn my approval, and when he didn't, well, it was safer for everyone if he was mad at me.*"

My heart breaks for Bruce. I thought he had ruined Amelia and Tarq's lives, but he had sacrificed any hope of happiness for Tarq and the entire pack. "You made him hate you so that he would take his anger out on you."

"*It was safer for everyone,*" Bruce repeats, sighing.

"I didn't know," I tell him, trying to apologize, but saying sorry would never be enough.

Bruce sits up. *"It's not like I could tell him. It would lose its desired effect."*

I hold my arms out, waiting for him to step into them. He slides his jaw down my back as I hold onto his neck. "He should know, Bruce."

"Maybe one day, Luna. But today is not that day." I feel him sigh and relax.

"I suppose you're right. Would you like me to tell Tarq you won't be there?"

Bruce steps back, rubbing his muzzle against my cheek. *"Would you?"* He bumps his nose against mine, which makes me smile. *"And good luck to you both. I hope to see you again."* He bows his head and jogs away, back toward the lake.

I remain frozen, sitting in the middle of the trail until Miles steps before me.

"Hey, are you ok?" Miles asks, sitting with me and taking my hands. He puts the back of his fingers on my forehead as I look down at his other hand. "Your mutant got worried about you."

Frowning, I look up at him. "Please don't call him that."

Understanding that this is more than he thought, Miles slides closer and puts his arms around me. "Do you want to talk about it?"

"I feel like I do, but I don't know what I want to talk about." My eyes mist as I turn to him.

Miles pulls my head to his chest. His hum starts as he rubs my back. "Why don't you tell me how you're feeling?"

My feelings spill out like they're pressurized. "I'm scared, Miles," I say, sobbing. "I'm marrying a man I couldn't love more if I tried, and I'm terrified I'll only be his wife for one day."

Miles pushes my hair behind my ear and gently runs his fingers over my neck, calming me. "I'm afraid, too," he admits. "I've been alive for a long time. I've gotten pretty good at it. I don't know how to be dead."

"Miles, I need you to promise me you'll accept Luna's deal." I snap upright, grabbing his cheeks. "Whatever it is, Miles, just accept it."

He nods his head, confused. "Ok, I promise."

I pull him back to me and hold his cheek to mine. My mind runs through every thought I could have but freezes when I hear leaves crunching.

"When I have to search for your search party, you've officially been gone too long," Tarq announces, making us jump.

I smile at Miles. "Thank you."

"Any time, Luna," Miles replies.

Tarq reaches out, helping us to our feet. He catches me in his arms and cups my cheek. "Are you ok?"

I take a deep breath as Miles tiptoes away. "Bruce isn't coming to the wedding."

Tarq's eyes roll, and he flexes his jaw. "Asshole can't just be happy for us?"

"He's not your father, Tarq," I spit out.

Tarq freezes. "What?"

"He told me that Amelia was pregnant when they met." I tighten my grip on him since I don't know how he'll react to my news.

I feel his fingers tighten on the back of my jaw. "Darya, next time, just lead with the good news. Now come on. Everyone's waiting for us."

I open and close my mouth a few times but end up just letting him escort me in my stunned silence back to the cabin.

He leads me through the door and straight to the couches, where Amelia sits on one with Dax's head in her lap. Miles is slumped in the oversized armchair with his feet propped on the table. Tarq lays down on the empty couch, pulling me with him.

"I assume you've at least seen electricity in your... travels," Tarq says. "I had some panels brought up here so we can have a movie night."

I've only seen electricity a few times. My favorite was the water heater that one of my buyers had. It was my first indoor shower, and it was wonderful. Rosalee had told me about movies when I was a little girl, but my jaw drops when the black screen lights up. I have never seen a picture move like that.

I stare at the screen as Tarq yells at Dax, and Amelia leans over to pass a bowl of popping corn. I've had that a few times, and it was delicious, but this baby I'm carrying does not like anything with flavor. Tarq grabs the bowl and sets it on my stomach.

"Why am I holding your food?" I ask Tarq as he stuffs a handful of popped corn into his mouth.

He looks hurt. "Darya, if I put it down there, Mom will eat it all."

"And what are you planning to do with it?" I ask.

Tarq pouts. "Eat it all."

I try not to, but I can't help laughing.

Tarq jolts upright, nearly knocking the bowl off me. "That, Dax," he shouts. "That damn thing is made of metal! How could it possibly fly?"

He's pointing at a helicopter. On TV, it's flying and loud. I'd seen pictures of them, and there is one that crashed a few towns over. They roped it off and turned it into a mini library a few years ago.

Dax rolls his eyes. "I don't fucking know," he barks. "It beats the air into submission." He rolls over to face away from us and the TV. "Fuck family movie night."

Tarq snickers and settles back into the couch. He moves down my body to put his face against my neck, breathing deeply.

"Oh shit, I remember this," Miles says. "Doesn't he get shot in the ass?" He gets up, grabbing the bowl from my stomach.

Tarq jumps back up. "Yes!" he shouts. "I remember when Dax shot me in the ass." He turns and looks at the back of Dax's head. "It sure would've been nice to have some ice cream."

"I did not shoot you in the ass," Dax grumbles, his face still buried in Amelia's hip.

Tarq smiles broadly, excited that he could get Dax to engage. "No, I was there," he starts. "Your arrow went into my ass, which clearly means you shot me in the ass."

Dax flops over to face us, looking quite aggravated. "You jumped in front of my damn arrow and stood there waiting for it. Therefore, you shot yourself, dumbass."

Tarq shakes his head with a smirk. "No," he says. "That's not how I remember it. I know damn well that's not how my ass remembers it." He pauses as Dax begins growling. "Don't growl at me, old man. I'm not the one that shot an innocent kid in the ass." Tarq ducks down near my ear to whisper to me. "I need you to roll off the couch in about five seconds. Dax is not playing over there."

"What the fuck? Innocent?" Dax shouts, red-faced.

Tarq flips his hand as he moves it down to my hip. "I was just some innocent kid with an extra hole in my ass and no fucking ice cream."

Dax flings himself at Tarq, who shoves me forward. I land on the floor and see Tarq launch Dax over the back of our couch. He crashes into the wall. Dax stands up, hauls Tarq off our sofa, and throws him toward the door. I hear the door slam, but they're both gone when I stand up.

"Shouldn't we go after them?" I ask.

Miles laughs, and Amelia shrugs. "They'll be back," she says. "Welcome to family movie night."

I look at Miles, but he just winks. "I'm sorry I missed these."

I lie back down and try to watch the movie, but my exhaustion quickly takes over.

* * *

It's quiet when I feel Tarq slide his arms around me. He pulls me under his shoulder, and I snuggle into his chest as he begins to heat up.

"No, you two," Dax says. "It's pack tradition. You can't be together tonight."

"Fuck off," we both respond, but Tarq's voice comes out with a growl.

Dax's boots retreat, and he slowly climbs the stairs behind the couch.

"Thank you for tonight," I whisper.

Tarq relaxes into me. "I love you."

"I love you too."

27

❧

I wake to someone shaking my shoulder. Tarq's chest is on top of me, and he tightens his grip as I sigh, enjoying his warmth. I know I'm marrying him today, but it doesn't mean as much to me as the love I feel when he holds me so protectively.

I'm shaken a second time.

"Take her out of my arms, and I will kill you," Tarq snarls.

"Tarq, honey," Edith says softly. "You both deserve more than a couch wedding."

Tarq sighs as he relaxes. He loosens his grip on me and looks down as I snuggle deeper into his chest. "Give us a minute." Edith's footsteps recede, and Tarq rolls back, pulling me onto him. "Talk to me."

I blink back my tears. "Why did I agree to this?" I ask him. "I just want to spend the rest of our time together. You and me."

Grinning, Tarq somehow understands my panic. "Because I want to marry you, Darya. I want to share our love with the world, even if it's just for one day." He pulls the tips of my hair.

I scowl at him. "You make everything sound so much better." Closing my eyes, I lay my head on his chest.

Tarq brushes my hair from my face and lies calmly underneath me. I can hear people walking through the cabin. Everyone leaves us alone while I collect myself and find the strength to give this beautiful man the day he deserves.

"I will lay here with you for as long as you need me to, My Love." Tarq kisses my head.

I smile at him. "How could I not give you what you want?" I put my hand on his cheek. "You are perfect."

"That's just part of my charm." Tarq kisses me so lightly that it could've been butterfly wings brushing against my lips.

I sit up, stretching my back. Tarq slides his arm behind his head and throws his leg over the back of the couch. He watches as I lift my arms over my head and roll my shoulders. His eyes shine even in the dim light.

I hold my finger out. "Don't you look at me in that tone of voice."

Tarq breathes out a laugh and licks his lips. "I'm not saying anything with my look."

"Just because I can't hear your thoughts doesn't mean I don't know what you're thinking," I say, lifting my eyebrow.

Tarq smiles. "Come here. I'll summarize, and we can compare notes."

I turn to kneel over him as he pulls my arms. Tarq pushes my chin up and inhales deeply when my hair drapes over his face. He lets out a deep growl, biting my neck. My eyes roll closed as he slides his tongue over the skin pinched in his teeth.

"TARQ!" Dax's booming yell reminds us that we are not alone. "Get your mouth off the Luna!"

When I look at Tarq, I cover us with my hair and smile at him. Tarq smiles back and rubs his lips against mine.

"See you in a little while?" I ask.

"You bet," he says, grinning. "I'll be the one in the tux."

I wink at him. "I'm sure I'll find you." I join Dax beside the stairs, putting my hand on his chest. "I need to talk to you, Dax."

Following me upstairs, Dax points to his room. "What's up?" he asks, shutting the door.

I look around the room, remembering the last time we were here. Luna was in charge, and she was hungry for Dax. I reach for his Blood Mark. "So much has happened."

Dax pulls me to his chest. He rests his chin on my head, threading his fingers through my hair. "I'm glad it was you," he whispers. "I bonded with her, but I wouldn't trade a single moment with you."

Dax's words cause me to completely lose control of my tears. "You've taught me so much, Dax, and I still have a lot more to learn. I'm not ready to lose you."

He pushes me back, grabbing my tear-soaked face. "Listen to me," Dax commands. "I will come back to you, Darya. I don't care what kind of deal I have to make. I won't leave you." He runs his thumbs over my cheeks, wiping away my tears as I sniffle and collect myself.

I sigh, ready to move on. "Bruce has decided not to attend the ceremony."

"Does Tarq know?" Dax asks with wide eyes.

I nod. "I told him last night before the movie."

"He didn't seem upset." Dax furrows his brow, confused.

I squint my eyes. "Bruce told me he's not his father. I think Tarq was relieved."

Dax twists his face but then sighs. "Alright, I'll keep an eye on him." He pulls me to his chest and kisses my head before letting me go. "I'll send the girls up. I love you, Darya."

"I love you too, Dax."

Dax barely makes it through the door before Edith and Amelia bound past him, squealing and clapping. They both hug me excitedly.

"What am I missing?" I ask them, confused.

Edith hugs me again. "We've just been working nonstop on your dress, Darya," she says, sighing. "I've outdone myself."

Amelia runs her fingers through my hair. "Luna, we'll wash your hair downstairs," she tells me. "I can braid it tighter with it wet." She hooks her arm with mine and escorts me back downstairs.

Miles stands behind a wooden chair when Amelia opens the side door. He places a water pitcher on the table and rolls up his sleeves. "I know women would traditionally help you get ready, but I used to do this for my wife."

I pull him into a hug. "I would be honored if you'd help."

Miles' hands are surprisingly gentle as he skillfully washes my hair. Whenever I look up at him, his eyes intently stare at what he's doing, even when talking to the women. Amelia seems nervous about Miles, but both women stay and talk to him while he works. I still haven't figured him out, and I know I'm running out of time, but I feel I'm close.

Once done, Miles kisses my forehead and passes me to Amelia's skilled fingers. She begins pulling and pinning sections. Edith distracts me by talking about Anthony's tux and how hard it was to find shoes. I barely notice when Amelia finishes.

Edith gasps, and I look up to see what's wrong. "You are so beautiful that I want to marry you," she says, making me giggle.

As we collect Amelia's tools, laughter filters in from nearby. Putting my finger to my lips, I motion for Edith to follow me to the end of the porch. I lean against the railing and point to a clearing on the side of the gazebo area.

"This is my favorite thing to watch Dax and Tarq do together," I whisper to Edith. Amelia leans against the railing beside me. Dax is standing in the middle of the clearing with five or six wolves. He holds up a single ball and shouts something.

"What are they doing?" Edith whispers as the wolves all fall in line beside him. She gasps as he hurls the ball, and all the wolves take off, with Tarq in the lead. The wolves bite and shove each other while Dax lets loose his arrow and leans on his bow.

"They'll do that for hours," Amelia says, smiling at them.

I put my arm around her shoulders. "Amelia, would you like to join them?"

She takes a sharp breath as if pulled from a distant memory. "Oh no, Luna," she replies. "Let the boys have their fun."

I pull her slightly away from Edith, who's fascinated by the wolves playing catch. "Amelia, I don't know what will happen tomorrow, but until then, I want you to spend as much time with Dax as you would like." She shakes her head, trying to object. "Do not worry about me. I have your son. I know you care about him, and I will not call for you."

Amelia hugs me tightly and looks back toward the wolves. Tarq is in the field, rolling around. "Dax must've thrown the ball you covered with your scent last time we played." She laughs and leans back down on the railing.

I had forgotten about that. I close my eyes, feeling Tarq take a deep breath of my scent. *"I love you."*

"I love you too," Tarq tells me. I open my eyes and see him jump up in the field. He turns toward the cabin.

I smile. "Alright, ladies, dress me because I need to marry that man."

We return to Dax's room to find Jules leaving a basin of steaming water. I smile and reach out to her. She looks confused but steps in for a hug anyway.

"Oh, Luna," Jules whispers. "This was not where I thought your story was going."

I pull back, cupping her cheeks. "I appreciate everything you've done for us."

"Luna, if this works, there are things we'll need to discuss," she tells me. "There is a lot written about the Luna."

I smile. "I'm sure there is, but for now, I want to spend time with my Alpha, which means I need to marry him."

Jules bows, leaving the room.

Edith is rinsing rags in the water. "Alright, lady, strip," she commands. "It's time to clean you up."

I wrinkle my nose. "You know this isn't necessary. I know how to wash."

"This, Luna, is pack tradition," Amelia says, smiling.

They help me out of my clothes, and I hold my hair out of their way as they run the rags over my skin. The crisp feeling of the water cooling on my skin is mesmerizing. I may have told them I didn't need this, but it's thoroughly enjoyable.

Edith pulls me from my daze by mentioning Miles. "Oh yeah, my brother is on his payroll. He didn't want to help and wouldn't tell me why." She rubs her rag a little harder against my leg. "And Miles just happens to ask if I know his witch?"

"Ok, ouch," I say as she takes another swipe at my leg. Edith hurls her rag across the room. It hits the window and falls to the floor. "Listen," I tell her. "I will get your rag, but you cannot wash me anymore."

She continues to complain as I cross the room to retrieve her rag.

Peeking out the window, I spot a very muddy Tarq. He's biting at Dax's arms, and it appears that Dax might have one of the balls in his hand.

"I know you do not have mud all over you on our wedding day!" I angrily say to Tarq.

He steps off Dax and shakes his coat out. *"Dax threw me in the mud. I wasn't doing anything!"*

I slide the window open and lean out. "DAX!" I scream. "Why are you making my groom muddy on my wedding day?!"

Dax sits up and looks back at me. "I had nothing to do with this." He laughs and shoves Tarq away. "He fell in the bog trying to get the ball covered in your scent."

I cross my arms over the window sill and lean further out. My breasts fall over my arms for all the world to see. "Shouldn't you be getting him ready?" I yell back to Dax. They stare at me as if viewing my goods for the first time. "Quit staring at me. This is nothing you both haven't seen before. Tarq had better be beautiful and in a suit the next time I see him!"

Tarq snickers. *"Yes, ma'am."*

I turn back to see Amelia has slipped into the beautiful blue dress Edith selected. She looks stunning, and Dax will appreciate Edith's choice. Edith is still in her jeans and T-shirt, sitting on the bed beside a gorgeous white dress with floral lace and silk ribbon. The beads are sewn in floral patterns.

"They say you smell like a beautiful bouquet," Edith says, smiling. "I thought you should look like one." She carefully fluffs it on the floor, and both women help me step over the fabric. They slide it up my body, zipping the back and fastening the buttons of the choker collar behind my neck.

They're beaming as they move me in front of the mirror. Edith probably wasn't thinking about the pregnancy since it smashes my chest, but the two straps that reach up to the choker make it look on purpose. I've never worn a fancy dress before, and I'm not sure I will ever wear anything more beautiful than this in the future.

"This is gorgeous," I whisper.

Edith kisses my cheek. "You make it beautiful."

A knock on the door makes us jump. "I'm coming in," Miles yells. "You better not be naked." When he barges in, Miles stops and runs his eyes over me. "Well, that is not naked."

I'm blushing, but I still flash him a crooked smile. *Miles can make anything sound like a compliment.* "You're not looking too bad yourself, handsome."

Miles laughs and hands a bouquet to Edith and Amelia. "Have some flowers, ladies, and let me get the door for you," he says, excusing them from the room. "Edith, you can attend the reception after sunset." Edith squeals excitedly on her way out the door.

In true Miles' fashion, he's dressed in the parts of a tuxedo that suit him. The pants and jacket fit him well, but the shirt is only halfway buttoned, and I'm positive there will never be a tie around his neck. He will probably be the only casually dressed person at my wedding, and I couldn't love him more for it.

"I love the casual look, Miles," I say, reaching for him.

He steps up and slides his arms around me. "I'm just here for the food, baby girl," he whispers. "No one's gonna be looking at me." His hum started while he was talking.

Keeping my arms tightly around him, I try to recall the first time I'd heard it. "Miles, your hum started when you tasted my blood," I say, holding him close so I can listen to it while we talk.

"Yeah," he says, drawing out the word. "That's some good stuff. I bet it makes your mutant loopy, doesn't it?"

"Don't call him that," I snap, letting my anger flash. Even though his hum stops, Miles stays where he is and chuckles. He tugs at the hair tips that cascade down my back. While focusing on him, my anger dissipates, and I tighten my grip on him. When his hum starts up again, I smile. *It's love. This old softy just wants to feel genuinely loved.*

Pulling back from Miles, I reach for his face. "Come here, Miles," I say, pulling his lips to mine. I give him one simple kiss, and he takes it, like everything else, in stride. "Now, let's go find my groom."

Miles puts his arm out for mine, smiling. "I only have one job. I probably shouldn't screw it up."

I take his arm, allowing him to escort me down the stairs, through the kitchen, and out a back door. We're suddenly standing at the beginning of the aisle. There is a person in every chair and many people around the outskirts. Hundreds of eyes turn in my direction as my breath catches in my chest. My grip on Miles tightens, and I try to take a step back. *I don't recognize any of these people. Why are they all smiling? I can't do this.*

"Don't look at them," Miles whispers. I turn to look up at him, and his smile calms me. "He's the only one here that matters, Luna. Look at your Alpha and breathe."

Turning my head toward the gazebo, I first notice how long the aisle is, but then my eyes land on Tarq. He's not calm, and Dax has a firm grip on his shoulder, but his smile is all I need. I take a deep breath, letting everything else disappear. "Miles," I say, still looking at Tarq. "Get me to that man."

Miles pats my hand and tucks my arm more securely around his. From our first step to our last, I can't take my eyes off Tarq. His perfectly fitted tuxedo does little to disguise how tense he is. He looks as though he's moments from running to me.

Although it seems like forever, I know it's only a few minutes before we make it to the first step of the gazebo, and Miles stops. He holds my arm, not allowing me to go to Tarq. I look up at Miles feeling my chest tighten again. He shakes his head and puts his finger to his lips.

I turn toward Tarq and see that Dax's hand is no longer on his shoulder, but his tux is now tight across the front of his body. *Ok, that's a little funny.* When Anthony steps into the gazebo, Dax moves to the side, pulling Tarq by the back of his suit.

"Ladies and gentlemen, we are here to join your Luna, Darya, and her Alpha, Tarq, in the ever-lasting bond of marriage. Does the Elder bless this union?" Anthony asks.

"I do," Jules says from behind me, making me jump. I hadn't even noticed she was there.

"Does the Alpha bless this union?" Anthony asks, eyeing Tarq as he starts to fidget.

"I do," Dax replies, winking at me.

I'm about ready to burst. *Why is this taking so long?*

"Who is here to escort this bride?" Anthony asks as if he doesn't know the answer.

Miles clears his throat. "Miles of the Blood Pack."

"Do you give this woman freely to the man she desires?"

Someone should have warned me that Anthony would ask so many questions because I'm one more question away from strangling him.

"I do," Miles answers before kissing my cheek. "This is it, Luna. Go slow so you don't trip," he whispers.

"Luna, please step forward and join your Alpha." Anthony finally says the words I've been dying to hear.

Miles lets go of my arm but holds my hand to help me up the two steps of the gazebo. I look back at him when he squeezes my fingers instead of letting them go. He shakes his head slightly, points to where I'm standing, and then lets me go. I try to step toward Tarq, but Dax shakes his head, and I see Tarq's suit tighten.

"In the tradition of the Lunar Pack, the Luna's Alpha may say his vows," Anthony announces.

When Dax lets go of Tarq, he's instantly in front of me. He stares into my eyes, and his hands tightly grip mine. I take a deep breath and exhale, directing it toward his face. Tarq's eyes gently roll as he relaxes.

"When a wolf is born, he's not whole," Tarq starts calmly, opening his eyes. "His missing piece is waiting for him to find her somewhere in the world. He walks this earth dreaming of what life could be like until he finds his mate. Darya, you make me all that I want to be.

"I will cross the depths of hell just to stand by your side. I will protect and support you through everything you do and love you beyond the day of my death. You've seen me at my worst, felt my bite, and accepted my flaws. You are everything good about me. For this, I vow to be yours forever."

I'm frozen as Tarq puts his hands on my neck and wipes the tears from my face. He smiles gently, and I take a few slow breaths.

Anthony clears his throat. "Luna, if you'd like to speak your vows."

I hang onto Tarq's wrists. "When we met, I didn't belong anywhere. I didn't have a home, and then you happened." I swallow hard and let out a deep breath. "You've been my rock when I needed support, my quiet place when I fell, and you've held my heart together when it otherwise would've broken. You've become everything I needed in my life.

"I couldn't imagine a morning I wouldn't wake up to you or a day that wouldn't end in your arms. I would do anything just to see your smile. I crave your words in the silence. And, above all, my Alpha, I vow to breathe for you."

There isn't enough restraint in the world to hold Tarq back. He crashes into my lips, and I feel our tears mixing on my cheeks. He takes a breath and leans his forehead against mine. "Woman, I could not love you any more than I do at this moment."

"Do y'all want to be married?" Anthony whispers.

I can't take my eyes off Tarq, but we both take a small step back.

"With the blessing of the Elder and the Alpha, we bind you in this union," Anthony announces. "Tarq, will you accept this pack?" he continues, causing Tarq to tense. "Will you protect and guide them? Will you govern them in the way of your ancestors to promote solidarity and unity?"

Tarq's staring at Anthony. He wasn't interested in being Alpha this whole time. Everyone said it's a job that comes with being my mate, but no one said anything about vows or accepting it. I glance at Dax, who nods with a grin.

I reach for Tarq's cheek and whisper, "We knew this was coming. You are our Alpha. It's time to accept our wolves and take your place beside me."

Taking a deep breath, Tarq straightens his back. He licks his lips and turns to Anthony. "I do."

Our guests erupt, clapping and stomping in a celebration that seems to last forever. Tarq turns to me, smiling broadly. Fresh tears fall as

I realize how he must feel. Tarq felt alone and disconnected from the pack for his entire life. Now, he will spend the rest of his days respected and loved by everyone.

The beauty of Tarq's happiness distracts me from the noise, but when it settles, Anthony continues. "Then, I bless this union with the power vested in me. May your bond be mighty, your love eternal, and your voice be one."

Tarq steps forward, wrapping his arms around me. His tongue slips past my lips, and I melt into him as he leans me backward. I run my tongue over his, threading my fingers in his hair.

"So, people are still staring at you," Dax whispers. "Feed them so you can sneak out of here."

Tarq carries me to the front of the cabin, where the wolves set up tables and chairs with buffets stretching along the deck. He sets me down beside a table with five chairs. We watch as our guests follow us, many of them still clapping.

Tarq sits and pulls me down into his lap. "I didn't think you could get any more beautiful," he says before licking my lower lip.

I reach up to my head. "Your mother did my hair," I say. "I think Edith did most of the work on my dress."

Tarq shrugs. "Yeah, those are nice, too," he says, rubbing his lips over my jaw. "But I was talking about how you look as my wife."

I release a raspy exhale as Tarq slides his tongue down my neck. My eyes roll closed when he blows hot air on my wet skin.

"What did I tell you two?" Dax barks.

Miles chuckles. "Leave them alone, Dax," he tells him, winking at me. "They outrank you now."

Amelia joins us, sitting between Tarq and Dax. Someone brings us food, but Dax makes a separate trip to grab me a bowl of soaked bread. Miles makes several trips to the buffet and steals some of my bread until Tarq points his knife at him.

Our guests approach our table, offering their congratulations. Dax announces their name and pack. He motions for me to touch them, so I make it a point to shake their hands, pulling them closer to cup their cheeks. After a while, I've had enough. I want to be with my husband, not my guests.

Tarq nods to Nate, who picks up a guitar and sings a beautiful slow song. Tarq stands, reaching out to me with a smile. Just beyond him, I see Dax do the same thing to Amelia. I tilt my head slightly and smile as I accept his hand. Tarq pulls me out to the grassy area between the tables and woods.

He twirls me once before putting his right arm around my waist. Looking into my eyes, Tarq slowly slides his left hand up my body from my hip and down the entire length of my arm. As he reaches my hand, he smiles. "Mom loves to dance and needs a partner sometimes."

I kick off my shoes and let him lead me around the dancing area. I've hardly ever danced, but he expertly guides me, making me look like a natural. After a short time, someone else joins Nate and begins singing a faster song. Tarq spins me away from him and lets go of my hand. Pretty sure I'll end up on my ass, I reach my arms out and land against Dax's chest.

There's a pause, and Dax looks down at me. "My turn," he says, smiling. He twirls me around the dance area with only a bit more grace than Tarq. I tuck my head under his chin, breathing him in and enjoying our moment. As the song ends, Dax spins me just as Tarq had, but I land against Miles this time.

The next song is slower, and Miles pulls me against him. He guides me softly, keeping me away from the crowd as my tears spill. I reach up to cup his cheek. "Miles," I start, sniffling. "I hope you know how much I'm going to miss you."

Smiling, Miles brushes his hand over my cheek. "There's no frowning on your wedding day, Luna." He kisses my temple. "It'll be dark soon, and you'll be able to sneak out of here."

"Where will you be spending your last day?"

"Dax has invited me to the lake," he tells me. "I thought I'd go down there with him."

I smile, sliding my thumb over his cheek. "I like that idea."

"I thought you might." Miles continues dancing with me until his gaze focuses on Tarq as he talks to some people I don't recognize. Miles stops and lets my body go but takes my hand. "Come with me, Luna." He holds me close to whisper to me as we approach Tarq. "These are some members of my pack. You should probably get your hands on them while you can."

Miles steps beside Tarq, clapping him on the back. He introduces his pack members, allowing me to hold their hands and touch their cheeks. They are sweet and cordial, which isn't what I expected from anyone in Miles' pack, especially when he told me I'd have to kill them. After we make it through Miles' pack members, others begin to line up, and Dax has to take over introductions.

Tarq wraps his arms around me from behind as the sun begins sinking. "Are you ready to get out of here?"

I lean against him, sighing as he rests his chin on my head. "Can you handle all of them if this doesn't work?" I ask, looking over our wolves.

Tarq lays his cheek on my head, and I can feel the weight of what he's about to say. "No," he says sadly. "So it better work." He takes a deep breath and turns me around. "Come on. Let's get out of here."

28

I sit on the Friesian as she thunders through the forest following Tarq. With the occasional cloud cover and the thick canopy of leaves overhead, the horse is my eyes, and I'm just hoping I don't hit a tree branch. Our destination is a new lake Anthony had shown Tarq on a map.

When the horse slows, Tarq appears before us in a clearing. Behind him is a small, perfectly still lake. I stare at it as I slide from my saddle. Walking to the water, I run my fingers through Tarq's fur.

"It's like there are two skies," I whisper, afraid I might cause a ripple. "I've never seen water that still before."

"Hey," Tarq says. *"Get back here with my necklace."*

Smiling, I turn and take in the scene. I'm looking forward to when he can shift without magic, but I love my beautiful wolf. He's perfect.

"Fine, I'll just wait here." Tarq lies down, setting his chin on his crossed paws. His lips fluff as he breathes out a sigh in a full pout.

"Aw," I say, faking a frown. "Don't be like that." I walk across the clearing and drop to my knees before him.

Tarq looks away. *"Nope, I'm good,"* he grumbles. *"I'll just spend our last night as a wolf."*

"Get over here," I say, pulling his crystal from my pocket.

Tarq jumps up and walks a wide circle around me. He stops behind my back, scooping my hair off my neck with his nose. *"I can make you beg me to put that on,"* he boasts.

I raise my eyebrow and smile like I stand a chance against him.

Tarq moves in front of me, putting his nose beside my throat. His fur and whiskers slide under my hair across the back of my neck, stopping below my left ear. As he twists his body around to face the opposite direction, he takes a deep breath, and my eyes roll closed while my entire body fires up.

I'm already getting the ribbon necklace ready when I feel his tongue on my skin. He slides it painfully slow across the back of my neck. I hold out the ribbon and feel his fur under my fingers.

Tarq slides his hands up my hips and under my shirt, pulling it over my head. I open my eyes to find him kneeling before me. I touch my fingers to his jaw and guide his lips to mine. Tarq slides his arms around me, hooking my knees, and lays me back to pull off my boots and jeans. Lying beside me, he props on his elbow and looks over my body.

"I love you, my Alpha," I say, running my fingers over his lips.

Tarq kisses and nips my fingers. "I love you too."

"You are forever putting parts of me in your mouth," I say, giggling. "You even chew on my fingers whenever I hold your muzzle."

"Yeah," Tarq says whimsically with a goofy smile.

"What is that? Do I taste that good?"

Tarq chuckles. "I was talking to Jules while we were at the cabin," he says. "She dug up some stuff about the Luna and her Alpha. The Luna's scent is enticing to all but is especially appealing to her Alpha. Since you taste even better than you smell, it just makes sense that I would enjoy putting you in my mouth."

Smiling, I shake my head. "If I didn't know you were a wolf, that would sound strange."

"Jules didn't know that our teeth can't puncture your skin, but honestly, I think that's an essential safety measure." He laughs when I raise my eyebrow. "I'm sorry, My Love, but I would probably eat you if I could. You taste that damn good." I squeal as he leans down, latches onto my neck, and scrapes his teeth along my skin.

"What about the pad rubs? Do all wolves like them or just you?" *I'm on a roll now. I want some answers.*

"I don't know, Darya," Tarq scoffs, laughing. "I'm not gonna run around offering foot rubs to find out."

"Fair enough," I say. "What else did Jules tell you?"

Tarq's face scrunches for a moment. "Oh, here's one. I find it good and bad," he says. "We stopped aging the moment we bonded."

"What?" I ask, confused. "As in, we're immortal?"

Tarq shakes his head. "No," he answers. "Normal things can still kill us. We can get sick and such, but we don't age. I'm kinda pissed that I don't get to grow old with you and sit on a porch swing grumbling about the youngsters."

I click my tongue and wrinkle my nose. "I think you'd be a sweet old man," I tell him. "Bringing me flowers with your crooked knees. Oh!" I shout excitedly. "Would you have gray fur? That would be so cute!"

Tarq looks down at me with a blank stare. "I want a divorce."

I grab his face as I burst out laughing. "No, you don't."

"Yeah, Darya, I kinda do," he says, wiggling his face to remain serious. "It's either that or I need to be inside you. One or the other."

Tarq soon begins laughing with me. Our bond affects every part of our lives. I yearn for his words just as much as his touch. I wake up every morning excited to know I will have a moment like this. He will make me laugh when I least expect it just by being himself.

Tarq, my Alpha, my husband, is everything in my life, and I never want to know a day without him again. So when he rolls on top of me, I'm ready to accept him and take all he's willing to give. "I love you," I whisper into his ear.

He pulls my leg over his hip and leans down to slide his tongue over my neck. Tarq's muscles shake as he satisfies my nerves' cravings. I appreciate his slow movements as each nerve fires one at a time in response to his attention.

Our hands rub over each other's bodies, ensuring every part can experience pleasure from our touch. Tarq's growl overtakes his hum, and he pulls my hip, triggering me. My muscles instantly lock down on him, claiming all of him as my back arches off the ground. He forces his way through my release and matches me moan for moan as we echo through the trees around us.

Tarq rolls us to our sides when we've caught our breath. "You ready for a swim?" he asks.

Before I can even register his words, Tarq's lifted me off the ground. He cradles me in his arms and marches straight for the water.

"Wait, Tarq," I plead. "Do you even know anything about that lake?"

He laughs and heaves me across the water as far as he can.

"SHIT!" I scream as I fly through the air without knowing what will happen when I land.

The water is surprisingly warm and has a considerable depth I wasn't expecting. As I drop below the surface, I make a decision I'll probably regret later and swim as far as I can from where Tarq threw me. I don't resurface until I need air, doing my best to keep my movements minimal.

I remain quiet as he watches the surface, waiting for me. When his panic takes over, he runs into the water and dives. Within moments, something grabs my leg and yanks me under the water. Tarq catches me by my cheeks and pulls me back to the surface.

I spit the water out of my mouth and frown. "You're an ass."

Tarq laughs as he drapes my arms around his neck. "Yeah, but I'm your ass, and you married me knowing who I am."

I shake my head at his cocky grin and push down on his shoulders, shoving him back under the water. I lie back and float to watch the fluffy clouds interact with the moon. Tarq surfaces and joins me, holding my hand. I close my eyes when I catch a hint of the comet.

"Did you know that water was warm?" I ask.

"No," Tarq answers. He pulls me closer, hooking our arms. "Who taught you how to swim?"

"Rosalee," I answer. "She said a girl who doesn't know how to swim was a girl asking to drown." I turn to him to see that he's watching me. "How about you?"

"Dax," is his only answer before turning back to the stars.

"I'm not picturing a calm lesson in paddling," I press.

Tarq bites his lip when he doesn't want to talk about something, and I'm about to change the subject when he responds. "I pissed him off one day, and he threw me in the pond."

For some reason, he doesn't want to talk about this, but I'm not going to be able to let him drop this subject for multiple reasons. "Why do all of your Dax stories start with you pissing him off?" I ask, laughing. I love him, but his mission in life is to piss Dax off.

"Why are you laughing?" Tarq turns to me, raising his eyebrow. "It was very traumatic!"

I try to frown, but it doesn't work out. "It can't have been that bad. You're always in the damn water."

Tarq's brow furrows. "Wait," he says. "You kinda have a point. I do piss him off a lot, don't I?"

I turn back to the clouds, thinking about their bond. *I'm so stupid. They fight like cats and dogs, but he's about to lose the man who taught him everything he knows, created a game to have something to do together, and saved him from himself every time he got mad. Tarq has to be feeling something.*

"Do you think there's any way Dax knew you'd be Alpha?" I ask.

Tarq drops into the water, resurfacing underneath me. His body feels hot against my back. "How could he? He's immortal. Why would he think anyone would need to take his place?"

His body dips down into the water slightly, giving me a moment to turn over and lay my chest on his. I hook my left arm under his shoulder while trailing my right hand down the length of his body. I wait until he starts to hum before I press him again.

"Since he learned that I was the Luna, everything Dax did was to teach me how to lead the wolves. Even when I didn't know that's what he was doing." I lay my cheek on his collarbone. "I feel like he's been training you to take his place your whole life."

Tarq chuckles. "Why would he pick me? All I do is piss him off." He slides his hand down my arm. "Did he tell you about my vows?"

I push off him enough to be able to look at his face. The playful glint in his eyes matches his genuine smile. "No, my Alpha, Dax does not tattle on you as much as you think he does." I lift my eyebrow. "But now I want to hear about your vows."

Tarq laughs, laying his head back in the water. "I was gonna start with, 'Get over here and get naked,' but Dax said, and I'm quoting here, 'I will rip your head off and shove it up your ass.'"

I can easily picture Dax's glare and Tarq's laughter. "It's like you do things just to push his buttons." I let my hand trail down his body, slipping it into the water to graze his hip and dig my fingertips into his thigh.

He lifts his head to look down at me. "If that were true, then we'd be two of a kind." He snakes his body, shifting me higher up his chest. Tarq pulls me upright with him and pushes his tongue into my mouth. I grab his face, matching his need as my legs wrap around him. He pulls at the water, bringing us closer to shore as I massage his tongue with mine.

Tarq stands up once it's shallow enough and walks out of the water with me still latched onto him. He grabs my face and pushes me back enough so he can form words. "I love you, Darya."

"Tarq?" I say breathlessly.

"Yeah?" His grin nearly annoys me because he knows what he's doing.

"Shut up."

He growls and slams me against a tree. Using his hips to hold me in place, Tarq moves my hair and bites down on my neck, making me cry out. I grab his face and pull him off my neck. He slides his hands down my body, heating up to dry us off.

Tarq licks his lips, moving his hands to my thighs and dropping me onto him. My head rolls back against the tree as Tarq claims me. His hands cling to the bark so that he won't hurt me as his growl builds to vibrate the air around us. He repeatedly enjoys my body as I stay pinned to the tree and at his mercy.

The pressure builds deep within me as I lose myself to the sensations. I bury my face into Tarq's neck but still hear my moans echoing in the distance. He doesn't even pause as I scream, but the force of my release triggers his.

When Tarq finally stops, he lets his arms fall and tickles my thighs with his fingertips. He curls his face into my neck, slowly catching his breath. "You finally rode the energy out of me." He lifts me away from the tree and carries me back to where he had thrown my clothes. "The sun will be up soon. Why don't we get some sleep, My Love?"

Tarq puts me down and unties the blankets from the mare. He lays them near the trees so we can have shade in the morning. Since he doesn't bother with clothes, I put my skin against his and relish his heat when he lies down with his arms extended.

"Are you happy?" I ask him as he pulls a blanket over our legs.

Tarq sighs, looking at the fading stars. "I know what we have to do tomorrow, but I've never been happier." He looks toward me and kisses my forehead. "I married the perfect woman, and she's in my arms." He lets his body heat up.

"I'm glad you're my husband," I whisper before falling asleep.

* * *

The sun is high when I wake. I'm wrapped in Tarq's arms, and his chin rests on my head. I flex my fingers against his chest and try to roll away, but he tightens his grip and ducks to my ear.

"Don't move," he whispers. "There's a bear behind you."

I raise my eyebrow. "And what are we going to do about this?" I whisper back.

I hear him lick his lips and roll my eyes. "It's been a long time since I've had bear, Darya," he whispers.

"Are you hungry?"

Tarq leans back, looking down. "Have you met me?" he hisses.

I shake my head slightly. "No, I haven't. I'm Darya, and you are?"

Tarq just stares at me. The one thing he won't joke about is his stomach.

"Alright," I tell him. "Go get your bear. Just be careful."

He smiles broadly. "I love the shit out of you right now."

Tarq tries to move away but freezes and looks down at me. "It's looking over here now. I need you to pull the crystal for me." He threads his legs with mine.

I reach up for the crystal but then realize what he's doing. "Are you sure about this?"

Smiling, he kisses my forehead. "You just have to watch my back claws."

I pull the ribbon over his head, and he shifts in my arms.

"Holy shit! I can't believe that worked!"

"I thought you said you were sure," I hiss, narrowing my eyes.

Tarq freezes. *"Well, I guessed it would. I don't know how I'll get up without crushing you, though."*

I grab his muzzle and pull it down so that he's looking me in the eye. "You are incredibly fortunate that I am in love with you," I growl. I help him curl his back legs so he won't cut me. "Ok, roll toward me, and don't put pressure on this leg until you're upright." I run my hand down his left front leg.

Tarq gently licks my forehead. *"Be still. I'll be right back."* He rolls upright and takes off after the bear, kicking dirt up as he leaves.

Sitting up, I shake my head and look around. The Friesian is grazing on the other side of the clearing. She made sure to keep Tarq between herself and the bear. *Smart horse.* "I bet you've seen some crazy shit, haven't you?"

The horse sneezes in reply.

"Yeah, that's what I thought."

I stand up and stretch before walking to the center of the clearing and picking up my clothes. The sun is high, so it must be about midday. I pull my clothes on and look at the reflecting pond. *Maybe I'll swim in the clouds.* I smile at the idea and shake my head, turning back to the horse.

"I could go for another swim."

I turn and see Tarq coming out of the woods. "Hey," I say, dropping to my knees. "I know that bear didn't get away from you."

"She had cubs," he says, poking my belly.

Smiling, I pull his jaw and kiss his nose. "You softy."

"Whatever," Tarq grumbles. *"I thought I'd ride back with you. Take it slow."*

I can't stop my eyes from misting, but I wiggle my face to stop the rest of my emotions. "I'd like that."

I step into my boots and walk with Tarq to the blanket where I'd left his crystal. I kneel as I slide it over his neck, and he shifts right into my arms. I take a few deep breaths before pulling away from him.

He runs his finger under my jaw and smiles. "Are you ready to take a ride?"

I kiss his hand. "I'll go anywhere with you."

Tarq dresses while I tie the blankets back to the mare. He helps me into her saddle before jumping up behind me and turning her into the forest. Tarq wraps his arms around me, and I absentmindedly run my fingers over his arms as I watch the horse.

"She's got some pretty neat tricks," I say, pointing at the mare's head. "Who trained her?"

Tarq snorts. "I did."

I turn around to look at him. "I thought she was Dax's?"

"She is," Tarq says. "He taught me how to train horses with her."

"I don't see that," I say, smirking. "I know Dax taught you a lot, but I don't see him trusting you to train one of his horses."

"Well, it did piss him off that I taught them to come to my call," he says, chuckling.

I lean against his chest. "She seems to trust you," I whisper.

Tarq doesn't answer me. Instead, he takes a deep breath and puts his chin on my head. We ride in silence for a while. As I'm staring off into the trees, I try to remind myself that Edith said this would work with every bit of confidence she has ever had.

I turn to Tarq, seeing he's lost in thought. "You're going to miss Dax, aren't you?"

Tarq tucks his head down beside mine. He presses his forehead to my temple and sniffles. "I can't recall a memory that doesn't have him in it," he whispers.

"He did seem to have a big part in shaping you into who you are to-day." I let him stay hidden and close my eyes, reaching up for his cheek.

"He kept sending me off with other pack members, saying he

couldn't train me," Tarq says. "I used the skills he taught me to follow their orders."

"So then, maybe we honor him by passing on his lessons?" I suggest.

Tarq shakes his head. "I'm not ready for that, Darya."

I twist my body to hold both his cheeks. "Dax is ready, My Love. He's tired and ready to pass the pack to the man he taught how to lead them."

He smiles faintly and kisses me. "Thanks for trying."

I kiss him back and frown. "I'm here for you as much as you are for me, but I will not push you." I rub my thumbs over his cheeks. I know that he won't talk to me. His pain is so deep that I could never understand it in the short time we have left.

I turn around and melt into his chest for the rest of the ride. The silence is deafening, but any word attempt would only end in tears. I recall my last conversations with everyone. I wonder if I hugged the Alphas tight enough. *Do they know that I love them?*

The horse steps down onto a road, and the cabin appears. I suddenly can't breathe as my chest tightens. Tears begin streaming down my face, entirely out of control, and I start hyperventilating.

"Breathe, Darya," Tarq whispers. He slides from the horse's back, and I look down at him as he reaches for me.

I shake my head and bury my face in my hands. "I can't do this," I wail. "I can't leave you. I can't lose Dax and Miles. I can't... I just can't."

I could've babbled on forever if Tarq didn't reach up and pull me off the horse. I land in his arms, and he cradles me. I curl against his chest, crying as if it would save my life. He carries me to the porch and sits in the chair where Miles washed my hair. After a while, Tarq starts crying with me.

I'm out of breath and energy when we've finished feeling our emotions. I lift my finger and rub it over his cheek, wiping a leftover tear. "I'm not ready to leave you."

Tarq picks his head up, and I cup his cheek, surveying his red eyes. "This has to work," he says, lifting me. He carries me into the cabin and puts me down on the couch. Sitting beside me, Tarq pulls me to his chest. "Dax gave me this cabin."

I sniffle and look up at him, confused. "Why did he think you needed another house?"

Tarq grabs my face. "Dax obviously believes it will work. He said, and I quote, 'When you undoubtedly fuck up, you're gonna need a place far away to hide from her.' So, if Dax can believe in his weird way that this will work, it has to."

Tarq kisses me and walks over to a cabinet by the dining table. He pulls out a long dagger and a corked bottle. He sticks them both in his back pocket.

"It's sundown, My Love," he says, returning to my side. "We can't wait any longer. It's time."

No matter what I do, I can't breathe normally. When my body starts to shake, Tarq scoops me up from the couch and carries me to the door.

"Close your eyes," he tells me.

My eyes blur with tears as I close them. I feel Tarq open the door and walk outside. His lips brush against my forehead when he steps down the stairs.

"Do you remember the beach I showed you?" he whispers.

The beach from our night in his house begins to appear. It's not an image I would think could calm me, but Tarq somehow makes the waves match his heartbeat, and my breathing begins to slow.

"Maybe we could just go on a boat somewhere," Tarq says as the image changes to the night sky on a boat's deck. "We'll just lie there and refuse to come back until we've counted all the stars."

I focus on the sound of the water hitting the side of the boat until Tarq lays me down on something soft, and the image fades. He kisses my forehead and pulls his arm out from under my legs. "I don't want to do this, but I need you to open your eyes."

I open them to see that he's leaning over me. We're in the middle of the field where he played ball yesterday, but now something is burned into the ground.

"Edith says this symbol will amplify the comet's effect," Tarq tells me so I don't have to ask.

"I suppose we need all the help we can get." I try to smile, but he sees right through it.

Tarq pulls me to his chest, letting me listen to his heartbeat. "I'm afraid if I try to make this easier with images, Luna will retaliate, and I couldn't handle her doing that to you."

He lays me back down on the ground.

"I'm scared," I tell him, calmed by his heartbeat.

Tarq leans over and kisses me gently. "I am too, but you vowed that you would breathe again. I'm gonna hold you to that."

As he sits back on his heels, I glimpse the comet. "It's time, isn't it?"

"Can you do me a favor?" Tarq asks. "Can you tell Dax that I love him? I don't think I ever told him, but he should know."

"I will," I promise.

I hear the blade clinking against the bottle and turn to see what he's doing.

Tarq catches my chin, stopping me. "Look right here, ok? Just look in my eyes. I've got you." He smiles sweetly through his tears and kisses me lightly. I feel him apply pressure to my chest as he places the tip against my skin.

I can't see Tarq anymore because of the blur my tears create, but I'm hanging onto him with all my strength. "If I don't come back, just know that I love you more than my words could say, and I will always be with you."

Tarq slides his hand down the blade, but I can still feel the tip resting where he left it. I reach for his hand that's on the handle and squeeze it. He hesitates, his tears dropping onto my arm.

"It's ok, My Love," I whisper. "I'm ready."

Leaning down, Tarq rests his cheek against mine and whispers shakily, "Please come back to me."

Pain shoots through my body as he thrusts the dagger deep into my heart. Every movement is excruciating, so I can only breathe in tiny bursts. My fingers dig into Tarq's skin until he twists the knife, and the last of my air slips away.

29

29

I'm sure there was a time when birthdays were happy. They wrote a song about it, so I figure it must be true. One year, Rosalee gave me something she called an evening gown. I used to think that was the worst birthday present ever. Enter birthday number 25, July 29, 2061, and the man I love gave me a dagger to the heart, officially making this one the worst birthday ever.

"Holy shit," a voice I never wanted to hear again shouts. "The dog actually did it!"

I open my eyes, or at least I think I do. It's all just black around me. *Maybe my eyes were already open.* I shake my head. *That's not important. Where is that bitch?* I turn until she finally shows up. "Oh, hell no," I shout at her. I stick my arms out because now I'm dizzy from spinning. "I am not going to be stuck here with you forever."

Luna smirks. "You are stuck here for as long as I say, Baby Luna."

"Fuck!" is all I can think to shout at her. It's hard to describe the environment in which she thrives. This blackness is stifling and feels like it is trying to smother you without touching you. Of course Luna would thrive within something so hateful. "Luna, how about you fix this? Why do I have to ask you every time? Do you like the color black?"

Luna scowls. "Fine," she sneers. "Let's watch some shows."

She brings me back to the field at the cabin. Tarq has removed the dagger and is now cradling my lifeless body. He mumbles that he's sorry in between sobs. I try to move closer, but Luna won't let me. It breaks my heart when he starts to rock me in his arms.

"He's so weak," Luna says, laughing. "He's crying over a kill. How could he ever be an Alpha?"

"Stop it!" I scream at her.

"I didn't cry when I killed my mate," she boasts, raising her eyebrow as if proving a point. "That's what real leadership looks like in our world, Baby Luna."

Looking back at Tarq, I wonder if I could ever do it. I love him with every fiber of my being. I would do anything to protect him. I don't know that I could ever kill him for any reason. "How could you do it, Luna," I ask her as I crouch down to watch Tarq. "Didn't you love him?"

When Luna doesn't answer, I look over my shoulder and see she's wearing a shocked expression. "No one has ever really cared. Why would you?" she asks.

I turn to Tarq and frown. "I couldn't imagine killing Tarq," I say sadly. "Going on each day would be excruciating."

Luna giggles. "Yet he had no problem killing you." She smiles broadly and wags her eyebrow. "Seems your relationship was a little one-sided."

Standing up, I narrow my eyes at her. "Look at him, Luna. Does he look ok to you?" I yell. *She's like a toddler trying to prove her toys are better than mine.*

Luna pouts. *Yep, a toddler.* "So? He still did it," she argues.

She turns toward the trees and hurls a rock at them. It appears she's missed everything because it makes no sound as it travels into the woods beside the field. While she's distracted, I move closer to Tarq to slide the back of my fingers across his cheek. My chest swells as he leans onto my hand and whispers that he loves me.

"Um, no!" Luna shouts, instantly changing our environment to a snowy cliff. The wind howls around us, threatening to shove us over the edge at any moment.

"Fuck, Luna!" I scream. "What is it with you and snow?"

"You shouldn't have touched him," she says, smirking.

Giving up, I sigh and sit down in the snow. "Aren't you cold?" I look up at her furs. She has no sleeves, her chest is exposed, and the skirt only falls halfway down her thighs.

"We're dead," she says, eyeing me curiously. "We don't get cold."

"It's just you and me in this frozen hell, Luna. Will you tell me about your mate?" I ask.

She narrows her eyes and backs up to lean against a boulder or gigantic snowball. *Fuck. Everything is white now. Who gives a shit?* "Why are you asking about Cathal?" She shakes her head. "Who cares?"

"Someone should, Luna," I plead. "He died by your hand, and no one speaks of him." I watch her momentarily, but she continues staring into the distance. "This is the first time I've even heard his name."

Luna hangs her head with a sigh, and the environment changes again. "Let's take a walk," she says as she turns to follow a dirt road.

We're still cliffside but in a much warmer area. The water at the bottom of the cliff must be the ocean, judging by the salt in the air. Luna must visit here often because she's not staring at the water like I am. *Oh shit. Let me pay attention.* I jog to catch up to her as she begins to answer my questions.

"Cathal means 'Ruler of Battle.' He was so strong." Luna smiles at her memory of him. "He used to launch me halfway across the lakes. He had this need to throw me into them."

I smile at my memory. "Tarq does that too," I tell her. "What is that?"

Luna giggles. "I don't know, but it never got old." She walks along quietly, kicking at rocks on the road. "I'm from a different time, you know. If you didn't eat them, they'd eat you. If you were stupid enough to love, they'd rip you apart."

I think about my wolves and how much I love them. They calm under my touch, loving me in return. "You could have used your power to change things, Luna."

Luna glares in my direction, making it obvious that I've said the wrong thing. "You are so delusional," she snaps. "How have you survived this long?"

Scowling, Luna brings me back to the lake. Miles lies with the back of his head against Edith's chest as she mops up blood from his mouth. Edith is silently rocking him with tears streaming down her face. She looks up to the sky, taking a few calming breaths and trying to hide her emotions from Miles.

"What's happening to him?" I ask.

Luna shrugs. "I imagine 150 years of decay is catching up to him."

I frown at her. "Can't you do something?"

"I don't understand why you people think I can help you," she shouts angrily. "Dax's mother called upon me to break the curse. That's all."

I crouch beside Miles, feeling his fear. "Tell me more about your mate, Luna."

She throws a rock into the water, and Edith looks up when it splashes.

"Will you let me touch him?" I ask.

Luna turns to Miles. "I will permit it with this one," she says, nodding. "He was a strong leader."

I shift onto my knees and run my hand down Miles' face, cupping his cheek. A tear slips from his eye as he leans against my hand and smiles faintly.

"Like you, my mate offered himself as a sacrifice," Luna says, watching how Miles reacts to me. "He would do anything for me, and I would do anything for a baby."

I move my hand to Miles' chest and feel his heartbeat slow. He puts his hand over mine and squeezes. I can still feel his fear, but I can also sense that he's comforted by my presence.

"It worked, you know," Luna says, looking back over the lake. "I became pregnant."

I pause for a moment but then turn to her, leaving my hands on Miles. "But the elders said you couldn't carry on the Luna line," I say, shocked. *I'm not sure she'll ever stop surprising me.*

Luna's eyes flash with anger, but she quickly settles and frowns as she rubs her belly. "They locked me in the tomb cells before they asked why I did it." She looks up at me, and I can clearly see the pooling of tears in her eyes before she blinks a few times, forcing them back. "I was starved and lost my baby."

I feel torn. Miles is dying under my hands, and it's breaking my heart that I can't save him. I love him so much, but Luna is hurting over losing her baby. I feel like I want to go to her. I could've been in her situation if Dax hadn't known what was wrong with me. Of course, my love for Miles wins, and I hang my head. "I'm sorry, Luna."

Miles grips my hand tightly, taking a few more shallow breaths before falling limp against Edith. I hold his hand in mine and lay it on his lap. Edith openly sobs and clutches Miles tightly to her chest. I try to comfort her or at least let her know she's not alone, but Luna moves us again before I can.

We're in Dax's bedroom, and Luna walks around the bed staring at him. He's lying on his back with Amelia curled up beside him. She's humming with her head on his shoulder. Gazing at the ceiling, he calmly rubs his fingers over Amelia's arm.

"Why isn't he dead?" I ask. "It didn't work?"

Luna sits on the bed, running her hand over Dax's cheek. He closes his eyes and sighs. "This one is mine," she says, looking at him lovingly. "I couldn't let him suffer. He is dying, though, Baby Luna."

"You could've helped Miles?" I spit out.

Luna rolls her eyes. "No sense in getting mad about it now," she says, shifting her gaze to me. "What would you like me to do? Go back in time? Deal with it."

Dax's breathing turns more and more shallow. His body becomes too weak to hold his arm up to rub Amelia, and it falls to the bed.

"He'll be here soon," Luna whispers, turning back to Dax.

I sit in the chair, giving her this time to comfort Dax. "Luna, how would you handle Miles' pack?" I ask while we wait.

She looks up thoughtfully. "Ah, the Blood Pack. They are a ruthless bunch, aren't they?" Her face scrunches. "Why do you ask?"

I look down at Dax and see he's leaning his cheek against Luna's leg. "Miles said they'd be a problem for me," I tell her. "That I'm basically just the woman who killed their Alpha."

Luna smirks. "Well, you kinda did."

I roll my eyes. "Yeah, thanks," I sneer. "Thank you for that, but maybe you could try to be helpful?"

Luna shrugs. "Well, Baby Luna, when something stands in your way, you kill it." She looks down at Dax, watching him exhale for the last time. Amelia grabs his shirt and begins sobbing and crying out to him. "It seems this one was in love with him. How tragic."

"Luna, don't be mean," I snap, glaring at her.

She laughs. "You're so sensitive."

She brings me back to the field. Tarq has propped me up in his lap and cradled my head against his chest. He rocks my body and leans down as he repeatedly whispers, begging me to return to him. *I'd be lying if I said I didn't want to hear his heartbeat right now.*

"Luna, if I could just comfort him —"

"No!" she shouts, cutting me off. She points at Tarq and sneers at me. "You don't touch him! That is a mutt!"

"That is my son!" a voice yells from behind me. "And I've had about all I'm gonna take of you disrespecting him."

The environment jumps a bit as Luna's taken by surprise. I fall to my knees, and Dax reaches out to me. My emotions instantly get the best of me as I take his hand and let him lift me off the ground.

"You did it, my beautiful," he tells me, cupping my cheek and wiping my tears away. "The curse is broken."

I look down at Tarq. "He did it," I tell Dax, watching Tarq quietly rock my body. "He's the strong one."

Dax pulls me over to my body and moves my shirt to show me the half-healed wound. Tarq notices the movement and runs his fingers over the puncture.

"You're his father?" I ask slowly.

Dax sits next to Tarq, eyeing Luna as she walks in a wide circle around us. "I couldn't tell him," he says as I sit beside him. "Amelia begged me not to, and she was right. If anyone knew, he'd be in danger."

176 years and the man only has one kid? "Dax, how is this even possible?" I ask.

Dax looks confused. "Well, Darya, when a man loves a woman —"

"Seriously, Dax?" I scoff.

Dax holds his hands out in frustration. "You're pregnant," he states.

"How do you not know how this one came along?" His finger points at Tarq.

I frown and roll my eyes. "Why do I even bother?"

"You mean because I was immortal?" Dax asks.

"Yes, Dax," I sputter. "If you can make them, how do you not have kids all over the place?"

Dax laughs and throws a clump of dirt at me. "Is that what you think of me? That I just spent my days whoring around?" He shakes his head. "No, I spent most of my time alone."

"Did you love her?"

He turns to me and tries to grin. "I loved Amelia. I still do." He sighs as he straightens his back. "I wasn't her mate, though. Tarq would've been hunted down and used against me if anyone knew."

"He told me to tell you that he loves you," I tell Dax, remembering my promise.

Dax puts his hand on Tarq's arm. "I did the best I could for him," Dax whispers.

"Is that why he's so different?" I ask. "His strength and the shifting?"

Dax sighs. "I don't have the answers for you, Darya. It's not like I have other children to compare him to." He looks at Tarq, smiling softly. "He's made me proud and ready to be Alpha. I bet he doesn't believe in himself yet, though."

I reach toward Tarq's back but stop, afraid Luna will take Dax away if I touch Tarq. "He doesn't," I tell Dax. "I'm afraid he'll falter if I don't make it back to him."

Dax looks at Luna as she continues to walk in her circle. "It's her decision," he says. "The spell will heal your body, but you have to convince her to send you back."

Luna stops her circling and smiles crookedly. "So you better start begging, Baby Luna."

Wolves begin howling in the distance, and Tarq looks up. His face glistens from tears, and his eyes are red and swollen. He pulls the crystal off his neck and squeezes my body tightly as the howls sound again. They are closer this time. Tarq puts his cheek against mine, promising he won't leave me. He whispers that he loves me and lays my body down.

Dax takes my hand as he stands up, pulling me with him. We step back as Tarq rises to his feet, never taking his eyes off my body. He pulls his shirt over his head and slides his pants to the ground. Tarq attempts to pile them neatly but can't look away from me. *He's probably afraid he'll miss a sign that I'm waking up.* I frown, wishing Luna would let me touch him.

"Luna, we need to leave," Dax says, pulling my attention, but not my eyes, from Tarq.

"What's happening?" I ask.

When the howls call out again, they are right at the edge of the trees. Tarq shifts, standing over my body. He crouches, snarling in the direction of the howls.

"The wolves are coming to claim the Luna's body," Dax explains quietly.

A few wolves filter out of the trees. I don't recognize any of them, but they appear older, as if they are from another time. They seem calm and slowly move to circle Tarq. He crouches lower, completely covering my body, and continues to snarl at them. Tarq's larger than they are, but they outnumber him.

"Luna?" Dax growls.

"Whatever!" she barks back.

She brings us to the room that she created in her mind. The room, she believes, represents what her parlor would look like today if it weren't a pile of rubble somewhere.

"What the fuck is this?" Dax snaps, making me giggle. *She has met her match with Dax.*

"Fine," Luna says, glaring. "Where do you want to go?"

Dax thinks for a moment and then winks at me. "The flower fields," he says.

Suddenly we're there, and Luna scoffs. "Are you...? How the hell am I going to survive an eternity with you?"

Dax laughs as he reaches out for my hand. "Flowers aren't so bad,

Luna. Get over it." He leads me through the fields as he holds out his other arm for Luna. She scoffs at him and follows at a distance.

"Is Tarq going to be ok?" I ask.

Dax puts his arm around me and pulls me to him. "Trust him," he says, smiling. "He's strong." He leads us to the spot where we had spent the afternoon trying to reach Tarq after he'd left. "Let's take some time to reflect. Luna, would you like to join us?" Dax lays down and holds his arms out to us.

"Give us a chance, Luna," I say, smiling at her. "We don't have to be enemies. There isn't a reason for it." I roll down onto Dax's shoulder and look up at the clouds. Luna sits nearby but refuses to come closer. "I appreciate the attempt, Luna. Thank you."

Luna doesn't respond, but Dax leaves his arm out for her.

"Do you know how to shoot a bow?" he asks, turning to me.

I frown. "No."

"So you'll have to practice," Dax tells me. "I made my bow myself. It's yours now."

"You assume I'll be going back." I turn to look at Luna. She winks as a sly smile spreads across her face. "Luna, what happened to your mother?" *She seems to respond better when I remind her that she was once a normal person.*

Luna turns away from us and stares across the field. "Your questions are annoying."

Dax runs his fingers through my hair and joins me, staring at Luna. "It's a fair question," he remarks.

Luna wrinkles her nose in a failed attempt to scoff at him and turns around to flop onto his shoulder. He smiles and winks at me as he wraps his arm around her. He pulls Luna's furs up to run his fingertips over her stomach.

"My mother was the most beautiful woman I've ever seen," Luna tells us. "They say she smelled like leather, and I remember her touch calming the wolves."

I roll slightly onto Dax's chest, grabbing a handful of his shirt. Luna has never been forthcoming with information, yet she's suddenly freely sharing details with us. *If I breathe too hard, it might startle her back into bitch mode.*

"She said I would grow into it, but I never could calm them," Luna continues. "If anything, my touch made them angry and more aggressive."

I remember the first dream I had after I met Dax. It was the night after our first time together. I had dreamt that Nate attacked me after I touched him.

"What was her name?" Dax asks, pulling me from my memory.

"Maylene," she answers him. "Her name was Maylene." She tucks her hand under Dax's shoulder, snuggling into him. "Once Cathal and I were married and bonded, she tried her best to prepare me to take over but fell ill."

I roll onto Dax's chest to look at Luna. I threw my leg over his in the process, which Luna noticed. She looks over at me and narrows her eyes.

"Knock it off, Luna," Dax growls. She turns back toward the sky and scowls as Dax continues rubbing her exposed skin with a grin.

"When she died, my father ran off with his tail between his legs," she grumbles. "He left me to fend for myself without any guidance."

We wait quietly, hoping she'll continue on her own, but Luna is generally angry. Her story hit a moment that would anger me, so I understand why she stopped.

"What killed her? Was it the illness?" I ask quietly, trying to nudge her along gently.

Luna closes her eyes and sighs. "Who knows? Probably." She puts her hand on Dax's, stopping him. "Of course they blamed me. Why not? I created hatred and evil."

Before I know what I'm doing, I place my hand on her shoulder. Luna tenses at my touch. "That sounds horrible," I whisper. "I'm so sorry." She relaxes her shoulder back onto Dax, and I watch a tear roll from the corner of her eye. I squeeze my hand on her shoulder. "Luna, what is your name?"

She wipes her face and stands up. "Annalisa," she says before walking away from us. She holds her hands out to her sides and runs them over the tops of the flowers.

I jump up and jog after her, falling in step once I catch up. "You weren't dealt a fair hand. I'm not sure I would have done anything differently in your situation. The world was cruel to you, taking everything you loved, twisting and turning it until all that was left was pain. You didn't deserve that, and I'm so sorry that your life contained such horrible things."

I move to stand in her way. "I forgive you," I say. I wrap my arms around Luna's shoulders, holding her head beside mine. "I forgive you for how you acted toward Tarq and me. I forgive you for the things you've done to us."

There's no accurate time measurement in Luna's world, but we remain still as I allow Luna the time she needs to feel my love. I'm nearly startled when I feel her arms slide around my waist. Luna squeezes me tightly and whispers, "Thank you."

* * *

Suddenly I'm bolting upright, coughing hard, and slamming my head into Tarq's furry chest.

30

Three Months Later

"Come on, Tarq!" I yell up the stairs. "It's almost time. What are you doing?"

Tarq walks out of our bedroom, pulling on a shirt. He laughs and leans over the balcony to look for me at the bottom of the stairs. "Woman, go get on that horse. I'll be there in a minute."

I shake my head and walk across the living room. "We only have the full moon with him," I remind Tarq. "You need to hurry." Pulling the door open, I grab Dax's bag and bow. I step outside, leaving the door open.

"Do you need some help, Luna?" Nate asks.

I smile at him, cupping his cheek as he takes the bag from me. "I'm pregnant, Nate, not useless. Thank you for helping out tonight, though."

He takes the bow off my shoulder. "It's my pleasure."

I step into the Friesian's saddle and turn her back toward the house. Nate looks up at me as I lean down for the bow.

"We're gonna be late," he remarks.

The mare's neck nearly crashes into my forehead as her head bolts upright when a low howl sounds in the distance. Nate jumps onto her back behind me and wraps his arm around my waist.

"TARQ! HE'S HERE!" I yell.

The front door slams shut, and Tarq jumps over the railing. He shifts mid-jump as the second howl sounds. The mare spins and dashes toward Dax's house. She slides to a stop at the back door, and Nate helps me drop from her back. Tarq jogs up, pushing his head under my hand.

"We're gonna run out of clothes," I tell him.

"Edie's supposed to be back today," Tarq says. *"She can make some more. Or I could just walk around naked all the time."*

I smile at him as we walk through the back door. "Tempting," I say, lifting my eyebrow. "So very tempting."

Tarq wraps his body around me as I stop at the table to remove my jacket. He slides his nose over my growing belly. *"I love you."*

"I love you too," I say, rubbing his ear between my fingers.

"I wasn't talking to you, but I guess I kinda love you too."

I stop and scoff at him. Tarq licks my belly and runs out the front door.

I follow him and sit on the porch's top step to admire the view. Tarq is out in the field wrestling with some of the younger wolves. They gang up on him but still lose.

Amelia and Chase are never far but have joined us for a game of ball tonight. Nate sits beside me and hands me a glass of sweet tea. He rummages around Dax's bag, looking for the extra balls we keep stashed.

After a few minutes, a wolf as black as night walks around the corner of the house. My vision blurs as tears well up. He walks straight to me, never taking his eyes off mine. He steps into my arms when I reach them out, sliding his jaw down my back. "And what have you been up to today, my beautiful," I ask Dax.

As I hang onto him, a large dark gray wolf with white flecks approaches us. Dax backs up. *"I brought a friend,"* he says. *"I hope you don't mind."*

I cover my mouth with both hands as tears begin freely falling from my eyes. The wolves in the field stop to watch. "Miles?" I whisper.

"I've missed you, Little One," Miles tells me.

I fall to my knees at the bottom of the steps and wrap my arms around him. "No more than I have missed you," I say through tears. "I am so happy to see you." I reach out to Dax and pull the fur under his throat. "I miss my Alphas all the time."

"Um, Alpha, right here," Tarq reminds me.

"Hush up, you know what I mean," I tell him. *"Let me give your father and uncle some love."*

Tarq chuckles and runs to his father. He immediately mentions a time Dax shot him in the ass, and Dax bites his leg. Tarq bounds off to the field, laughing at Dax's attempt to catch him. I shake my head at them and turn back to Miles.

"Will you stay for a game of catch, Miles?" I ask as he rubs his muzzle against my cheek. "It's how they like to spend their full moons these days."

Miles bumps his nose against mine. *"It might be interesting."*

Dax jogs up to sit beside me while Tarq rubs his face in the grass, trying to remove Dax's slobber. *"Has my son been taking care of you?"*

"You know he does," I tell him with a smile. "He's always good to me."

Nate stands, holding a few balls up. "Y'all about ready?" He steps off the porch and walks out into the field.

Amelia bows her head to me as she steps up to Dax. She slides her head over his neck in a hug. Dax leans into her briefly, closing his eyes. I hear him tell her she should prepare for the game, and she backs away. I'd asked Dax to help her move on and maybe connect with her mate. It's not going well, but I still have hope.

There's a commotion behind us as Edith and Anthony crash through the house. "Sorry we're late," Edith says, plopping beside me. "We brought snacks." She smiles, holding out a tray of egg wraps.

"Edith," I say, giggling. "I don't think my wolves are interested in wraps."

Edith waves her hand. "These are for you, Dar. If they're hungry, they can go hunting." She leans in closer to whisper in my ear. "I did bring a duck, though." She points behind us to a bag Anthony is carrying.

Out in the field, I see Tarq's head shoot up, turning in our direction. *I love my family.*

"So, have we decided on a name for the little Luna?" Edith asks, rubbing my belly excitedly.

"Annalisa," I tell her, winking at Dax.

"Oh, that's beautiful!" Edith exclaims.

I bump my shoulder into Dax's as Nate sets up with the first ball. All of the wolves except for Dax and Chase line up beside him.

"Where did you get that name from?" Edith asks.

Nate hurls the ball, and the wolves at the line take off after it, kicking dirt up in their wake.

I stand up with the bow and look back at Dax. "I'm just honoring an old friend."

Dax takes off after the ball, and I set my arrow on it, letting it loose to race the wolves.